DYING FOR
A young woman is h
twelve days of

'Packs a killer twist'
Prima

FIRST ONE MISSING
The parents of missing children club together for
support. But all is not as it seems.

'Astonishingly good'
C. L. Taylor

WHEN SHE WAS BAD
Nasty things are happening at work. Can they figure
out who is the guilty co-worker, before it's too late for
all of them?

'Unsettling, tense and utterly unputdownable'
Woman & Home

THEY ALL FALL DOWN
Hannah's in a psychiatric clinic. It should be
a safe place, but patients keep dying. Can Hannah
make anyone believe that there's a killer on the
loose before they strike again?

'You'll devour this book in one sitting'
Erin Kelly, bestselling author of *He Said She Said*

Tammy Cohen (who previously wrote under her formal name Tamar Cohen) has a growing backlist of acclaimed novels of domestic noir, including *The Mistress's Revenge*, *The War of the Wives* and *Someone Else's Wedding*. Her break-out psychological suspense thriller was *The Broken*, followed by *Dying for Christmas*, *First One Missing*, *When She Was Bad* and *They All Fall Down*. She is also the author of *Clean Break*, a Quick Reads novel.

She lives in north London with her partner and three (nearly) grown children, plus one badly behaved dog. Chat with her on Twitter @MsTamarCohen or at www.tammycohen.co.uk.

STOP AT NOTHING

Tammy Cohen

BLACK SWAN

TRANSWORLD PUBLISHERS
61–63 Uxbridge Road, London W5 5SA
www.penguin.co.uk

Transworld is part of the Penguin Random House group of companies
whose addresses can be found at global.penguinrandomhouse.com

Penguin
Random House
UK

First published in Great Britain in 2019 by Bantam Press
an imprint of Transworld Publishers
Black Swan edition published 2020

A CIP catalogue record for this book
is available from the British Library.

ISBN
9781784162474

Typeset in 10.57/13.50pt Sabon by Jouve (UK), Milton Keynes.
Printed and bound in Great Britain by Clays Ltd, Elcograf S.p.A.

Penguin Random House is committed to a sustainable future
for our business, our readers and our planet. This book is made
from Forest Stewardship Council® certified paper.

MIX
Paper from
responsible sources
FSC® C018179

1 3 5 7 9 10 8 6 4 2

For Billie, whose story this happily isn't

You know when you have a song stuck in your head that you can't shake off? Earworm, they call it. Something that wriggles into your brain and gets lodged there. Well, you are my earworm. You have eaten your way along my neural pathways and into my frontal lobe and now my thoughts itch with you.

'Just say no, you can't come in,' Mum says. As if it was a question of looking through the video intercom and deciding not to press the buzzer.

She doesn't understand that you're already installed, feet up, kettle on.

I had nits not long ago. When you're in and out of school every day it's pretty much inevitable. I can still remember that sensation of my scalp crawling, of something living, uninvited, on my skin.

And now that's where you live too.

Some days I think I would wash myself in bleach if it would get rid of you.

1

'You must not speak.'

That was directed at me.

I nodded. I was there only as a silent support.

I was sitting about six feet behind Em, slightly to her right. I could see the rounded slope of her shoulders, the heavy fall of hair over her face, the curve of her right cheek, the hand resting on her jeans, one finger worrying away at the ragged skin around her bitten thumbnail.

There is something about your children's hands, isn't there, that goes straight to the most primeval part of you? Some muscle memory ingrained from the very first time their tiny baby fingers gripped on to your own, or when a soft toddler palm reached up for yours in the street – that unquestioned trust that you would be there, waiting to receive it.

As I watched, a small bead of blood blossomed on the side of Em's thumb, and I had to look away.

The room was windowless. Less a room, really, than a partitioned area off the main floor. Fluorescent strip lights, the same drab dark blue carpet as everywhere else in the building. The air stale and mint-edged from

3

the gum the policewoman chewed so her breath didn't smell of cigarettes, although her clothes reeked of them.

There was another woman in the room who'd been introduced as the defence solicitor. She had a moon-shaped face and an impassive expression, as if it was all the same to her. My daughter. The ugly thing that happened to her. All the same.

A video camera was bracketed to the wall up near the ceiling, and I deliberately didn't look at it, though I was conscious of it the whole time.

The policewoman read through the script, explaining what was going to happen. A video would play showing nine different men and Em was to watch the entire thing through twice without commenting, after which she'd be asked if she recognized the man who'd assaulted her.

'Is that clear?'

Em nodded, but then was asked to say 'yes' out loud, for the camera. Then she had to confirm her name. Her voice sounded very small and my stomach felt tight.

The video started. A man with heavy-set features and a pronounced underbite turned slowly to show first his left side then his right and then finally face on.

I sat up straight. Made my expression neutral.

This first man looked nervous. Licked his lips. Concentrated. They weren't actors. I'd already googled it. They were volunteers who'd agreed to go on a national database in return for a tenner or something. VIPER, they called this identification process. I knew it was an acronym but it also suited the sense of menace I'd felt since this whole nightmare started.

The second man could hardly hide his smirk. I pressed

my top teeth down on to the bottom ones so those at the back ground together. Did he think this was funny? My daughter. Only sixteen years old. Was it a joke to him?

Neutral face. Silent support.

I was sure I'd have coped with it all better if I'd had more sleep. I'd gone to bed deliberately early the night before, chamomile tea, half an hour's reading, then lights off. Nothing. Lying in bed, I'd tried being mindful, focusing on the here and the now, the way each part of my body felt in contact with the sheet, relaxing each muscle one by one.

But anxiety whined in my ear like a mosquito.

By the time the alarm went I was a wreck. And now my nerves buzzed like faulty wiring.

Man number three was way too skinny. I could have told them that for nothing. 'Chunky' is how Em had described her attacker in her statement to Detective Byrne, the nice policeman, who was currently sitting at a desk in the main area outside. He'd explained why he wasn't allowed to come in with us. Something about having to be sure the whole process was impartial. He'd worked so hard trying to track down the guy from the CCTV they'd taken from the bus. Perhaps if he was here in the room with us he wouldn't be able to resist sending some kind of subtle signal when he turned up onscreen. You couldn't blame him for that.

It was Detective Byrne who came to the house the night it happened. He found Em sitting, crying, on my lap – how long had it been since she'd done that? – the bruising already coming out on her cheek and forehead.

'Had you been drinking?' the other policeman had asked her, and I'd been glad she was on my lap because otherwise I might have flown at him, my body charged with shock and worry and all the broken nights.

We were both relieved, when we got to the station a few days later so that Em could give a statement, that it was Detective Byrne who came to buzz us in at the door. Even so, the process had been traumatic.

'What colour was he?' he'd asked. And my daughter, taught from birth to be wilfully colour-blind, had been frozen with awkwardness. Even after he'd extracted the description 'mixed race' from her, it wasn't enough.

'But what complexion exactly? Was he black like me?' Detective Byrne had skin the colour of the bark chippings outside on the front section of the forecourt.

Em shook her head. In the end he'd used what he called the 'sliding JLS scale'. He'd called up a photograph of the boy band on his computer screen. 'Is he more like Aston or Oritsé, would you say?'

Like I said, Detective Byrne was nice.

But Em had definitely used the word 'chunky'. By the end of her statement I'd built up a pretty good idea of what the bastard looked like. He'd approached her from behind, so she'd only seen a glimpse of him when, before running off, he'd turned to see if anyone was after him. Stocky. Short hair. A pungent aftershave that got up her nostrils.

'His chin was shaped like a "w",' she'd said, and the tissue of my heart had torn softly. She didn't know the word for 'cleft' so she was making up her own description. She wanted so much to be helpful, forcing herself to build pictures of the face she least wanted to visualize.

He'd been wearing a dark padded jacket, she told us.

Of course, he would be, I recall thinking, along with ninety-nine per cent of the male population. 'But it had some kind of logo on the sleeve,' she remembered suddenly, jubilant at having something to give us. His arm had been around her neck and she'd tried to prise it off with her hands and felt something hard and round on his sleeve. She'd seen it only from the corner of her eye. Some kind of symbol. White, she thought, though she couldn't be sure.

Now another detail came back to her. When she'd been trying to twist his arm away she'd grabbed his hand and she'd felt a ring. She was sure of it. A metal ring, flat on the top. Chunky, just like the man who wore it.

No, she didn't know if it was gold or silver. It'd been dark.

Em kept returning to how dark it was, yet in my mind's eye I saw him crystal clear.

He did not look like man number three.

Man number four had longish dreads. I frowned at the screen over Em's shoulder. She had described his hair as short. Hadn't mentioned dreadlocks. Hadn't they been paying attention? Or was the database really so short on volunteers they had to approximate so wildly?

The fifth man was more like it. Broad, fit, but wary. Barely glancing towards the camera as he turned his head first to one side then the other. As if he had something to hide. I saw a muscle throbbing at his jaw.

I looked at Em, trying to gauge her reaction from the angle of her head. Her right hand was still resting on her leg, though the blood on her thumb was smeared now from being rubbed on the thick denim of her jeans. From the back she could have been twelve years old and I had to fight the urge to reach out and stroke her hair as I used to do when she was little.

Man number six was also promising, though he had the look of someone taking his role too seriously. Frustrated actor, perhaps. People like that must gravitate towards these types of gigs, I guessed. A chance to appear on screen, perhaps for some stranger hundreds of miles away to remark, 'That one is particularly good.' He was self-consciously relaxed, if that makes sense. His chin was square, with a hint of a dent. Like I said, promising.

Number seven was a flat-out no. Too dark, too slight. I looked at his delicate mouth. Tried to imagine him hissing, '*Stop, bitch*,' in my daughter's ear. Impossible.

Then came eight.

It was like a physical punch in the guts, that first sight of him.

I knew him, you see. I recognized him in some primordial part of me where my daughter and I were still one, where our consciousnesses had not yet divided, where I felt what she felt and knew what she knew.

He was so exactly how Em had described him. Squat, muscular. Skin stretched tight over the bones of his face. He had green eyes. Now that was a surprise. But then it had been dark and she hadn't seen his face up close. The chin, though. A perfect 'w', as if, while he was still being formed, someone had taken a finger and pressed hard. Each corner a mean point of bone. I imagined how it must have felt for Em when he gripped her from behind, those nubs of bone digging into her skull. Of course there was no jacket, and no ring. None of them wore any accessories. No jewellery or distinctive clothing.

But it was him. I knew it instantly.

I glanced at Em. Adrenaline was charging around my body and I wondered if I'd be able to see it in her too. She was sitting up rigid. Where her shoulders had been sloping a moment ago, now they were tensed. I looked at the hand resting on her jeans and saw how the fingers were digging into her thigh, knuckles protruding, anaemic, through the skin. Was I imagining how pale she looked suddenly?

There was a tugging in my rib cage as I watched her concentrating on the screen, just as she'd been told. Not looking away, no matter what it must have cost her to see him again, this man who'd smashed his way into her life, looming up out of the darkness. The bogeyman of her childish nightmares come to life. She knew she had to watch the video twice. She mustn't give away any reaction. She was doing exactly what was asked of her.

But, oh, I wanted to get up then and cross that horrible blue carpet and put my arms around her. My blood felt like it was boiling in my veins. There was no air in that room. Sweat popped on my skin.

This man's neck was meaty and thick. His arms bulged and strained under his T-shirt. I imagined him hooking one of them around my daughter's pale, narrow neck from behind. Acid rose up in my throat.

Face on, he looked straight at the camera. Those green eyes shockingly direct. A smile twitched at the corners of his mouth, as if he were saying, *Come on, then. What have you got?* And I had to dig my nail in my palm because a pulse of hatred shot through me so strong it almost propelled me right out of the chair.

Neutral face. Silent support.

I don't remember anything about number nine because number eight was still papered all over my eyelids.

After the tape had run, they reminded Em not to speak until she'd seen it a second time. Then they replayed it. This time I didn't pay any attention to the first seven men. Impatience knitted my muscles together, set my foot tapping against the chair leg.

Even second time around the physical reaction to him was visceral.

I'd reached fifty-two years of age without wishing serious harm on anyone.

I wanted him dead. Wanted to split that cleft chin open, rip tissue from bone.

Afterwards, the policewoman stopped the tape.

'Did you recognize the man who grabbed you around the neck at 00.15 hours on Friday 12 January on Brownlow Road and repeatedly hit you around the head while trying to pull you away from the main road?' she asked my daughter. Her voice was flat. Matter of fact. She could have been reading out her shopping list.

Now it was coming. I bit down on my lip, already anticipating the sweet relief of it all being over. Now he would get what was coming to him and we could move on with our lives. For the last four weeks since it happened, we'd felt powerless. Em frightened to come home on her own, even to walk to school. *What if he's still out there?* Now the tables had turned.

'No.'

So certain was I of hearing 'yes' that I thought at first I'd misheard, then that Em must have got it wrong. Must have said 'no' when she meant the opposite. I sat up straighter, leaned forwards, trying to tap her on the back with my mind, alert her to her mistake. Emma was always inclined to be cautious, particularly where other people were concerned. *This isn't the time for niceness*, I wanted to tell her. Number Eight. *You saw him*.

But instead I remained impassive, my hands on my lap, while the video camera recorded the scene.

Neutral.

Silent.

As we left the video room I saw Detective Byrne sitting at a desk behind a glass partition. He raised his eyebrows in a question then lifted his hand to Em. I remembered how excited he'd sounded when he called to say they'd got an identification on the CCTV taken from the bus that night. Another officer had recognized the man who'd gone through the doors behind Em on the tape. He had spent time inside. Common assault. ABH. There were hints of something more serious, though Byrne wouldn't be drawn. No sexually motivated convictions. Yet.

'Isn't that par for the course?' I'd asked. 'Criminals graduating from one crime to another?' I'd watched enough TV.

Now, I could hardly meet Detective Byrne's eyes. I felt we'd let him down.

The policewoman showed us out. There were various complicated buzzers that had to be pressed and cards to be swiped.

She told Em not to worry, that she'd done her best. And that if she wasn't a hundred per cent certain, she'd been right not to guess.

As she held the door open, she stared at me just a moment too long.

'You look familiar,' she said.

'I was here with my daughter a few weeks ago when she made her statement.'

'Ah, okay. That must be it.'

I turned aside sharpish, but I still felt her eyes on me.

Outside, I threw my arms around Em.

'You did really well,' I told her.

There was a knot tying itself inside me, ends pulling tighter.

We started walking, and I couldn't stop myself.

'Was there anyone you thought it could be?'

Could she hear it, that knot in my voice?

Afterwards, this moment was something they asked me about again and again. Whether she'd said it unprompted or whether I was the first to mention him.

And even after I told them, they kept coming back to it. How can you be so sure? Wouldn't it have made sense for you to . . . ? Trying to corral the truth into something different.

But I know what happened. I was there when Em turned to me, hesitant. 'There was that one guy,' she began, uncertainty thinning her voice like paint stripper. 'The one with the eyes. Number . . .'

'. . . Eight,' I said. 'I know.'

I grabbed her hand and squeezed.

'So why didn't you . . . ?'

'I just didn't feel completely sure. They said I had to be certain. But now I feel bad for Detective Byrne, after he went to so much trouble.'

Again that tearing of the soft, worn fabric of my heart.

'Darling, you did your best, that's all you could do.'

I kept hold of her hand as we walked on, as if she were once more a child, half surprised that she let me. Her palm was warm in mine, but my mind was elsewhere, focused on a cleft chin, skin stretching like canvas over sharp bones, muscles knotted and obscene under a thin cotton T-shirt.

Where was he now, this man who'd tried to take my daughter from me? Was he going about his life as if nothing had happened? Was he a son, a brother, a husband, an employee, to people who hadn't the first idea what he was really like? Was he even now hiding in plain sight?

Injustice burned a path across my brain until my head throbbed with it.

2

'Frances is coming round.'

'Oh. Right.'

'Honestly, Mum, could you please try sounding a bit happier about it? She basically saved my life.'

'Sorry. Obviously, it's lovely that she's coming. I'm just surprised, that's all. I didn't know you two had been in touch.'

'She called me just now. She wanted to know how the identity thingy went earlier. You know she did one too. Oh my God, can you stop looking at that thing? Do you know how creepy it is?'

Guiltily, I stopped the Granny-Cam, my parents frozen in place in their living room. Snapping the laptop shut, I glanced over to where Em was standing, feeding bread into the toaster. She was wearing an oversized hoodie printed with the names of everyone in her year that she got after GCSEs last summer and the baggy sweat pants she'd changed into the minute we got home from the police station. Her hair was scraped back into a ponytail and there was a fresh spray of spots on her chin.

She looked heartbreakingly young.

'You didn't tell Frances about Number Eight, did you?

Because I'm pretty sure it's illegal for a victim and a witness to swap stories.'

'God, Mum, I'm not dumb.'

Sometimes, Em sounded so angry with me, not for any particular reason. Just for the fact of me. Perhaps all teenage girls were the same.

The prospect of a visitor forced me to clean the house. The bathroom was disgusting, the grouting on the tiles in the corners stained an orange that no amount of scrubbing could get rid of. I even vacuumed the dog hairs off the sofa with the special attachment I'd never used before. Dotty's fur was black and white so it showed up on everything.

'She's not the queen, you know,' Em said, watching me from the doorway an hour or so later. 'Anyway, she's been here before, remember?'

I hadn't remembered.

What I mean is, I tried not to remember.

That night. The banging on the door jolting me out of a sleep I had no memory of falling into. Feeling like it was all in my dream. Dotty barking wildly, Em's face milk-pale, her shoulders shuddering. A young woman I'd never seen before standing on my doorstep with her arm around my daughter.

'Something's happened.'

Can there be two more terrifying words for a parent to hear?

'Do you feel all right about seeing Frances?' I asked Em now, vacuuming under her legs as she sank down on to the freshly dehaired sofa and picked up the remote. She folded them up underneath her, as she used to do as a child. 'It's not going to bring back bad memories, is it?'

Em shrugged. 'I'm okay.'

'Because we can put her off, if you're at all unsure. Tell her it's not a good time.'

'Yeah, because that's nice, isn't it? Thanks for saving my daughter from being raped and murdered but you can't come round because it's not convenient.'

'That's not what I—'

The doorbell cut through my justifications.

'How are you doing . . . Tessa, isn't it? Oh my God, I can't even imagine how hard all this must have been for you.'

I hadn't properly registered the last time how attractive Frances was, in a wholesome, head-girl kind of way. Thick chocolate-brown hair broken up by tawnier streaks falling to her shoulders. Hazel eyes set well apart in a wide, open face. A small neat nose above a large mouth whose top lip bowed and dipped extravagantly like a mountain range. Strong white teeth, with just the right degree of gap in the front when she smiled, as she was doing now.

'Oh, I'm fine.'

But then tears were blurring my eyes, and I thought, *Really? Is that all it takes? Someone being nice to you?*

Of course, it was more than that. Seeing Frances brought it all back. The horror of that night.

I'd been fast asleep. Em said afterwards that they'd banged on the door for ages before I finally woke up, but I'm sure that was an exaggeration. I'd left my phone downstairs. There were seventeen missed calls.

My head still sluggish from sleep, I'd pulled on my dressing gown, but my feet were bare and cold as I padded down the stairs. Dotty was going frantic so I shut her in the living room before opening the front door. 'Something's happened,' said the strange woman who turned out to be Frances. And for a moment I just stood and stared and felt the wind on my bare toes and it all felt wrong and I could not make sense of any of it.

Then instinct took over and I opened my arms, and Em fell into them and buried her veal-white face in my neck. And she was crying. My girl who never cried.

'Shall we go inside?' the woman suggested.

We went into the kitchen, me stumbling with my cargo of sixteen-year-old girl. The light seemed blindingly harsh as I sank on to a kitchen chair and pulled Em on to my lap. She buried her head in my neck, her shaking body setting my own blood quivering.

'Sweetie?' I asked, moving my head back so that I could see her more clearly. 'Oh my God!'

A bruise was breaking over her right cheek, livid and purple. White lumps pushed up under the skin of her forehead like knuckles. Her face was stained with mascara tears. My stomach contracted and I felt for a moment that I might be sick.

'What happened, sweetheart?'

Something's happened.

The police arrived then. Frances had called them on the way. There were two of them, one black, one white, both wearing big dark jackets and bringing with them a waft of cold from outside. I was conscious suddenly of my dressing gown and bare feet, my legs left unshaven through the winter months.

I felt Em stiffen and take a deep breath. Pressed against me as she was, when she swallowed I felt it as if it were me gulping myself calm.

'I got on the bus at the top of Muswell Hill Broadway,' she said in answer to their questions.

'On your own?' asked the white policeman, who introduced himself as Detective O'Connell. It felt like a rebuke.

'We moved recently,' I said, defensive. 'Her friends live in Muswell Hill.'

'And you didn't feel you should pick her up?'

'I don't have a car. I gave her a strict curfew, though. Home by twelve thirty at the latest.'

See how I'm a good parent? See the boundaries I set?

Em explained how, as she'd got on to the bus, she'd been half aware of someone getting on behind her but hadn't paid it any mind. Her voice was small, but steady. *Good girl.*

'You'd been at a party,' said Detective O'Connell. 'Had you been drinking?'

I felt myself stiffen, anger rearing up inside, but my thickened thoughts and the solid weight of Em on my lap left me slow to react. Not so Frances, who glared over at the policeman.

'I really don't see how it's relevant whether or not Emma had been drinking.'

I felt myself dissolve with gratitude for this unknown young woman, and she shot me a brief look of support.

'I'd had a bottle of beer,' Em said. 'Maybe two. I wasn't drunk. I got off at the stop after the Tube.'

Again, she'd been vaguely aware of someone getting off behind her.

'He'd been sitting at the back, I think. But I hadn't noticed him.'

I imagined him then, this faceless man. Watching from the shadows.

Then what? Detective O'Connell wanted to know. He was younger than his colleague and slighter and the gel in his fair hair glinted where it caught the light.

'You're doing great,' added Detective Byrne. He looked tired, as if he'd been working a long shift, but his eyes were kind. Both policemen were standing, leaning against the kitchen worktops, as if they wouldn't be stopping long enough to sit. There were a few drops of tea on the counter just inches from Detective O'Connell's elbow, and I stared at them distractedly to see if he would put his sleeve in them.

'I stepped off the bus and started walking away,' Emma continued. 'Then as the bus pulled away I heard something behind me and, before I could turn, an arm was locked around my neck and someone was dragging me backwards.

'I started screaming, and he was hitting me, telling me to shut up.'

Hitting her. I'd spent sixteen years keeping my daughter safe and a strange man had come from nowhere and hit her. Over and over. Oversized knuckles connecting with child-soft skin. I felt sick.

'What exactly did he say?' Detective O'Connell wanted to know.

'Stop, bitch.'

Em's voice cracked, as if she was embarrassed to say the word, ashamed even. Rage burned an acid path down my throat, immediately followed by a rush of pity. My poor, poor girl.

'My head was jerked back but I could see that he was trying to pull me towards a side road.'

The policemen muttered to each other and Detective O'Connell got out his phone and called up Google Maps. 'Maidstone Road?' he asked, flashing the screen towards Em, as if she was in any state to see.

She shrugged. 'I guess so.'

'We haven't lived here long,' I said, repeating myself.

'He kept dragging me back and I was fighting him and he was hitting me and I could see the side road getting closer. It looked really dark down there. I was so scared.'

Em twisted her face towards me as she said this last part, and then she burst into fresh tears and buried her wet cheeks in my neck, and I squeezed her as hard as I could because I couldn't think of anything else to do. There was a pain in my chest. Tight and sharp. I stroked Em's hair and felt more raised bumps on her scalp where he'd hit her.

'Didn't anyone go past?' asked Detective Byrne.

'I heard at least two cars go by.' Em's voice was muffled against my neck. 'I thought they would stop. But they didn't.'

And now there were lumps of fury forming inside me to match the ones on my daughter's head. Two people drove past where my daughter was being attacked and did nothing.

'And then you came along?' Detective O'Connell was looking at Frances now. She was sitting across the table from me. Her face was very pale against her dark hair and I remember wondering if it was always that colour or if she was in shock, just like Em.

'Yes. I was on the opposite side of the road, driving home from a work thing in Cambridge, when I saw them. At first I thought it was two men fighting but then I realized it was a man trying to overpower a young woman.'

'So you stopped.'

Frances blinked at him. I noticed then that her hands were around a mug and I wondered who'd made her tea, or had she made it herself.

'Of course I stopped. Anyone would.'

'That isn't true,' said Emma hotly. 'The other two didn't.'

'I leaned on my horn, and when that didn't stop him I got out of the car with my phone in my hand and shouted that I was calling the police. And that's when he ran off.'

'Which direction?' Detective O'Connell was writing it all down in a small notebook which had a loop in the top to slide the little pen into.

'Down that same side street. What did you call it? Maidstone Road? I ran over to Emma to see if she was okay. She was upset, as anyone would be. So I brought her home and rang you on the way.'

The younger policeman frowned.

'See, if you'd called us straight away and waited where you were, we'd have been with you in minutes and we might have been in time to go after him.'

'I thought Emma needed to be at home with her mum.'

'I'm so grateful to you,' I said, my arms tight around my girl. 'If you hadn't come along . . .'

Now Detective O'Connell was looking at me. His eyes were that curious colour that is no colour at all, like the translucent dough of Chinese dumplings.

'Had *you* been drinking, Mrs Hopwood?'

COHEN

'Me? No.' Surprise neutralized the outrage I ought to have felt.

'Only you seemed a bit out of it when we arrived. Sleeping pill?'

I should have said no. It was in my mind to say no. But it's one of those ingrained things, isn't it, not lying to the police?

'Just half,' I said. My face was burning. 'Not even half. I have trouble sleeping. I don't suppose I've had more than five hours over the last two nights. Tomorrow's the one day I can lie in, my chance to catch up.'

'Even though your sixteen-year-old daughter wasn't home yet?'

Now the outrage came, front-loaded with guilt.

'Emma is very sensible. She never misses a curfew. I trust her absolutely.'

'The problem is, though, Mrs Hopwood, unfortunately, you can't trust all the people Emma might come across while she's out. There are some not very nice characters out there.'

22

3

Even four weeks later I carried the memory of that night on the surface of my skin, so the slightest reminder, like now, with Frances walking through the front door and along the hallway, as she had done that first time, caused the shame and fear to flare up again.

If Frances hadn't driven past . . .

Frances sat down at the kitchen table, with Dotty excitedly circling her chair and bringing her discarded shoes from various bedrooms. Em, head down, shot furtive glances at her from under her hair. I wondered if she felt intimidated because Frances was so pretty and confident and I worried that I hadn't told my daughter enough how lovely she was.

'I hope you don't mind me coming over,' Frances said. 'I've been thinking about the two of you so much, and what you must be going through. Then being in the police station this morning watching that video brought it all back.'

I noticed how big her eyes were and how they were flecked with amber.

'Did you get him?' Em wanted to know. Then she blushed at the way it sounded.

Frances nodded and, though her lips were pressed together, a smile was pushing against the corners trying to escape.

'You did? Oh, that's brilliant.'

In my excitement, I reached across and put a hand on Frances's arm. Her jumper was cashmere, a soft coral colour that complemented her peach-toned skin.

Em was beaming, her usual wariness momentarily forgotten in the relief of hearing that her attacker was on the way to being brought to justice.

'Was it him?' I asked. 'Number Eight? Although he might not have been eighth in your line-up. Distinctive chin?'

Frances hesitated.

'Green eyes?' I continued.

'Yes. That's right. Green.'

We drank tea in celebration. Em had been to the shop for biscuits, which she offered, shyly.

'Blimey, you get the plate treatment. You should be honoured,' I said to Frances. 'Normally, we eat them from the packet. Well, I eat them, Em inhales them.'

I noticed Em's cheeks flush pink and wondered if she minded being teased in front of Frances.

Frances lived with her mother in Muswell Hill, she told us. I was surprised. I'd imagined her with a boy-friend in a flat with stripped floorboards and house plants and a sleek blue-grey cat. Or sharing with other professional twenty-somethings, all of them sitting around in their dressing gowns on a hungover Sunday watching box sets and drinking stupidly expensive coffee from the farmers' market at Alexandra Palace.

'Mum has MS,' said Frances. 'I help her out at home.'

'Oh, I'm sorry,' I said, reminding myself yet again that you can never judge what goes on behind the closed doors of other people's lives. 'That's so tough for you. My parents are also ill, but at least they're in their eighties so you kind of expect it.'

'Mum spies on them on her laptop.'

Emma was getting her own back at me about the biscuits.

'It's not spying. I keep an eye on them, that's all.' My voice sounded shrill. Defensive. 'My mum has dementia and my dad has diabetes. I have a webcam set up in their sitting room so I can check Mum hasn't given him the slip or Dad isn't lying in a diabetic coma. It's perfectly legal, and it reassures them, knowing they're not entirely alone.'

'She's obsessed,' said Em. 'She watches them for hours.'

'Hardly.'

I couldn't explain even to myself the fascination of observing my parents when they had quite forgotten they were being observed. Certainly, I did it primarily out of love and to make sure they were safe, but I couldn't deny there was also an element of voyeurism, of which I wasn't proud. More than that, it took me back to my childhood, eavesdropping on grown-up conversations. Hoping to hear an insight into the adult world but also an insight into me, some objective sense of who I was.

'I didn't know you had another daughter.'

My chest froze.

Frances was looking at the family photograph on the fridge. The four of us. Back in the days when we were four.

'Rosie doesn't live here any more,' said Em quietly.

'She's away at university,' I added quickly, looking away so neither of them would see the heat that rushed into my cheeks. 'Manchester.'

Changing the subject, I asked Frances what she did for a living, even though it was a question I'd come to dread myself. I'd have pegged her for something in media or marketing but it turned out she worked as a business systems analyst for an investment bank called Hepworths. Em made the mistake of asking her what a business systems analyst was and we both spent the next few minutes glazed over, emerging none the wiser. Something to do with computers and data.

'What about you, Tessa?'

There it was. The reflexive surge of panic that question always induced. I was annoyed at myself for having brought it up.

'I used to edit women's magazines,' I began, as I always did. I might as well have had it tattooed across my forehead: *I used to be someone.*

'And now?'

'I'm a kind of freelance editorial consultant.'

I didn't want to get into it. The slow death of print magazines coinciding with me becoming the 'wrong demographic': *We just feel we need a figurehead who better reflects the readership.*

Younger, is what they meant.

Now I went into offices to fill maternity cover or to consult on new projects. And the rest of the time I sat at home pitching features to a dwindling number of publications or chatting in private Facebook groups with other dispossessed journalists still lamenting the end of the blank-cheque era and complaining about how rates were going down instead of up and how long it took for invoices to be paid.

'Freelance is good, though, right?' said Frances. 'Being your own boss.' I realized she'd guessed something of my discomfort and a lump formed in my throat at how tactful she was.

I went to the loo, listening as I climbed the stairs to the low murmur of conversation. It was heartwarming that Em felt so comfortable with Frances, despite an age difference of more than a decade. When I came back into the kitchen, Em was taking a selfie of the two of them on her phone and some muscle that had been tensed inside me relaxed at the sheer normality of it.

As Frances left, I couldn't help asking her exactly where she lived. One of the Avenue roads, it turned out. Beautiful, big houses, many of them worth millions, though she was quick to explain theirs had been converted and she and her mum lived in the upstairs flat.

'We used to have a house not far from there,' I told her. It was my own hubris, of course, wanting her to know we didn't always live here, in this nondescript terrace in this nondescript street in the no-man's-land just south of the North Circular, only a mile from our old house, though it might as well be five hundred. 'Sold it when we got divorced. Em still goes to school around there.'

'Dad still lives in Muswell Hill, though,' added Em.

It shouldn't have hurt. Not after all this time.

Later, I was watching on my laptop as my parents ate a TV dinner that had been prepared for them earlier by one of the agency care workers when my ringtone startled me. So few people called any more that having to talk to someone live now seemed startlingly exposing.

It was Detective Byrne.

'You're working late,' I said, anticipation fluttering in my stomach. The news that Em's attacker had been charged and was safely behind bars would be such a boost for Em – and for me.

'Eight p.m.? Believe me, Mrs Hopwood, I wish that counted as late. Anyway, I'm really sorry to have to tell you that we've reached a dead end with the case.'

'What?'

On my screen, my mother speared a boiled potato with her fork and glared at it with the utmost suspicion.

'As you know, resources are really stretched. The only way I managed to get the manpower to track down the CCTV from the bus and then send it around all the different forces was by calling it an attempted abduction rather than an assault. Putting together the identification tape, showing it to witnesses, it all takes time and money. And now Emma hasn't been able to make an identification.'

'Not officially, but you know afterwards she was sure it was Number Eight.'

There was a hesitation. Then:

'Unfortunately, we can't do these things in retrospect, as I'm sure you understand. And since Miss Gates made a false identification, well, we're at a—'

'Frances made a false identification?' My voice was shrill, echoing my complete surprise. 'You mean she picked the wrong guy? But that's not possible. She described him. I know it was him.'

Detective Byrne exhaled softly.

'The thing is,' he said, 'this is not an exact science. We're all of us only human. Sometimes our memories play tricks on us, convincing us we saw something that wasn't there. Or we are so desperate to help we persuade ourselves into something that we're not a hundred per cent sure of. And sometimes we get it wrong our end. Maybe the guy we captured on the CCTV wasn't the one who assaulted your daughter. Maybe once he got off the bus he went in the opposite direction to Emma and it was some other opportunistic criminal who just happened to be walking past who followed your daughter.'

'What are the chances of that?'

'At quarter past midnight on a Friday night in inner London? Higher than you might like to think.'

'So that's it, then?'

Onscreen, my mother had thrown her potato on the floor. It stared up from the carpet like an eyeball.

'We're not closing the case, Mrs Hopwood. It's only that there are no further active lines of inquiry we can pursue. I'm really very sorry. We all wanted to get him for you.'

Only after he had hung up did it occur to me that I should have corrected him.

It wasn't for me. It was for Emma.

Barely ten minutes later, the phone went again.

'Oh, Tessa, I'm so, so sorry.'

Frances sounded on the verge of tears.

'Detective Byrne just rang. I feel awful. I didn't want to tell you this afternoon, but the truth is, when I was in the police station earlier, I was torn between two of the men in the video. I went back and forth between them. Obviously, I chose the wrong one.'

'But you sounded so certain earlier.'

'Because I knew how upset Emma was that she hadn't been able to identify him. And I wanted to give her some hope, you know? And now I feel like I've let you both down.'

I reassured her as best I could and hoped she couldn't hear the disappointment in my voice.

I've never been good at hiding my feelings.

Later that evening, while I was doing my best to forget about the collapsed case by scrolling through Rosie's friends' Facebook pages on the off chance of seeing a new photo of my elder daughter, my phone pinged with a notification. *Frances Gates has sent you a Friend request*, the blue-and-white wording said.

I clicked confirm, touched that Frances wanted to keep in touch.

Less than a minute later a private message popped into my Facebook inbox.

I really am so sorry.

The profile picture was a close-up of Frances that looked to have been cropped from a larger group photo. A suggestion of other people's sleeves pressing against hers, a stray strand of fair hair on her shoulder.

It's okay, Frances. Honest, I wrote.

But really, it wasn't. Not at all.

4

'Everything would be all right, I think, if I could just get some sleep.'

The locum doctor nodded, but he was looking at his computer screen rather than at me. He was reading the notes from the last GP I saw here, a few weeks ago now, and from the one before that. Each time, a different doctor; each time, the same story told all over again. Not that there was much to differentiate it from all the other stories they must hear in here. I wondered if we became interchangeable in the end, us middle-aged women, with our flushes and our anxieties and our bursting into tears at the supermarket checkout.

'It must be very frustrating, I'm sure, and obviously, if you were a candidate for HRT, that would be something we'd try next, but given your family history ... However, perhaps if you tried to reframe how you view the menopause?'

'Reframe?'

'Try not to view it as a collection of unpleasant physical symptoms and accept it instead as a natural fact of life that will pass. Surely knowing that every woman goes through the same thing must be some sort of comfort? Strength in numbers, after all!'

The doctor had a smattering of raised purple bumps on his neck. Despite the wedding band on his left hand, which he touched regularly with the fingers of his right, like a talisman, he didn't look much older than Rosie.

And now I'd let myself think of Rosie the tears came. The young doctor glanced at me, then back to the screen, as if out of delicacy.

'I'm sure it must seem quite overwhelming sometimes,' he said, not unkindly. I wondered if the notes he was reading mentioned all the other times I'd fallen apart in front of one or other of his colleagues. *Unstable*, they might have written. *Histrionic*, even.

'Have you tried talking to friends?' the doctor suggested, as if this possibility might have somehow slipped my mind. 'I know there's still a stigma and sometimes women are embarrassed to bring it up but . . .'

I let out a noise that wasn't very attractive.

'I assure you, the hard part is getting my friends to shut up about it.'

He tried to give me a new prescription for temazepam, but I told him I'd stopped taking it. I could still hear the unspoken judgement in Detective O'Connell's voice on the night of the attack, five weeks before, when he'd said I'd seemed out of it. That list of seventeen missed calls viewed through a sleeping-pill fug.

The GP surgery was in Muswell Hill, near our old house.

Phil had suggested at one point I might prefer to find a doctor closer by. 'You're supposed to inform them when you move postcode,' he'd said sanctimoniously.

He thought it was healthier for me to break all the links with our old life and move on. Start again, as he'd done.

I'd stayed more out of spite than loyalty to a practice that had always seemed a bit impersonal. He'd taken everything else. He did not get to keep the lacklustre GP.

My journey home took me past Phil's house.

Well, that's not entirely accurate. One possible route home took me past his house and, although it was longer and I knew it wasn't good for me, I still took it because, sometimes, you can't help ripping the corner off a scab, despite knowing it isn't entirely healed. Sometimes, a clean, sharp pain can take your mind off a low-level, festering one.

There was an overhanging bush on the pavement opposite and I paused underneath it, my phone out as if I were checking it.

Phil's house wasn't exactly his house. It belonged to his 'girlfriend', which was a term that always made me laugh because there was nothing girly about Joy. Apart from her name, maybe.

When we'd sold our family home and divided up what was left after the monster mortgage was paid off, the plan was that we'd each have enough to buy a small place in the area where I live now. Fair, and easy for the kids, we decided.

Except afterwards, Phil maintained I'd decided that all on my own in my head, while he'd been non-committal. I'd heard what I wanted to hear, he said, as ever refusing to countenance any narrative outside my own. In the end, that was what convinced him he was doing the right thing, he told me later, the fact that there

had been two of us in our marriage but, even in the dis-
mantling of it, I'd managed to make it all about me.

I'd gone ahead and bought my place, my head in such
a state I shouldn't have been allowed to choose the next
Netflix movie, let alone a house.

And then Phil had moved in with her. Joy. Into her
house, just a few roads away from our old one, this red-
brick villa with its extra-wide front door with the
stained-glass panels and its deep bay window with the
plantation shutters, and the black-and-white tessellated
front path and the wisteria and the fucking brass welly
cleaner. My life had imploded, but nothing changed for
him.

Only the face on the pillow next to him.

There was a movement in the top window. A flash of
fair hair that was gone in a nanosecond. Rosie? I shrank
back into the shadow under the bush and stared and
stared, my heart racing. But nothing.

I moved off down the road, my chest tight, as if someone had sewn a line of stitches through the middle of it,
cutting off the air.

Rosie would be at university. It wouldn't be her. It
would be one of Joy's anodyne twins with their long,
shiny hair and netball-player legs.

Even so, every step hurt.

Safely two streets away, I stopped and fumbled in my
bag for my glasses so I could text Kath, trying to make
myself forcibly normal again. *In Muzzie. 12-year-old
GP tried to ply me with drugs but I said no, no, no.*

The answer pinged back almost immediately. I imagined
Kath at her desk in Pimlico at the head office of the housing association where she is chief press officer, surrounded

by people half her age who'd do her job for half the salary.
I knew she'd be desperate for a distraction.

*Excellent work. Now listen carefully. DO NOT GO
NEAR EVIL PHIL'S HOUSE. Do not pass go. Do not
collect £200. Understood? In other news, LOOK!!!*

There followed a screenshot from a phone app. Even
before I magnified it, I knew what it was.

*In the 15 days since I stopped drinking I've saved
£120 and lost 5lb in weight.*

I sighed.

Ever since Kath signed up to NoMoreDrinking.com,
she'd become horribly evangelical.

I don't recognize you any more, I texted back.

*That's because I've lost 5lb and bought a whole new
wardrobe with all the £££s I've saved.*

I replaced my phone and specs and set off, feeling
calmer. I'd always valued my friends but, in the last
couple of years, since everything started going wrong,
I'd come to depend on them more than ever.

The thing was, these days, all of us had bad stuff in
one way or another. Kath's adored older brother dropped
dead of a heart attack three years ago while training for
his first ever marathon. Our other university friend,
Mari, who hadn't long completed the painfully slow
process of becoming a fully-fledged grief counsellor,
found herself very nearly having to counsel herself after
her oldest son attempted suicide. Drugs-related, it turned
out. He's fine now, thank God, but those things leave a
mark.

Even seemingly perfect Nita, the one school mum I was
still in contact with, hadn't got through fifty completely
unscathed. The last time I saw her she told me her mum

had been diagnosed with aggressive inoperable liver cancer and given just months to live.

What I'm saying is, bad stuff came with the territory.

On my way home, I called into the garden centre. Not that my house had much of a garden. More like a yard with a fence around it. As it faced north-east, the yard got no direct sunlight during the winter months so the concrete flags were green and slippery with algae, while summer days saw us migrating southwards as the day progressed, chasing the sun, ending up flattened against the back fence by five forty-five, when it disappeared altogether.

What our yard needed was lots of big, colourful pots with big, colourful plants in them, I decided. Or maybe I could deck it in sections and lay down lots of that purple slate that was so popular.

In the event, I wandered aimlessly around, stroking the leaves of plants whose names I didn't know and baulking at the price of the giant, colourful pots. I saw some bedding flowers I liked the look of, then realized I had no way of getting them home. I bought some seeds instead, which I knew would simply join the other packets in the kitchen drawer.

Em was at home when I got in. There was a time, not so long ago, when she was hardly ever home, always out with friends, or at the library revising, or at any number of after-school activities or else staying with her father. 'Hello, stranger,' I'd say when I encountered her by the kettle or on the landing. On the rare occasions where she had an evening free, I felt like I'd won an unexpected prize.

But in the weeks since the attack, particularly the last week, since the case collapsed, she'd been at home more often than not, coming directly back from school, rarely going out, apart from to drama club or to her dad's. And rather than being pleased to have her with me, I worried about what her near-constant presence meant.

'Are you sure you're okay?' I asked her as we sat together at the kitchen table over a cup of tea.

'I'm fine,' she said, rolling her eyes good-naturedly – it was far from the first time I'd asked her.

'It's just that you're home so much more now than you were before . . . well, before *it* happened.'

That's how we referred to the attack now, Em and I. *It. That thing. What happened.* As if taking away its label somehow reduced its power.

'That's because exams are getting closer,' she said, which was true, although they were still months away. 'It's easier to study at home.'

'And you're sure it's not because of—'

'No. I told you. It's because of work.'

She twiddled a strand of her long hair around her index finger, which is something she'd done since she was a child in times of stress. 'Stop,' I said softly, reaching out to tap her hand. Since she'd confided in me a couple of days before that she was worried her hair was falling out, I'd been scanning her scalp anxiously, and now I was sure I could see patches on her head where her hair was noticeably sparser.

'Em, sweetie. You know you can talk to me.'

Emma stared down at the floor and I realized she was trying not to cry. She'd always been this way. Fiercely protective of her own feelings but also not wanting to put other people in a position where they felt something was demanded of them.

'It's okay to put your own needs first for once,' I told her, shuffling my chair around the table so that I could put my arm around her. 'Come on, tell me what's going on.'

'What, so you can pass it on to Dad and try to find a way to make this his fault too?'

I flinched at the unexpected barb, hurt burning behind my eyes. I wasn't proud of the way I'd acted during the break-up. There were occasions when I'd thrown the girls' suffering in Phil's face, used things they'd told me in private to guilt-trip him about what he'd done. But that was then. I'd apologized so many times since. I knew I hadn't acted well.

'Sorry, Mum,' said Em, in a small, lumpy voice, leaning her head so it rested in the crook of my neck and I could smell her apple shampoo. 'I didn't mean that. But I don't want to talk about it, because that means I have to think about it and I just want it to go away. I want *him* to go away.'

Now, of course, I know I should have pressed her, despite the tears she was trying so hard not to shed. But you can't force teenagers to open up, can you? You have to let them come to you in their own time.

That's what I tell myself, anyway.

Sometimes I catch Mum looking at me with an anxiety that both melts me and sets my teeth on edge, at the same time.

'Why don't you go out?' she suggests, and I pretend to consider it. I don't tell her how my neck aches from looking out for you or how I steel myself before going around corners in case I bump into you or how I avoid shop windows for fear of seeing your face reflected back behind me.

I've stopped listening to music while I'm out on my own. With headphones in my ears, how would I hear you coming?

Yesterday, I was on my way home and the sun was shining and I leaned against the park railings and raised up my face to the warmth, and for a moment I forgot myself and closed my eyes. Then I felt goosebumps on my skin, as if a shadow had fallen across me, and my eyes sprang open, but not before I'd convinced myself that when they did I'd find you standing in front of me.

'Are you okay?' asked a woman with a pram standing nearby. I realized I was hyperventilating. I must have looked insane.

Last night, I dreamed I was back there next to the park with my eyes closed, and that cold feeling came and I knew that you were there, just inches away, but my lids were glued shut and my legs wouldn't work. When I woke up my breath was ragged and my skin felt ingrained with you, and even after I dragged myself to the bathroom and ran the water scorching hot in the sink I couldn't wash you off.

5

I kept an eye on Em while trying not to make it obvious that was what I was doing.

The problem was, she had always been hard to read. Meeting her at the school gates when she was small, I'd inspect her little face when she came out of the classroom, my anxious mother's heart searching for clues as to what sort of a day she'd had. But there would be nothing, just the same *Mona Lisa* smile as always.

'Yeah, it was fine,' she'd answer, and it would take a tap on the shoulder from a teacher or another parent to find out that there'd been some incident where she'd got hurt or fallen over. Getting her ready for the bath one evening, I'd been horrified to discover a bruise on one milky shoulder in the shape of a perfect bite mark, but when I asked about it she'd shrugged it off. 'It's fine now.'

'She'd make a brilliant poker player,' Phil and I used to joke. Well, it wasn't so funny now, I thought, scanning her face at breakfast-time, a little over five weeks after the attack, trying to work out what was going on behind that placid exterior.

She'd always bitten her nails, but the hair thing was more worrying. When she wasn't twirling strands of it absently around her finger, she was compulsively patting her head to see if it was getting thinner. One night she came to me, her hair still wet from the shower. 'Look,' she said, holding out her hand. We both stared at the small clump of hair lying across her palm as if it were the body of some once-living creature. When she parted the top sections, I could now see two or three coin-shaped patches where the scalp showed through. But when I suggested she talk to a counsellor about what had happened, she insisted there was no need.

Still, in most other respects, she gave the appearance of having put it behind her. True, she was still around more often than she'd been before, but that could easily have been down to a heavier school workload, as she said. She'd always been conscientious about schoolwork, often stressing far out of proportion to the importance of whatever essay she was working on. It would have been out of character for her not to be preoccupied and subdued with important end-of-year exams looming.

Of course, I still worried, but I tried not to dwell on it. 'Don't let that man take any more from you – or Em – than he already has,' Mari counselled me over the phone when I confided how much Em's attacker was still on my mind. 'When he comes into your head, deliberately shut him down, and that way you restore your own power.'

So, for a few days, I persuaded myself that things were getting back to normal. *See how Em is walking around the house with her phone in her hand, laughing with her friends on FaceTime, showing them the disgusting tuna sandwich she made or the weird way Dotty is sleeping? Isn't that exactly as it should be?*

Then one afternoon, just under a week since I'd last

tried to broach the subject of the attack with Emma, it all came rushing to the surface again in the most agonizing way.

It was mid-afternoon and I was, for once, upstairs, working at my desk, which was in an alcove on the landing. There were three bedrooms in our house, but I couldn't bring myself to set up my office in Rosie's room. It would have felt like I was admitting she wasn't coming back.

So I was sitting at my cramped desk, facing the wall, when I heard Em's key in the lock and the sound of her bursting in through the door, breathing noisily, as if she'd been running.

'Hello, darling!' I called down.

There was no answer, although I could still hear those painful, rasping breaths.

Puzzled, I got up and peered over the top of the banister, racing down when I saw that Em – my normally stoic daughter – was leaning against the wall in the hallway with her head in her hands.

'What is it? What's happened?'

I flew down the stairs and put my arms around my daughter's shaking shoulders.

'Em, talk to me. What's the matter?'

'I've seen him, Mum.'

The words were muffled and, though I instantly guessed what she meant, still I pretended I didn't, as if I could force reality down a different channel by merely refusing to recognize it.

'Saw who? Is it a boy? Is that it?'

She shook her head and finally raised her tear-streaked face so that I could hear her properly.

'*Him.* Number Eight. I saw him while I was crossing

the road outside the Tube station. He'd come out of a doorway somewhere on the opposite side and then crossed straight over right next to me.'

There was a tightening then, in my chest, but still my first thought was that she was mistaken. I wanted her to be mistaken.

'Darling, you must have seen someone who just looked similar. He's obviously in your thoughts, so it wouldn't be at all surprising if you thought you saw him.'

'Mum, it was him. I know it was. He was exactly the same height and he had that weird chin and those exact same eyes and he was wearing that same jacket with the badge thingy on the sleeve, and then when he passed me I smelled that aftershave and I started shaking all over. I know it was him, Mum. What if he recognized me? What if he followed me?'

Her eyes were wide, locked on mine, searching for reassurance, just like she was small again.

I took her into my arms and held her for a while, the solid warmth of her. I was glad she couldn't see my face so I had a chance to neutralize the shock from it.

'He didn't follow you, Em. You said yourself he was going the opposite way. And there's no way he would recognize you. It was dark the night it happened. He came up to you from behind. He probably didn't see your face the entire time. You're perfectly safe, sweetheart. You're home now.'

All those platitudes I told her as I rocked her to and fro like a baby, wanting to give her comfort, hoping she couldn't feel my own heart pummelling against my ribs.

It was what I'd feared, right from the night of the attack. That the man who'd done it would turn out to be local. Since the failed ID parade, after the bogeyman had a face and we knew he'd got away with it, those fears had only intensified.

It used to drive Phil mad, this compulsion I had to jump right to the worst-case scenario. 'My wife, the catastrophist,' he'd say, rolling his eyes, as if I were deliberately dramatizing my fears for effect. He never understood how thinking through the very things I most dreaded was my way of guarding against them happening. Everyone knows bad news takes you unawares, so making myself confront the direst outcomes rendered them impossible.

Except, of course, it didn't.

I felt sick. But still I forced my features into a smile and took Em into the kitchen to make her some tea, telling her all the time that she was safe, that nothing bad would happen to her.

After a while she calmed down, the pink blotches fading from her cheeks.

'You're right, I don't think he ever saw my face,' she said at last. 'I mean, he couldn't, could he, if he was grabbing me from behind?'

'Exactly.'

'And just because I saw him coming out of that doorway today, it doesn't mean he definitely lives around here, does it? I mean, maybe he was working here and getting the Tube home. That's a possibility, isn't it?'

'Of course it is.'

'Will you call that detective, though, to double-check? You've still got his card, haven't you?'

Detective Byrne had given me a business card with all his contact details on that first night when Em was attacked, telling me to call him any time I needed to find out what was going on with the case.

'Darling, I really don't think the police will—'

'Please?'

I shrugged and took out my phone, rummaging around in my wallet to find the policeman's white, functional card.

I was expecting to leave a message. Like most people brought up on a diet of TV cop shows, I imagined the police to be constantly on the move, out and about investigating crimes, and that idea was proving hard to shift, despite having witnessed at first hand the mountains of paperwork on the desks at our local station, the shiny patches on the upholstered office chairs hinting at long, sedentary hours. Instead, Detective Byrne – Detective *Sergeant* Byrne, as it said on his card – answered on the second ring.

'Mrs Hopwood. What can I do for you?'

He had one of those voices, deep and gentle, that somehow release tensions you hadn't even known you were carrying, and I found myself exhaling softly before speaking.

'I'm sorry to bother you,' I started, remembering too late how I'd read on Twitter that women – and it was mainly women – who started conversations that way immediately lost ground.

'It's just that' – 'just', another disempowering word – 'Emma thinks she saw the man who attacked her – you know, Number Eight from the video you showed us – not far from here, actually. I thought maybe you could put her mind at rest that it couldn't be him.'

Detective Byrne sighed.

'I'm sorry, Mrs Hopwood. I can understand your concern. And Emma's too. But I'm not at liberty to tell you where a suspect in a case lives, let alone one who has not been charged with any crime.'

'But surely you're allowed to reassure us that he's not living right here, practically around the corner?'

'All I can say is you don't need to be concerned.'

Em was watching my face, so I smiled brightly as I put my phone down.

'He says we don't need to be concerned,' I told her. 'So that's good, isn't it?'

Em nodded, and my heart contracted as I watched her swallow hard behind the soft, pale skin of her throat.

We sat and chatted for a little while then she said she had to go upstairs to work. And when she came down for dinner a couple of hours later, she seemed to have put Number Eight out of her head. We talked about a teacher from school whose husband was facing deportation after fifteen years living in the UK. 'They can't do that, though, can they, Mum?' asked my big-hearted girl. 'Not after all this time?'

Later, we watched TV together, a show about couples meeting for a blind date in a London restaurant. We agreed that the women were uniformly in a different league from the men.

'How about you?' I asked her, nudging her in the ribs. 'Any boyfriends on the scene?'

At one point before the attack I'd been convinced there was someone. Just little things. Spending longer in the bathroom before school. Texting furiously then clicking off abruptly if I came near.

'Shush, I'm trying to listen.'

I glanced at Em and saw she was blushing, which made me think my suspicions were right, but I knew better than to push her. If there was a boy, I'd have to let her tell me about it in her own time. She'd always been that way.

At eleven, we both went up to bed, meaning, of course, that I lay in bed reading, then trying to sleep, then giving up and reading again. I tried to remind myself of what Detective Byrne had said, about us not having to be concerned, but his words sounded hollow in my memory, as if he'd been telling me what I wanted to hear.

The more I thought about it, the less likely it seemed that he'd have told me anything different, even if Em's attacker *was* living around the corner. No charges had been brought, after all. He was still a free man.

Whenever I closed my eyes I pictured my daughter passing inches away from the man who might have attacked her and the horror of it made them ping open again.

Around one in the morning I heard the sound of Em's door opening. I expected her to go into the bathroom but, instead, I heard her padding softly down the stairs.

I got up, walked over to my door and opened it a crack, listening for her heading into the kitchen for a drink of water. But in place of the sound of the tap running I heard a clicking noise coming from the front door and the sound of keys jangling.

Hearing Em coming back up, I pulled my door gently to and dived back into bed.

Then I lay staring at the ceiling and tried not to think about what it meant that my daughter was double-checking the locks on the door and setting the latch we never used in the middle of the night.

6

'I didn't know who else to tell. I hope you don't mind.'

'Oh my God, not at all. I've thought about Emma loads since I saw you both last. Wondering how she was getting on.'

I didn't let on to Frances that I knew she'd texted Em directly, checking to make sure she was okay, or that she and Em often 'liked' each other's posts on Facebook and Instagram. Besides, it was good if there was someone else Em could talk to about what happened if she needed to. I suspected she hadn't been completely open with her friends. 'I don't want to make a big thing out of it,' she'd told me. And if my suspicion was right and there was a boyfriend she was confiding in, she wasn't about to tell me.

'Oh, Emma's all right. I think. Not that she'd tell me, probably. She's at that age.' I stood up from the kitchen table, tucking the phone under my chin while I rinsed out my coffee cup at the sink. 'I only thought I should warn you that she might need a bit of reassuring, now that she's seen him. Or seen someone who looks like him.'

'You think she's wrong?'

I shrugged, nearly dislodging the phone.

'I don't know. I mean, it would be such bad luck, wouldn't it? To see the man who'd tried to abduct you while you were walking home, minding your own business.'

I think I was waiting for Frances to agree with me, hoping for reassurance that, no, fate would not be so unkind. Instead, she said:

'It can't be uncommon, though, I would guess. Don't you think it stands to reason that most opportunistic crimes would be committed locally? Someone taking advantage of a situation that presents itself as they go about their day-to-day lives?'

A situation. Had Em been a 'situation' to this man?

'So I expect it must happen a lot,' Frances went on. 'Victims of crime coming across the perpetrators in the street. Poor Emma, though. What a traumatic thing to happen. I think I'd struggle if I saw him again. I can't imagine how much worse it must be for her.'

A cold chill caused the skin on my arm to come up in small bumps. I'd called Frances after Em had left for school, hoping to have my fears allayed. Instead, as I said goodbye and pressed the phone off, they felt far more real.

Whenever I thought back to the previous night, hearing Em's soft footsteps padding downstairs and the click of the night latch going on, the jangling of the keys, I ached with impotence. Just how much was my daughter bottling up?

I rang Nita. Her daughter, Grace, had been friends with Em since they started in reception class, two little girls in light-up trainers and with their hair in plaits. I wanted to ask her if Grace had noticed any changes in Em since the attack, and to warn her that Em might need extra support over the next few days while she got over the shock of seeing the man who attacked her walking in the street.

Nita's phone went straight to voicemail and I left her a rambling message asking her to call me back.

Then I sat down at the kitchen table, phone still in hand, wishing there was someone else with a link to the school that I could call, needing to close that gap between my world and my daughter's.

Belatedly, I remembered the school mums' WhatsApp group. We'd started it years before when Emma and her friends were in secondary school and we were no longer all meeting up at the school gates every day, as we had when they were younger. We wanted a way of staying in contact so we could talk through any concerns about changes in behaviour or fallings-out, or ask questions about homework or exams or how it felt that our daughters were growing away from us. Since its inception we'd dealt with bullying and a burgeoning eating disorder and whether fifteen was too young to allow your daughter to sleep with her boyfriend under your roof.

Over the last two years, after losing my job and then Phil, my contributions to the group chat had more or less dried up and then, after the estrangement with Rosie, I'd muted it completely, unable to face going back on. For all I knew, I might have been ejected from the group. Even if I hadn't been, I was sure they'd have forgotten I was ever part of it, as it had been so long since I last actively contributed. But perhaps there'd be some mention on there of what had happened to Em, some clues Em's friends had dropped to their parents about how she was coping with it, or even whether I was right to think there might have been a boyfriend in the picture.

I clicked on the WhatsApp icon. There were various chats there. One with Emma from last summer when she'd gone away to a festival with her friends, one with Kath and Mari and a couple of our other friends where we posted silly photos and lots of 'send gin'-type messages. An old family chat between the four of us with the last comment from Phil just before it all fell apart – *Stir-fry tonight??* – the poignant mundanity of it making the breath catch in my throat.

And now, here it was: *Year 8 Mums.* Although, of course, Year 8 had turned seamlessly into years 9, 10 and 11 since the chat started, children growing into semi-adults in front of our eyes.

The current conversation was about tutoring. Who was doing it. How much it was costing. Everyone agreed it gave our kids an unfair advantage over kids whose parents couldn't afford tutoring, but no one, it seemed, felt strongly enough to give up that advantage out of principle.

I started to scroll backwards until I got closer to the date of Em's attack five and a half weeks ago, scanning the comments for mention of her name. There was a conversation about arrangements for picking up a group of girls from a party and then another one about the deadline for delivering English coursework.

I scrolled further and found a conversation that was different in tone from the others, less brisk and practical. I caught the words 'dreadful' and 'awful' and then 'poor girl' and my heartbeat quickened. I scrolled up the thread to where it started with someone – Tilly's mum, Selina – saying: *OMG, have you heard about the attack?* and then Ruth's mum, Ayesha, chipping in, *What happened???* with a goggle-eyed emoji. Then the reply: *Emma Hopwood was assaulted on her way home from the party on Friday night.*

I was surprised how much it hurt, seeing it laid out so bluntly in black and white, just a thing that happened to someone else's child. At least it proved my hunch was right and they'd forgotten I was ever in the group.

Those first comments were followed by a string of horrified responses from those who hadn't yet heard about the attack. Lots of *OMG!* and *that poor girl.* Others who'd already heard the news from their own daughters jumped in, adding the extra information they'd gleaned. Where it took place. What exactly happened. How she managed to get away.

Thank God she's ok, wrote Ellie B's mum, Mel, *only . . .*

Instantly, my hackles rose. That word 'only', with everything it implied.

. . . I can't help wondering why she was on a bus alone at that time. I would never let Ellie come home alone.

Now it came, the chorus of assents.

Absolutely!

Exactly.

I understood what they were doing, distancing themselves, so that this became something that happened to other people's children, not to theirs. But still their words were like elastic bands snapping against my skin.

No way would I have let Tilly go if she had to come home alone, said Selina. *Me neither*, wrote Mel. *WTF didn't they get her an Uber?*

Now Nita chimed in for the first time:

Em refused Uber, didn't feel safe.

I mouthed a silent 'thank you', though my stomach was clenched tight.

In that case Tessa shouldn't have let her go at all, wrote Ayesha.

Then it came. As I knew it would.

Unfortunately, as we all know, this isn't the first time Tessa has screwed up.

My eyes swam as I read Selina's comment and I was assailed by a hot rush of guilt and shame. The things the women were saying were only the same things I'd been berating myself with ever since that awful night. Why did I let her go? Why didn't I insist she got a cab? But to know that other people had also been levelling those same criticisms, even implying there was some sort of a pattern of neglect, felt unbearable.

I don't want to be a bitch, wrote Ayesha. *But sometimes I think Tessa thrives on the drama.*

An icy blade of shock sliced through my brain. Is that really what they thought of me? That I'd brought all of this on myself somehow – the divorce, the move, the rift with Rosie, the terrible thing that had happened to Em? All of it an attempt to thrust myself into the limelight?

There was one more comment on the thread. I hoped it might be Nita again, defending me. But instead it was Mel. And what she wrote broke me into tiny pieces.

It's those poor girls I feel sorry for.

*

The WhatsApp messages played on my mind for the rest of the day. These were women I'd once counted almost as friends. We'd shared playdates when the girls were too young to stay on their own and taken each other's children to ballet lessons and pantomimes. I'd helped with face painting at their daughters' parties and sponsored countless charity walks and climbs and swims and silences. Even though my job had meant I wasn't around as much as some of the others, I'd tried to make up for it with sleepovers at weekends and trips to the cinema. I'd even managed to get Ayesha's oldest daughter, a wannabe designer, into London Fashion Week, pulling every magazine-editor string I possibly could.

And now it was as if none of that history had happened, as if I were some stranger from a foreign country, who didn't belong and couldn't get things right. Worse was the worry that some of the opprobrium would be deflected on to Em. That if I was now an outsider, maybe Emma would be too, merely by association.

It's those poor girls I feel sorry for.

The hurt I felt was the raw, flayed hurt of the playground.

I'd only just resumed work after the body-blow of the WhatsApp messages when Em came home. I glanced at the clock on the computer screen. Three twenty. She wasn't usually this early.

'I had a headache,' she said when I asked her. I scanned her face anxiously. She did look pale, but still I wasn't sure I believed her.

'Are you okay, Em?' I persevered. 'Are you still upset about seeing that man yesterday?'

'No, honestly. This has nothing to do with him. I just have a headache.'

I couldn't remember the last time Emma had complained of a headache. I stood up to hug her and she submitted stiffly before heading upstairs.

That night, as I lay waiting in vain for sleep to claim me like a forgotten suitcase, I heard muffled sounds coming from Em's room. I went to my door and listened and was horrified to hear what sounded like stifled sobs.

But when I crossed the landing and opened her door, whispering her name softly, she pretended to be asleep.

Back in my own bed, now wide awake, a ball of fear and worry formed in my gut, solid as a fist.

7

Until that week, I'd never really noticed that there was a café practically next to the Tube entrance on Brownlow Road. It was a bit of a greasy spoon, to be fair, and when Nita ordered a flat white the waitress looked at her blankly and said in a heavy accent, 'So I give you Nescafé with milk,' but it was clean enough. And there was a table in the window overlooking the street.

'I don't get why we're meeting here,' said Nita, taking a baby wipe from her bag and surreptitiously running it across the white plastic table top.

I thought about lying. The stinging WhatsApp chat I'd read the day before still weighed heavy on my mind, and I was reluctant to give Nita and the other school mums any more reasons for distancing themselves from our family. They already believed drama clung to us like a bad smell.

But Nita was still my friend, the one school mum who'd stuck by me, even after all the madness surrounding the break-up, the sobbing in the playground, the fixation on Joy and her family and her house, the awful estrangement from Rosie. And though it still hurt that Nita hadn't been more vocal in standing up for me on that WhatsApp chat, she had at least not piled in with the others. Plus, with her daughter Grace and Em long-time friends, she was a valuable link to the life my daughter led when she wasn't with me.

So I told her about the ID line-up and how Em was sure she'd seen the man she'd failed to recognize right here on the street.

'He was coming out of a doorway somewhere over there,' I said, gesturing to the parade of shops directly across from us, separated from the main road by a small lay-by in which cars could park to load or unload.

Nita frowned. Or at least that's what I presumed she was doing. Since she'd started having regular Botox, I found I had to guess at some of Nita's facial expressions. That's not to say she didn't look amazing, her neat features perfectly set into her small, smooth face like tiny jewels in a ring, only that she looked occasionally as if she'd been varnished.

'So we're here to spy on him?'

'Just to keep an eye out, that's all,' I said. I didn't mention that I'd been in this café since it opened. Sitting at this very table. Keeping watch. 'The police say they can't get involved, so I feel like it's up to me to make sure she's all right.'

Nita reached out and put one of her small hands on my arm.

'Tess, I know how hard this must have been for you. If something like that happened to Grace, I don't know what I'd do. But what do you think would happen if you saw this guy? What are you going to do, perform a citizen's arrest?'

'No, of course not.'

'So why not leave it? There's nothing to say the guy lives around here. He could have been visiting or passing through. Or it could have been some random man who happens to look like the guy from the video. You need to focus on Emma, not him.'

Nita called the waitress over to ask if they had smashed avocado on sourdough toast. The woman shook her head blankly. 'No avocado. But we have brown bread,' she said helpfully.

'With what?' Nina asked.

'Butter?' the woman suggested.

Normally, Nita and I met up in Muswell Hill, where she still lived and where it would be unheard of for a café not to sell avocado. I remembered the first time I'd seen her across the classroom on Em and Grace's first day of primary school, all perfect glossy hair and good teeth, one of those stay-at-home mothers who arrived at pick-up with a Tupperware container full of home-made cookies and who knew the name of every kid in the class by the end of the first week, and I'd just known we wouldn't get along.

Yet somehow, despite everything, Nita and I became friends. And remained friends. Even through these last two turbulent years, and in spite of the rumours about my erratic behaviour that spread around the school like wildfire. In spite of the judgements of Rosie's friends' parents.

'I'm worried about you, Tess,' said Nita now, her huge brown eyes liquid in her unnaturally smooth face. Would this be the way it was now? I wondered. Half the women I'd grown up with remaining preserved in aspic at some indeterminate age while the rest of us grew wrinkly and saggy until one day we looked in the mirror and no longer recognized ourselves?

I didn't even mind my lines. Not really. I ate well, I exercised a little. I took care of myself. What I minded was that it wasn't a level playing field and that nobody ever admitted it. And that by the time I realized how many women I knew were secretly slipping off every three months to have botulin injected into their faces, I was twenty years behind the curve, unable to catch up even if I wanted to.

'No need to be,' I said, but my attention was fixed on a point out of the window and across the street, where a door had opened up.

Nita followed my gaze.

'Is that . . . ?'

But the man who came out was old, with a white beard and a back bent almost at a right angle. I smiled, wanting Nita to know I was well aware I was being ridiculous.

'Has Grace said anything about Em?' I asked her now. 'Has she mentioned a boyfriend at all?'

Nita shook her head.

'Well, has she been acting out of character at all since the attack?'

'Not that I can remember,' said Nita. 'Although I know Grace was upset that Em pulled out of the play.'

I'd been biting into a greasy croissant, but now my head shot up. Emma loved drama club. She wasn't a born actress, hated drawing attention to herself, but she'd always enjoyed being part of a big school production. She'd even mentioned the possibility of going into stage management or theatre directing at some point.

And she'd been thrilled at this year's choice – the music-al *Cabaret*.

'What do you mean, pulled out of the play? Why would she do that?'

Nita widened her already wide eyes.

'Oh God, I'm sorry, I had no idea she hadn't told you. I don't know why. She announced it a couple of days ago apparently.'

A couple of days ago. So it would turn out to be about *him*. I knew it would.

The croissant solidified in my mouth and burned as I swallowed it down.

Back at the house, I waited until Emma had come home and made herself a cup of tea before broaching the subject of the abandoned school play.

'I've just got too much work to do, with exams and everything.' Em was looking at something on her phone and didn't meet my eyes. Needles of unease pricked my skin.

'Who are you messaging?'

'Frances. She's been really nice about making sure I'm okay.'

I was touched at Frances's kindness. She'd already done so much to help.

'Did you tell her about seeing him in the street?'

Still, Em didn't look up.

'No, not yet.'

'Are you sure you dropped out of the play because of work and not because of what happened? Because if you're worried about coming home from rehearsals or from drama club, I'll happily come to meet you.'

'I'm not eight years old, Mum. And it's not about him. Honest.'

She tried to smile and her hand went up to her hair. I caught sight of a new bald spot, just behind her ear, small as a five-pence coin.

A memory blazed in my mind of holding Emma as a hairless newborn and feeling that heartbreakingly soft patch of skin at the front of her head where the bones of her skull hadn't yet fused, and something tore inside me like damp paper.

I turned away so that my daughter wouldn't see my face.

8

It was two days later that I saw him.

I'd told myself that this would be the last day I sat in that café. The last weak coffee, the last time the tired-looking waitress would greet me without recognition, as if she'd never seen me before. But the fact is I'm not sure that's true. I felt so helpless at that time, so powerless to help my hurting daughter. At least being in the café gave me the illusion of taking control. Besides, what would I do at home? After a string of broken nights my concentration was shot, and when I sat at my computer to work, the words I was searching for floated out of reach, like fruit flies that I grabbed at in vain.

The thing that no one tells you about insomnia is how, in the middle of the night when you're lying in bed, your mind feels scalpel-sharp, thoughts dazzling as crystals, too bright to sleep. But as soon as the alarm goes off – if you're lucky, waking you from the light, restless state you slipped into what seems like only min-utes before – they turn turgid, crawling sluggishly through the bog of your mind.

Coming to the café gave me an escape from hours I'd otherwise spend staring blankly at the computer screen.

And like I say, it made me feel like I was doing something, even if all I was doing was looking out of a window.

Which was exactly what I was doing when a door opened between the mini-market and the fried-chicken shop, halfway along the parade of shops directly opposite and *he* came out.

Just as with the ID tape, I felt an instant thump of recognition in the pit of my stomach, even though he had his back turned, double-locking the door he'd stepped out of.

The dark puffa jacket he wore emphasized the solid breadth of his shoulders. Even from across the street I could see the white flash of a logo on the sleeve. When he turned around I saw his distinctive-shaped face, the cheekbones wide, the chin with those jutting twin points.

Now he came forward to stand on the opposite side of the crossing. Eyes that even from this distance away I knew to be startling green. That same *Come on, then, I dare you* set of his head as in the ID tape.

Fumbling with nerves, I pulled my phone out of my bag and took a photo through the glass of the café window, zooming in as far as I could. First, I focused on his meaty hands, imagining them folded into fists, pummelling my daughter's head. Was that a glint of metal on his finger? I couldn't be sure. I moved my attention to his face – the full mouth, lips moving silently in sync with whatever he was listening to on the headphones plugged into his ears. *Stop, bitch*, that's what he'd said, and I pictured that cruel mouth saying the words. I couldn't smell his aftershave from all the way back here but still I imagined how it would be, heady and overpowering.

I put the phone down and followed his progress across the road until he disappeared from view in the direction of the Tube entrance. When I picked up my discarded coffee, the cup shook in my hand.

'You poor thing,' said Frances. 'And poor Em. It must have been such a shock for her. On top of everything else she's had to cope with.'

We were sitting in the pub on Bounds Green Road, in the coveted window snug – a table that had been fitted into a tiny bay in the wall with padded seating following the contour of the glass.

I nodded, for a minute not trusting myself to speak. Frances seemed to be offering sympathy entirely without judgement, and it almost overwhelmed me.

'That's why I didn't want to show Em the photo,' I said eventually. 'It's all so raw, and the last thing I want to do is give her more to worry about. I thought maybe you could take a look.' I started rummaging in my bag for my phone. 'So you can tell me if I'm going completely bonkers.'

'Of course. Anything I can do to help.' Frances took a sip of her lime and soda. She didn't usually drink during the week, she'd explained. Liked to keep a clear head for work.

I was grateful to her for coming at such short notice. I'd called her at work and when she'd said she could meet me on her way home I'd almost cried from relief. I'd watched her park her car – a pistachio-green Fiat 500 – from the pub window and felt as if an unbearably tight belt I'd been wearing had been suddenly loosened a notch or two.

I called up the photograph of him. It wasn't a great picture. The angle was strange and there was a blur of a car bumper in the bottom right. But when you scaled it up, there he was.

Frances inhaled sharply when I showed her the image. First, her face drained of colour and then a pink stain crept over the contours of her cheeks.

'It's him, isn't it?' I said.

She nodded, bit down on her lip.

'Sorry,' she said after she'd composed herself. 'I don't know what right I've got to be upset. It's just such a shock seeing him. I still can't get it out of my head, you know. That night.'

I couldn't either. Lying awake during the long, stomach-churning hours, I went through it again and again. What might have happened if Frances, driving home tired after a two-day work conference in Cambridge, hadn't noticed what was happening on the other side of the road. Or if she'd carried on assuming, as she did at first, that it was two men having a fight.

'I couldn't have held out any more,' Em had said. 'If Frances hadn't come . . .'

That was our mantra now. *If Frances hadn't come.*

'So the doorway you saw him come out of was near the Tube, practically opposite the bus stop where he assaulted Emma?' Frances asked now, her hazel eyes darting to the photo and then away, as if she couldn't bear to linger too long on his face.

'Yep, talk about shitting on your own doorstep.'

'And the police won't do anything?'

I shook my head. 'How can they? They can't have a second identification. The guy hasn't been charged with anything. They don't have the resources to pursue it any more, that's what Detective Byrne said. The case fell apart.'

'When I got it wrong,' said Frances wretchedly.

'No. You mustn't think that. Em couldn't ID him either. It was the set-up that was so stressful. That bloody video suite. It was all so formal and so impossible to breathe in there. It's a wonder anyone ever gets it right.'

For a moment or two we sat in silence, sipping our drinks. I was in the window seat, facing the bar, and Frances was opposite, gazing past me at the now-dark street outside. She was wearing a brown polo-necked jumper that brought out the warmth in her eyes. She looked so downcast and I felt awful that she was blaming herself when she'd done so much to help.

'So what will you do?' she asked eventually.

I shrugged.

'Nothing I can do. I just wanted someone else to look at the photo, to prove I'm not going mad. I have trouble sleeping and some days I'm so tired I can't work out what's real and what's in my head.' I tapped the side of my skull to demonstrate.

'Now you know where he lives it wouldn't take much to find out his name,' Frances said. 'I could help you, if you like.'

I was thrown off guard.

'Why would I do that? What good would it do?'

'You're absolutely right,' said Frances, looking embarrassed. 'Forget I spoke. You know, Tessa, I'm so impressed with how calm you are. If I were in your position, I'd want to march straight round there and confront him.'

'Believe me, that's crossed my mind.'

I said goodbye to Frances outside the pub. She tried to insist on driving me home and looked almost disappointed when I said no, but it was in the wrong direction for her and she'd put herself out for me quite enough already. Besides, I wanted to walk, to clear my head.

The walk from the pub took me past the Tube station and the crossing where I'd stood earlier that day. Had that featured in my refusal to accept a lift? The knowledge that I'd almost be passing the door he'd come out of? I'd like to say no.

The Tube station at Bounds Green stands on a crossroads and has two entrances, one fronting on to Bounds Green Road and one on to Brownlow Road, a short distance from the café in which I'd sat earlier that day. If I stood just inside the Brownlow Road entrance, I had a direct view across the road to the mini-market and the fried-chicken shop.

The thing was, I was in no hurry. Emma was at Phil's and, really, there was nothing I had to get home for. True, it wasn't exactly balmy out, but if I put my hands in the pockets of my jacket it wasn't so bad.

I noticed that the little row of shops had a road sign stuck up on the front wall above the window of the rental agents on the end. Taking my distance glasses out from my bag, I was able to read the letters: Regency Parade. The doorway the man had come out of earlier was a few doors down, of nondescript brown wood, with a thin, mean letterbox and '17A' marked out in stick-on numbers. From looking at the other doors between the shopfronts – the kind you walk past hundreds of times every day and don't even notice are there – I worked out that 17A was the flat above the mini-market.

That didn't mean it was where the man lived, though, I reminded myself. It could be anyone's place – a friend's, a relative's. He could work there. It could be his girlfriend's, or his drug dealer's.

Yet still I stood in that entrance, looking over at the first-floor window, which was set back from the level of the shop underneath, creating a kind of narrow terrace in front, on which two wooden dining chairs sat side by side. There were net curtains in the window, but the light was on behind them. I willed the window to open and for him to come clambering out. He looked like a smoker. Wouldn't it make sense for him to sit on one of these chairs, light up a fag?

Come on, I urged him in my head. *Show yourself.*

But he didn't appear. And when I next looked at my phone I was shocked to see that forty-eight minutes had gone past.

9

Back home, the house felt empty without Em. Even Dotty seemed subdued, stretching out languidly on the sofa.

I powered up my laptop and tried to concentrate on work. I'd just had a feature out in one of the homelier women's monthlies that had gone down gratifyingly well, so they'd commissioned me to write a different one, on women who radically overhaul their lives. 'We started over and look at us now!' was the kind of headline they'd use. I could do this feature in my sleep. Except that, nowadays, there were so many criteria for the case studies they wanted me to find. No one too highpowered, but not downbeat either, and must provide a photograph so I'd know they were 'the right sort'. 'On the glamorous side of relatable,' the features editor told me, straight-faced.

Resolute, I went online to research new case histories, determined to make the most of Emma being away, being able to work without worrying about her up there in her room.

Instead, somehow, I found myself googling 17A Regency Parade, N22.

I was hoping for an entry from the electoral roll,

showing the names of the occupants of the house, but I
didn't find one. There were a couple of estate agents' par-
ticulars from a sale way back in the distant past, a
planning-permission request for an extension to the shop
downstairs.

Then, halfway down the page, I saw an entry from
Companies House, listing a business registered to that
address: *J. L. Stephens Painting and Decorating. Company Director, James Laurence Stephens.*

I stared at the name, waiting for something to jump
out. Was this him, this James Laurence Stephens? Was
he the man with the green eyes and the sinews thick as
rope under the skin of his neck?

I put 'James Laurence Stephens, Bounds Green' into
the search box and waited. To tell the truth, I wasn't
expecting much. It was a common enough name. The
first entry that came up was an article from the local newspaper from March 2013 reporting on a match between
Haringey Rovers FC and a team from Waltham Abbey.
It didn't look promising. So I wasn't prepared for the
acid rush that came when I clicked on it and saw the
photograph of a young man in a football strip squatting
on the grass next to a leather ball. 'James Stephens: Man
of the Match', read the caption. The features were slightly
slimmer, the hair longer. But still those eyes, still that
arrogant tilt of the head. The cruel mouth. The chin.
That sense of power in the breadth of his shoulders.

I looked at the hand that rested on the ball, a chunky
silver signet ring wrapped around one of the fingers.

It was him. Number Eight.

For a long time I stared at the picture of the man
who'd attacked my daughter. I imagined him seeing her

at the bus stop, thinking what an easy target she was. Em has always looked younger than her age, minimal make-up, in jeans and T-shirts. Did he look at her standing there and think how vulnerable she was? Was it that very vulnerability that excited him? I pictured him following her on to the bus. Sitting behind her, staring at the back of her head where sometimes she misses a bit with the hairbrush so it's still rough and tangled from sleep.

When she rang the bell to get off just after the Tube station, did he think this was fate, the fact that she was getting off at the same stop as him? Was it so opportunistic after all, his decision to grab her around the throat and try to drag her away? Or would he have done it anyway, staying on the bus after his own stop, waiting for her to make a move so he could follow her off?

The questions clotted in my brain.

I scanned through the accompanying text, which was mostly a recap of the match with a brief mention of Stephens at the end and his winning goal.

I clicked off the photograph and read through the other search results. There wasn't much. A couple of other football references after his team performed well in the local league and a few reviews of his painting-and-decorating company. He got a solid four-star rating on Yell.

Respectful, professional, very accommodating, read one.

James really goes the extra mile, read another.

Only one two-star brought down the average.

Can't fault the work, but a word of advice. Make sure you have the money to pay up straight away. I had a slight cash flow problem and, fair enough, that was my fault but I saw a very different side of him. I'm a single mum and I felt quite threatened, to be honest. Something to be aware of.

The initial rush of vindication – *it was definitely him* – was eclipsed by dread.

All the things that might have happened. With a man like that.

I looked again at the photo of him with the football, rigid tendons snaking across his biceps, and pictured him watching my daughter ring the bell of the bus, his breath quickening with adrenaline as he stood to follow her off.

A pressure was building up in my skull, my brain being fed through a mangle bit by bit.

I clicked off the link and went back to researching the magazine feature, but even while I was making notes and looking up experts online he was in the back of my head, pressing tightly on my chest. James Laurence Stephens. The naming of him had made him real, and now he didn't want to be ignored.

I started playing around with an introduction. Always best to go straight into a case history for an opening scenario – the most dramatic one – and then posit the argument in the second paragraph. But though I wrote and rewrote, the words wouldn't flow.

Getting up, I paced aimlessly around the house. I told myself I was stretching my legs after sitting for so long, but I don't think it was an accident that I ended up in Emma's room.

I sat down at the desk where she did her homework. It was messy, piled up with text books and notebooks and a long printout made on a school printer that was clearly running out of ink held together by a large pink plastic paperclip.

It wasn't the first time I'd come to sit here in the twenty-two months since my marriage ended and I'd had to learn to share my daughter with another household where she had another bedroom, another desk, another life. Sitting where Emma spent so much time, touching her things, helped me feel close to her while she was away. Deep down, I was aware I was trespassing, but it was such a little thing, and I always left everything just as it was.

I picked up a blue notebook. English literature. She'd written the title of an essay and underlined it but hadn't got any further. *Evaluate the view that Iago doesn't destroy Othello, he provokes Othello to destroy himself.* I thought about that one for a moment or two, wondering how much all of us ultimately bear responsibility for whatever happens to us, regardless of provocation and circumstance.

There were some loose pages tucked into the back of the notebook. A letter from the head of English about a forthcoming theatre trip. I frowned when I noticed the form at the bottom, still not filled in. A history printout bearing the prominent instruction to STICK THIS worksheet INSIDE YOUR BOOKS. There was also a stiff sheet of paper folded over into thirds. When I opened it I recognized it as the letter Em had received from Victim Support soon after her attack, offering emotional and practical support to her as a victim of crime. Em had refused to call the number.

'But wouldn't it help you to talk about it?' I'd asked.

74

'I don't need to talk about it,' she insisted. 'I just need to put it behind me.'

When the letter disappeared I'd assumed she'd thrown it away, and yet here it was. More disturbing than the fact that she'd kept it were the biro markings on the page. Every incidence of the word 'victim' had been underlined twice, or sometimes three times, in blue pen.

I could see more writing coming through the page and when I turned it over my heart shattered like an eggshell. In letters so deep she'd almost gouged a hole through the paper my beautiful daughter had written over and over: *I hate myself. I hate myself. I hate myself.*

Back at my laptop, I felt flayed, the surface of me left raw and exposed. Nothing strips a parent bare like the hurt of their child.

Em was someone who internalized her feelings. I knew she'd been rocked by the divorce and the house move and then the rift between me and Rosie. How could she not be? The last two years had made her anxious. She worried about me being lonely when she was at her dad's and I had to make a big show of how much I was enjoying the freedom to meet up with friends or work late into the night.

Perhaps if the attack had happened in a different context, where Phil and I were still together and life at home was stable, it wouldn't have had the same effect, but coming on the heels of so much upheaval, it seemed to have lodged in her mind like a tumour. I knew she was cross with herself for not picking her assailant out of the ID parade, but this self-loathing rocked me to the core.

Shaken, I clicked back on the tab for James Laurence Stephens's Yell page and read through the comments again. *Respectful. Extra mile. Nice guy.* Then the lone two-star review and that word: *threatened.*

I remembered Emma's bitten nails, the skin ragged and bloody around them. I thought of the small bald patches on her head and the words gouged into the paper.

He had done this to her. This thickset man who had seen a young girl on the bus and decided he had the right to hook his brutish arm around her neck and drag her along the street for the fulfilment of some perverted fantasy or need.

I clicked on the link that said 'leave a review'.

James Laurence Stephens is a sex attacker.

I stared at the words for a few moments while something screamed in my head. I'd typed them out as a way of releasing the rage that had built up in me, intending to delete them, but the screaming wouldn't stop.

So I pressed send. To silence it.

If it wasn't for Henry, I don't know if I'd still be here.

It sounds melodramatic, but it's true. Knowing that you're still out there, still walking around, still free after what you did, might have pushed me over the edge.

One night I actually emptied a packet of paracetamol into my hand, popping them out of their foil blister packs one by one until I had a mound of white pills in my palm.

I could make this all stop now. The thought was intoxicating. An end to the low-level fear that buzzes in my ears like tinnitus. An end to dreaming about what happened and waking up with my heart bruised from slamming itself against my ribs. An end to you and the hold you have over my life.

I was so tired of it all.

I don't know how long I sat there, looking at the pills. I was in the bathroom, sitting on the side of the bath. I'd just had a shower so the air was steamy and there was mist on the mirror of the bathroom cabinet. I imagined running the tap in the basin and swallowing down the pills two or three at a time, then lying down on my bed, still wrapped in my towel, knowing that it was over. For a moment, I imagined the peace of not having to think about it any more.

Then I thought about Henry. In my mind I traced his face with my fingers. I imagined his warm breath on my neck.

I threw the pills into the bin, and then I fished them out and flushed them down the toilet, a handful at a time. Just in case.

Afterwards, I felt awful, thinking about Mum and what it would have done to her.

But I still can't get it out of my mind, that split second of blissful peace when I imagined being rid of you.

10

This is how I found out my husband had met someone else.

It was nearly two years ago, and I hadn't long been made redundant. I had also just turned fifty. You could say my confidence was at an all-time low.

Phil was at work. He is a sound editor so he often worked late. Deadlines on post-production are a killer. He'd already told me he wouldn't be back that evening. When there was a rush job on he sometimes used to sleep on the sofa in his Shoreditch studio. Or so he said.

Anyway, this day, I was home for once in our lovely old house, sitting at my actual desk in my upstairs study, working on putting a few pitches together for a magazine I'd once edited. I was still in shock about losing my job but determined to see it as a temporary setback, telling myself something else would come along shortly. We could get by financially on my redundancy and Phil's income, at least for a year, but I wanted to keep working, to keep *relevant*. Now I look back and wonder if it was genuine naivety or just denial. The girls were at school. Dotty was sitting by my feet, gazing up at me adoringly. My being at home all day was still a novelty and she would stare at me for hours, as if she couldn't believe I was actually real.

A text alert sounded on my phone. The noise of a bird whistling.

I glanced over and saw it was from Phil. I considered leaving it for a few minutes, until I'd finished what I was working on, but it would have whistled again a few seconds later, so I clicked.

You know how sometimes your life divides into 'before' and 'after'? And later, when you're looking at a photograph or an old film comes on the television you'll feel a twitch of pain remembering the last time you saw it and how it felt to be in that 'before', to not know the things you now know?

That text was the door between everything I'd known and the new alien reality I've inhabited ever since.

I can't wait to be inside you.

That's all it said. But that was enough.

At that point, Phil and I hadn't had sex in around four months. I wasn't too concerned. It was a fallow period. We'd had them before.

So I knew instantly that text wasn't meant for me.

I sat in a daze, feeling sick. My husband was cheating on me. Shock stripped my nerve endings raw. The GP I saw before the twelve-year-old once read through my notes with a serious expression and then asked me if I'd ever heard of post-traumatic stress disorder. I made a joke about how being in your fifties wasn't exactly the same as being down the trenches, but she'd been quite serious. 'You've been bludgeoned over the head by major life events,' she'd told me. 'You lost your job, your home, your husband left you and you reached a milestone birthday all within a year of each other. Add in ailing parents and the menopause and that's quite a potent cocktail of psychological blows.'

Looking back now, I wonder if she was on to something. And if she was, I wonder if this is where it started, if this moment staring at my phone screen in the study of my beautiful Muswell Hill house might actually turn out to be the still point of my turning world, the axis around which my life shifted into something I could no longer recognize.

But at the time, I wasn't thinking in those terms. At the time, I thought this would be a dip in the road – a pretty major dip, to be sure – but beyond it the road itself would carry on just as it always had. In fact, you know something mad? After half an hour or so of noisy devastation where I yelled out every filthy word I could think of, I started almost relishing the situation I'd found myself in. Oh, I was still upset, don't get me wrong. But I knew what I'd found out would change things. And even I could recognize that our lives were crying out for change. Phil and I had been married for twenty-two years. We'd got into a rut. Here was something that would force us out of our stagnant status quo.

I was furious, hurt, all those other things. But I also wasn't a complete hypocrite. I'd been tempted myself in the past. Flirtations I'd allowed to go further than they should. Sure, I'd pulled myself back, but I understood how it could happen.

While I was still working out how to react to the text I heard the sound of a key in the lock.

'You're back early,' I said, ironing my expression smooth.

'I thought I'd come back for a couple of hours. Pick up a few things. Head back in later.'

And all the time his eyes were anxiously scanning my face, looking for clues. I could read him so well I saw the thought pass through his head as surely as if it were ticker-taped across his forehead: *She hasn't seen it yet.*

Much later, he admitted he'd come home ready to pretend he'd meant to send that text to me, ready to mount a seduction scene to back it up. But then I hadn't reacted and he'd thought himself safe. 'You must have been so relieved,' I'd told him bitterly. 'Not to have to go through with it.' He hadn't said anything, just looked sad and guilty, which remained pretty much his default expression throughout our separation.

I'd gone downstairs to the kitchen to make coffee, still not mentioning the text but deliberately leaving my phone out on the coffee table in the living room where Phil was sitting. Then I'd brought him a drink and we'd chatted about this and that before he went upstairs to grab some things.

Looking back, I can't believe I was so calm. It was as if my brain had entered a state of suspended animation while my body carried on going about its normal business, like a chicken with its head cut off.

When I checked my phone the text had been deleted.

After Phil left for the studio again I went through everything. His social media accounts, email addresses. Old phones. He hadn't made much effort to hide his tracks. But then, why would he? We weren't the sort of couple who checked up on each other. Who would, after all this time?

It had been going on over a year, it turned out. I'd

assumed she'd be some young, cool producer he'd come across through work, but no, Joy was a wealthy Muswell Hill divorcee he'd met at the gym. A year older than me.

And he really did love being inside her, as his many texts and emails on the subject attested.

I'm not going to pretend those messages didn't hurt, the ones where he rhapsodized about how sex with her had opened his eyes to how sex could be. Ditto the ones that talked about how me and him were just 'going through the motions' or how he was developing feelings for her. Or how he felt like he'd been sleepwalking through the last twenty years and now she'd woken him up. Is there some cheaters' handbook where they get these lines from? I wonder.

But still I thought I could win this one. He'd have to do a lot of grovelling. We'd have to make plenty of changes. It would take a long time. Counselling. The works. But we could recover.

It never occurred to me that he might not want to recover.

Recently I read that by the time one partner first brings up the prospect of separation, they've already been thinking about it for an average of six months. But at the time Phil sent that text I assumed the prospect of splitting up was as shocking to him as it was to me and that, after he'd had a chance to let it sink in, he'd come to his senses.

I had no inkling that, after he arrived home the following day and I confronted him, puffy-eyed through lack of sleep and high on the self-righteousness of being the wounded party, that after he'd apologized again and again and cried a little and said how awful he felt, that after all that, he would turn to me and say, 'But you must admit we've run our course, Tess.' As if I might simply agree and shake his hand and we'd wish each other luck and say it was all for the best and go our separate ways.

People talk about being blindsided. Well, I was blindsided and blind-fronted and blind-behinded.

Within forty-eight hours, he'd gone.

'My husband left me,' I'd tell anyone who'd listen – random strangers in the GP waiting room, Twitter acquaintances I'd never even met. Because spoken out loud or written baldly down, it sounded so preposterous. I was waiting for them to tell me not to be so absurd.

I was thinking about all this as I waited for Phil to bring Em home the evening after I'd posted the review on Yell. Normally, he dropped her outside the house but I'd texted to ask him to come in. After two years and everything that had happened, we'd just about managed to coat a thin veneer of civility over our interactions.

As long as we stuck within set parameters.

Set by him, obviously. Despite everything he'd done, my own more recent behaviour superseded his, meaning I'd forfeited the right to dictate terms.

Dotty was beside herself when Phil came in, bringing him offerings of shoes and making that semi-orgasmic noise she made when everything she wanted most in the world had unexpectedly fallen into her lap. Phil dropped to his knees in the narrow hallway and she jumped excitedly around him, licking his face.

He misses the dog more than he misses me.

The realization was sobering.

In the kitchen, Em dithered by the kettle, darting looks

at us both from under her hair. She wasn't used to seeing us together. Wasn't sure what it meant.

'Dad and I have a few things to discuss,' I told her, smiling. 'Nothing sinister.'

It broke my heart to see how my sixteen-year-old daughter had become so protective of her parents.

After Em had disappeared upstairs with her tea I launched straight into it, so there could be no question in his mind of why I'd asked him in. How, at the police station, Emma had been drawn towards Number Eight but had lacked the strength of her own conviction. The absolute certainty I'd had when he came on the screen that it was him, that instinctual recognition. Then how Em had spotted him first and not long afterwards I'd seen him coming out of the doorway while I was in the café across the road.

'Look,' I said, calling up the camera roll on my phone. 'This is him. This is the man who attacked our daughter.'

I thrust the picture at him. And then had to wait while he felt around in his jacket pocket for his glasses.

I don't know what I was hoping for. The same kind of visceral reaction I'd had, I suppose. But I'd forgotten about Phil's analytical nature, how he never gave a gut response but took time to digest the facts, processing them through his brain until they arrived packaged and labelled and itemized with an introduction and a conclusion. And footnotes. I'd forgotten how crazy it used to drive me.

Finally, he put the phone down and removed his glasses. Rubbed the bridge of his nose between his finger and thumb in a familiar gesture that made my heart ache a little.

'I don't understand where you're going with this, Tess.'

'What do you mean?'

'I mean, this could be anyone. Those men on that identification video. They're from all over the country. What are the chances, really, that one of them is living practically round the corner?'

I gaped at him. Incredulous.

'I can't believe I have to explain this to you. I know eight of the men were from all over the place, but the actual criminal isn't. The actual criminal probably *does* live right round the corner, seeing as that's where the attack happened.'

'But Emma didn't recognize this man when she saw him on the video – if he is the same man from the video. And neither did the woman who came to her rescue.'

'No, but Frances said afterwards she'd been torn between two of the choices. You should have seen her face when I showed her the photo, Phil. She went completely white. She definitely recognized him. He was wearing the same jacket, for God's sake. Look, with that funny little logo.'

Phil shook his head. It was galling to me that, though his hair was more silver now than brown, it was still as thick as ever. He wore it long in the front, so he was constantly pushing it out of his eyes. 'Joy's welcome to you,' I'd flung at him once. 'She'll end up with the dregs of you, bald and incontinent.'

I wasn't proud of myself. Some of the things I'd said.

'Please tell me you haven't shown this photo to Em,' he said now. 'Or, God forbid, told her which door you saw him come out of.'

'Not yet.'

'Promise me that you're not going to burden her with this. The chances of this being the right man are so minuscule. But even if it was, what good would it possibly do for her to have her worst fears confirmed – that he's living right here, in her neighbourhood? Neither Em nor Frances picked him out of the identification tape. The case is effectively closed. What Em needs now is to get on with her life.'

'She's not getting on with her life, though. Have you seen her hair – those little bald patches? She's stressed and she's blaming herself.' I stopped short of telling him about the letter I'd seen from the Victim Support agency, that *I hate myself* gouged into the page. I didn't want him to think I'd been snooping.

'I know about the hair. Joy's been talking to a brilliant hair specialist she knows and he's sure it's just a temporary reaction. But you know, all this makes it even more pressing that she rebuild her confidence, without being scared that every time she goes out of the door she might bump into the man who attacked her.'

'But she's already seen him.'

'Yes, but that was only once. He could have been passing through. She doesn't need to know where he lives.'

'Surely we need to warn her, though?' I persisted, with less certainty. One of the worst things about menopause for me was that I lost the thread of a thought so easily, leaving it snagged and trailing, while I scrabbled to remember what my argument had been. 'So that she can avoid going near where he lives?'

'It's right opposite the Tube, Tess. That's what you

told me. Are you going to stop her getting public transport during the day now?'

We'd already made a rule that Em now had to get an Uber home if she went out in the evening. Though one heard such awful stories about that too. Frustration made me lose my temper.

'So you're suggesting we just ignore it? For God's sake, Phil, you're her father. Why aren't you round there right this minute, pounding on his door? Our daughter could have been—'

'I don't need you to tell me what could have happened. I think about it every bloody day. But I'm not about to turn up at a complete stranger's house, accusing him of harming my daughter, purely on some whim of yours.'

We glared at each other. I thought for a moment of telling him what else I'd discovered. That this complete stranger had a name. A profession, even. *See*, was what I wanted to say, *the lengths I'll go to for our daughter?* See how much I love her? But then Phil threw me by reaching out across the table and covering my hand with his own.

My skin felt weird where he touched it, as if his fingers weren't made of living tissue and blood and bone but some inanimate material encasing my hand.

'Tessa. I know you feel powerless. We both do. But getting yourself into a state is not going to help anyone.'

Just like that, I felt tears burning the backs of my eyes. It might have been the sympathy in his voice, or the mere fact of the two of us sitting there like that, as we used to do, as if the last two years had never happened.

'I don't want to let her down.'

'I know that. But the way to help her is to be here and

listen to her and support her. This isn't about you galloping in to save the day. In actual fact, it isn't about you
at all.'

The words were harsh but the tone was gentle.

'You look tired. Are you still having trouble sleeping?'

I nodded. And bit back the words, *Thanks to you*.
Bitterness had become so much a default setting in my
dealings with my ex-husband that it was almost always
my automatic response, even though, these days, it
didn't reflect how I felt most of the time.

Phil got up to go, sending Dotty into a panic.

'How's Rosie?' I'd promised myself I wouldn't ask,
but the words came out before I had a chance to check
them.

'She's fine. In fact, she's home at the moment for reading week.'

Home.

'Perhaps if I just came—'

But Phil was already shaking his head.

'We've been through this so many times. I'm sorry, I
know this is hard on you, but you have to let Rosie come
to you.'

'Do you remember when they were small and still
thought we were the centre of the world, and how it felt
like we were the only people who really knew how to
look after them and keep them safe?' I asked. 'And now,
sometimes it seems we're the ones they need keeping
safe from.'

Phil didn't like that. I could tell he wanted to correct
me and tell me not to lump him in with me. But I was
right. We'd both hurt them in different ways, these girls
we'd rather die than see hurt.

'Can you at least tell her I love her? Please.'

My voice sounded strange. There was a lump in my throat, as if my heart had come loose and got lodged there.

Phil's face softened, the features blurring around the edges.

'Oh, Tessa, she knows that.'

Phil was right. There could be nothing gained by trying to find out more about Number Eight. Best to forget I ever saw him.

I was thinking exactly this after he'd gone and I sat down at the kitchen table, powered up my laptop and sought out that photo of the young James Laurence Stephens in football kit squatting next to a ball.

That instant tug of anger at the sight of those probing green eyes. The sheer, dense mass of him.

On impulse, I took out my phone and sent Frances a text, telling her what I'd found out so far. I needed to share the information with someone who understood what it meant that this man now had a name, that he was real.

After I hit send, I went back to my laptop and called up the Yell page for his painting-and-decorating business and my heart thudded when I noticed there was a reply to my review.

As my fingers hovered over the link, my mouth was dry. I glanced across the table, my eyes coming to rest on Phil's half-full tea cup, which made it look like he'd left the room for a moment and would be back to finish it. As if he still lived here. The sight was oddly comforting.

Calmer, I clicked on the link.

Reply from J. L. Stephens Painting and Decorating:

To my loyal customers, please be informed I am in the process of getting this slanderous review removed.

To the person who posted it, people are tracking down the IP address as we speak.

I slammed shut the lid of my laptop.

The IP address. I hadn't even thought.

Could he find me? Could he find out where I lived?

Oh, Emma. What had I done?

11

What did we do before Google?

The morning after Phil's visit, when I was finally thinking straight, I googled 'what can you find out from an IP address'. To my enormous relief, I discovered it wasn't possible to find a name or address, though someone who knew about computers might be able to discover the area the review had been sent from.

I sent up a silent prayer of gratitude to the god I didn't believe in and took Dotty out for a walk, even though I actually felt like going back to bed, having spent half the night awake, anxiety binding itself around my brain until every last bit of calm had been squeezed out.

We walked up to Alexandra Palace, the big London landmark strung out across a hill in the very north of the capital. Dotty adored humans but regarded other dogs with suspicion, so we tended to lurk in the upper part of the palace parkland, where it was less populated.

It was a Sunday, and though it was only late February, it felt like spring. Already there were yellow clots of daffodils around the bases of the trees, yet still as I threw the ball for Dotty I felt jittery and nearly jumped out of my skin when my ringtone sounded. I usually ignored my phone when I was out with the dog, in case she misbehaved while I was distracted, so it was only when we were on the way back that I glanced at my screen and saw a missed call from Frances. No voicemail. I'd only recently discovered via Em that no one under thirty listens to voicemails any more. 'So all those times I've left you long, complicated messages, you haven't listened to them?' I'd asked her.

'Nah. Sorry. It's not personal, though.'

I was planning to call Frances back, but I was running late to meet up with Kath and Mari down on the South Bank and it slipped my mind. As it was, my old friends were both there already waiting for me outside the entrance to the vast monolithic brick slab that was Tate Modern. Since Mari and Kath had got Tate memberships, it was something we did quite often on the weekend. A quick whizz around an exhibition, a leisurely stroll around the gift shop then up to the members' bar for a drink and something to eat. Sometimes we even left out the art and just did the shop and the bar.

Amazingly, we managed to nab one of the prized window tables in the bar. It was something I never got blasé about, the majestic beauty of that stretch of the Thames with the creamy dome of St Paul's Cathedral rising up straight ahead above the gleaming steel ribbon of the Millennium Bridge and, to the right, the outline of the Gherkin and the other City skyscrapers probing the watery-blue sky.

Kath had her iPad out and, despite my vociferous objections, was creating a profile for me on a dating website.

'It's time, that's all. You've moped around too long.'

'I'm fifty-two. All the men my age will be pretending to be forty and looking for women between twenty-five and thirty-five. The only people who'll click on my profile will be seventy-year-olds who figure I'll be grateful for whatever I can get.'

'Don't be defeatist,' said Mari.

'That's easy for you to say.'

Mari had been with her second husband, Niall, for twelve years. He was nine years younger than her and his eyes still followed her around the room as if he couldn't believe his luck.

Mari had long dark hair liberally streaked with grey and she never wore make-up as she claimed it brought her out in a rash. At university, Kath and I used to chase her around the flat the three of us shared, trying to daub her with mascara or blusher or whatever else we had to hand, to prove her wrong, but we'd long since given up on that. Besides, whether it was the lifelong aversion to cosmetics or simply good Irish genes, Mari, who had looked like our mothers when we were eighteen, had stopped ageing somewhere around her thirty-eighth birthday. You could already see how she would turn into one of those enviably baby-faced old women, all long white hair and smooth skin and clear eyes.

'A good shag would sort you out,' said Kath.

'Or quite possibly kill me.'

Kath frowned and squinted at the screen through her tortoiseshell cat's-eye glasses.

'I've put that you like long country walks with your dog. They always like that kind of thing. Makes you sound non-threatening.'

'Makes me sound like Clare bloody Balding. Anyway, I *am* non-threatening. And I hate walking my dog. She's a nightmare.'

Mari asked me how I'd been and I found myself telling them about James Laurence Stephens. Of course, they already knew all about the attack. In fact, Mari had been the first person I'd called the following morning, when I'd got up, stiff and heartsore, from Em's floor, having spent the night wrapped in my duvet, watching her while she slept. And Kath had sent Em a box of posh chocolates after the case collapsed nearly three weeks ago.

So I expected them to be fully supportive, but when I got to the bit about leaving the online review, Kath sucked in her cheeks.

'Are you mad? I mean, are you literally insane? First, you have no proof this is actually the same guy from the video.'

'It's him. Em was shaking all over when she came home after seeing him. And Frances – you know, the woman who came along and scared him away – she recognized him immediately.'

'And secondly, if it is the right man, he's a psychopath and you are basically provoking him.'

When Kath was riled two bright pink spots appeared on her cheeks like a kid's doll, clashing with her flame-red hair.

'I know, I know. I've deleted the review. You don't need to worry.'

'It's completely understandable that you want to get revenge,' said Mari. 'Bloody hell, I want to get revenge too. Em's my god-daughter, don't forget. But you have to go through the proper channels. Take it to the police if you really think you have something. How is she, by the way? Emma?'

I tensed, fingers gripping on to the handle of my coffee cup.

'Not so good, really.' I told them about the hair loss, and that letter with the word 'victim' underlined again and again, that phrase on the back: *I hate myself.*

Mari leaned forward and held my hand.

'Do you think she'd talk to me? It is my job, after all.'

I shook my head.

'No offence, but I've begged her to talk to someone and she won't. She insists she's fine.'

'And she probably will be. She's made of stern stuff, your Em. She'll be okay.'

For a moment, as Mari looked into my eyes and pressed my hand, I felt calmer, but then I was distracted by Kath pointing her phone in my face and taking a photo.

'For your profile picture.'

During the ensuing tussle while I tried to grab the phone to delete whatever monstrous photo she'd taken and she in turn tried to upload it to the site, my own phone started ringing.

I glanced at the screen. Shit, Frances. I'd forgotten to call her back.

'Hi, Tessa.' Frances sounded bright and excited. 'I'm so glad I got hold of you. Listen, can we meet up?'

'Now? Oh, I'm sorry. I'm in town having lunch with a couple of old friends.'

There was a pause, as if Frances was surprised to discover I had a social life. Then she recovered herself.

'Oh, how lovely. It's just that I've been doing some investigating and I found out more information. About our guy. I tracked him down on Facebook. His personal account is locked but he DJ's in his spare time and he has a professional account for that as well as his painting and decorating and, get this, his DJ name is J-Lo. James Laurence. Get it?'

Though I'd turned away from the table, I could sense Kath and Mari staring at me.

'Actually, Frances, I've decided to drop this. My friends here nearly bit my head off when I told them I'd written a review on Yell. Em says she's trying to move on and put it behind her, and if she can do it, I should probably do the same.'

'Oh. Right.'

Frances sounded momentarily deflated, but she rallied quickly.

'Of course, you know best. You're her mum.'

After we'd finished in the bar, we went to the gift shop, where Kath bought a colouring book for the granddaughter I still couldn't believe she actually had. Grandmother. How was that even possible? Well, I knew how it was possible. She'd had Jemima when we were only a year out of uni – the product of a brief but very satisfying liaison with a Dutch PhD student. And now Jemima had become a mother herself at not very much older. The thing was, though, I looked at Kath and still saw the girl with the bright red backcombed hair and biker jacket I'd met in the Student Union where we both worked behind the bar to make some extra cash.

At Bounds Green Tube, I deliberately kept my gaze averted from Regency Parade while waiting to cross the road, focusing instead on the opposite pavement, where a man with a ginger beard was trying to press flyers into the hands of passers-by.

I was a few minutes from my house when my phone rang again.

'Tessa?' Frances sounded hesitant. 'Is it a better time to talk now?'

'Yes, of course. Sorry.' I felt absurdly guilty for having been caught out enjoying myself.

'Oh God, no need to apologize. The truth is, I've been in two minds whether to call again. Ever since we last spoke I've been going backwards and forwards, trying to work out what to do for the best. But in the end I asked myself what I would want in your situation.'

'I'm not sure I understand.'

I'd stopped by a house with a low brick wall that separated the small front garden from the street. The heavy lunch, followed by cake, combined with the lack of sleep, made me feel suddenly exhausted and I sank down on to the wall next to an old toaster bearing a Post-it that read 'Take me, I work.'

'I don't want to worry you, but Emma has been texting me quite a lot the last few days,' Frances said carefully. 'I think she feels a bond between us because of what happened. And of course I'm very flattered that she feels she can confide in me. She hasn't wanted to burden you because she seems to think you're fragile at the moment, but the truth is she isn't over this. Not by a long way. Since she saw him she's been having nightmares where she's back by that bus stop, being dragged towards the darkness. She's scared of walking anywhere, even in the daylight. She says she's constantly listening for footsteps behind her.'

I felt a tearing of tissue somewhere deep in my chest.

'I know she's struggling,' I said. 'But why won't she talk to me? I'm not being rude, Frances, and I'm so grateful to you for being there for her, but she's only just met you. I'm her mum.'

My voice cracked on the last word, and there was a brief silence before Frances replied, gently, 'She's incredibly protective of you, Tessa. She's a very special girl.'

Frances made me promise I wouldn't say anything to Emma.

'She trusts me, and if she thinks I've betrayed that trust by talking to you, she might close up completely. But I thought you ought to know. So you can keep an eye on her.'

After Frances had rung off, I stayed sitting on the wall, still with the phone in my hand. A couple with a baby in a buggy stopped to consider the toaster, but I hardly saw them.

I thought of Emma's pale face across the breakfast table that morning, spooning cereal into her mouth without taking her eyes off her phone screen. She'd been wearing her fluffy navy-blue dressing gown, and her head, poking out from the outsized towelling collar, seemed disproportionately small, like a tortoise's.

The radio had been on and the presenters were talking about the latest school shooting in America. 'What makes someone do something like that,' one of the presenters asked about the seventeen-year-old gunman, 'to kids they've known all their lives?'

I didn't think Em was even listening, she was so intent on her phone. Then she said:

'I think he must have been very lonely.'

And I'd thought how she was absolutely right. Loneliness. Disconnection. Feeling excluded from a life in which everyone else seemed to have a place.

And I'd thought how perceptive she was, my daughter. And how kind.

What I should have thought was, *Why are you worrying about everyone else except yourself?*

I hurried back home, propelled by guilt. But when I walked in through the front door, panting, to be met by a semi-hysterical Dotty, who barrelled into my leg as if she'd been abandoned alone for months, it was obvious Em was out.

'Gone to study at Grace's,' read the note she'd left on the kitchen table.

I sank down on to a chair. For a moment I considered calling Em, just to hear her voice and try to get her to confide in me, as she had done in Frances, but I was mindful of my promise and of Frances's warning about Em shutting down altogether. Besides, I was glad Em was at her best friend's house instead of moping around on her own. It was a sign she was feeling better, wasn't it?

But all I could hear was Frances's voice telling me about Em being scared of being dragged into the darkness.

I fired up my laptop, which was sitting on the kitchen table, as usual. It was old and the battery needed replacing so it had to be more or less constantly plugged into the wall socket, which kind of defeated the object of a portable computer.

The poleaxing guilt that had followed me home after my conversation with Frances was slowly giving way to a new emotion. Rage was snaking through my veins from the bottom of my legs up through my body, building in intensity as it progressed through until it arrived in my gut like a burning fireball.

Not only had that man tried to drag my daughter off the road when all she was doing was trying to get home in time for her curfew, now he had destroyed her peace of mind, polluting her day-to-day life, haunting her sleep so she turned to strangers for comfort.

And he had got away with it.

I called up Facebook and typed 'James Laurence Stephens' into the search box, adding the term 'Bounds Green' as an afterthought. He came up immediately. A recent photo, from the looks of it. He looked older, his features harder, more defined, his hair shorter. Bare-chested on a beach somewhere, all dense muscle and attitude and Maori-type tattoos on his bulging biceps.

Smiling, as if he deserved to be happy.

There was a sharp, metallic taste in my mouth and I swallowed hard.

As Frances had said, the privacy settings on his account meant I couldn't get any further, so I went back to the search box, this time entering the words 'J-Lo DJ'.

A different photograph. Blurred around the edges in acid tones of purple and green. Him behind a deck with a huge pair of headphones on and his hand up by his ear. I zoomed in on his face, on the deep groove in his chin. Then I shifted the mouse to his hand. There was a ring on his index finger, silver and chunky with a flat surface.

He looked like he was dancing behind that deck. Like he didn't have a care in the world.

I bet he didn't have trouble sleeping.

I bet he wasn't worried about walking the streets in his own neighbourhood.

I googled 'create new Facebook account' and followed the instructions. I used an old Gmail address and the name of a girl I'd gone to school with, Natasha Barker. I had one of those anonymous shadow figures as a profile picture. The whole thing took less than five minutes, and all the time my blood was pulsing with an elemental rage.

By the time I'd logged into my new account and navigated back to J-Lo's page anger was a white-hot knife in my brain.

Write something . . . Facebook invited me.

I've tried many times to work out what was going through my head as I sat there in front of my computer scanning the face of the man who'd attacked my daughter. Did I have a concrete plan at that point to drive him away so that she could walk around without fear, so that her hair would grow back and her eyes would shine like they used to? Or did that come later? Did I actually, at the beginning, want only to frighten him, as he'd frightened her? To wipe from his face that arrogant belief that he could do whatever he wanted, to whomever he wanted?

Whatever the reasoning, I set my cursor in the empty box. Clicked the caps-lock key on my keyboard. Then I wrote a post to J-Lo the DJ.

I KNOW WHAT YOU DID.

12

'I can't tell you how grateful I am to you for coming. I don't dare tell my friends I'm doing this. They'd be horrified.'

Frances and I were squashed into a corner of the crowded Peckham pub, sharing a table with three lads in matching Joe's Ho's T-shirts who had managed to escape from the rest of their stag group and were lying low, hoping not to be found. They kept boasting about the excesses of the day and then shooting glances at Frances, trying to gauge if they'd impressed her.

She was wearing a patterned silk long-sleeved top with tight-fitting jeans and boots. I'd told her we should try to blend in, but we both knew that was unlikely. I was also wearing jeans, teamed with a grey T-shirt and trainers. In the safety of my own bedroom, I'd thought it looked cool in a low-key, not-trying kind of way, but now I felt dowdy and underdressed. Already I was clammy and hot and was dreading how I'd cope if the club was rammed with people.

Frances pressed her lips together, as if trying to stop herself speaking.

'What?' I asked her. 'I can see you're worried about something.'

'It's just, well, do you think your friends might have a point? We know what this guy is capable of. But unless we catch him in the act of doing it to someone else, there's not much we can realistically do, is there? Don't you think you might be upsetting yourself unnecessarily?'

I knew she was right. And yet whenever I thought of my daughter walking to school fearful of shadows or lying in bed in the dark reliving what had happened to her while the man responsible strutted around unscathed, anger lodged in my throat, heavy and dense.

'I want to get an idea of who he is, how he lives. You know. It's mad but I feel like if I keep an eye on him, keep tabs on him, I can make sure he never gets near Em again. I'm like the Catcher in the Rye – you know that book? – standing way off on the sidelines just in case someone needs saving.'

It was the truth. But it wasn't the whole truth.

The real reason for me trekking across London on a cold Thursday night in early March, preparing to go to a sweaty nightclub full of teenagers and twenty-somethings, was to let him, James Stephens, know he hadn't got away with it, that he'd been seen. Even if I did nothing but stare at him, he'd know there was something amiss.

He'd *feel* it.

Frances was still looking at me quizzically, so I pushed on, the words coming out in an unrehearsed rush. 'But what I really want is for him to be gone. Do you know, every time Emma leaves the house, I think, *Is this the day? Will she see him today?* And if that's how I feel, God alone knows how she must be feeling.'

'Have you thought about moving yourself?' Frances asked. 'That might be more realistic.'

I shook my head. 'We can't afford to. I used up my half of the equity of our old house and most of my redundancy buying the house we're in. I stretched myself to the limit taking out as big a mortgage as I could get. I don't have the money to move again – estate agents' fees, stamp duty, solicitors. Anyway, we're only just getting over the upheaval of the last move – why should we have to move again, because of him? He's the one who should leave. I can't help thinking there must be a way to shame him into it.'

The pub was around the corner from the bar where J-Lo was DJ'ing. When we arrived outside the venue my heart sank. It was smaller than I'd imagined and already jam-packed.

The girl taking money on the door flicked me a questioning glance. I avoided looking at her face in case she was smirking and held out my arm so she could stamp my wrist with a purple star.

Inside, we were hit by a tsunami of noise. An insistent bass that rose up through the floor, passing through the soles of my feet and reverberating through my blood, making my liver and kidneys shake, another conflicting rhythm over the top of it, then someone spitting out words without any discernible melody. And above and beyond the music, the shouting and screaming and screeching of dozens of excited young people high on youth and two-for-one cocktails.

'I've died and gone to hell,' said Frances in my ear.

Though she wasn't far off the age of the majority of the clientele, Frances stood out in her silk top with her freshly scrubbed complexion and her expensive leather handbag clutched to her side. I felt a sharp tug of affection mixed with gratitude, seeing how far she was pushing herself out of her comfort zone for a woman she hardly knew.

'You know, there's a Chinese proverb that says if you save someone's life, you're responsible for them!' Frances shouted as we squeezed into a gap near the bar.

I must have looked as blank as I felt because she elaborated.

'That's how I feel about Emma. I know it's crazy, but I feel responsible for keeping her safe from that monster.' She jerked her head in the direction of the dance floor, where a heaving crowd blocked our view of the DJ box just beyond.

A lump formed in my throat.

'Being responsible for Em is my job,' I told her, glad that the loud music covered up the cracking of my voice. 'You've done quite enough already. We can never thank you enough.'

Up until that point, neither of us had laid eyes on Stephens, who'd been bent over his decks behind the crowd, but at that moment the music changed and he suddenly shot upright. An electric charge passed through me at the sight of him, the sheer powerful mass of his chest and shoulders, the hard angles of his face.

'Feel,' said Frances, holding out one of her surprisingly small hands.

I took it between my own and felt how it was trembling.

'It's seeing him,' she said. 'It brings it all back, as if it's happening all over again.'

'So it is definitely him?'

Of course, I'd known it was all along, I just needed to have it confirmed.

'Oh, yes.'

Her voice was quiet and her features seemed frozen on to her face. I felt a brief flash of vindication, of which I was immediately ashamed.

I was right. But then I'd known from the start that I was.

For a few moments we both stood, shoulders pressed together, and stared over the heads of the dancers at the figure in the DJ box. He was wearing a white T-shirt, fitted enough for his biceps to strain the fabric. His forearms, one of which he kept raised, jerking it in time to the music, were knotted with muscle under a sleeve of black-and-white tattoos and the skin on his face stretched cling-film tight over his cheekbones.

'He's smiling,' Frances commented, as if she'd imagined his crime somehow precluded him from showing pleasure.

I nodded, my throat too choked to speak.

The noise was a hammer, pounding my sleep-deprived brain until I could no longer think. After half an hour or so, when my head felt ready to explode, Stephens announced he was going to take a twenty-minute break. It was the first time I'd heard him speak. His voice was higher than I'd expected. I imagined how it had sounded in Em's ear.

Stop, bitch.

Stephens sauntered across the dance floor, high-fiving

as he went, as if he was some sort of rock star. By this stage, Frances and I had managed to nab a tiny table and two high stools on the raised section by the bar, from where we had a good vantage point over the rest of the club. At one point during his slow progression, someone tapped him on the shoulder and he swung around furiously, causing Frances to gasp out loud.

'What is it?'

She put her hand flat against her breastbone and briefly closed her eyes.

'That gesture. When he turned round like that. It was so exactly what happened after I stopped the car and shouted at him that night. My skin just came up in goosebumps.'

I reached out to pat her arm and was taken aback to find that she was trembling again. How had I forgotten that Emma was not the only victim in this whole thing?

Stephens had reached a table on the edge of the dance floor where five or six twenty-somethings sat behind a barricade of empty glasses and beer bottles. A woman with long dark hair sitting with her back towards us reached out her arm and hooked it around his thick neck, drawing his face close enough for a long, lingering kiss.

Anger scuttled across my chest on tiny, hard feet.

If she only knew what he was really like. What he was capable of.

The next time I looked over, the dark-haired woman was standing up. I wished she would turn round so I could see her face. I'd bet she was young. He liked them young.

She set off in the direction of the women's toilets.

'Just going to the loo,' I said to Frances, sliding off my stool. 'Don't worry, I won't be long.'

The toilets were downstairs, along a narrow, scruffy corridor, past a closed door with a piece of paper gaffer-taped to it on which someone had felt-tipped 'DO NOT ENTER' in uneven letters. As I turned into the corridor, the woman with the dark hair was just disappearing through the door of the ladies' loo at the end. Though the music was muffled down here, my head was still thumping and the cumulative lack of sleep made me feel curiously disassociated from myself, so I had to rest my fingertips on the wall briefly as I followed in her footsteps, simply to touch something solid.

Inside, miraculously, there was no queue. And no sign of the dark-haired woman.

I went into one of the middle cubicles. On the back of the door someone had drawn a row of five stars and shaded in the one on the far left and written 'One star. Would not shit here again.' I slumped down on the loo and put my head in my hands, wishing I was back home.

Then I remembered why I'd come in here in the first place and forced myself back up to standing, the blood rushing to my head. Had I missed her? Exiting the cubicle, I cast my eye anxiously over the row of basins, feeling a rush of relief and adrenaline when I recognized the back of the woman's dark head at the end, nearest the hand-dryers.

I moved towards her, hoping I could squeeze into the basin next to hers, but there was another woman there, laboriously reapplying her make-up. So instead I went up behind her.

'Excuse me.'

She glanced up and our eyes met in the mirror. She was older than I thought she'd be. Mid-twenties. Pretty in a very delicate way. Huge brown eyes. A tiny, well-defined mouth. A fragile bird of a woman.

My heart was thudding uncomfortably in my chest. What should I say?

'The guy you're with. The DJ. He's bad news. I just want to warn you. He tried to attack my daughter. He's dangerous.'

The words fell out in a rush, like dead fish slipping from a net.

Her eyes widened.

'What're you talking about?'

And now she turned around.

'*Oh.*'

The exclamation came out before I'd had a chance to check it.

'I'm sorry,' I stuttered. 'I didn't know.'

Then I turned and fled, back along the corridor, heat flooding through me until all my nerves felt like they were on fire.

Back at the table, I snatched up my bag and coat.

'We have to go,' I told Frances, shouting to make myself heard.

'But I haven't finished my drink.'

'We have to go. Trust me.'

Down near the dance floor I could see the dark-haired woman arriving back at the table. She looked like she was crying. Stephens leapt to his feet, put his arm around her narrow shoulders. I saw her say something and his head jerked up, the veins on his thick neck raised and angry.

'Quick!' I urged Frances, anxiety a sour taste in my mouth.

And now the woman was scanning too, and her eyes locked with mine.

Now she was pointing, and both of them were looking, and I turned and plunged into the bodies that surrounded us, hoping against hope that Frances was behind me. I knew we were a lot nearer the door than Stephens, but he was faster and he knew the layout.

My chest was a tight line as I pushed my way through the crowd, past the woman on the door, who shot me a look as if to say, *I could have told you this wasn't for you*, and out on to the street.

To my huge relief, Frances followed on almost immediately after.

'What?' she began.

'Run. I'll explain everything. Just run.'

We set off down the street, past the queue of people waiting to get into the club. I felt sick with nerves and fear as we pounded along the pavement and turned the first corner, whereupon I pulled Frances into a shop doorway. We leaned against the glass, our hands on our knees, our breath fast and shallow.

'What's going on?'

Frances sounded scared and pissed off. And I couldn't blame her. What an idiot I'd been. What a stupid idiot.

'I'm sorry,' I said. 'I've made everything worse. I wasn't thinking straight.'

I told her about the confrontation in the toilet. The woman with the dark hair.

'Tessa!' Frances exclaimed, but to my relief she seemed

more surprised than angry. 'You said you only wanted
to watch him. Just to see him. That's all.'

'I know,' I said, wretched. 'But that's not even the
worst thing.'

I had a flashback to the woman's shocked brown eyes
in the mirror, then how she'd turned slowly around. I
closed my eyes, remorse and regret flooding my brain
until I thought I would drown in them.

'She's pregnant.'

13

Everything felt bad.

Since the previous Thursday I'd had a knot in my stomach, tight and fibrous. The broken nights were racked up behind me one after the other and now my brain felt sluggish and my body was coated in a clammy sheen of exhaustion.

Frances had hardly talked to me on the way home from Peckham. She'd said she was tired, but I worried she was angry, and I didn't blame her. I'd assured her we were only going to observe. Then I'd put us both at risk by not being able to keep my mouth shut.

But worse than that was the memory of Stephens's girlfriend's expression in the toilets when she'd turned around, her belly huge under her loose black top.

I imagined Rosie in her place. Pregnant, scared. Out of her depth. And was taken aback by how fierce the urge was to scoop this fragile girl-woman up and protect her. To keep her safe. The odds were already stacked against her, having a baby with a man like that. And now I'd made everything worse.

I tried to put all that out of my mind and focus on finding new cases for the women's magazine feature I was writing on fresh starts, but my sleep-starved thoughts scattered in all directions like spilled beads and I could not gather them back in.

I'd had several notifications from the internet dating app Kath had signed me up to and I spent fifteen dispiriting minutes sifting through the men who had liked my profile. Kath had already told me to add a decade to any photographs I was sent, but even allowing for that, they were a grizzled lot, most with that look of having been resoundingly beaten by life. Either that or they were brimming over with themselves. A moody photo wearing mirrored sunglasses and leather jacket. An invitation to me to tell them something about myself that would impress them. One looked okay, but then I noticed a line saying he'd joined the site in 2011. If he hadn't found love in seven years, he must be pretty fussy, I thought. Or else there was something very wrong with him. Either way, I wasn't interested in finding out.

I clicked off the dating site and logged into Granny-Cam instead. My father was in his chair, pen in hand, filling in a crossword on a neatly folded broadsheet newspaper. My mum was asleep so, for once, the television was off. I zoomed in on her. She looked so young. It was a funny thing about the dementia, that it had erased the care lines and laughter lines that had built up over the years, so that in repose she had the untroubled face of a baby.

Hard to believe that only a few years ago Mum would have been the first person I'd have turned to with my worries about Em. God, what wouldn't I give, I thought now, to hear her measured, musical voice again with that faint Welsh accent saying, *Oh, poor Tessie, but you know* . . . followed by something that would instantly put the world into perspective.

Fifty-two years old and I was missing my mum, even while she was right there in front of my eyes.

My dad looked at his watch, a gesture that took me right back to childhood, my father's watch as much a part of him as the wrist it sat on. He got heavily to his feet. When did he start having to lean on the arms of his chair to get up?

I felt a sharp prick of guilt. I knew Dad was finding it harder and harder to look after Mum. For the first time I could remember, he'd rung me the previous day, asking when I could come to visit and when I'd asked him how things were, instead of saying, 'Fine,' as he usually did, he'd replied, 'I'm managing,' in a gruff voice quite unlike his own. When I'd told him I'd be over at the weekend, he sounded so relieved.

I had to make more time for them, I reprimanded myself, watching him shuffle out of the room, straightening slowly as he went. For a few seconds I watched my sleeping mother. So peaceful. I imagined that she was her old self, nodding off in the evening in front of the television but refusing to go to bed. 'I was never asleep,' she'd protest when she was nudged awake, and Rosie and Emma would quiz her on what had happened in the TV programme over the last five minutes.

All of that gone now.

She was clearly dreaming, her eyes flickering beneath the latex-thin membrane of her eyelids. As I watched, she called out, something unintelligible, and Dad came to the door. He had his insulin pen in his hand, as if he'd just extracted it from the drawer. My father's diabetes had been such a fixture in my life since I was a teenager I no longer even registered what an odd thing it must be to inject yourself three times a day every day of your life. Like his watch, it was part of what made my dad himself.

For a moment he watched my mother, frowning behind his wire-framed glasses. Then, seemingly reassured, he ducked out of the room again. Without warning, I was so flooded with love for them both it seemed possible I might drown.

Dotty was sitting by my feet, gazing up at me hopefully. 'Come on, then, silly old thing.'

I didn't have a plan when we set out, but my feet took me up to Muswell Hill and I didn't have a good enough reason to make them go in some other direction.

The heart of Muswell Hill is a roundabout at the highest point from which the major roads in the area radiate out. There are two main shopping arteries. The more upmarket of those leads down to a church at the bottom and a cinema, from where it bends right. Along there are bookshops and some quaint half-shops selling cheese and jewellery and the like. The locals like to believe they live in a village, rather than a suburb of London, and this is the road that helps sustain the delusion. It was here I ended up, lurking outside a shop I'd always loved that sold stuffed animals in glass cases and other period curiosities.

I was eyeing up a wooden case with jewel-coloured butterflies pinned out in rows and wondering how ethically wrong it was to want it in my living room when I became aware of Dotty making the high-pitched whining noise she does when she's agitated about something.

Looking around, I noticed a figure standing alone

further along the street. My heart thudded to a stop as I recognized my elder daughter.

Rosie was outside a shop, gazing into the window. I was too far away to see her face but I could see she looked thin. Anxiety pinched me. Rosie had flirted with anorexia while she was a teenager, though thankfully it had never got serious enough to require treatment. Wasn't she eating at university? She'd had her hair highlighted blonde the year before, and the roots were growing through in her natural brown, against which her skin looked unnaturally pale. Might she be ill? I was sure Phil told me her reading week was last week. Why hadn't she gone back to university?

But oh, good God, she was lovely.

Rosie was delicate-boned and slight, but with such force of will that people were always surprised to find out how small she actually was. From the very beginning she'd never taken anything on faith. Always questioning, challenging. She was one of those rare people who properly held your gaze, not afraid to keep on looking until she'd worked out whatever it was she was unsure of. She had always had a hugely developed sense of what was fair and what wasn't, but the downside was she could be ridiculously cut and dried about things, unbothered by mitigating factors or context.

She was loving, but exacting. And, as I'd found out to my cost, she was agonizingly slow to forgive.

All the childhood and adolescent versions of Rosie spooled through my mind as I stood in that Muswell Hill street and gazed at my daughter. The young girl with the blonde plaits who'd been incensed that her teacher hadn't made her star pupil of the week again, even though she'd been far more helpful and better behaved than Owen, the latest recipient of that accolade. Not understanding until we'd explained it to her carefully that it was only right for everyone to get a chance. And then taking up 'fairness' like a crusade.

Her courage in overcoming her fear of water, her little face terrified but determined over the top of her pink arm bands. Her loyalty to her friends. The way she'd stand behind me in her pyjamas as I sat on the sofa at the end of a long day and massage my shoulders with her small, soft hands. How, as a teenager, she'd mounted such an impressively forensic case against her eleven o'clock curfew that we'd ended up agreeing to extend it, despite our own better judgement.

My heart was a water balloon, swollen with love.

All this time, Dotty's whining had been getting increasingly frantic. When Rosie lived at home she'd been the only one who let the dog sleep on her bed, putting up with her nocturnal changes of position and her endless fidgeting. Now Dotty had smelled her and was straining at her lead to get to her.

Desperate, Dotty let out a high-pitched yelp of desire.

Immediately, Rosie looked over. Our eyes met.

I broke into a smile. I couldn't help it. I was so happy to see her.

Rosie at first seemed frozen with surprise, but then she too smiled and opened her mouth as if she was about to say something.

As I took a step towards her the shop door opened next to Rosie and a woman stepped out. Blonde hair twisted up, expensive pale pink coat, suede boots with a heel. Joy. How could I have forgotten that her florist shop was along this stretch?

I stopped. Uncertain. Watching as my husband's girl-friend linked her arm through my daughter's and, not seeing me standing there all those yards away, steered her off in the opposite direction.

Rosie, silent and uncharacteristically submissive, threw me one last look over her shoulder but allowed herself to be led.

I remained motionless, every nerve and sinew and atom in my body straining to follow my estranged daughter, even while my head warned me to turn away. Poor Dotty pulled and pulled on her lead as the figures of Rosie and Joy became smaller and then disappeared altogether.

I knelt down to comfort my distraught dog, burying my face in her wiry fur so that passers-by wouldn't notice that my cheeks were wet with tears. A rush of heat came out of nowhere. Suddenly, my thin denim jacket, which earlier had seemed so flimsy against the cool March breeze, was like a thick, suffocating blanket and I tore it off, the long-sleeved T-shirt I had on under-neath sticking to my skin with sweat.

Back home, I went straight up to my room, threw myself on my bed and let the sobs rip from me until my throat was stripped raw.

That afternoon I prepared a lasagne from scratch, roasting the vegetables, whisking the béchamel to a smooth, silky paste.

'Wow, what's this in aid of?' asked Em when she came through the door, her face lit up. Sometimes I forgot how easy it was to make my daughter happy – the smell of her favourite dinner cooking when she came home from school.

'You, of course,' I told her, putting down the cheese grater to give her a big, tight hug.

'All right, all right, no need to squash me.'

Em dumped her bags next to the kitchen table and sat down in front of the cup of tea I'd made her. She looked tired.

'Are you sure you're okay, sweetheart?'

She glanced up, frowning.

'Why wouldn't I be?'

'And you're not still thinking about what happened? Because if you are, you can always talk to me. That's what I'm here for.'

'Mum, I've told you, I'm fine. I'm just stressing about exams, that's all. Please stop worrying about me.'

The lasagne was lovely, and then Emma told me a funny story about something that happened at school and I laughed probably more than the story merited.

'It's not *that* funny,' Emma said. But I could tell she was pleased by my reaction.

I hadn't always been home at dinnertimes when my children were growing up, hadn't always been on hand to hear the small details of their day. I regretted that now, all those tiny threads in the fabric of their lives that I'd missed out on.

'I saw Rosie today,' I said, head bent over my plate.

I sensed Emma go very still. She and her sister were very close, staying in regular contact whenever they were apart, but Em didn't talk to me about it and I didn't push her. I never wanted her to feel pulled in two directions, or that she had to vet what she said to me.

'I don't think she saw me,' I lied. 'And then *Joy* turned up.'

I emphasized the word 'Joy', as if it weren't really her name. I couldn't help it.

Emma put down her fork.

'She's all right, you know, Mum. Joy, I mean. She's nice, actually. We play board games.'

'Oh, well, *board* games.'

I said it sneeringly, even though when the girls were younger I used to fantasize about us being the kind of family that played board games. When I saw Em's face I regretted my childishness.

'Sorry, darling. I'm glad she's nice.'

But after Em had gone up to her room and I was clearing up I started thinking again about Rosie and how she'd looked, and whether she'd been about to say something to me, and an ache started low in the pit of my stomach. I flopped down on the sofa in the living room. The television was full of reality shows and food programmes, so I began scrolling through Netflix. I clicked on the first film that had a good rating, just to escape from my own head for a while. It starred Robert Redford and Jane Fonda as elderly neighbours, both desperate for human connection, and I watched for a while, wondering if Hollywood stars ever got lonely.

I was waiting to feel tired enough to go upstairs. Like most insomniacs, I dreaded the prospect of getting into bed only to feel suddenly, horribly alert, the worries and anxieties of the day like a relentless clock ticking loudly in my head.

I fetched my laptop from the kitchen table and sat back down on the sofa. I'd check in briefly to Facebook, just to see what my friends were up to.

But as I scrolled down my home page, I felt as if I were play-acting, going through the motions of being interested in Mari's search for chiropractor recommendations or someone else's photos of their weekend in Northumberland.

Finally, I gave in. I'd look on Stephens's DJ page. Just to see what was going on. That wasn't hurting anyone. Maybe he'd have photographs of last Thursday night.

Even the thought of it, that young woman's stricken face in the toilets, made my stomach lurch.

I could see right away there weren't any photographs. Nothing to show our paths had crossed. Nothing to indicate he'd been inconvenienced in any way.

I looked again at his picture – blades of cheekbone pushing through smooth, tight skin, the cocky jut of his jaw. My gaze snagged on that chunky silver signet ring on the hand that had hooked itself around my daughter's neck and my stomach twisted.

Scanning down the page, I noticed that my comment, *I KNOW WHAT YOU DID*, had been deleted. I shouldn't have been surprised, and yet I bristled with outrage. Why should he be allowed to erase the things he didn't like, while my sixteen-year-old daughter had to relive what he'd done to her again and again?

I wanted to keep up the pressure on him, to make sure he couldn't forget that there was someone out there who knew who he was and what he was capable of. The conversation I'd had with Frances was still fresh in my mind. I wasn't about to move house again – couldn't afford to even if I wanted to – but maybe, just maybe, if I made things difficult enough for him, he might decide he was better off somewhere else.

After logging out of Facebook I signed back in under my new fake account and reposted my comment.

Almost immediately, there came a reply. From him. *Who r u?*

Adrenaline shot, caffeine-strong, through my veins. He was there. If I stepped through my screen, I could step out through his and be face to face with the man who'd hurt Em. My breath quickened and I even put my hand to my screen, as if I expected to encounter that mocking smile, those blade-sharp cheekbones.

Almost immediately, he came back again. *Whoever u r, this is harassment. Think of this as a warning. U need to stop.*

Or what? I wrote. My fingers felt charged with electricity.

Or u will regret it.

For a moment I stared at the words, exultant. A threat. In writing. Quickly, I googled 'how to screen-shot' but before I had a chance to follow the instructions, the whole exchange disappeared.

A post appeared on the page, from a woman I didn't recognize who'd clearly witnessed the whole thing – *U ok, J?* – and the reply, almost instantaneous: *Yeh, some nuttaz around.*

Helpless with rage, I typed in, *YOU SHOULD BE LOCKED UP.*

The woman who'd commented before shot back with a sarcastic *6 years too late, hun. U need to try harder.*

Again, the whole exchange was deleted almost before

the last letter appeared, but now glee had replaced the anger. He'd been in prison. That woman, whoever she was, had just confirmed it. I remembered what Detective Byrne had said about our suspect having a criminal record. Any lingering doubts I might have had about Stephens being the man who attacked Em were instantly snuffed out.

Adrenaline meant I stayed up for another hour before going to bed and miraculously falling asleep. But I woke up a couple of hours later, my head thick, the sheets sticking to the backs of my legs. Restless and hot and unable to get back to sleep, I went over what had happened that evening, feeling frustrated all over again at how easily he'd erased me, my accusations disappearing before my eyes.

Then I thought about my phone charging by the side of the bed.

I picked it up and saw it was 2.38 a.m. He wasn't going to be policing his FB notifications in the middle of a Tuesday night.

I navigated to his DJ page, feeling a thrill of power at the thought of having free access to his page while he slept on unaware.

I KNOW WHAT YOU DID, I wrote again.

Then, when that stayed exactly where it was, I typed, *JAMES LAURENCE STEPHENS IS A SEX ATTACKER.*

Propped up on my elbow, I watched my screen to see if anything would happen. When the messages remained untouched, I clicked off my phone, flushed with triumph. So what if the messages were gone tomorrow

124

morning? Who knows who might have seen them by the time he next checked?

Unusually for me, I fell back to sleep after that, but when I woke up in the morning it was with a clammy sense of having done something wrong. My head throbbed with the hangover from my broken night as I trawled back through the events of the previous day. The encounter with Rosie came back to me and I fought back a wave of panic until I'd reassured myself I hadn't done anything to upset her.

Then I thought about the exchange with Stephens. How he'd kept deleting me. Then how I'd sent him those messages from my phone in the middle of the night when he was safely asleep.

Oh no. Oh no, no, no, no, no.

I snatched up my phone from the floor, nausea rising from some point deep inside me.

I called up Stephens's DJ page, my eyes scanning wildly through, looking for my comments of last night, but they had disappeared.

A red number one had appeared on my notifications and I clicked with a dense feeling of dread.

Even before it came up, I knew.

On my phone, I was still logged in as the real me. Not the fake account I'd been messaging from downstairs.

J-Lo Stephens posted in Tessa Hopwood, read the top line in my notifications.

I clicked on the link and a high-pitched alarm went off in my head as I read his message, sent first thing that morning.

I KNOW WHO YOU ARE.

Mum asked me about you today.

She never says your name but I know it's you she's talking about.

We were standing in the kitchen. I was making tea and she was sitting at the table behind me. She prefers to have serious conversations without eye contact. We aren't a soul-baring sort of family. She asked me how I was 'in myself'. Then she said how brave I was and how well I was dealing with everything. Then she said, 'Have you put it behind you now?'

And I knew she really meant you. Have I put you behind me.

I smiled and said something encouraging because I knew that's what she needed to hear, but inside I was screaming at her not to talk any more.

And now all day the dark cloud of you has been hanging over my head.

Only Henry calmed me down.

On the way home from school he took my hand and my thoughts were so full of him there was no space for you.

14

There's a pub at Alexandra Palace with outside tables from where you can see over the whole of north London, past the Post Office Tower to the west, and all the way to Canary Wharf to the east. Today, though, a thick, low-lying layer of cloud was obscuring all beyond a radius of two or three miles, making the air feel clammy and padded.

In any case, Frances and I weren't much in the mood for admiring the view.

'How much could he have seen from your Facebook page? I mean, presumably, you had your privacy settings up high,' said Frances, bending down to pet Dotty, who couldn't understand why we'd choose to be sitting in this gravel courtyard when there were grassy slopes to be run down and balls to be chased.

'Yes, of course! Well, maybe not as high as I'd thought.'

I'd been horrified when I'd gone up to my privacy settings and realized that, while my posts were protected, anyone could access my friends list or, worse still, my biographical details.

He now knew my birthday was in October.

He knew I was a journalist.

He knew I had two daughters.

And he knew who they were.

Oh, Emma.

I hadn't intended to tell any of this to Frances. After what had happened at the Peckham club I had assumed Emma's rescuer would give me a wide berth. And the last thing I wanted was to give her even more reason to think me dangerously out of control. But then she'd called, to see how I was. And as it was only a few hours after I'd seen Stephens's comment on Facebook, I couldn't stop myself telling her what had happened.

What I'd done.

I half expected, maybe even hoped for, some kind of rebuke from Frances. It was what I deserved. Instead, probably hearing the note of desperation in my voice, she told me she had that afternoon off work and asked if it would help to meet, and I found myself nodding, even though I was on the end of a phone and she couldn't see me, because I couldn't trust myself to speak.

So here we were. Sitting at one of the wooden picnic tables outside the pub, while joggers and dog walkers and the occasional high-vis-jacketed member of the Palace grounds staff passed to and fro in front of us. Frances was well wrapped up, although the thick cloud meant it wasn't really cold but kind of damp and muggy. She had an emerald-green mohair scarf around her neck, and her long thick hair was tucked into the folds of the scarf in that cute, casual way some women manage.

'Have you warned Emma and your older daughter to change their privacy settings to high?'

Fear gripped me by the throat.

'You think he'll go after them?'

'It's as well to be cautious, that's all. Listen, Tessa, don't you think you ought to tell the police what's going on?'

I'd guessed she was going to say that, but still I cringed at the thought of it. Having to explain to Detective Byrne, with his tired, bloodshot eyes, how I'd stalked James Stephens. The confrontation with his pregnant girlfriend in the toilets. How I'd put my girls in danger.

As I was thinking about it, a neat figure in a close-fitting black tracksuit with a subtle fuchsia flash on the lower outside leg jogged towards us, long, sleek ponytail swinging.

'Tessa!'

Nita extracted her headphones from her ears while jogging on the spot. Aside from a faint pink flush on her smooth cheeks, there was no other indication that she'd just run up one of the steepest hills in London.

'Nita!'

I got to my feet and stepped towards her.

'Oh God, don't come too near. I'm all sweaty and disgusting and I probably stink.'

She was none of those things.

As I sat back down, my mind was racing ahead, trying to think of how to introduce Frances without giving away how deeply embroiled in the fallout of Emma's abduction I'd allowed myself to become. Instinctively, I knew Nita would disapprove. I remembered that Whats-App chat, that stinging accusation that I was getting off on the drama of it all.

But now Nita was eyeing Frances expectantly.

'This is Frances,' I said, slapping a smile on to my face like a sticker. 'My friend.'

I felt Frances stiffen beside me.

'Hello,' she said in an off-hand voice, quite unlike her usual one. I glanced over and saw that she wasn't even looking at Nita but was concentrating on a point on the table that she was scraping with her thumbnail.

There was an awkward silence.

'Well,' said Nita, hopping from side to side. 'Better press on. I'm doing the half marathon in a couple of weeks.' This last was addressed to Frances. 'Raising money for Macmillan nurses. My mother has terminal cancer.'

'I'm sorry to hear that.'

The words were friendly but the tone was flat. Disinterested, even.

'Right then. Offski!' Nita, who was one of those people who prided themselves on knowing the appropriate thing to say in any given situation, was not used to encountering indifference.

After I'd watched her jog away, ponytail swinging angrily, I turned back to Frances.

'Hope you didn't mind me introducing you as a friend. I didn't really want to get into it. Do you know what I mean?'

'Of course. I completely understand.'

But she still sounded subdued and, just a few minutes later, she told me she needed to be going. Her mum was having a bad spell and she didn't like to be away from her longer than necessary.

'You're a good person, Frances,' I said, putting my hand on her arm. 'Not many people your age would put their own life on the back burner to look after their parents.'

I thought about my own mum and dad and how it had been weeks since I'd seen them, and I felt a warm flush of shame.

'Oh, I don't do much, really. Besides, it's the least I can do after everything she did for me, bringing me up single-handedly after my dad died. She's been brilliant.'

'You do make sure you have time for you, though, don't you?' I persevered. 'Time to hang out with your friends, and enjoy being young?'

Frances nodded. 'Oh yes, definitely. Well, I mean, my best friend, Claudia, moved away quite recently so I don't go out as much as I did. But that suits me, really. I'm a home-bird at heart. Anyway, you have enough on your plate without worrying about me.'

Frances was heading back home, in the opposite direction to the way I was walking. She'd gone a few steps before turning back.

'You will think about what I said, won't you, Tessa? About telling the police what's been going on? You might have your privacy settings on, but what about your friends, your family? You'd be amazed how much someone could piece together from all the different parts of your life.'

Walking home with Dotty, the fear and anxiety I'd felt that morning while scanning through my Facebook feed returned as I imagined scenarios where one or other daughter woke up to threats, or else damning messages about their mother. I pictured Rosie as I'd seen her the day before. She'd been about to make a move towards me, I was sure of it. The first step towards a reconciliation. Getting caught up in something like this would kill any chances of that happening. How could I have been so stupid?

On impulse, I didn't take the normal route home,

instead diverting via Wood Green, which took us up the main high road from Wood Green station, past the fast-food restaurants and the minicab companies.

I usually avoided going this way, and deliberately kept my face averted from the junction outside the Tube. Even so, I could feel the sweat beading on my forehead and a cold, clammy dread building. As I passed, I could hear in my head the sickening crunch of metal on metal. I quickened my pace but the sounds followed me. A girl crying in great, tearing sobs. A man's voice shouting. The deafening thunder of my own heart in my ears.

I stopped a few hundred yards up the road in front of a charity-shop window and bent my head, trying to shake the memories loose from my head, like I was getting water out of my ear after a swim.

This route also happened to pass the police station, housed in a former pub on a corner between the timber yard and the depressing-looking civic centre. This wasn't the kind of station to encourage public drop-ins. In fact, unless you knew where to look, you probably wouldn't even notice it was there. The car park in front obscured the Metropolitan Police noticeboard and the doors were locked, with no visible means of entry. It was on the closures list, I'd been told. Soon there'd be no police stations left.

Standing outside in the tiny car park with my phone in my hand, I made a bargain with myself. If Detective Byrne was here, I'd tell him everything and not hold back. But if he wasn't, well, at least I'd have tried. And I could go home and deactivate my social media accounts and just focus on being a good mother to my girls and keeping my head down and earning some money.

One hand absently stroking Dotty and trying to calm her down, I scrolled through my contacts until I found Detective Byrne. Took a deep breath.

He was there.

Five minutes later I was sitting opposite him on a plastic bucket chair in that anonymous open-plan office that could have been any office anywhere in the country, with the dark blue carpet and the cheap grey desks and the bulky desktop computers that looked ten years out of date. We were next to the window, which had slatted white blinds, allowing me to keep an eye on Dotty, who was tied up outside and staring balefully at the door through which I'd disappeared, as if she might will me back out again.

I started, hesitantly, to tell him what had been happening. To my own irritation, I could hear myself apologizing in advance for what I was about to tell him, making jokes at my own expense. 'Call it a mad, middle-aged menopausal moment,' I said at one point. I was minimizing it, trivializing it, as I had a tendency to do when talking to people I didn't know well, even though I knew, fundamentally, that this was neither minimal nor trivial.

Why did I do that?

I was telling him about the door I'd seen James Stephens emerge from, the one opposite the Tube. I was looking for some kind of recognition in the policeman's eyes. Some confirmation. A way of making Detective Byrne complicit in what was going on. Instead, he held up a hand.

'Whoah. Let me stop you right there.' I noticed for the first time an angry, pink patch of psoriasis on his wrist, the skin raised and scaly. 'I thought we'd been through this before, Mrs Hopwood. I cannot tell you the address of a man who has not been charged with any offence and who your daughter failed to pick out of a line-up.'

I stopped, nonplussed.

'No. Of course not.'

'And please remember that eight out of the nine men in that video were recruited from all around the country. Only one, the man captured on the CCTV from the bus, is local.'

Something must have shown in my eyes, because he instantly corrected himself.

'I mean, might be local.'

I was so exhilarated by his unwitting confirmation that the suspect lived locally that I wasn't thinking properly.

'It's definitely him. Frances has already identified him.'

The change in Detective Byrne's demeanour was instant. Gone was the gentle, tired smile. And in its place an expression of the utmost seriousness. His eyes, without their usual crinkled fan of laughter lines, appeared hard and unnervingly direct. For a moment I thought I could see how intimidating he might seem to a newly arrested criminal or a suspect brought in for questioning.

'Frances Gates is involved in this? Let me tell you something, Mrs Hopwood, we do not condone vigilante-style behaviour in any way, shape or form. *If* you or your daughter have had threats made against you, rest assured, we will take them very seriously. However, if you start taking the law into your own hands and rop-ing in a witness in order to harass a member of the public, we would also have to take that very seriously. Do I make myself clear?'

I nodded, not trusting myself to speak. I found I couldn't meet Detective Byrne's eyes, so I focused instead on looking through the window at Dotty, who had given up her vigil at the door and was lying down in an attitude of abject misery.

Detective Byrne showed me out.

'It's not that I'm not sympathetic, Mrs Hopwood,' he said as he held the door open. 'Believe me, we are as keen as you are to get the scumbag who attacked your daughter. But without a positive ID there is really nothing more we can do. The best thing you can do for Emma is to put this all behind you and move on with your lives. Agreed?'

I nodded and shook his outstretched hand, which encompassed mine like a baseball glove, rigid and strong.

When I bent to unclip Dotty, I was mortified to find I hadn't actually tied her up. I'd looped the lead around the railing then pulled it through the handle but had forgotten to clip it on to her collar.

Idiot, I muttered under my breath. As I straightened up and turned to leave, I saw that Detective Byrne was still standing there, watching me through the glass.

15

It used to take an hour and twenty minutes to drive to my parents' house.

Over the years I'd been making the journey from north London to north Oxford I'd travelled in torrential rain, in snow, once in extreme heat that had us pulling on to the hard shoulder, black smoke belching from the engine.

I'd driven there on my own in the early hours, doing ninety miles an hour on the empty road, listening to hush-toned radio DJs hosting late-night call-ins, and I'd sat in bank-holiday jams with Rosie and Emma, singing along to Amy Winehouse at the top of our voices.

In the early days with Phil, we'd drive with our hands clamped to one another's thighs, chatting about everything and nothing, a far cry from the silence of the later trips, both of us wrapped up in our petty resentments, our relentless point-scoring, the distance between us as wide as the motorway itself.

In between those points were all the times we'd driven with babies, slumped in their car seats, heads lolling, plump lips still sheened with milk, and with squirming toddlers fractiously trying to free themselves from restraining belts. We'd had the years of squabbling in the back seat, with Rosie drawing an invisible line down the middle and complaining every time Em put a toe or a finger over it. Then the years of headphones plugged firmly into ears, lost in their own thoughts and the anthems of their lives.

Since I'd got rid of the car, I missed those journeys. Sealed up together without escape, I'd had some of my most open conversations with my daughters, boredom and proximity combining to tease out secrets and mend bridges. Now we took the train, which doubled the travel time when you included the Tube journey and the bus the other end.

At least today I'd managed to bag a table seat. It was Mother's Day and the carriage was full of men self-consciously clutching bunches of flowers and elderly women dressed in their Sunday best. I was sitting next to Em, who had her headphones in. I asked what she was listening to and she obligingly took one earbud out and gave it to me by way of reply.

Johnny Cash was playing, which surprised me, although it probably shouldn't have. My children were constantly revealing layers I couldn't even guess at. And besides, everything comes full circle in the end. Even Johnny.

After the song finished we chatted about this and that, nothing important, but I was glad to see Em was in a relaxed mood, hardly touching her hair. Even though the car, traditionally, was the place my children had allowed themselves to be most unguarded, physically close but without embarrassing eye contact, the train still came a close second.

'How are you feeling now?' I asked her. 'About what happened?'

We still didn't refer to the attack directly, only in the most oblique terms. *What happened. That thing. The incident.* As if not naming it might make it easier to forget.

Gaze fixed on her phone screen, Em shrugged.

'Okay, I guess. I mean, I still think about it some-times, especially since I saw him that time in the street. But then I tell myself he was just visiting, or it wasn't even him at all, and I try to forget it.'

'And do you talk to anyone about it? Your friends?' I hesitated. 'Frances?'

Em whipped around to glance at me, as if trying to guess how I'd found out, before returning her attention to the screen again.

'Sometimes. She was there, you know. So she kind of understands.'

That was typical Em. Worrying I'd be hurt that she'd confided in someone else instead of me.

'It's all right, Em. I'm just glad you have someone you can talk to. Though you know you can always talk to me, don't you?'

She nodded.

'Are you still having nightmares about it?'

'Not really.' She swallowed audibly. 'Only sometimes.'

I pressed my lips together, suddenly conscious of a painful lump in my throat. She was being so brave. But it killed me that she felt she had to be.

Emma said something quietly that I didn't catch, so I asked her to repeat it.

'I said, I wish they'd caught him. I wish I'd just said it

was him. You know, Number Eight, or whatever he was. Even if I wasn't a hundred per cent sure, I wish I'd said it anyway. I hate the thought that he's still out there, maybe even living around the corner.'

For a moment I was tempted to admit I knew exactly where he lived. But then I remembered my last meeting with Detective Byrne and realized it would do more harm than good for her to know that he was so close by and that we were powerless to do anything about it. She didn't travel by herself after dark any more, and he was hardly going to target her in broad daylight. Better not to freak her out more than she already was.

So I kept quiet and watched out of the train window as anger calcified inside my chest.

My parents lived on a modern executive housing estate in north Oxford in a house they'd bought off-plan in the mid-1980s when it would still have been possible to buy a beautiful rambling Victorian villa around the corner for the same money, a fact that could still make me weep all these years on.

As always, I had to steel myself before going inside, pulling in all my core muscles like we were taught to do in Pilates, trying to make myself inviolate.

Even though a cleaner went in once a week, at my insistence, and an agency carer came daily to get Mum up and prepare food, the house still smelled bad – a combination of the heating kept on too high for too long, lax personal hygiene and a nursery-food diet – overboiled vegetables and tinned mushroom soup.

'Here we are!' said my dad, rushing into the hall to meet us.

I watched my parents most days on the webcam at

home but it wasn't until I saw them in the flesh that I properly noticed the physical changes they had undergone since the last time I visited them. Dad had a nick on his skin-saggy chin where he'd cut himself shaving, and the stiffness I'd noticed on the webcam was pronounced. My eyes filled with tears, and I had to quickly step forward to hug him so he wouldn't notice.

Dad had trained as a hydraulic engineer and later in his career had travelled the world, advising private companies and local authorities on the design of water-treatment plants. As a child I'd kept a diary, where I wrote down bits of news so I wouldn't have forgotten them by the time he got home from wherever he'd gone. 'I can see why that would upset you,' he'd say solemnly when I related some trivial or imagined slight perpetrated by one of my friends from school. From the earliest age, he'd made me feel like someone who deserved to be taken seriously. Only now could I see what a great gift that had been.

'How is she?' I asked him now.

'Oh, you know. Good days and bad days.'

My mother was sitting in her chair in the living room watching *Midsomer Murders* on the television. There had been occasions over the last couple of years where I'd gone in and she hadn't recognized me at all. One time I'd taken Em and Mum had looked her up and down with an expression of the greatest contempt, before asking, 'Who, or *what*, is that?'

Today, though, she seemed to know who we were – well, apart from confusing Em with Rosie. But then I did that sometimes.

Used to do that.

'Happy Mother's Day,' I said, plastering on a jolly smile and pressing a small, wrapped parcel containing an unimaginative woollen scarf into my mum's hands.

'Thank you, dear,' she said, beaming. 'Good journey?'

It was what she always said on her better days. One of the stock phrases she'd memorized to trot out when people came round. No longer able to empathize, she had to search for cues in social interactions – people appearing in the living room greeting her with a smile, or a particular tone of voice dipping or an expectant pause in the conversation, during which she might interject, 'Well, we must wait and see,' or 'We must hope for the best,' or, if someone sounded more upbeat, 'That's nice.' Innocuous phrases she'd learned by heart so that she could still participate in life.

As ever, my heart contracted with pity and regret at the sight of her, even as I curled my fingers into my palms in irritation, noticing how she was stealthily increasing the volume on the remote control. This was the story now of my relationship with my mother, sympathy and frustration existing simultaneously so my emotions lurched from side to side like the bubble on a spirit level.

'Hello, Grandma!' Em shouted, struggling to be heard over the sound of the television. She went over and put her arms around her grandmother and I was struck all over again by the contrast between my daughter, rude with health and the power she didn't yet know she possessed, and my shrinking mother, with her papery skin that always seemed like it would crumble to powder if you pressed too hard, like a moth's wings.

My father insisted on making the tea, which meant

the drinks arrived with a grey scum floating on the top. I don't think I breathed the entire time it took him to walk from the kitchen to the living room with two steaming cups in his unsteady hands.

While we drank, I was conscious of the monitor fixed in the corner of the ceiling, winking red. For a moment, it amused me to think of a parallel me opening up my laptop back in London and watching us all politely sipping our scummy drinks. Then an image flashed through my mind of James Stephens, breaking in and creeping along the narrow hallway, opening up my laptop, spying on me, and I felt weak with dread.

How much could he have found out about me from my Facebook page?

Did he know where I lived?

'Are you feeling unwell, Tessie?' my father asked over the top of *Midsomer Murders*. 'You're looking very pale.'

'No, I'm fine, Dad. Honest. Just a bit tired. I don't sleep terribly well.'

'I never sleep,' announced my mum. 'Up all night long, while he' – she jerked a thumb in my father's direction – 'slumbers like a baby.'

Dad rolled his eyes. 'Chance would be a fine thing,' he said under his breath, and we exchanged a small smile. 'But seriously, Tess, what you need is fresh air. Take that dog of yours out a bit more often. That'll sort you out.'

As my father detailed his other failsafe methods of getting to sleep – no tea after 4 p.m., in bed directly after the ten o'clock news – I scanned his face, noting the violet shadows under his eyes and the deep lines that went down from the corner of his mouth like those on a ventriloquist's dummy. Had those always been there?

When he took our cups back into the kitchen I followed him.

'How are you, Dad? Really?'

He opened his mouth as if he was about to reply, 'Fine,' as he always did. But then he closed it again and wiped a hand across his face.

'I'm tired,' he said finally, and something inside me caved in. I'd never heard him sound so defeated.

'Is it time to consider other alternatives?' I said gently. 'Dr Ali said he'd recommend some good nursing homes when the time came. I could come with you to look at them.'

My father sighed then pulled back his shoulders and straightened up.

'Not yet,' he said. 'If you'd asked me yesterday when she didn't know who I was and kept shouting for help, I might have said yes. But just look at her today. It's almost like the old Judy is back. I can't do it to her.'

'But you have to think of yourself too. Your own health.'

'I shall be all right. Don't worry about me.'

I cooked lunch from ingredients I'd bought at the Sainsbury's in town, a fish pie that Mum looked at with suspicion and refused to eat until I fed it to her a spoonful at a time.

I washed up afterwards while Dad and Em played Scrabble in the living room and Mum dozed in her chair. Once again I found myself thinking about Stephens and what he might have been able to discover from my Facebook page.

I tried to reason with myself. I was sure I'd never had to give an address to Facebook, so there was no way

Stephens could have found out where I lived. So all he had really was a name, a photograph, a job description and a list of my friends. Nothing that could lead him to us.

I wiped my hands on my jeans, got out my phone and googled Tessa Hopwood, journalist. Pages of results came up and I scanned through, feeling weak with relief when I saw that after the top result, which was my own website, they were almost all links to features I'd written for various publications or quotes from me when I was still an editor and people still cared what I thought. Nothing that gave away my address.

I picked up the brush to resume washing up but stopped, pan in hand, when something else occurred to me.

If he'd been able to access my biographical details in the 'about' section, he'd have seen links to Rosie and Emma, who were listed as my daughters. But what would he see if he looked up *their* biographical details?

I fished out my phone again, my hands still soapy, and clicked on Rosie's Facebook page. She'd unfriended me ages ago, but I could still view her public profile. To my relief I saw that the entire biographical section was blank. *Good girl.* Now Emma.

Like her sister, she'd added only sparse personal details, but my heart stalled as I saw that under 'current home town' she'd put Bounds Green, N22.

With unsteady fingers, I called up Google again, this time typing in 'Tessa Hopwood journalist N22'. The first entry was from Companies House. My accountant had persuaded me to register myself as a limited company the previous year. And here was my entry, Tessa Hopwood Ltd, with myself as director.

Followed by our full address. How ironic that the thing that had first led me to James Stephens might be the very thing that now led him to me.

My mouth felt suddenly sandpaper dry, and for a moment my parents' kitchen blurred as my mind emptied.

He knew where I lived.

He knew where Emma lived.

'Penny for them,' said my father, coming into the kitchen.

I shoved my phone into my pocket and turned back to the sink.

'Oh, it's just work.'

I took a deep breath in and let it out slowly. There was nothing to say Stephens had made those connections. He didn't seem like the type who spent a lot of time online. Those biographical details weren't on the first page you came to. You had to click a couple of times to get to them. It probably wouldn't even occur to him to see what was on there, much less to follow it up. As a journalist, it was second nature for me to dig around and follow up all leads, but most people wouldn't bother.

Finally, I felt calmer, my pulse no longer racing. I was overreacting. Increased anxiety was an age-related thing, the twelve-year-old GP had informed me with regret that last time I'd visited the surgery and tried to explain how, sometimes, in the dead, still hours of the early morning I listened to my heart racing and it sounded like the drumming of distant horse's hooves. Lots of women in their fifties experienced it, he said. Had I tried yoga?

Menopause: the gift that kept on giving.

Later, we went for a walk. My mother allowed me to

put on her coat and her new scarf then looked at me coyly from under her lashes, asking: 'Are you taking me out somewhere?' as if I were some long-distant beau. We walked around the beautiful university park, lingering on the bridge over the river, where, in a different lifetime, my mum used to play Pooh sticks with the girls.

As we walked over the lawn my phone beeped with a message alert.

It was an email that had been sent via my website. The address was unfamiliar, a series of seemingly random letters and numbers. But the image that filled my screen when I clicked on the message was anything but. A photo of the front of our house with Dotty framed in the window, looking over the back of the sofa, observing the goings-on in the street, as she often did when we were away from home.

The message was short, written in bold capitals:
PEEKABOO

16

'Were you threatened at all?'

'Well, no, not in so many words.'

'And was the photograph taken from inside your garden gate – on your property, if you like?'

'No, from the street.'

I could hear a loud tapping, as if the woman on the other end of the line was hitting the keys of a computer as I spoke.

'Okay, well, what I can do is log your report, so there's a record of it, and if you have any further communication, take a note of it, date and time and that sort of thing, and if anything else happens where a concrete threat is made to you or to your daughter, you get back in touch with us. All right?'

'So you can't trace the IP address?'

'Not unless there's been a credible threat made, no.'

'But, like I told you, I'm pretty sure I know who sent the photograph – the guy who attacked my daughter. And if you could just trace the IP address, I could prove it was him.'

'I'm afraid it's not as easy as that. Data protection means the providers won't give us that kind of information without a court order. So a crime would have to have been committed. And I'm sorry to say, if someone has gone to the trouble of making an anonymous account, they would more than likely use a public computer anyway, like in a library, that sort of thing. So the IP address would be next to useless anyway.'

I hung up and sat for a moment with my head in my hands as frustration fizzed along my nerves.

Twenty-five minutes I'd been on hold to the 101 non-emergency number, and all for nothing.

I rang Frances. To tell the truth, I didn't much feel like talking to anyone, but I'd told her I'd get back to her once I'd called the police.

'There's nothing they can do,' I told her. 'Not without any overt threat. And even then I get the feeling it would have to amount to major harassment for them to take action.'

'I'm sorry to hear that. But look, all you can do now is put it out of your head. I mean, there was no sign of damage when you arrived home, was there? He's just trying to spook you, that's all.'

'I know you're right, but I keep jumping out of my skin every time someone walks past the house.'

It was Frances I'd called from Oxford station earlier on having sent Em off in search of cappuccinos. There'd been a moment where I dithered about calling Kath or Mari instead. The two of them had always been the ones I'd turn to first in any crisis. But then I'd have had to own up to sending Stephens those messages online and following him to the club in Peckham, and I couldn't face having to go through it, knowing they'd warned me to keep clear of him. Couldn't face admitting to that shameful moment in the toilets, his pregnant girlfriend's face crumpling. Mari's voice in my ears: *Oh, Tessa!*

So I'd called Frances, because, out of everyone, she would understand. And she'd made me promise to call Detective Byrne when I got home. But even after I'd got into the house, my fingers fumbling with the key in the lock, fearing I might find the place ransacked or, even worse, Stephens waiting inside, having somehow broken in, I'd still had to wait a couple of hours for Emma to go up to her room, so she wouldn't overhear. And then Detective Byrne hadn't answered his mobile and when I called his office number he hadn't been there, and the man I'd spoken to had interrupted my rambling explanation to tell me to call 101 if I wanted to report harassment.

And now it was nearly nine o'clock in the evening and it had all been a waste of time.

After saying goodbye to Frances I got out my laptop and called up the message again. That photo of my house still shocking in its incongruous familiarity. I studied it, searching for clues. There were the tops of car roofs just visible in the lower part of the picture, so he must have been standing on the other side of the road when he took it.

I walked to the window and stared out over the low wall that separated our front garden from the pavement, then over the cars parked on either side of the road. The house opposite, which was occupied by an ever-changing cast of Polish labourers, was plunged into darkness, apart from one window at the top that was lit by a greenish flickering light like an eye winking.

17

The dating site Kath had signed me up for notified me every time I had a new message, and even though I kept vowing not to click on them I always gave in, with predictably negative effects on my self-esteem.

'I'm sure they're probably very nice people when you get to know them,' I told Mari when she called for an update, 'but really, if I want to hang out with octogenarians I'll just visit my dad. Again.'

Though it at least took my mind off Stephens and the anonymous email, you could say my expectations were scraping-the-bottom low. So I was taken aback when, a couple of days after the trip to Oxford, I clicked grudgingly on the link to my profile page and found a message from a man in his early fifties who didn't begin by listing his achievements or all the ways the women in his life had let him down but simply told me his name was Nick and he was a university lecturer. One ex-wife. One ex-stepson. Originally from Edinburgh, he now lived in west London and he wasn't expecting stars and rainbows, just hoping to meet someone interesting to have a laugh with over dinner, or go to see movies with and be able to talk about them afterwards.

I peered at the thumbnail photo then enlarged it as much as I could. A handsome face, with lively eyes set into lightly tanned skin, and plentiful dark hair, turning silver at the temples. Well-cut blue suit worn with a crisp white shirt. If you asked a random person to put together an identikit of a middle-aged woman's fantasy boyfriend, he'd pretty much be it.

It was probably taken years ago, I told myself. But no, at the end of the message, he apologized for his formal attire, explaining that the picture had been taken at his mother's eightieth birthday party the previous year.

I dashed off a reply before I had a chance to talk myself out of it. Non-committal. The barest biographical facts about me then more questions about him. Like how, when he seemed perfectly normal, had he ended up on a dating site? And why, come to think of it, was I here too?

Within minutes, I had a response. It was, Nick told me, a matter of logistics. He had met someone lovely through the normal channels, but it was too soon after his divorce and he wasn't in the right head space for a new relationship. The break-up had been bitter, he said. His wife had got back together with her first husband, an old friend of Nick's, informing Nick she'd only really married him on the rebound. She'd moved back to their home town, taking her young son, whom Nick had raised as his own, with her. Nick hadn't reacted well, and for a long time afterwards he felt poleaxed by loss. Then, by the time he'd dealt with his demons and was ready to start dating (wasn't that a terrible word, he asked? Like we were school-age again?), the lovely woman had got engaged to someone else and he hadn't found anyone else who came close.

Logistics are a bastard, I wrote back. *That's why my social life mostly consists of sitting on my sofa watching* Masterchef *with the dog. The logistics of being in the right place at the right time to meet the right man are so complicated at my age, it's easier to stay put. Plus, the dog is pretty good company. As long as she hasn't been eating the remains of our curry again. In which case, wide berth.*

I asked him how often he saw his stepson, who he'd obviously loved immensely. *I don't*, came the reply. *The divorce was brutal. Lots of regrettable things said and done on both sides. But that's a conversation for another time.*

We messaged back and forth a few times, me flicking between my profile page on the dating site and the piece I was writing for a women's lifestyle website on whether middle-aged women were the true activists of the twenty-first century. I had been really enjoying writing the feature, which tapped into many of my own personal experiences and those of my friends, but now I found myself distracted, and I was annoyed to find my heart was fluttering every time Nick's name appeared in my inbox.

'Idiot,' I said out loud.

I decided to take Dotty for another walk. Who knew, perhaps my father was right and the fresh air would miraculously cure my insomnia? I took my shopping bag so I could kill two birds with one stone and call into Tesco on my way home.

It was one of those unseasonably warm March days that make you start thinking of bagging up your winter jumpers and trying to work out when you last waxed your legs. The exchange with Nick had buoyed me up and everything looked more promising. Even the crisp wrappers on the street and the used mattress leaning up against the house at the end of our road didn't dent my mood. It was all part of the vibrancy of living in London, I told myself. The richness of urban life.

With the sun pooling on the paving stones, it was easy to tell myself that the fear I'd felt just two days before, looking out of my front window on to the pavement, where the anonymous photographer had stood, was out of proportion. There was no definitive proof it was Stephens. And even if it was, Frances was right. He was just trying to scare me away. Of course, I worried for Em. But she never came home at night on her own any more, and it wasn't as if he could keep watch on the house without sticking out like a sore thumb. There were no trees on our road, no overhanging greenery. Besides, the attack on Em had been opportunistic, as had the other crimes he'd been convicted of. Assault. ABH. Stephens just didn't seem the type, I told myself, to plan ahead.

Dotty and I strolled around the neighbourhood. Up the New River, a man-made waterway that would have been picturesque were it not for the beer cans and used metal canisters of amyl nitrate that littered its banks. There were geese on the river – huge, scary creatures – and I dragged Dotty towards the far side of the path so that she couldn't antagonize them.

On the high road, I tethered her to the bike rail outside the Tesco Express. I didn't normally do it. You heard stories about dogs being stolen from outside shops, but Dotty was no expensive pedigree and, besides, the bike rack was just outside the automatic doors, where I could keep an eye on her while I was whizzing around. I only needed a couple of things. Bread and milk, mostly. I'd be out of there in minutes.

But, as usual, I remembered other things as I was going around. Dishwasher tablets, those energy bars Em really liked. And then I had to take the baked beans back to exchange them when I realized I'd picked up the ones with those hideous mini-sausages in them by mistake. And there was only one person on the tills, so the queue stretched back along the soft-drinks aisle. All the time, I was checking on Dotty regularly. Each time I looked, there she was, staring at the doors.

The cashier on duty was the eccentric one who sang at the top of his voice and engaged in long chats with the customers. The woman in front of me was talking him through all the different times she'd tried to give up smoking while he fetched her a pack of twenty Marlboro from the shelf behind him. One of the times, she'd given up for over a year then someone offered her a fag and she took one just to test herself. 'Because I was so sure I was over it. I thought I'd take one puff and be all, like, disgusted, and chuck it away on the floor. But instead it was the most fucking lovely thing I ever had in my life.'

When it came to my turn, the paper ran out in the till receipts machine and a manager had to be summoned to bring a replacement roll. Then it turned out the barcode sticker had come off the avocado I'd picked up so someone had to be dispatched to fetch another one. By the time I picked up my bag to leave, my good mood of earlier had all but evaporated and I was looking forward to getting back home and closing the front door behind me.

A couple with a buggy walked ahead of me through the automatic doors, blocking my view. As I followed them out I expected to hear Dotty's high-pitched, excited whine – she always smelled me before she saw me. The realization that there was no whine came at the same moment as I stepped through the doors and saw the empty bike rail.

No lead.

No Dotty.

I didn't panic straight away. Instead, I looked around, certain there'd be some obvious explanation. Maybe someone had let her off the lead and she was nosing around at the base of the shop's outside wall, where discarded food generally ended up. Then I started doubting myself. Had I even tied her up properly? Or had I perhaps looped the lead around the bike rail and then, just like at the police station, neglected to clip it on, in which case Dotty had probably taken herself home?

That would be it. I ignored the bubbles of alarm that had started to pop in the pit of my stomach. She'd be at home, I told myself firmly. I'd walk down the street and see her strangely proportioned black-and-white spotted form sitting dolefully by the front door.

But when I arrived, panting, there was no dog.

Now I did start to panic. Dropping my bags down inside the gate, I ran back to Tesco. Why hadn't I properly searched around before haring off back home? Crossing the supermarket forecourt, I turned left into the car park. Might she be there, sniffing around the bins, blithely unaware? But there was no small black-and-white dog. No red lead. Nothing.

I charged into the shop.

'My dog's been stolen from outside,' I said to the security guard.

'Stolen?' he repeated back to me, after a delay.

'Yes. Or else she got free. Anyway, she's disappeared. Has anyone reported anything?'

He shook his head slowly.

I ran back outside again and stood next to the rail, looking up and down the street.

Now I could no longer ignore the fear shooting up from the base of my stomach in long, fizzing streaks.

Where was she?

I ran back home and burst through the door. Powering up my laptop, I googled the number for the Haringey dog warden, leaving my details when I was told no dog matching Dotty's description had been brought in. Then I rang around all the vets in the area. Nothing.

I called the police, once again holding on the phone for what seemed like hours, and made an official report into what had happened, priding myself on how steady my voice was, only to crack when I admitted I couldn't be a hundred per cent sure I'd tied her up properly. 'So she could have run away?' the woman said. 'But she wouldn't have,' I said. 'She just wouldn't.' There was a silence from the other end. Then: 'Still, it's a possibility, isn't it?'

When Em came home from school I was posting a picture of Dotty on the Facebook page of the local dog walkers' group. *MISSING!* I typed in capital letters over the top of the picture, then felt nauseous at the sight of the word in all its awful uncertainty.

'What's the matter?' asked Em, freezing in the kitchen doorway.

'Darling, I've got bad news.'

Em was inconsolable.

'Why did you leave her there? Of course someone would take her.'

She insisted on ringing around all the vets again, just in case. And the rescue centres. When it started getting dark, she became hysterical in her grief.

'She's out there all alone,' she sobbed. 'She'll be wondering why we don't come to find her.'

Em had always been soft on the dog, but this felt like something more. As if Dotty's disappearance had opened a valve inside her and all the pain and fear she'd been storing up since the attempted abduction were gushing out.

She rang Phil and he came over after spending half an hour driving around the streets looking for her.

'I'm so sorry,' I said wretchedly. 'It's all my fault.'

'You drowning yourself in a vat of self-blame is not going to help anyone,' he said, rubbing the back of his neck with his hand, as he sometimes did when he was upset or agitated. I glared at him. Did he think I enjoyed feeling so guilty?

After he'd left and Em had finally gone to bed, where I heard her sobbing softly into her pillow, I went back on to the dog walkers' Facebook page to see if anyone had any information. There were no sightings, only a barrage of recriminations. *Why are people still leaving animals tied up outside shops? Was it really worth putting your pet in danger, just to save yourself the few minutes it would have taken to drop her off at home?* Someone else just commented, *Shame on you.*

That night I hardly slept at all. Every slight movement

or noise outside – the slamming of a car door, the sound of footsteps further up the road, one time a pair of cats fighting two houses up – brought me rushing to the window, hoping I might see a flash of white and black or hear that distinctive excited, high-pitched whine.

In the morning we overslept without the usual alarm call of a wet nose nudging bare hands or a plaintive yap from outside closed bedroom doors.

Downstairs, I tried to ignore the empty basket in the corner of the kitchen.

Making my way to the front door, I paused for a minute. *When I open the door, she'll be sitting outside on the doorstep, tired and hungry and happy to be home.* Positive visualization. Wasn't that supposed to work?

I turned the key in the bottom lock then opened the latch and flung the door open.

The doorstep was empty.

I scanned the tiny front garden, craning my neck so that I could see behind the wheelie bins. Then, with fading hope, I looked up the path to the gate.

And cried out.

Tearing down the path, I stopped just short of the gate, my breath coming from me in short, shallow, horrified gasps.

There, buckled to the gatepost, was Dotty's padded pink collar. Except it wasn't really pink any more, because splattered all over it were sickening, spreading patches of red.

18

I'd hidden Dotty's collar in a drawer in my bedroom so Em wouldn't see, but still I couldn't stop thinking about it. I'd tried telling myself it wasn't blood, but I knew it was. When I'd first found it and pressed my finger to one of the stains, it had come away smeared with something dark red and glutinous. I'd had to run to the bathroom to wash it off, but the sick feeling had lasted way after the blood had disappeared down the plughole.

Em, though blissfully ignorant of the collar in the drawer, was heartbroken. She insisted she didn't blame me, but I didn't entirely believe her.

'But who would have taken her?' she kept asking.

I'd shake my head, as if stumped. But the truth is, I had a pretty good idea.

He must have been following me. The knowledge was a tight metal band around my skull.

He must have followed me when I walked Dotty and then when I went into Tesco. I imagined him watching me loop her lead around the bike post, give her a quick rub behind the ears and walk away without a backward glance.

I remembered that photo in the anonymous email.

Dotty framed in the window, peering out over the sofa back.

PEEKABOO

'Surely the police will listen to you now?' said Frances over the phone. She was the only one I dared tell my fears about Dotty. I'd kept so much from Kath and Mari by this stage that, for the first time in thirty years, it felt like there was a disconnect between us, like jigsaw puzzle pieces that ought to fit together but were marginally misaligned.

I thought about Detective Byrne's face the last time I'd seen him. The disapproval in his voice when he'd used that word, *vigilante*.

'I don't have any proof,' I told her. 'We told the police when Dotty went missing, of course, but quite honestly, they've got bigger things to worry about.'

'But this isn't missing. This is—'

'Yes, I know,' I cut in before she could finish. I didn't want to hear her say it. I didn't want to face up to all the things that might have happened.

Two days after Dotty's disappearance, I went down to breakfast after a virtually sleepless night and looked first at Em's red-rimmed eyes, then at Dotty's empty food dish and water bowl, and something in me snapped like an elastic band.

Em only had one class on Thursdays, in the afternoon, so all morning I waited, this ball of burning fury building in my gut. As soon as she'd left the house I set off on foot, habit making me pick up the ball thrower from the terracotta pot by the front door. When I realized, at the corner of the road, that I had it in my hand, I laid it down on top of the nearest garden wall, walking away quickly with my hands in my pockets and my head down, heavy with guilt, as if it were Dotty herself I was leaving behind.

By the time I arrived outside number 17A Regency Parade I was overheated, fired by a fury that boiled the very blood in my veins. Em's tear-stained face was imprinted on my mind, along with Dotty's bloodstained collar. Without stopping to question myself, I pressed on the white plastic doorbell to the right of the door. A shrill bell sounded somewhere up above. When there was no sign of response, I pressed the bell again. I was ringing for a third, desperate time when I finally heard movement inside. Footsteps slowly descending the stairs.

I stiffened, fortifying myself. *Here it comes*, I thought. *Now we will get this over with.*

From inside the door came the sound of a metal bolt being slid across. Adrenaline came funnelling to the surface in anticipation of release.

But when the door finally swung open, in place of Stephens's bulky frame and mocking eyes, there stood one of the smallest women I'd ever seen. My fury drained away in the space of time it took to take in her cloud of white hair, domed shoulders and walnut-wrinkled face.

'Yes?'

There was no smile. The greeting of someone who resented having negotiated the stairs to find a complete stranger on the doorstep.

'I was looking for James. James Stephens?'

Still no smile.

'He's at work.'

'Oh. Right.'

For a moment we stood staring at each other. Sizing

161

each other up. I knew I should leave the old lady in peace. But then I thought about Dotty, and about Em's red-ringed eyes, and my resolve hardened.

'Look, are you related to James? His grandmother, maybe?'

She nodded warily, as if I'd forced the confirmation out of her against her will.

'I'm Mrs Stephens,' she said eventually.

'I wonder if I could come in and have a quick chat with you. It's about James. It's . . . well, it's personal.'

She looked me up and down then, as if wondering how personal I was going to get. Her brown eyes were sharp and I realized she wasn't as old as I'd first assumed.

She folded her arms and leaned against the door frame. She did not let me in.

'Let me guess. This is about your daughter.'

Shock slammed the air clear out of my chest.

She knew.

This woman knew what her grandson was and did nothing.

'How did—?'

'You're not the first mother who has come to see me.'

There were others. What kind of monster was I dealing with, who could talk about her grandson's victims so casually? The blood was rushing so loudly in my ears I couldn't believe she couldn't hear it.

'He's a good boy, really,' she went on, oblivious. 'I can see you don't want to believe it, but I brought him up since he was little and I know what's in his heart. Now, that's not to say he can't be a little bastard where girls are concerned . . .'

Now, finally, the rage came.

'A little bastard? Your grandson tried to abduct my sixteen-year-old daughter, dragged her off the street and beat her up when she resisted, and you act like he's some kind of naughty kid who needs his wrist slapped.'

Now it was her turn to look like she'd been physically struck, her head jolting up, the knuckles on the hand gripping the door turning white.

'What are you talking about? James would never . . . Look here, he's no saint. I know that. He got into a bit of trouble with the police when he was younger – plenty of boys do. It wasn't his fault. Wrong crowd. He's always had a quick temper on him. When that poor man died after that fight, no one was more cut up about it than James, especially when he found out he'd left a baby behind. He tried to make amends, but the wife refused to hear him out, wouldn't have anything to do with him. But it was an accident. The CPS said there was no case to answer.'

Now the old lady narrowed her eyes. 'You aren't his mother, are you? The man who died?'

I shook my head, confused. 'I already told you. My daughter—'

'Oh yes. Well, like I said, James doesn't always play fair with girls. I'll hold my hands up to that. If you'd come to tell me that he'd broken your daughter's heart, I'd say, *Uh-huh. Yeah. Okay.* You know, he has a lovely young girl about to have his baby, but that hasn't stopped him running around like he's a free man. But this, what you're talking about now. Nuh-uh. That's not him. That's not my James.'

She was wilfully blind to his faults. I could see it instantly. Yet still I persisted.

'I understand you don't want to believe it, but I'm afraid it's true. Your grandson is a very dangerous individual. I also have reason to believe he has done something to my dog.'

The old lady blinked.

'Your what now?'

'Dog. I tied her up outside Tesco. I was only gone a matter of minutes. And when I came out she'd vanished. Then someone left her collar on our gate, covered in blood.'

My voice tailed off towards the end, conviction wavering as I recognized the relief dawning on Mrs Stephens's wrinkled face. Mentioning Dotty had tipped the balance of credibility. Now I could be dismissed as a crank, some nutter her grandson had done work for, perhaps, who had an axe to grind.

'You'd better go,' she said, drawing herself up to her full height, which was still hardly level with my shoulder.

'But—'

The old lady started fumbling in the pocket of her dress and produced an ancient phone.

'I'm callin' the police,' she said.

I had a momentary flash of Detective Byrne's serious brown eyes when he'd warned me to stay away from James Stephens. That word again: *vigilante*.

'Don't. I'm leaving.'

The encounter had left me rattled and I found I couldn't face going straight home to that unnaturally silent house. There was a pub further along Bounds Green Road that I'd never been in before. Trendy, with high ceilings and walls painted the dark grey of wet concrete. It wasn't really on my way home, but it wasn't too much of a detour. There were only two other customers in there, both sitting alone, an older man reading a newspaper and drinking a pint of something cloudy and another woman my age, at the bar ordering a gin and tonic. Not her first, judging by the empty glasses and bottles on the table where she was sitting.

I eyed the drink greedily, imagining the bite of the gin as it slid down, that faint aftertaste of lime. But I knew I couldn't. Wouldn't. Then I ordered myself a sparkling water, asking for ice and lime as an afterthought. When the woman left not long afterwards I slipped into her table, which was the only one with a clear view out of the huge pub window, allowing me to gaze out across the narrow strip of grass that separated the pub from the busy main road. As I sipped on my drink I started to reframe what had just happened in my mind.

Stephens was out of control. That much was clear. The assault convictions. Someone had died, for God's sake. Wasn't it better in the long run, I told myself, that Stephens's grandmother was made aware of exactly what her precious grandson was capable of? Even if she chose not to believe me now, at least the seed had been planted and she'd be warier from now on. On the lookout for anything amiss.

By the time I reached the front door, I'd almost convinced myself I'd done a good thing. At least I'd acted, I told myself. I'd taken back control.

I blocked out the doubts that tugged at my skirts, telling me I'd overstepped a line, taken things too far. Asking how I could be sure it was him, what proof did I have.

Entering the house, I was hit all over again by the absence of a welcoming bark at the sound of my key turning in the lock and the unwanted novelty of being able to hang up my coat and take off my shoes without a hot, furry body throwing itself against my legs, desperate for attention.

At first I thought the low voices I could hear were coming from the television in the living room, but then I recognized Em's soft laughter and someone else talking, fast and animated.

When I walked into the room Frances was sitting on the sofa with Emma on the rug on the floor across from her. The coffee table that lay between them was littered with the detritus of tea and biscuits. I noticed that Em had dug out the teapot we hadn't used in over a year and the cups that used to belong to my grandmother.

I was surprised at the relief I felt on seeing Frances again. Conviction returned, settling around my shoulders like a warm coat. I was in the right here. My daughter had been damaged by that man. The young woman sitting on the sofa in the soft green sweater dress was proof of that.

Emma was looking flushed and happy and I found myself both grateful to Frances that she had managed to cheer her up, and disappointed with myself that it wasn't me who'd been able to make her laugh again.

Stupid, I reprimanded myself. To mind, when Em needs all the friends she can get.

'Any chance of some fresh tea, Em?' I said, eyeing the teapot with distrust. 'As opposed to so stewed the spoon stands up on its own.'

I didn't really want tea, but I needed to speak to

Frances alone. Em made a face but, to my relief, she got up and took the teapot back into the kitchen, giving me a chance to update Frances on the events of the afternoon.

'I can't believe you did that. Just turned up at his house!'

Frances was leaning towards me, her eyes wide and her whole body rigid.

'I know. I'm an idiot. You don't need to tell me. But I wanted to have it out with him. I wanted to look into his eyes when I confronted him about Dotty.'

'You're very brave and—'

'Yeah, I know. Stupid.'

'I wasn't going to say that. I actually think it's amazing what you're doing for Em. The lengths you're going to. To protect her. I wish my own mother . . .'

Her voice tailed off and I instinctively moved over to sit down next to her on the sofa, putting my hand on her knee.

'It must be very hard, having to be the carer to your own parent. When sometimes you must be desperate for a little bit of looking after yourself.'

Frances's lovely eyes filled with tears then and she dabbed at them clumsily.

'She was such a perfect mum before she got ill. Just really warm and supportive of everything I did. I know there are some women who should never be mothers, and that makes me feel so lucky.'

Some women who should never be mothers. For a wild, terrible moment, I thought Frances was referring to me.

Em came in then with a fresh pot of tea and I took my hand off Frances's knee and made some inane comment

about how she'd used the best china. I had snatched at
the first thing to say to change the subject and distract
attention from Frances's pink-rimmed eyes, but I could
see from the way Em's face coloured that I'd embarrassed her. I seemed to do that without trying these
days.

Frances stayed longer than I'd expected and, though it
was a comfort to have her there, it meant I couldn't get
Em on her own to apologize for joking about the china.
Then when Frances did finally go home, Em disappeared up to her room to work before I could think of
what to say.

I took the cups into the kitchen and washed them by
hand, trying not to think about the confrontation with
the old lady earlier on. Already, there was a sour taste in
my mouth and I realized it had been a mistake.

Back at the table, I took out my phone to watch my
parents on webcam, knowing that would make me feel
calmer. Instead, I noticed there was an icon flashing to
show I'd missed a call.

My heart stopped as I saw the name.

Rosie.

19

I spent the rest of the evening trying to call Rosie back, but she didn't pick up. In the end, I rang Phil, who sounded irritable. He and Joy were binge-watching a series on Netflix, he told me. It was 'insanely gripping'.

Insanely gripping. When did the man I was married to for over two decades start sounding like a tabloid film reviewer?

I asked him if he'd heard from Rosie and was surprised when he said she was out.

'So she's still at your house? How come she's not back at uni?'

Phil said she'd gone back to Manchester for a bit after reading week but then returned saying she had an important paper to write and she couldn't work in her student digs, which she described as 'party central'. Plus, he thought there might be a new boyfriend on the scene bringing her back here, though she wasn't admitting to anything.

'So she's all right?' I wanted to be absolutely sure. 'Because she rang me.'

I couldn't keep the excitement out of my voice and

Phil must have heard because he replied in a warmer tone, 'That's great, Tessa. I'm really pleased for you.'

That night I woke as usual in the early hours with the events of the day churning around in my head like a washing machine I couldn't turn off. The old lady, Frances, Em, Rosie. Not for the first time, I wished I could reach into my head, take out my brain and stash it in the bedside cupboard like I did with loudly ticking alarm clocks. I threw off the duvet, feeling I would spontaneously combust from the heat if I had it on a second longer. But within minutes my feet were freezing cold.

It was so exhausting, all of it. The endless flip-flopping between extremes.

The next morning I tried again to call Rosie. And again.

Eventually, my phone pinged with a text.

Sorry, Mum. Not quite ready for an actual conversation just yet but wanted you to know I'm really sorry about Dotty. I hadn't even finished reading the first when another pinged in: *PS No one blames you.*

I sat and stared at my screen for ages, tracing the text with my fingertip. Happiness inflated inside me like a balloon. Rosie didn't blame me for what had happened to Dotty. And though of course I was disappointed she didn't want to speak to me, it was a start. The window that had been locked tight for the last six months had just opened up a crack.

I actually managed to work that day, my broken night all but forgotten. I put the finishing touches to the feature about middle-aged women being the new activists. I'd really enjoyed writing it and I was sure it showed. Next, I started putting together a list of articles to pitch to a features editor I'd worked with a few years back and who'd just been appointed to a weekend supplement I'd been trying to get commissioned by without success.

A quick perusal of the papers online sparked some interesting trains of thought and soon I had five strong ideas. I also received an email offering me a week's holiday cover on *Silk*, a glossy monthly magazine I'd all but given up hope of working on ever again.

Then I wrote a detailed list of instructions for the new care assistant who'd just joined the agency team that looked after my parents. Even though I knew the others would talk her through what needed doing, it was always as well to have things written out, so there could be no excuses if things didn't get done. I told her how my mother didn't like spicy food, and where my dad kept his diabetes medication. I wrote down the practical details of their day in brisk bullet points, and all my contact details, conscious the whole time of what I wasn't writing: *Please be kind to them.*

Satisfied with my morning's work, I spent the afternoon creating a Missing Dog poster. Though I was secretly convinced something terrible had happened to Dotty, it felt important for Em to know we were doing everything we could to find her.

Going through the photos was heartbreaking. We'd taken so many of her as a puppy and it was hard to look at pictures of her sleeping on Phil's chest as he lay on the sofa watching TV or being rocked in Rosie's arms like a baby without feeling as if all that was part of some halcyon era that would never come again. There was a video where a small, soft-bellied Dotty ran alongside Em in the park, tripping over her too-big paws, and I had to stop it before the end because I was crying too hard to see the screen. Not just crying for Dotty, but for all of us. That young, hopeful family with everything in front of them.

I bought some clear plastic sleeves to put the posters in from the mini-post office around the corner then walked around the streets between our house and Tesco, attaching them to trees and lampposts with strong tape.

Some time later Em came in, clutching one that she'd found lying face down in the street, having already come loose.

'These are great, Mum,' she said, throwing her arms around me in a rare spontaneous show of affection. 'You know, I'm sure she's around here somewhere. Someone must have untied her as a joke, or else she broke free and somehow she's got shut up inside some-one's shed, or else someone took her in, thinking she was a stray. We'll find her, won't we?'

I nodded, glad that my face was buried in my daugh-ter's hair so she couldn't see my expression.

'Why don't we watch a film this evening?' I suggested, wanting to do something to take our minds off every-thing else that was going on. 'We could make it a movie night.'

It's something we used to do a lot when Rosie and Phil were still at home, but we'd let the tradition slide now it was just the two of us. To my quiet joy, Em readily agreed and we assembled all the required elements – a pack of popcorn that had been mouldering in the back of the cupboard for the past year or so, duvets to snuggle under – and settled in on the sofa.

'I wish . . .' said Em, eyeing the space in the middle of us where Dotty would usually have insisted on going.

'I know.'

I scooted up so that there was no longer any space between us and put my arm around her. She rested her head on my shoulder and I stroked her head, glad to feel that the bumps which had come up like boiled eggs under her scalp after the attack had now smoothed away to nothing and there was a soft fuzz growing in the patches where her hair had fallen out. We watched a thriller. We both agreed within the first ten minutes that it was pretty terrible, but we carried on watching anyway, scooping up handfuls of popcorn from the huge mixing bowl on the coffee table and absently feeding the individual kernels into our mouths one by one.

I'd left my phone in the kitchen and was conscious of it bleeping to show incoming texts, but I didn't want to disturb this rare, easy interlude. My experience of being a parent was that there was so much drudgery, so much painstaking negotiation and accommodation, so much conflict and onerous resolution, that these moments of closeness, of completely peaceful coexistence, were like tiny lumps of hard-won gold glinting amid the dirt. Each one to be treasured.

As the movie was coming towards its predictable conclusion, there was a long ring on the doorbell which made both of us jump.

My immediate thought was Stephens. My own feelings of guilt had made me try to wipe the encounter with the old lady from my mind, but I knew someone like him would never let that go. I'd gone into his territory, exposing him to his family. Sooner or later I would find out what the punishment would be.

The photograph flashed into my mind of the front of my house. *PEEKABOO*

Another ring, this time more prolonged. My nerves, already on high alert, now crackled as if electrically charged.

'Aren't you going to answer it?'

I nodded at Em and attempted a reassuring smile, which tightened into a grimace.

There was a dark shape silhouetted behind the opaque glass panels of the door. I stepped on to the doormat and hesitated.

'Yes? Who is it?'

My voice was small and squeaky.

'It's Phil. For fuck's sake, Tess, I've been calling you all night. Can you just let me in, please?'

I opened the door to find him glaring at me, as if it were my fault he was on my doorstep at half past ten on a Friday evening. He was wearing the sweat pants he used to change into when he came home from work. 'Just getting into my lee-zure-wear,' he'd drawl in a cod-American accent. I felt a pang of regret for the me who'd rolled my eyes behind his back, secure enough in my marriage to be utterly dismissive of his tired old jokes.

Phil seemed surprised to see Em there on the sofa, snuggled under her duvet, surrounded by the evidence of a movie night, and I couldn't help a rush of satisfaction at the cosy domestic scene he'd just interrupted. Let him see what he was missing.

But my satisfaction was short-lived.

'Can I have a quick word in the kitchen?'

I locked eyes with Em, saw her eyebrows rise.

'Sure.'

'Don't worry about me,' said Em, standing up to gather her things. 'I've got to work anyway. So you two can have your *quick word* in peace.'

After she'd gone Phil reached into his jacket pocket (a jacket I'd bought him several years back, I couldn't help noticing) and withdrew an envelope on which his name and studio address appeared neatly typed.

'This arrived this morning. No postmark. Read it.'

'What does it say?'

'Just read it.'

The letter was typed and unsigned.

Mr Hopwood. You need to know that your ex-wife is an unfit mother. She made your daughter an easy target by letting her come home alone and then she left your dog outside a shop for anyone to take. Are you going to risk something worse happening???

'That's ridiculous.'

Fear squeezed my voice out of me in lumps like old toothpaste.

'There's more.'

Phil reached again into his jacket pocket and withdrew a photograph, which he handed to me in stern-faced silence.

At first I couldn't work out what relevance this picture of an urban street had to me, then I recognized the outside of the pub on Bounds Green Road, and finally I saw myself. In the window of the pub, drinking on my own, with two empty glasses and two small bottles of tonic in front of me. There was a time printed on the side of the photograph: 16.45. And yesterday's date next to it.

'I thought you'd learned,' said Phil. 'After what happened with Rosie.'

'I have. That photo doesn't show anything. I was having a sparkling water. That's all. While I was waiting for Nita.' The lie came out before I'd even thought about it. 'Those empty glasses are from the woman who was sitting there before.'

'Oh, come off it. Do you think I'm stupid? You're getting pissed on your own in the middle of the day while our daughter is at school. Are you really going to tell me that's acceptable?'

The combination of the sanctimoniousness of that 'acceptable' and my frustration over not being believed, plus my need to shut him down before he brought up the whole Rosie thing again made me react with fury.

'So that's it? You're going to take the word of some anonymous busybody over the woman you were married to for twenty-five years?'

'Twenty-two, actually. And I'm not taking anyone's word. That's why I came round here. So you could have a chance to put your own side of things. But frankly, Tess, I'm worried. First Em gets attacked and she can't even wake you up, then you lose the dog. Now this. You know, I really hoped we were all getting back to normal. Putting the past bad feeling behind us. Rosie has mentioned you two building bridges. But now I'm really not so sure. Who would have sent this?'

'I don't know. Someone with an axe to grind. Someone who wants to turn my children against me. Have you asked your precious Joy if she knows anything about it?'

It was a low blow and undeserved. Of course, I had a very good idea who'd really sent that letter, but my own abject terror at the thought of losing Emma made me lash out.

The effect on Phil was instant. His face closed up like a fist.

'You know, Tessa, all I want is for our family to heal and move on in a healthy way. Believe it or not, I carry a lot of guilt for what I did. I want to believe the best of you. But make no mistake, if I believe you're acting in a way that undermines our daughters' interests, I *will* take action.'

'Dick!' I said as he walked away, louder than I'd intended.

After Phil had gone I sat at the kitchen table, shaking. Only one person hated me enough to do something so vindictive. I'd known Stephens would retaliate for what I'd said to his grandmother. But this?

She must have telephoned him as soon as I'd left his house. Perhaps he'd already been on his way home, or maybe he was just working nearby. I imagined him following me as I made my way along Bounds Green Road. Then standing outside watching me through the pub window. Taking the photo then going home to work out how to inflict maximum damage.

Stephens had already discovered my identity on Facebook. Though my posts and photographs were set to private, my relationship status was visible to everyone, so he'd have seen I was divorced. He'd also have been able to go through my friends list, also public, and

Emma's and Rosie's, which meant he could easily have worked out that Phil Hopwood was my ex.

I got out my phone and clicked on Phil's profile. He'd always been so scathing of social media when we were together, adopting Facebook only to keep in touch with scattered uni friends while still roundly decrying its sinister qualities, but since he'd been with Joy all that had changed. Now there were almost daily updates that pinpointed his exact location on a map and arty photographs of sunsets and footprints in the snow.

My heart sank as I clicked on the 'about' section of his profile and saw that he'd dutifully listed his occupation as sound editor under 'current career'. 'So much for your sodding principles,' I muttered under my breath.

My fingers were unsteady as I typed 'Phil Hopwood sound editor' into Google, and I had to input the last word twice to get the right spelling. The very first result was from Companies House, giving the address of his studio. The studio through whose letterbox that vile letter had dropped earlier that day.

I'd considered myself a private sort of person. But now it transpired that every detail of my life was laid bare for the picking.

20

Leave my family alone or you'll be sorry. You're a monster.

When I fought my way out of a fitful sleep the next morning I didn't remember writing the message at first. Then, when the memory came to me, it had a nebulous quality, as if it might have been part of a dream.

So when I checked Stephens's Facebook DJ page, I wasn't completely sure I'd find anything. But there it was. To be honest, I was surprised the post was still up but, after the initial jolt of shock, I found I didn't regret writing that message. Sure, it was part-fuelled by fury with Phil for his high-handed reaction, and with myself for everything I'd so carelessly given away online. But he *was* a monster. I wasn't proud of upsetting his grand-mother, but it was *his* actions, *his* attempt to drag my daughter down a dark street simply because he felt he was entitled, without any thought for what it might do to her, and then *his* ruthless efforts to scare me off, that had driven me to it. He'd proved himself a danger to everyone around him.

What kind of person would I have been if I hadn't warned the woman who lived with him?

Even so, I was nervous when I saw the string of comments from Stephens's friends underneath my post. More so when I started scrolling through them.

U better back off, bitch.

Hey JLo, the crazy lady is back. She got the hots for you, bruv.

Then, finally, a message from the man himself.

OK. No more being nice. Your mental but you crossed a line.

I slammed shut the laptop, adrenaline heightening every movement. *You crossed a line.* It was undeniably a threat. But what did he have in mind? No matter. Let him bring it on. The anonymous letter was a tipping point. Being a mother was at the very core of me. He wouldn't challenge that and get away with it. I felt charged and ready, fuelled by the sudden certainty of being right.

The feeling of being pumped up and energized lasted the whole of that Saturday. I tried to work, but concentration eluded me, the blue-and-white Facebook icon drawing me in like a call to prayer. The exchange from earlier was deleted not long after the last post I'd read, but still I waited for his next move, sure I would find it there.

But when nothing more happened that day, or the next, I relaxed, my guard lowering little by little like a slow-motion sunset until, by the following Monday morning, the whole thing seemed once again unfeasible. Like something that had happened to someone else far removed from me.

It was Em's parents' consultation meeting that afternoon and I was trying to cram in some intensive work beforehand when a sharp ring on the doorbell interrupted me, bringing on a shudder of irritation. It would be something from Amazon, I was sure, that I'd ordered in a fit of boredom, feeling I couldn't do without it – a pack of cardboard folders in rainbow colours to help keep my accounts in order, special spectacles for applying eye make-up, with only one magnifying lens that you could flip from one side to the other.

Instead, there were two uniformed police officers on the doorstep, a man and a woman, neither of them looking particularly glad to be there.

'Mrs Hopwood?' The woman had an indeterminate accent, stressing and elongating the second syllable of my name so it felt unfamiliar. 'We're responding to a harassment complaint that's been made against you. Can we come in?'

I showed them through to the kitchen, where we all stood awkwardly around the table. It hadn't yet sunk in, just what they were doing here, and I felt only a kind of removed interest, as if they might be coming to tell me about a new parking scheme, or ask if I'd witnessed a car accident. I was a middle-class, middle-aged woman. I had no concept of being on the wrong side of the law.

'I assume you might have some idea why we're here,' said the man, whose nose bent slightly to the right, as if it had been broken at some point in the past. 'We've received a call from a Mr James Stephens, who claims you have been harassing him online and also in person. Attending the gigs where he DJ's, following his pregnant girlfriend to the toilets, and now calling at his house and intimidating his elderly grandmother.'

I was still looking at them both with a polite smile on

my face, as if waiting to hear how I could help them. *Harassment. Intimidation.* These were not words that related to me.

'You do realize, Mrs Hopwood, that these are very serious allegations,' said the woman sternly.

Only now did the first prickles of alarm make themselves felt. But surely they'd see, these two police officers, that I was respectable. Just one look around the kitchen would prove that. Would a woman with a fresh sourdough loaf sitting on a wooden butcher's block go around harassing old ladies?

'I don't think you understand,' I told them. 'James Stephens assaulted my daughter two months ago. He was caught on the CCTV footage and appeared in the video line-up, only, unfortunately, my daughter was too overwhelmed by the occasion to pick him out at the time. And now he's wandering the streets, free to do it again to another young girl. People need to be warned about him.'

'So your daughter failed to identify him as her attacker?'

The woman had a way of making everything sound like a challenge, like she didn't believe what you'd just said. I felt myself growing hot.

Oh, please, not here. Not now.

Sweat began to break out on my forehead, under my arms.

'Like I say, she was thrown by the situation,' I said, shrugging off the woollen cardigan that was already sticking uncomfortably to my arms. 'But I know it was him, and Em and Frances both confirmed it. That's Frances Gates, who was a witness to the attack.'

'So you're saying Ms Gates picked him out of the line-up?' asked the wonky-nosed policeman. 'In which case, why isn't he—'

'No, she picked the wrong guy.' By now, sweat was trickling down my back and I felt as if I was about to explode from heat. I was conscious that everything I was saying was coming out wrong, but I couldn't work out the right words to make them understand. 'Look. Someone attacked my daughter half a mile away, in this neighbourhood. And that someone is still at large. And he's dangerous.'

I needed to make them appreciate the seriousness of the threat Stephens posed. His grandmother's words came back to me. The man who died following a fight.

'He killed someone,' I said.

Now they were interested.

'So he has a murder conviction?' asked the policeman, taking his notebook out. His fingers were poised, holding the pen. 'Manslaughter?'

'No, I mean, I don't think he was ever charged. There was no case.'

The officer closed his notepad, tucking the pen back inside the loop at the top.

'He stole my dog,' I blurted out.

'Your dog?'

The woman again, with her flat, sceptical voice.

I strode to the back door and opened it.

'It's hot in here, isn't it?' I asked, tugging aside the neck of my T-shirt to waft in the colder air. 'Aren't you both hot?'

The police officers exchanged a glance but didn't reply. Then the man spoke again.

'Mrs Hopwood, if the two witnesses both failed to pick a man out of a line-up, the chances are that case is now concluded and that man is now at liberty to go about his business. May I remind you there is such a thing as due process in law. And you are in very big danger of finding yourself on the wrong side of it. How can you even be sure it's the same man – if the two witnesses couldn't identify him?'

'He sent me a photo. Of my house. As a threat. Look.'

I scrolled wildly through my emails, relief flaring as I found the photograph.

'See how my dog is right there in the centre of the picture. Then, just days later, she goes missing. That's not a coincidence.'

The two police officers bent over my phone screen.

'And this came from Mr Stephens's personal email account?'

The woman's expressionless voice was getting under my skin.

'No, it was from a weird fake account with just jumbled numbers and letters. But I know it was him.'

Again, they glanced at each other. Then back at me.

Just like that, the heat abated and I felt my arms go goose-pimply with the cold. I slammed the door shut, trying to disguise a shiver.

'I'm afraid there's nothing to prove this came from the person in question,' the man said evenly. 'And even if it did, there's no threat made.'

I tried one more time to appeal to them, addressing myself to the woman.

'My daughter is only sixteen. She still has nightmares about that night. Can you understand how it feels, knowing the man who did that to her is still strutting around the neighbourhood without any repercussions for what he did?'

The policewoman looked back at me through wary blue eyes.

'We're very sorry about what happened to your daughter,' she said, 'but you can't go around taking the law into your own hands. Consider this a warning.'

After I'd shown them out I went back into the kitchen and sat at the table. The whole thing seemed too surreal to have actually happened. Did two police officers really just come into my house, into my kitchen, and stand in front of the fridge covered in school timetables and photographs of my daughters and accuse me of harassment?

What had happened to my life?

I wanted to shower and get out of my now damp clothes before going to Em's parents' consultation, but the unexpected visit from the police meant I didn't have time. I had a quick look in the hall mirror as I dashed out and cringed at the sight of my lank, sweat-straggled hair and the dark shadows under my eyes that gave my irises the appearance of being mired in mud.

For a moment I wavered, torn between my need to be on time and the temptation to nip upstairs and try to slather make-up over the worst of it, but I knew what those afternoons were like. If you missed your slot, you were put to the back of the interminable queue, forced to watch everyone else's consultations, trying to gauge from their expressions whether it was good news or bad.

I called an Uber as I was running so late. Belted into the back of a Prius – why was it always a Prius? – my thoughts circled back to Stephens, as they always did these days. Once again, doubt came crawling into my mind. Why would someone who already had a criminal record involve the police in a dispute in which they themselves might be incriminated? Might I have made a mistake?

I got out my phone and scrolled to Kath's number, needing to talk it through, but my finger hovered over the call button. There was already so much I hadn't told her and Mari. So much I wasn't proud of. Better to save it for the next time I saw them in person, where I could explain it all properly.

On impulse, I called Frances. She was at work, but she said she could talk for a few minutes. I think she could hear in my voice how wound up I was. I told her about the malicious note sent to Phil's studio and how the police had turned up on my doorstep.

'Would he really do that,' I asked her, 'if he was guilty?'

'Maybe you're right,' said Frances. Then she paused. When she resumed, her voice was hesitant, but kind.

'But Tess, the thing you have to remember is you have no idea what kind of person you're dealing with. This is someone who has been in prison before, he's familiar with the law and what the police can and can't do. He knows what he can get away with.'

When I arrived at the school Em was waiting outside the gates, glaring at her phone screen.

'You're late,' she said, then looked me up and down. 'Is that what you're wearing?'

'Of course it's what I'm wearing. Did you think I brought a change of clothes in my bag?'

There was a time when I enjoyed these occasions. Having a full-time job meant school remained an enigma, a place whose rooms and corridors my daughters knew like the backs of their hands but to me were unknown and imbued with mystery. I used to love stepping inside those locked front doors, making my way past reception to meet the teachers who gave me an outsider's view on my own children so I saw them as the world might see them. I loved walking past a wall display and catching sight of 'Rosie Hopwood' or 'Emma Hopwood' on the bottom of a piece of work, loved this glimpse into the people they were becoming separate from us.

But that was before my family was split down the middle like a ripped ticket stub.

The first meeting was with Em's English teacher. Em had always been good at English, so I was looking forward to this one. Before I had children, I hadn't considered it possible to love someone so much that hearing them praised, knowing other people recognized what was special in them, brought you more pleasure than any amount of glory for yourself. But my optimism soon turned to dismay when Mrs Malik put her head to one side in the time-honoured fashion of those about to deliver unwelcome news.

'I'm afraid we've had a bit of a rocky time this term, haven't we, Emma? The last three or four assignments have not been up to her usual standard and she's appeared very distracted in class, which is not like her. Is everything all right at home?'

I glanced at Em, who had gone a deep wine-red and was busy staring at her hands.

'Well, I'm sure you know that Emma had an *unpleasant* experience a couple of months ago,' I said. 'And to be honest, I think it's had more of an effect on her than she's letting on.'

'I'm *fine.*'

Em looked furious. Though the school had been informed at the time of the attack and, obviously, she'd talked to her friends about it, she'd been emphatic about not wanting a fuss made. I knew she'd hate me discussing with her teacher things she considered private.

Mrs Malik's head remained on a tilt, her black hair swinging, mouth scrunched up in concern.

'I do understand Emma has been through a horrible ordeal, and we'll all help in whatever way we can. But this is a critical time academically and it would be such a pity for her grades to start slipping now.'

The rest of the consultations followed the same depressing narrative. Em had appeared to be working well, certainly on target for her predicted grades, but then in recent weeks something had gone badly wrong. With each encounter, pity for my daughter wound itself tighter around my heart.

'Why didn't you tell me?' I asked her after we said a terse goodbye to the fourth teacher.

'I'm dealing with it,' snapped Em. But I could see she was shaken by what she was hearing, the incontrovertible evidence that the attack had affected her on a more fundamental level than she was willing to admit to.

For the first time, I wished Phil was there and not stuck in his studio on the last crucial stages of an edit. I felt like I needed an ally, someone who knew how sensitive Em was, how conscientious, and could help me find the words to make the staff understand how precious she was to us. Alone, I felt unequipped for the task of protecting her.

By the time we got to the queue for maths, always Em's weakest subject, we were both reduced to a kind of numbed silence, just wanting the whole thing to be over with, standing side by side, staring ahead in a daze.

Which is why I didn't see Anna Cunningham until it was too late.

'Oh,' she said, clearly having failed to notice me also. She recovered first.

'Tessa. It's been a while.'

Her eyes, perfectly made up as always, with those flicks of liquid eyeliner that some women manage to pull off, looked me up and down, distrust written into every subtly bronzed and shimmered pore.

I remembered with a sharp feeling of loss how, when she first found out I was a magazine editor, when Rosie and Anna's daughter, India, were in reception, she used to seek me out at school events as if I were some sort of minor celebrity, and how grateful she'd been in Year Ten when I gave India work experience on my magazine. And in return I'd been able to call her when I was running late, asking if she could keep Rosie an extra hour or drop her off on the way back from orchestra.

She was one of the stay-at-home mums, one of the PTA mums, and we didn't have a huge amount in common, but I knew that she and her husband slept in separate rooms and she'd seen me break down after I was made redundant, and those things, plus our mutual love for our daughters, seemed to be enough.

Until they weren't.

'We're just here seeing my teachers,' said Em, her jaw set in that way she had when she was anxious and trying to be brave.

Anna seemed to see Em for the first time.

'Yes, of course. Michael's too.'

She gestured towards her son, a sullen teenager in Emma's year, with a pronounced Adam's apple, a scattering of wispy facial hair and his hands wedged deep into his pockets.

How is India? The words formed on my lips, but I couldn't say them.

'Well, goodbye, Emma.'

The very obvious slight made my face burn as Anna Cunningham turned and walked away, steering her reluctant son in front of her.

Emma stared miserably straight ahead of her. I knew I should try to make everything all right, but I didn't trust myself to speak.

The maths teacher's comments were just as bad as I'd feared. Em had been trying really hard, not top of the class but certainly holding her own, then in the last few weeks everything had gone to pieces. Again I had to listen to my daughter claiming everything was fine, and this time I didn't even attempt to justify and explain to the concerned-looking teacher.

A single thought tattooed itself painfully across the inside of my head.

Him.

This was all his fault.

It's just a glimpse of blue. That particular blue of a shirt you wore one time. I see it from the corner of my eye while I am standing at the school gates. And that's all it takes.

When Henry comes out I grab his hand and haul him away, even though he doesn't like me holding his hand any more, not when his friends might see.

'Can we go to the park?'

'Not today.'

My voice sounds weird, like I am out of breath.

'Stop!' says Henry. And when I don't comply, he yanks his hand from mine and stands in front of me so I can't go any further.

'I don't like you when you are like this, Mummy.'

His bottom lip is wobbling and his brown eyes are huge with reproach and worry.

Love pricks the balloon of my fear and I hold out my arms.

'Sorry, bubba. Forgive me.'

We hug. Henry's sweet nature means he can never stay angry for long. Hurts are instantly forgotten.

I wish I had the luxury of forgetting.

We go to the park and I buy him an ice lolly then watch him on the swings. He's met a friend from school and I chat with the mother as the boys kick out their legs with all their strength, racing to go highest. Sometimes I feel awkward with the other mums. All of them in their happy family groups.

'Are you waiting for someone?' the other mum asks. 'Only you keep glancing around.'

'No. No one,' I reply, smiling, and force my eyes straight ahead.

But that's not exactly true.

I'm waiting for you.

21

Just suffering from post-parents-consultation blues, that's all.

Parent consultations are why afternoon drinking was invented.

I'm liking your style.

The truth was, I was liking more than Nick's style. It was only a week since we'd started messaging each other, but already his emails had become the highlight of my day. You know how there are some people you might have known for years but, somehow, the deeper connections aren't there? You're friendly, affectionate even, but essentially you're skating across the surface of each other. And then there are people you meet for one evening and somehow you recognize each other on a level that makes superficial conversation unnecessary, almost ridiculous.

Well, Nick was like that. Over the course of several long messages we'd talked about our parents (his dad was dead, his mum had a seventy-five-year-old toyboy whom Nick fell out with over Brexit) and our children. I'd told him about Emma's attack, and he knew my relationship with Rosie was difficult at the moment, although I hadn't been able to bear to go into detail. How could I talk to him about what I didn't even admit to myself? He knew I blamed myself for losing Dotty, and I knew he regretted the things he'd said and done when he'd discovered his ex-wife was having an affair and how much he missed being part of his stepson's life.

I found myself wondering whether, if I'd been as open with Phil over the last few years we were together as I'd been with Nick over just a few intense days, things might have turned out differently.

It's always the roads we don't take that come back to haunt us.

I'd tracked Nick down on social media. I knew he had a Facebook account but held back from sending him a friend request, not sure if I was ready to see photos of his ex-wife or her son. He was an infrequent poster on Instagram and Twitter. Mostly comments on things in the news or in films he'd seen, a few retweets of funny political cartoons. One Instagram post showed a photo of his departmental Christmas dinner, and I'd spent far too long scrutinizing all the women around the table, trying to gauge their body language in relation to him.

Nick was the main topic of conversation when I met up with Kath and Mari two days after the disastrous parents' consultation, at the chic private members' club in Soho that Kath belonged to. It was so private it didn't have a name on the outside and the first time I'd gone there I'd walked up and down the street for several minutes, in front of the crowds of twenty-somethings spilling out on to the pavement of the cocktail bar opposite, scouring the numbers, too scared to ring the bell.

'He sounds too good to be true.'

Mari was renowned for her caution, but even so I was irritated by her response. It was so long since anything had gone my way. Couldn't she just be happy for me?

'So when are you going to meet up with him?' Kath wanted to know.

'No plans. Don't want to rush things.'

Instantly, she was on the offensive.

'Don't be ridiculous. This isn't the bloody Victorian era.'

'Are you looking for a boyfriend – or a pen pal?' added Mari, who seemed to have overcome her earlier misgivings.

'I'm not looking for anyone. Anyway, I look too disgusting to meet anyone new at the moment.'

They both put on their reading glasses so they could inspect me properly.

'Mmmm . . .'

'Well . . .'

That was the problem with really good friends. They didn't lie to you.

'I did suggest a phone call, but he said he was enjoying the slow burn of the emails and we should just carry on with the written messages a while longer. He says I've got the sexiest sentence construction he's ever come across.'

'Definitely hiding something,' said Kath. Mari, on the other hand, thought it was cute.

Kath and Mari ordered cocktails. Kath had had enough of clean living and declared her intention of drinking back every one of the calories she'd lost. I eyed the cocktail menu greedily before asking for a Diet Coke. Then we ordered three salads and a huge bowl of chips, as we always did. The room was wood-panelled, with a roaring fire down one end, even though the mild March temperatures outside hardly merited one. The low-level lighting illuminated walls and surfaces covered with quirky objects and framed photographs and paintings.

I started telling them about what had been going on with Stephens, but their suddenly serious expressions stopped me well before I got to the part about me going round to his house and exposing him to his grandmother.

Mari leaned forward, wearing what I imagined was her therapist face, her features radiating empathy, understanding and concern.

'I know it must be tough knowing that the man who did that awful thing to Em is wandering around scot-free, but you have got to stop this obsession with him, Tess. It's really taking its toll.'

'You mean I look like shit.'

'What she means is you look like a woman who's been through the mill and who's desperately worried about her daughter,' interjected Kath, with untypical diplomacy. 'But you need to start looking after yourself, Tessa, or you're no good to Emma or anybody else. For God's sake, put this arsehole out of your head and start concentrating on you for a change.'

I nodded, because what else could I do?

Now there was no way I could face confessing that it had all got so out of hand. I'd told them, of course, that I'd lost Dotty, but they didn't know about the blood-stained collar, or about the anonymous letter to Phil or the visit from the police.

At the time I'd told myself it was because I didn't want

them to worry, but now I wondered if I just couldn't bear hearing what I knew they would say. And of course, the longer I put off telling them, the more impossible it became. It was as if a gap had opened up between my old life and this new frightening reality and Kath and Mari were on one side and I was on the other and the gap was getting bigger and bigger and I had no idea how to bridge it.

Back home, I sat at the kitchen table with my head in my hands. Em was at Phil's, so there was no one to hear the ugly, snorting sobs that tore from me in great gasps.

Kath and Mari had been my support system my entire adult life, and without them to lean on I felt acutely alone.

My phone beeped with an incoming email, my mouth turning suddenly ash-dry when I saw it was a message sent via my website.

Sure enough, when I clicked on it I saw that it had come from that same anonymous email account as the photograph of the outside of my house, the mixture of letters and numbers sinister in their randomness. The subject line read: 'NEW RECORDING'.

There was no written message, just an attachment in the main body of the email, a pink square titled 'New Recording.m4a'.

I stared at the file and thought about Kath and Mari's warnings, and their alarm when I'd started telling them what had been going on.

I was conscious of my breath coming out fast and shallow.

I shouldn't open it. Things had already escalated so far beyond my control. I should ignore it. Get on with my life.

But even while those thoughts were coursing through my mind, my fingers were over the screen, clicking on the blue lettering under the pink box. The download notification appeared at the bottom of my screen.

It wasn't too late. I could still ignore it. I *should* ignore it.

Instead, I turned the volume of my phone up to full and clicked on 'open'.

Immediately, there came a clicking sound. And then . . .

No, no, no. This couldn't be happening, it couldn't be.

Yet I knew it was. I was listening to a recording of a dog's high-pitched whimpering. And I knew, beyond any shadow of a doubt, that the dog I was listening to was Dotty.

22

I couldn't remember ever being this nervous.

I'd washed my hair and put on make-up and stressed over what I would wear, trying on various outfits until I settled on jeans and a new orange top from Cos. I didn't want to appear to be trying too hard, but really, who was I kidding? Desperation leaked from every pore until I felt sodden with it.

The one upside to my current state of nerves was that my thumping heart effectively drowned out the agonizing sound of Dotty's whimpering, which had been lodged in my brain since I'd pressed 'open' on that audio link the night before.

Rosie had suggested meeting at a small, achingly hip café in Muswell Hill rather than one of the bigger chains. I knew it was because she didn't want to risk being seen. Probably, she hadn't told her father or Joy that she'd agreed to meet me. Well, that was understandable. She was just testing the waters. I knew that.

But God, I was nervous. I'd messed up so badly with her. When her text had come through just a few hours before, while I was still grappling with what to do about that terrible audio recording, I'd been too excited to mind the clinical language. *I'm ready to take a first step to reconciliation.* I'd known that was Rosie's way of covering herself, allowing herself an opt-out clause.

Who could blame her?

She was five minutes late, and I was getting hot and breathless and couldn't tell whether that was because of Dotty or hormones or because I was so anxious about seeing my own daughter.

I found myself remembering the last time I'd talked to her, when I'd turned up at the hospital.

'You can't be here,' she'd said, bundling me down the corridor away from the ward. 'What are you thinking?' And then, 'Please don't come here again, Mum. I just can't see you for a while.'

Rosie always was true to her word.

And now here she was. Wearing a denim jacket over a vintage dress in a style that was purely her own.

This beautiful girl who somehow, impossibly, had come from me.

I stood up, overcome by a wave of emotion that left me quite mute, and we faced each other awkwardly, not sure whether to shake hands or embrace. In the end, nature took over and I stepped forward to hug her. Though she held herself stiffly, I felt her arms close lightly around me. Somewhere in my mind, hope tentatively shrugged off its coverings and laid itself dangerously bare.

My girl. My precious girl.

We sat down and Rosie ordered an Americano. I asked for the same, just because I couldn't concentrate on the menu or on anything but her.

I asked her when she was going back to Manchester. I'd meant it as an ice breaker, an innocuous way of easing into the difficult conversation that surely lay ahead. I certainly wasn't prepared for her to say:

'Actually, I'm not going back to uni. I dropped out. It wasn't what I thought it would be. And really, what's the point of spending all that money on something that isn't all that?'

'All that what?'

Rosie studied me through narrowed eyes, as if testing to see if I was joking, but the truth was her bombshell had knocked the sense clean out of me.

'I just wasn't learning much, Mum,' she said.

'But what about all the money you've already paid?'

She waved her hand dismissively, as if all those thousands of pounds were a mere detail.

'I might be able to use the credits to switch into another course in the future,' she said. 'The main thing is not to waste any more money.'

No! I wanted to yell at her. *The main thing is to get a degree, to complete this rite of passage that opens up the world to you.* But I bit the words back. Our new-found connection was too gossamer-thin to risk putting any strain on it.

'And before you kick off, Dad only found out a few days ago and I swore him to secrecy. He and Joy are as anti it as you are. But they know it's pointless trying to change my mind.'

Rosie tossed her head of faded highlights as if her intransigence were a point of personal pride. She'd always had this need to appear completely in control of her own destiny. Hadn't yet realized that no one really is.

'But what will you do here?'

'I've got a job working at the cinema, and maybe I'll

start looking at courses I can do here in London in September. Please don't worry about it, Mum.'

She sounded so casual. This, the girl who'd plastered the walls of her bedroom with Post-its and sheets of dates before her history A Level, and who, unbeknown to us, had ordered 'smart drugs' over the internet so she wouldn't need so much sleep and could spend more time studying.

A cloud of suspicion formed.

'This isn't because of some new boyfriend?'

'Great that you have such a high opinion of me, that you think I'd change my life because of some man. Thanks a lot.'

'Sorry, it's just—'

'Actually, I have just started seeing someone. But it's only been a few days, so please stop looking at me like that. I'd made up my mind about uni way before I met him. Honest.'

Rosie's small, fine features were set in that way I recognized from old and I knew that if I carried on pushing I would lose her again, and I couldn't take that risk.

We changed the subject. Rosie wanted to know if there was more news about Dotty. I shook my head, hating how her eyes blurred with tears. She was so sensitive under that prickly armour she wore. There was no way I could tell her about the collar and the weird audio recording of the night before. She started reminiscing about the day we took Dotty home from the rescue shelter when she was still just a puppy. 'Can you remember, Mum, how she used to fall asleep standing up, just topple over on the carpet wherever she was?' I nodded, but really, I was only half listening to her, happy just to stare at her lovely face, as if I could commit it to memory so that, if she snatched herself away again, at least I'd have this.

Suddenly, I became aware of a shadow blocking the light. Looking up, I saw Frances standing on the other side of the window. She smiled broadly and pointed at the door to indicate that she was coming in, moving off before I could communicate that now wasn't a good time.

'Is that . . . ?' But Rosie's question was cut short by Frances's arrival.

'Tessa! How are you? I've been meaning to get in touch to see if you've got Dotty back yet.'

Frances was dressed down in a parka and jeans with her thick hair pulled back and her face scrubbed free of make-up.

I saw Rosie look at her appraisingly and for one self-ish moment I resented Frances for being there. I'd waited so long to be with my older daughter again. I didn't want to share her.

Introductions were made. 'I recognized you from Emma's Facebook page,' said Rosie, jumping to her feet. 'I was hoping I'd meet you, to thank you.' She stepped towards Frances and enveloped her in a hug. Frances was several inches taller and stood awkwardly, but I could see from the pink glow on her cheeks that she was touched. I invited her to join us and, for one agonizing moment, I thought she was going to say yes, but then she said she'd better not after all. She was just passing on her way back from the dentist's a few doors down and she had to get home to make her mother's lunch before heading back into work for the afternoon.

'So that's the famous Frances our Emma is so star-struck by,' Rosie said after she'd gone.

She smiled, but her face looked strained. Impulsively, I put my hand out to cover hers.

'Darling,' I said, emboldened by the fact that she didn't pull her hand away, 'I know it must have been hard for you to watch your little sister go through something like that.'

Rosie gave a single nod of her head.

'But maybe slightly worse for her,' she said, and laughed to show it was meant as a joke. 'You know, though, Mum, I really thought she'd be over it by now. I mean, he didn't actually *do* anything. Thank God.'

'You mean, besides bashing her round the head and trying to abduct her off the street?'

Rosie made a face.

'You know what I mean. He didn't do whatever it was he set out to do. But Em still seems really hung up about it. The other day, we were walking up to the shops and this jogger came running up behind us and she almost had a heart attack, I swear to God.'

I swallowed painfully. I'd wanted this meeting to be all about me and Rosie and building bridges, but worry about Emma was a loose thread on the surface of me – the slightest snag and I felt myself unravelling.

'I just feel,' I began thickly, staring down at the point on the table where my hand met Rosie's, 'that I've made such a mess of being a mother.'

Rosie took a while to reply, though I could sense that her direct gaze was fixed on me.

Eventually, she spoke, and though her tone was gentle, her words broke me a little.

'Mum, sometimes it just isn't about you.'

23

I hadn't been to Phil's studio in years. He'd got it on a long lease way before Shoreditch became the new Notting Hill, which in turn had once been the new Soho.

When he'd first signed the lease, we'd had two small children and a negligible bank balance but big dreams we'd discuss at night, lying in the dark with my head on his shoulder, his fingers stroking my arm. Even so, it had been a risk. I remember how drunk we'd got the night he signed, trying to drown our nerves in cheap cava.

God, I missed those two people.

I rang the top bell, telling myself there was no need to feel so anxious. I had a perfectly legitimate reason for coming to see him. Still, I knew I should have called ahead to warn him I was coming. Thing was, I wanted to catch him unawares, so that he wouldn't have a chance to discuss things with Joy. Oh, I knew they were a unit now, and I'd more or less accepted that, but I still missed getting his honest opinion, not the view he'd reached after careful consultation with the woman he left me for.

Phil did not sound terribly happy when he realized it was me at his door, but he buzzed me up anyway. I'd forgotten how steep those stairs were and the claustrophobic proportions of the rooms – the studio with all his equipment and an old three-seater sofa taking up the bigger space, with a tiny kitchen and bathroom off it.

He made me a cup of tea in a *Star Wars* mug that I knew for a fact he'd had for more than two decades, making a big thing of having to hunt around for a 'normal' tea bag, as he only ever drank green these days. If I'd wanted to, I could have traced the line of memory back to whichever distant birthday or Father's Day that mug originated from but for once I decided to spare myself the hurt of going back to that other life, that other time.

'I just don't understand why she'd want to screw up her future like this,' I said. 'And please don't tell me this is almond milk?'

He made a face.

'Joy and I are off dairy now. And believe me, we tried to talk Rosie out of it, but you know how she is when she's decided on something.'

'Have you met this boyfriend?'

'Not yet. And she swears it has no bearing on her dropping out. And to be fair, she has been talking about it for a few weeks now. Look, I'm no happier about it than you are, Tess. But she's nineteen now. Old enough to know her own mind.'

I took a deep breath then, trying to think of the words to broach what I had to say next.

'About that photograph you got sent in the post, the one of me in the pub.'

Phil glanced over, wary now.

'I honestly wasn't drinking. I just called into the pub to try to settle my thoughts. I'd had a really stressful day.'

For a moment I considered telling Phil my suspicions

about Dotty, and about going to confront Stephens and the encounter with his grandmother. It would have been such a relief to share with someone the horror of that audio recording. Dotty's high-pitched whimper that spooled through my mind when I lay in bed, trying to sleep. But I stopped myself.

'You know I would never do anything to hurt my children, don't you?'

'Oh, come on, Tess. Have you really forgotten what happened with Rosie?'

'No, of course I haven't forgotten. But you know what state I was in at that time, Phil. You'd just left us. I wasn't myself.'

'So it was my fault.'

'I'm not saying that. All I'm saying is I'm in a different place now. I won't let Em down. I'd do anything for those girls. You know that, don't you?'

Phil sat up straight, holding my gaze as if he were about to argue, but then he exhaled heavily, the fight going out of him.

'Yes. I know that, Tess.'

On the way back from Phil's studio I felt stirrings of optimism. The conversation with Phil hadn't been easy, but at least it had been honest, and on the way out he'd given me a proper hug and said, 'I know at heart we both want the same thing, Tess. For our kids to be happy.' I turned the memory of that hug over and over in my head like a precious stone I'd picked up on the beach.

Back home, I spoke to my dad on the phone while watching both parents on the webcam.

I could see from my mum's disapproving frown as my dad spoke that she was having a bad day.

'Tell them we don't want any,' she instructed him.

'It's Tessa, love.'

'I don't care who it is. Just tell them we're not interested. You always were too soft for your own good.'

'How are you managing, Dad?' I asked him. 'Honestly?'

On the screen my dad put a hand to his head and rubbed and the gesture made me want to climb through the computer and put my arms around him and comfort him the way he so often comforted me as a child.

'I do my best, Tessa,' he said. As if I needed convincing of that. 'But I have to admit I'm finding it hard.'

'Perhaps it's time to get that list from Dr Ali,' I said, trying to keep my voice down, even though my mother couldn't have heard above the sound of the television. 'The recommended nursing homes?'

My father closed his eyes.

'Maybe give it a little longer,' he said eventually. 'We can struggle on here for a while.'

After I'd hung up I carried on watching them, the elastic membrane of my heart stretched first this way and then that by pity, love and frustration.

A message pinged into my inbox from the dating site to notify me I had mail. Clicking off my parents, I logged in to find two more messages from Nick, one from earlier in the day asking what I had planned, and the next from just now. *Where are you?* He'd written. *I miss you.*

I stared at the last three words for a long time, a smile bubbling up and twitching on my lips.

Everything had been so shit for so long. Since Phil left it had seemed like that side of my life was over. The side where I existed physically for anyone apart from myself.

And I'd convinced myself I was glad of that, glad that I could walk the streets draped in the invisibility cloak of middle age. Glad that when I met a stranger on the near-deserted river bank while walking the dog I could smile and say, 'Hi,' without worrying he might see it as an invitation. It was a relief, I told myself, not to bother with the tiresome banalities of a physical relationship – caring if I'd shaved under my arms, wearing clothes based on aesthetics rather than comfort, seeing myself always through two pairs of eyes, mine and his.

But Nick's *I miss you* made me realize I wasn't quite done with all that yet.

And it came as a shock how happy that made me.

I was off dancing with wolves – I mean, negotiating with my ex.

The reply came back almost instantly.

And? You survived?

Bloody but unbowed.

There was a pause then, and I found myself glancing impatiently at my screen, irrationally irritated that he might have been called away, or just found something more pressing to do. But then:

OK. Deep breath. How do you feel about meeting up next weekend IN REAL LIFE?

My initial response was *too soon*, but I knew that Mari would say it was my fear talking. So instead I took a deep breath, just as instructed, and wrote back:

Why not? (On second thoughts, don't answer that.)

Emma came home, buzzing because her last class of the day had been cancelled. The weather had turned warmer, the sun finally pushing aside the last of the persistent cloud of earlier. I remembered we still had half a

209

box of mini-ice-creams in the freezer, left over from last summer, so we ate them sitting on the back doorstep, our faces lifted towards the sun.

For a moment I forgot and looked around for Dotty, expecting her to be hovering, tongue-lolling, eyes fixed on the ice-creams, before remembering about her collar and that awful recording. There was a split second where I teetered on the knife edge between the here and now – this sun-flooded doorstep – and the dark abyss of Dotty's unknown fate.

Deliberately, I pulled myself back into the present. The warmth of the sun on my skin. Emma next to me.

If only this moment could be frozen, I thought. So I could pop it into the freezer like those ice-creams and bring it out when things were going badly.

A ring on the doorbell shattered our peaceful slurping. Instantly, the feeling of wellbeing disintegrated, my throat closing up, thinking of all the people it could be. Phil, Stephens, the police again. None of the options was good.

Couldn't I have just this one perfect, intact moment?

'I'll get it,' said Em, jumping to her feet before I could stop her.

'Hang on—' But she had already disappeared through the back door.

I steeled myself for whatever was coming. Even before I heard Em cry out, 'Mum!' I'd got up and was running through the kitchen. But now I could hear her exclaiming. And another sound. It couldn't be. Surely . . .

A small black-and-white shape came barrelling in through the hallway, making high-pitched squeals of delight.

I dropped to my knees, speechless. While Dotty licked my face, I inspected her. She was thinner, and her fur was matted in places. I sucked my breath in through my teeth when I saw the deep cut to her abdomen, its length traced by a bumpy seam of dried, black blood.

Em appeared in the doorway, followed by a thin woman in an anorak that seemed excessive for this mild weather.

'I see poster and I bring back,' said the woman.

'Her name's Magda,' said Em, and a tear snaked down her cheek.

'She says she found Dotty in her garden this afternoon and recognized her from the posters. Isn't that amazing?'

I nodded and buried my face in Dotty's neck, realizing to my surprise that I too was crying.

After Magda had left, reluctantly accepting the twenty-pound note I pressed into her hand, Em and I stayed on the kitchen floor for a long time, taking it in turns to hug Dotty.

Apart from the cut, she seemed unharmed, though subdued, following us from room to room as if worried we might abandon her.

'But where's she been?' Em kept asking. 'And who's done this to her?'

I didn't tell her that I had a fair notion of exactly who'd taken her. And why.

'We should definitely tell the police,' Emma said, as we carefully washed off the dried blood to reveal the ugly pink cut. 'People shouldn't be allowed to get away with hurting animals.'

'I'll do it tomorrow,' I promised.

But even as I said it I was wavering. If I went back to the police with my suspicions, and they in turn went back to Stephens, where would it stop? He'd proved now how ruthless he was, as if there was ever any doubt.

The thought of being involved with someone like this skewered me with fear. That life, the life that Stephens represented – moving in the shadows where violence was normalized – was a life I didn't want any part of. If he could hurt our dog, what was he capable of doing to us?

I imagined the kind of knife he might have used to make that cut.

Then I imagined that same knife held against Em's throat.

What happened to Dotty was clearly some kind of warning to back off. Why didn't I do just that? I was just so tired of it all by that stage, you see. The lack of sleep, the constant anxiety over what would happen next. I just wanted it to be over.

In every other aspect of my life I felt I was making headway, for the first time in months. Reconnecting with Rosie. Being able to have a civilized conversation with Phil, recognizing that we both shared the same basic goal – to see our daughters happy. The gentle, warm flame that came from my interactions with Nick, my physical self unfurling as if from a long hibernation.

Now Dotty was back, Em might be able to put what happened behind her and move on. She needed to focus on getting her grades back up, without worrying about me or about any repercussions from all this. And I also needed to focus on my own life. Whatever Stephens was, whatever he'd done, it wasn't my concern. My job was only to keep my girls safe.

Looking back now, I can't believe my own naivety. To believe I was in control and that the choice to engage or switch off was mine to make.

Such hubris.

That evening, Em brought her laptop downstairs so she could work on the sofa with Dotty curled up on her legs.

I was sitting in the armchair opposite, writing up the feature on second chances and breaking off every few minutes to check on social media, as I always did these days. The news was full of the effect on young people's brains of constantly flitting from one internet site to another, but in my experience the women my age were just as bad. All of us watching telly with our laptops on our knees, jumping between tabs, grazing on social media like junk food, constantly dissatisfied but not understanding why, instead trying the next site and then the next, sure we would find it, that elusive thing we were searching for that opened up the door into the life we were meant to have.

On Twitter I followed several local accounts that broadcast headlines pertinent to our neighbourhood or those around it. Announcements of upcoming events or news about bin removals or road closures. That sort of thing. One of those accounts had just tweeted.

As I read the headline my heart froze in my chest.

I stared at the words for a long time, trying to will them into a different meaning, before conceding a sickening defeat.

Schoolgirl attacked in Bounds Green, the tweet read. *15-year-old dragged off the main road and sexually assaulted.*

He'd done it again.

24

'There's not much I can tell you, Mrs Hopwood.'

There was an open pack of Tesco chicken-salad sandwiches on Detective Byrne's desk, the plastic film ripped
off. Inside was one whole triangular sandwich and a
second that had been half eaten. A packet of salt-and-
vinegar crisps lay beside it, also open. I got the definite
impression I'd disturbed him mid-lunch.

'The girl was walking home from the Tube just before
midnight down Bounds Green Road and a man came
out of nowhere and pulled her off the main road and
assaulted her. But apart from that, we know nothing
more at this stage.'

'But there'll be CCTV on the street, won't there?'

I was trying to keep my voice steady, but I could hear
how it cracked with excitement. This might be a break-
through. If Stephens had attacked again and been picked
up on CCTV, they'd have to charge him this time,
wouldn't they?

Especially if this girl was able to positively identify
him.

'The camera wasn't working.'

'What?'

'The CCTV camera for that part of the road wasn't recording.'

'Oh, for fuck's sake.'

Detective Byrne's eyebrows lifted a fraction at my reaction, but he didn't say anything.

'At least you'll be able to pull him back in, won't you? St—' I stopped myself, before I said his name. 'I mean, the guy you picked up from the CCTV footage after Em was attacked? You can recall him and then the girl can ID him, right?'

'At this stage the girl is unsure if she wants to take things any further.'

'Pardon?' I stared at him, totally taken aback. 'But that's ridiculous. She has to take it further. She owes it to the other girls out there. You must persuade her.'

'Mrs Hopwood.' Detective Byrne's voice had a new, hard edge I hadn't heard him use before. 'Please remember this young girl is just fifteen years old and has been through a traumatic experience. How would you feel if it was your daughter?'

I felt ugly with shame then, seeing myself through his eyes. This vengeful mother so bent on getting back at the man who hurt her daughter she lacked the imagination to see what it might cost someone else's child.

Or worse, she could imagine, but just didn't care enough.

'Well, you can bring your own prosecution, can't you? Without the girl's assistance?'

'Only if the evidence is there, Mrs Hopwood. Look, I know you're concerned, but rest assured, finding this creep is a priority for us. We are taking all the steps we possibly can and that might well include bringing our initial suspect in your daughter's case back in for questioning. But you must also understand that this isn't the only serious case we're investigating. Do you know how many stabbings we've handled over the last six weeks alone? Last week, a sixteen-year-old kid was shot dead, just a few hundred yards away from here, standing on the pavement minding his own business. We had his mother collapse right where you're sitting now. Had to rush her to hospital. Suspected cardiac arrest. So yes, this case is a priority, but it's not the only priority. Do you hear what I'm saying?'

I'd intended to tell Detective Byrne about the cut on Dotty's stomach, but his demeanour made me change my mind. I could see he was stressed. The patch of psoriasis I'd noticed on his arm before had definitely got bigger, the livid pink crusted with white. I still had no evidence Stephens was involved in Dotty's disappearance and I guessed the policeman wouldn't welcome the extra paperwork for a complaint that had little chance of coming to anything.

Detective Byrne showed me out through the cramped waiting area. There was a woman sitting texting on her phone and, next to her, a heavy-set girl with hair pulled back from her head in pigtails that looked too young for her. Both of them had puffy pink skin around their eyes, as if they'd had a few long, difficult nights. The girl was dressed in a school uniform which stretched uncomfortably over her large frame. There was a school exercise book open on her lap and she held a biro in her hand with which she was absently doodling a heart on the skin of her inner wrist.

A heart. The sweet hopefulness of it made me want to weep.

'Is that . . .' I began as we reached the door, but the look on the detective's face silenced me.

I was outside and about to turn away when Detective Byrne stopped me.

'Mrs Hopwood? Please believe I mean this in the kindest way when I suggest that you do your job, which is to look after your daughter as best you can, and leave us to do ours.' As I began walking home, Detective Byrne's rebuke rang in my ears. Of course I should leave him to get on with the investigation in his own way. Everyone knew police budgets were being cut; obviously, they couldn't allocate all their resources to this one case.

But then I started thinking of the girl in the waiting room, the one with the pigtails and the biro'd heart. Of course, there was nothing to say for sure that she was the girl who'd been attacked the previous week, but the fact was, if it wasn't her, it was another girl just like her. Young and not yet fully formed, still doodling and dreaming. I remembered the girl's puffy eyes. How long would it take to recover from whatever it was Stephens had done? Could she ever truly recover? Could Emma?

The soft, pale, exposed skin under that biro heart.

Afterwards, I'd rack my brains, trying to work out whether I consciously decided to make the detour I did then or whether my feet genuinely took me there without my telling them to, acting on some subliminal impulse. Whatever the truth, I found myself, some ten minutes later, standing outside the sports field just off the high road where all the local teams played.

Rosie's best friend had once had a crush on a boy who'd played in a Saturday youth league and the two of them had spent a whole term shouting encouragement from the sidelines and hanging around the clubhouse hopefully after the end of the matches. I'd picked her up from there often enough to know that the kids' teams and adult teams shared the same very basic facilities.

On an overcast weekday afternoon in March, the fields were empty, apart from a dog walker desultorily flinging tennis balls from a thrower for an overweight and largely disinterested Labrador. But as I turned to go, the door to the clubhouse swung open and a wiry middle-aged man stepped out with a large nylon bag slung over his shoulder, which he placed on the floor while he locked up, using an enormous bunch of keys.

I hurried over.

'Excuse me, are you the coach for the Haringey Rovers over-twenty-ones?'

'Yeah, could be.'

His grey eyes, looking out from a weather-leathered face, were cautious.

'Can I have a quick word? It's about one of your players, James Stephens. I'm afraid it's quite a serious matter.'

Walking away some time later, I felt as if a weight had been lifted from me.

I'd done my duty by the girl with the soft inside wrist and by my own daughter, sitting in a classroom some-where not too far from here, hopefully thinking of exams or boys or plans for a future golden with promise.

The coach had been taken aback when I told him about Stephens, though not entirely surprised. 'Let's just say he has form when it comes to being on the wrong side of the law,' he'd said, his mouth set into a grim line.

I remembered what Stephens's grandmother had said about the man who'd died because of her grandson's temper.

The coach had agreed not to tell Stephens about my involvement but promised he would take action. 'I believe in second chances, but this is something I will not tolerate,' he said. 'I have daughters myself. This has crossed a line.'

Now, there would be consequences, I thought, relieved. And it was no longer my responsibility to deliver them. Without his precious football team, and with his own grandmother looking at him with suspicion, wasn't Stephens more likely to move away? He knew he was on the police radar now, knew it was only a question of time. Maybe he'd move in with the girl with the black hair who was having his baby. Of course, I felt bad for her, but it wasn't as if I hadn't tried to warn her.

She wasn't my responsibility. Rosie and Emma – they were my responsibility. And I'd do anything to drive him far away from them.

On the way home, I felt shaken in that way you sometimes feel when you've done something irrevocable, but the adrenaline was surging. Now, something would happen.

I wanted to tell someone about the events of the morning, to share the feeling of having passed on a great burden. On impulse, I sent Frances a text.

Just done something I might live to regret.

I knew she was at work so I wasn't expecting a response but, within a few seconds, my phone was ringing.

'So' – she sounded breathless – 'tell me.'

She suggested meeting after work in the pub nearest me, but it was the one where I'd been photographed drinking on my own in the afternoon and I didn't feel comfortable, so we agreed on one halfway between us that I usually avoided because it always seemed to have a pub quiz on or some lamentable local singer.

In the event there was neither. At just after six on a Monday evening it was still too early for the book clubs and the PTA meetings and the men wanting to wash away the dregs of the day on a tide of craft real ale.

'I hope I wasn't interrupting anything the other day when I walked past,' said Frances, dropping her bag down on the table. 'I know the two of you probably have loads to talk about.'

'Don't be silly. You weren't interrupting at all. Rosie was so happy she finally got to meet you. But you're right, we did have a lot of ground to make up. We haven't exactly been on good terms over the last few months.'

Frances scrunched up her face in sympathy.

'I did kind of get that impression.'

'But the good news is that things are looking much more positive now. Rosie and I have taken that first step towards making up, and my ex is being slightly less of a dick. Oh, and you'll never believe it, the dog came home!'

'I saw on Facebook. Emma posted a photo. I'm so happy for you. And she was completely okay? He didn't hurt her?'

''Fraid so. She had a big gash on her tummy.'

Frances's eyes widened in horror.

'Why would he do something like that, though – take her and then let her go like that?'

I shrugged.

'I think he took her to punish us, and the cut and the bloody collar and weird audio recording were warnings. Thank God she's home now. The man's unhinged.'

'So what's this thing you might regret, then?'

Frances had on a vibrant green top that brought out tones of red in her hair and she leaned across the table, as if anxious not to miss anything.

I hesitated. Now the bravado of earlier had worn off, I was already wondering if I had made a dreadful mistake in going to see Stephens's football coach. Even though I'd made him promise to leave me out of it, how could I be sure he wouldn't let something slip? Or that Stephens wouldn't somehow put two and two together. He knew where I lived. What if he retaliated?

Falteringly, I explained to Frances about the new attack and how I'd felt so helpless after seeing Detective Byrne – until I'd found myself outside the little sports hut.

I held my breath, waiting for her reaction, worried she might be disapproving, as Kath and Mari would be if they knew what I'd done. But to my relief, Frances seemed to think I'd done the right thing.

'If the police aren't going to act, what are you supposed to do except take things into your own hands?'

'Exactly!'

Then Frances wanted to know what my next move would be and seemed disappointed when I told her that was as far as I was going to go.

'Are you sure? I mean, he's clearly still a danger to young girls.'

My forehead felt tight when she said that, like someone was pressing hard on both sides of it. But still I replied:

'No, I can't keep going with this, Frances. I need to move on. It's not good for my mental health to keep obsessing about him. I need to concentrate on what's good in my life. For instance, would it surprise you to know I might finally have found a man who isn't married or a serial killer or still lives with his mum?'

I realized what I'd said and clapped a hand to my mouth.

'Oh God, I'm sorry.'

Frances laughed, showing that gap in her teeth.

'Don't be silly. I'm with my mum because I'm her carer. Not because I don't know how to wash my own pants. So, tell me everything.'

And though, really, I hardly knew her, Frances just had one of those smiles you couldn't help but open up to. And so I found myself telling her all about Nick and our plans to meet up at the weekend.

And, just for that moment, I felt normal.

25

Nothing fitted me any more.

Since hitting fifty, weight had stealthily crept on, extra pounds attaching themselves like stubborn barnacles to various parts of me, instantly making themselves at home, as if they'd always been there and had no intention of shifting.

My expensive pre-redundancy clothes stretched and strained unflatteringly, while my day-to-day dog-walking, kitchen-table-sitting wardrobe was barely fit to be seen outside the house.

I certainly had nothing to wear on a date.

We'd agreed to meet for brunch, figuring that made the whole event marginally less scary.

It's less loaded than dinner or lunch, isn't it? Nick had said.

Initially, I decided on a pair of skinny jeans with a forgiving jersey top but when I'd spilled a big dollop of foundation down my leg the whole thing had to be rethought. In the end I opted for a denim dress with a zip up the front and plenty of stretch and a pair of suede ankle boots I rediscovered at the bottom of my wardrobe. But even as I reached the front door I was having misgivings.

On the doorstep I hesitated, eyeing the darkening sky. Should I have gone for trousers instead?

While I dithered, a familiar pistachio-green Fiat 500 pulled up outside the house.

'Tessa! I'm so glad I caught you. I've been trying to call you all morning.'

I pulled out my phone from the pocket of my bag. Sure enough, there were five missed calls.

'Shit. Sorry, I forgot to turn it off from silent this morning. I've been in a bit of a state. What's up? Why are you here?'

'This is going to sound mad, but I just have a bad feeling about this date, Tessa. I've been feeling uneasy since you told me about Nick in the pub and I couldn't work out why. Then this morning it just hit me. What if Nick is actually James Stephens?'

Shock made me burst out laughing.

'That's bonkers. I've been talking to him. Chatting. He's funny and intelligent. I've seen his photograph. He's got a young stepson.'

Frances's face softened.

'Oh, Tessa. Doesn't he seem a teeny bit too perfect? Anyone can be who they want to be online. Steal a photograph, pass it off as them, adopt an identity. Be someone they're not. Think about the timing. When did Nick first get in touch?'

I tried to think back. It was not long after Emma and I had been to visit my parents.

'This is important, Tess. Had you mentioned anything about joining a dating site on Facebook?'

'I don't know.' I found myself getting angry. 'I might have done. But he can't see what I post.'

'No, but he might have friended other people in your network, set up a fake profile. If they comment on one of your posts, he might be able to read it.'

A horrible sense of deflation and disappointment was building. Could it be true, what Frances was saying?

But the timing made a sickening sort of sense. I recalled that Mari had tagged me in a jokey post with a clip from a sitcom where a woman joined a dating agency. Had someone in the comments mentioned this particular one by name, the one Nick had found me on? I had a terrible feeling that they had. All week I'd been waiting to find out what the fallout would be from my visit to the soccer coach. I reasoned he probably wouldn't find out anything until Saturday-morning training, which was today, so I'd thought myself safe. But what if he already knew? If Nick really did turn out to be Stephens in disguise, how would he make me pay for what I'd done?

'But why would Stephens want to meet me?'

Frances shook her head. It had started raining now and small drops of water flew off her hair.

'Who knows? To confront you? To humiliate you? Perhaps he plans to be watching from somewhere, hoping you'll sit there on your own like a lemon. Maybe he's hoping to see you cry. Men like him get a kick out of seeing women in distress. It's all part of their power plan.'

Already I felt it evaporating – the hope that had been shyly building inside me like the tiny popping bubbles before water boils, the fragile shoots of confidence that had started to push through the dry soil of my post-divorce life.

Trussed up in my uncomfortable boots, my face shiny with dreams and anti-ageing primer, I felt horribly vulnerable.

Could she be right? Was I being played for a fool?

'I could be wrong,' Frances said gently. 'But, well, I just don't think I am. Come on, how about we go back in and get a coffee?'

For a moment I wavered, the thought of Stephens's gloating face almost too much to bear.

But then my phone pinged with a text alert. It was from Nick.

I'm here already. Keen as. Was sitting outside but it started pissing down so headed indoors. I'll be the one with the damp patch on his shirt.

I tried to imagine Stephens composing that text, but it was impossible.

'Look, Frances. I really appreciate you coming over, and you might well turn out to be right, but I couldn't live with myself if Nick turned out to be genuine and I stood him up. I think I'd rather risk looking like a fool.'

Frances pressed her lips together then nodded.

'Gotcha. Whatever you think is best, Tessa. I was just worried about you, that's all. If you arrive and Stephens is there . . .'

'. . . Then I shall turn straight around and leave. It's a Saturday morning in King's Cross. There'll be enough people around that he wouldn't dare try anything. But Frances' – I paused until her eyes met mine – 'I want you to know I'm really touched by your concern.'

'No problem. I really hope you have a lovely time.'

Nick had suggested meeting in Granary Square, behind King's Cross station. When I first moved to London that whole area had been a no-go zone for anyone but the most hardened drug dealer or desperate street-walker. Once, waiting for Phil to pick me up around the back of the station when I was eight months pregnant with Rosie and big as a house, a car had pulled up and two men had asked, 'How much?' Now, it pulsated with mainstream hip and the fug of skunk had been replaced with the heady smell of prosperity, restaurants the size of Amazon warehouses teeming with Japanese tourists and the type of well-heeled Londoner who found safety in numbers.

My nerves were shredded by the time I exited the Tube by the strange neon-lit art installation of a bird in a cage and began making my way to our rendezvous. It didn't help that I'd only scraped a couple of hours' sleep, exhaustion no match for the combination of anxiety and excitement rampaging around my body. And now Frances had sowed seeds of doubt as well.

By the time I reached the restaurant I was so nervous I could hardly work out which was more terrifying – the possibility that Nick might not be there, as Frances had predicted, or that he would.

The restaurant was cavernous and loud, with music playing over the persistent hum of other people's conversations. Three enormous crystal chandeliers hung from the ceiling and the seats were upholstered in orange velvet.

My voice shook as I gave Nick's name to the maître d', but he didn't seem to notice.

'The gentleman is already here. Will you come this way?'

For a horrible moment I pictured Stephens sitting at a table for two waiting for me and almost turned around to leave. But then I forced myself to take a deep breath in and stand up straight. I'd done a few Pilates classes earlier in the year and now I heard the South African teacher's voice in my mind: 'Imagine there's a cord from the top of your head to the ceiling, and you're trying to touch your shoulder blades together like wings.'

I set off, following the maître d's back, past a long, dramatic bar to the left overhung by hundreds of upside-down wine glasses. And then, all of a sudden, the maître d' moved to the side, and there he was.

'Thank God you came, I thought you'd stood me up. You look so lovely.'

Nick was just as he'd looked in his photos. As always now with meeting new people my own age, there was an initial moment of surprise – *but this is an old man* – followed by an almost instantaneous recalibration, the younger man behind the greying hair and weathered skin materializing gradually as we looked at one another, like one of those magic-eye pictures.

Instantly, there was a feeling inside me of something relaxing, like when you get home and surround yourself with familiar things and everything decompresses. He was real. It wasn't a trick.

If anything, I decided after I'd sat down, he was more handsome than he'd looked in his picture, wearing a blue shirt that matched his eyes and dark blue jeans. He had a soft Scottish accent, which surprised me, as I'd completely forgotten he'd told me he was originally from Edinburgh, and his voice had a musical quality so that he stretched my name out over several notes.

We talked about being single and about how strange it felt to be on a dating site.

Then he asked me about my daughters, and I told him my worries about Rosie dropping out of university. I said I'd done something to upset her a few months ago and was still trying to make amends. I told him how bright she was and how funny and loyal and how, after Phil first left, she'd refused to meet Joy until I told her it was okay.

Then we moved on to Em. And somehow I ended up talking about the attack and how Em had then seen her attacker in the street. I didn't tell him about the messages I'd sent or about how the dried blood had clotted on Dotty's stomach. Or about my warning to the wiry football coach with the big bunch of keys. I still had enough perspective then to realize how mad it would sound and how much normal people feared being sucked into a world where those kinds of things happened.

'I feel like I let her down,' I admitted. 'I wasn't there when I should have been, and now I can't even manage to do the one thing that would make her feel safer, which is to get him to move away so she never has to see him again.'

We'd ordered our food by this time. Nick had a stack of pancakes topped with fruit, while I'd gone for avocado and poached egg, which I ate gingerly, in case of a rogue dribble of egg yolk. Now Nick sat back with a segment of pancake speared on his fork and fixed me with his very blue eyes, which made me realize how rarely anyone did that any more, that intense eye contact.

'You know, I'll bet you're a really good mum, Tessa.'

I swallowed hard and looked away so he wouldn't see

my eyes blur. I was such a mess these days, my nerves, rubbed raw by sleeplessness, overreacting to every scrap of kindness.

We finished eating and ordered more coffee, and when that was gone we still stayed sitting at our table chatting while the tables around us filled up with lunch-time diners until, finally, the waiter apologized and told us they needed the table for the next booking.

'Shall we find a pub and go for a drink?' Nick asked when we were outside, the rain falling more heavily now on the grid of mini-fountains that rose up out of the concrete of the square.

'I can't,' I said. After the incriminating photo that had been sent to Phil, I couldn't contemplate going into a pub again in the afternoon. 'I need to get back to feed the dog.'

I didn't add that I wanted to check up on Em too.

When we said goodbye outside King's Cross station, he stepped forward to kiss my cheek as I leaned in to give him a hug, so we collided clumsily, but when I moved away my shoulder felt warm where he'd touched it.

On my way home from Bounds Green station, I called Kath.

'I knew it,' she cried, when I told her how well the date had gone. 'I'm off to google wedding hats just as soon as we hang up.'

Then she wanted a blow-by-blow account. What did I wear? Where did we meet? What were my first impressions?

'I was a bit late getting there, so he was already waiting for me.'

That was the first time I'd remembered about Frances.

Excitement at being with Nick had all but swept her from my mind.

'Actually, it was Frances who made me late. I told her about Nick and she got it in her head that he might actually be Stephens. She thought the timing was too coincidental.'

'Paranoid much?' asked Kath.

I laughed.

'She was just watching out for me. I think she thinks my whole family need protecting 24/7.'

Kath was quiet for a moment. Then she sighed.

'You know, Tessa, personally, I worry this Frances might be getting a bit too attached to you and Em. But in this particular instance, I have to concede she might just have a point.'

Last night, after Henry was in bed, I made a list of everything you've taken from me. My home with the sunshine-yellow kitchen walls that everyone had tried to dissuade me from but made my heart sing every morning when I got up. The job I loved, special-needs coordinator. Well, I didn't always love it. Some days, when I was explaining to desperately worried parents why the latest cuts meant we had to axe their daughter's one-to-one help, I didn't love it. But I was bloody good at it and it made me feel like I was worth something. Matt. How I was the only one he'd allow to see him wearing glasses, the tops of his arms where they were so wide and when they went around me I felt protected from everything. He worried he was getting fat, but I loved the sheer breadth of them. The more the better. When I went to see his body, I focused on the tops of his arms, so I wouldn't have to see his face and know that it was him.

My list was never-ending. Feeling safe in my own home, feeling free from the guilt that woke me in the night gasping for breath, my chest crushed with it. Feeling able to trust my own judgement.

After I'd written my list I stared at it for a long time. Then I took my pen and crossed out the heading where I'd written <u>Things You Took from Me</u> and changed it to <u>Things I Let You Take</u>.

26

By the time my stint of holiday cover on *Silk* magazine arrived, I was feeling more positive than I had in ages.

Though I hadn't yet seen Nick again, as he'd been in California giving a keynote speech at a conference at UCLA, we'd been messaging back and forth and had spoken a few times on the phone. Each conversation went deeper than the last, both of us peeling ourselves slowly apart like the layers of an onion until I found myself viewing my everyday life through the prism of Nick's eyes, always conscious of how I could work up a random encounter into an anecdote or describe a thunderstorm or a particularly fine view. Every time we had contact I came away with fresh hope, and it was only those long, sleepless night hours that saw me pulling that hope out of shape until it resembled something else.

I was happy to be going into a magazine office again. I'd spent so much of my adult life in that environment that entering into the building through the revolving doors felt almost like coming home. I was wearing a suit from my editor days and, though it was tighter than it had once been, I still felt the confidence from its tailored lines and every one of its tiny tucks and seams.

I didn't yet have a security pass, so I had to wait down in reception for someone from the magazine to bring me up. I waited five minutes. Ten. Fifteen.

'Can you call up again to make sure they know I'm here?' I asked the receptionist, worried about being late on my first day.

She was new from the last time I was in this particular magazine building. I did some mental calculations and realized with a jolt that it was nearly a decade ago.

'Of course.'

She smiled and picked up a phone receiver, pressing some numbers.

'Tessa Hopwood is still down in reception for you. Yes, I know. I did tell her. Right. Fine.'

The receptionist looked up and her smile had dimmed a notch.

'They do know you're waiting, Tessa. Someone will be down just as soon as they can.'

The young girl who eventually came down to fetch me was apologetic.

'It's press week, so things are pretty crazy.'

'Don't worry, I remember what it was like.'

'You used to work here?'

'Yes, mind you, it was probably about ten years ago now.'

'Wow. I'd just left primary school.'

In the open-plan office, I was shown to the desk that would be mine for the next week. It was completely clear, apart from a list of instructions neatly typed on a piece of A4 paper.

'Geri left that for you,' said the girl who'd shown me up, who was revealed to be the current intern, by the name of Skye. 'So you can get stuck straight in.'

Geri was the features editor whose place I was taking while she island-hopped around the Caribbean on a press trip. I glanced towards the glass booth where the editor sat. Strange to think I'd once sat there myself, a decade ago, my penultimate job in magazines. Now the door was shut and all the white blinds were down.

'Should I go and say hello to Natalie?'

'Oh, I wouldn't. She knows you're here. I'm sure she'll be out shortly.'

I turned on the computer, using the password written in my handover notes. The first job was to edit the reviews section, something I could do in my sleep.

I was nearly finished when Natalie, the magazine editor, finally emerged from her office.

'Sorry, Tessa. I got bogged down in calls. You know how it is.'

Natalie had once been my assistant, so she knew I knew exactly how it was. Still, I felt a jab of something when she said that. A memory of the life I used to have, the non-stop meetings and snap decisions, the adrenaline rush of press week, the sheer exhilaration of producing a two-hundred-page-plus glossy magazine that a month ago hadn't even been thought of.

'How's the family?' she wanted to know. 'You had girls, didn't you? Are they okay?'

'Well, Em's doing fine. First year of sixth form. And Rosie . . .'

'That's great, Tessa, great. I do so admire you. How you've looked after your family. And you're looking so well. That lovely, leisurely freelance life obviously suits you. Now, how are you getting on with Geri's list?'

I told her I had nearly finished the reviews.

'Which of the subs should I send them to?' I said, looking over automatically to where the sub-editors' bench used to be.

Natalie laughed.

'God, you have been out of the loop a while, haven't you? We only have a skeleton staff of subs who have to cover several magazines. A *hub*. Most of our copy we sub ourselves now. And lay it out too. Please tell me you know how to use InDesign.'

'Of course,' I lied.

After she'd gone I had to email my friend Ben, who'd been my old production editor, to ask him to talk me through InDesign.

The day stretched on. I'd forgotten how long days could be in an office where you didn't really belong and all the in-jokes passed you by. The staff were over-worked. I was shocked by how few of them there were, turning out a magazine that was the same number of pages it had been when there were twice as many people working on it.

Ridiculously, I found myself missing Nick. I kept thinking of funny comments I would send him later. How he'd laugh when I told him about the features meeting we'd just had where I'd suggested an idea from the list I'd made at home and the deputy editor had made that face people make when they're trying to let you down gently and said:

'You see, the thing is – no disrespect – but we don't do features like that any more.'

They'd got excited about a couple of the others, though, and I'd felt myself growing lighter, like I'd been wearing a heavy coat and had just shrugged it off. I might have been out of the game for a couple of years, but there was still a value to be placed on experience.

I'd hoped that Natalie and I might go out for lunch, or at least there might be someone to grab a sandwich with. But it soon transpired that most people had brought their own lunches in plastic tubs – lots of spiralized vegetables and fruit salads and nuts and seeds – or else had already bought something from the sandwich man who came around from floor to floor mid-morning. They ate at their desks, assiduously working through lunch hour.

I decided not to bother with lunch. Without a security pass, if I'd gone out, I'd have had to call someone down to escort me back up, and I couldn't face it.

I forced myself to get back to work. To my delight, Natalie had told me the magazine was sending me out later in the week to do a celebrity interview. The celebrity in question was Ingrid Blackwood, a Hollywood actress who'd narrowly missed out on an Oscar earlier in the year. I knew the interview would have been hard to secure so I was flattered that they'd given it to me and determined not to let them down. I'd called up every in-depth interview with her over the last four years and was busy working through them, making notes on the line of questioning I was interested in pursuing and the possible angles I could take.

When my phone pinged some time later I had a momentary surge of hope, thinking it might be Nick, until I realized it wasn't my email alert but my Facebook Messenger.

I pressed my eyes closed when I saw the name in bold on the left-hand side of the page.

James Laurence Stephens.

I took a deep breath in then opened them again and clicked on the message.

You bitch. Suspended from footie thanks to you, bitch.

I won't forget.

I stared at the screen. At first I was furious with the coach for giving away that it was me, but when I calmed down I allowed that Stephens might just have worked it out on his own.

I kept re-reading the message. *I won't forget.* Such a strange thing to say.

Then it hit me. He was couching it in language that wouldn't leave him open to charges of threatening behaviour.

But, make no mistake about it. I knew what he was saying, what he was doing.

It was a threat all right.

27

Though Stephens's message disturbed me on a fundamental level, I didn't have time to analyse what it meant.
Work was so full on, and I was having to catch up on all
the new technological advances as I went along, which
took up all my brainpower.

I hadn't realized until I went into the office how much
I felt like I still had something to prove. That I was still
relevant. That I still had some status, outside of my
house and my children.

The morning of my big interview with Ingrid Blackwood I'd changed clothes so many times that in the end
Em had stood in front of my bedroom door and forbid-
den me to go back in. 'You look fine,' she'd said, eyeing
up the navy-blue suit and silk fuchsia top I hadn't worn
in two years. 'For God's sake, Mum, you used to do
interviews like this all the time. You know what to do.
You'll be brilliant. Just relax.'

But still I felt jittery in the office, making my last-
minute preparations.

'Does anyone have a spare dictaphone?' I asked the
features department in general. 'I thought mine was
working but looks like the batteries are dead.'

Skye gave me a look of confused concern.

'You do know you can record on your phone, don't you?'

After she'd shown me how, and then shown me again because I promptly forgot the first set of instructions, I went on to my email.

Since when can you use a phone to record interviews? I asked Kath and Mari. *If you want me, I'll be out stamping around the tundra with the rest of the dinosaurs.*

I'd already told them how nervous I was about this interview and complained about the paltry fifteen minutes I'd been allocated. I'd given them the name and address of the hotel where it was taking place so that they could go on to Google maps and work out exact timings of how long it would take to get there. They knew how important it was to me to get this right.

Twenty minutes before I was due to leave for my interview I slipped off to the loos. I'd brought my entire make-up bag with me so that I could apply full war paint. It wasn't as if I was trying to compete with Ingrid Blackwood, who was one of those impossible flawless beauties with cheekbones you could light matches off and huge, luminous green eyes. It was more that I was trying to give myself every advantage. Like in a battle. Make-up was the armour which would give me the confidence to go into that room and shake her hand and do the job I was being paid for.

Plus, naturally, I hadn't slept so I needed to cover the deep maroon shadows under my eyes. I'd run out the previous lunchtime and bought a concealer I couldn't really afford that came in the world's smallest pot. 'Ounce per ounce, this stuff must be more valuable than gold,' I'd said to the woman in the make-up department as she rang up the bill. 'The price we women pay for beauty,' she'd replied with a sigh.

The interviews were taking place in a suite in a hotel in Chelsea, tucked down a residential street a brisk ten-minute walk from South Kensington station. The journey by Tube was hot and uncomfortable. There had been a signal failure earlier and now the platforms were packed with disgruntled people, all believing their own delayed appointments took precedence over everyone else's. Two trains came and went, too packed to board. Those of us on the platform waited by the open doors, glaring at the passengers inside, willing them to get off so that we could squeeze on.

When I finally pushed my way into the third train, I found myself wedged into the corner by the door, hemmed in on all sides. As I stood pressed up against the glass partition, a familiar burning sensation spread out from my stomach, anxiety crawling all over me like a rash. And now came the fire, shooting up into my back, my neck, my face, until I was one mass of heat. I shrugged off my jacket and stared fixedly out of the window, trying to quell the panic, and to pretend that I was oblivious to the clamminess of my forehead and back.

I emerged into the daylight, crumpled and damp, the silk top I'd so painstakingly selected that morning looking like a wrung-out dishrag. I was also late.

There was a taxi idling outside the station so I jumped in, even though the journey only took a few minutes. Then I was out and hurrying up the steps and into the gloom of the lobby, which was decorated entirely in black with accents of orange, and where a publicist was standing watch, her expression pinched and anxious.

This threw me. Normally on these occasions, there'd be back-to-back interviews arranged, which invariably overran, so you'd expect to be kept waiting, sometimes for hours. I'd been depending on having time to dash into the loos to reapply my smudged make-up and then to sit quietly and go over some of the questions I wanted to ask.

Instead, I found myself being shepherded up the thickly carpeted stairs and along a muffled, darkly pan-elled hallway, eventually coming to a halt outside a door at the very end.

The publicist, who reminded me a little of Frances with her glossy, swinging hair and her English-rose complexion, knocked tentatively at the door.

'Come,' said a woman's voice.

We entered a small living room which was all done out in grey, with grey walls and a grey sofa, complete with grey-and-gold velvet cushions and heavy grey-and-cream brocade curtains. There was a doorway, the door just ajar, through which one could get a glimpse of the corner of a four-poster bed festooned with satin drapes and piled with throws and pillows, also, natur-ally, in grey. There were lots of pleats. Lots of gathers.

Lots of grey.

Facing the sofa with its velvet cushions was an arm-chair. And sitting in it was one of the most beautiful women in the world.

The thing about film stars, women particularly, is that they're always so much less substantial than they appear on screen. Ingrid Blackwood starred in movies where she usually portrayed powerful women, certain of their own agency, but in person she was slight and fragile. When I shook her hand it felt limp, as if the effort of raising it to mine had left it quite exhausted.

I smiled broadly. It was always so essential to make eye contact as soon as possible, to at least pretend that this was a normal interaction between two human beings, here to have a chat.

'I hope you're enjoying our weather,' I said, indicating the clouds outside, grey to match the decor.

She smiled wanly, and I reflected that I was probably not the first person that day to have made the same anodyne comment.

'Just reminding you,' said the publicist, 'you have less than fifteen minutes. We're on a very tight timetable and you were a couple of minutes late.'

The reproach stung.

'Right. Let's get started, then, if it's okay with you.'

Ingrid nodded her assent and sat back down on the chair. She was so slender the cushion didn't even seem to depress under her as she sat. Her trademark long dark hair was pulled up into a thin ponytail, and her face was pale and make-up free, the features so fine it was as if they'd been painted there with the most delicate of brushes by an eighteenth-century miniaturist. She had on a baggy white T-shirt over black jogging pants rolled up at the bottoms to reveal legs that looked as if you could snap them in half like twigs, and surprisingly long bare feet which she pulled up underneath her.

She looked like a thirty-five-year-old child.

I sat down on the sofa opposite and pulled my black cross-body bag on to my lap, feeling around inside for my phone. I'd been rummaging for a few seconds before I remembered it was in the pocket.

Ingrid Blackwood gazed on impassively.

Now I had to remember how to set it to record. Every movement felt clumsy and inept in front of this wraith-like child-woman.

The publicist stretched a tight smile across her face and glanced pointedly at her own phone, as if checking the time.

As I'd guessed, Ingrid Blackwood wasn't the most forthcoming interviewee. Mind you, I didn't suppose I'd be terribly expansive if I was answering more or less the same set of questions for the tenth or eleventh time that day, each time trying to bring the conversation round to the boring film you were promoting while knowing that the other person was doing everything they could to lead you in a different direction, hoping you'd let something slip you didn't really want the world to know.

I dutifully asked her about the current film, to ease into the interview and placate the publicist, at the same time trying to tease out more interesting quotes, pulling at every tiny thread in her answers, horribly mindful of the ticking clock. Just as I detected a slight lowering of her guard, there came a knock at the door.

The publicist frowned and rose to answer while I pressed my lips together in annoyance, trying to calculate how long I had left.

'So sorry,' said a hard-faced woman in a dark jacket with a subtle hotel-logo badge. 'There's a call for Tessa Hopwood. Urgent, apparently.'

I was so shocked it took a few seconds to realize that she meant me.

'I don't understand,' I said. 'Why wouldn't they phone my mobile?'

I picked up my phone, which was still recording. Might someone have been trying to call me while I was recording the interview with Ingrid Blackwood? Immediately, the possibilities started scrolling through my head. It must be the magazine. Who else knew I was here? But why would they be trying to get hold of me so urgently? Was it something to do with Emma or Rosie? Had something happened to my parents?

'I didn't think you'd want the call to be put through to the room,' the woman was saying to the publicist. 'It's not terribly private.'

I got to my feet.

'I'm so sorry,' I said, my mouth suddenly dry. 'I'll be as quick as I can.'

I followed the hard-faced woman from the room, trying not to notice Ingrid Blackwood's subtly raised eyebrow as she exchanged a look with the publicist.

'Did the person say what it was about?' I asked the receptionist on the way down the stairs.

She shrugged.

'My colleague took the call,' she said. 'But he's been called away.'

On the main desk in the reception area an old-fashioned phone receiver lay on its side next to its cradle. I picked it up and took a deep breath before speaking, nerves pricking at my skin like tiny needles.

'Hello?'

There was a thick silence, but not the clean void when there's no connection.

'Hello?' I repeated.

Again, there was nothing.

The receptionist surveyed me coolly. She had neat stud earrings in the shape of butterflies and my gaze fixed on them while I waited for someone to speak.

Eventually, I replaced the receiver, feeling churned up and anxious.

'Did your colleague say if the caller was a man or a woman?' I asked. The receptionist shook her head.

I took out my own phone and called the magazine while I headed back towards the suite where the interview was taking place.

'Skye? Did anyone try to call me from the office?'

'Hang on.'

There was a clunking noise and then I heard the intern's voice, sounding further away. 'Has anyone been trying to get hold of Tessa?'

A woman's voice answered in the background. 'Isn't she supposed to be doing an interview?'

It sounded like Natalie.

I took the stairs two at a time and burst back into the interview room.

'So sorry,' I said, preparing to sit back down where I'd been sitting before. 'I have no idea what that was about.'

The publicist made a face, pulling her mouth down at each corner.

'The thing is, Tessa,' she said, 'we're on a really strict schedule. Otherwise, it's too tiring for Ingrid. I'm sure you understand.'

'Of course,' I said, not understanding at all.

'And with you starting late and everything, I'm afraid you've run out of time. Sorry!'

She stretched out the last word as if it had several e's on the end. *Sorr-eeeeeee.*

'But I've only asked a couple of questions. I haven't got nearly enough for a cover piece.'

The publicist threw a fleeting glance at Ingrid Blackwood and I realized, with building panic, that this must be something they'd agreed between themselves before I'd even returned to the room.

'Like I say, I'm very sorry,' the publicist said.

Ingrid Blackwood held out her limp hand for me to shake again and, before I quite knew what was happening, the publicist was herding me out of the door of the suite and back down the stairs to reception, where the next two journalists were waiting to take their turn.

'Apologies for keeping you,' she told them pointedly.

On the way back to the office I listened on my headphones to the recording of the interview, desperately hoping there'd be something I'd missed. Something that would immediately jump out as a great cover line or at least something I could be fairly sure the other thirty or so interviewers wouldn't have got. But to my growing dismay, I realized there was nothing.

When I got back to the office, hot and sticky and eaten up with worry, I tried to sneak back to my seat, but Natalie came bounding out of her office.

'Well?' she said, beaming. 'Did you get something juicy? Tell all.'

I felt the heat surge into my cheeks.

'The thing is, they hardly gave me any time.'

'Still, you must have got something, surely?' Natalie's smile had faded a few notches by this point.

'A little,' I lied. 'But not much. She talked a bit about the film.'

'And?'

'And that's about it.'

Now Natalie was stone-faced, holding out her hand.

'I'd like to have a quick listen, if that's okay.'

It wasn't a question.

I handed over my phone, my movements dull and heavy. Natalie put in the headphones and listened in silence for a few moments. Then:

'Is that it?'

I nodded.

'There was a call. I thought it was the office so I—'

'Four or five comments about the fucking film? For a cover story? Oh fuck. This is a monumental fuck-up. I'm going to have to put in some calls, see if there's any way we can get another shot at this. Maybe squeeze in at the end of the day.'

I looked up at Natalie, full of relief at the lifeline she was throwing me. A second chance. That's all I needed.

'Thanks, Natalie. I promise I won't mess it up this time.'

But Natalie wasn't even looking at me. Her attention was focused behind me, on Edie, the deputy features editor.

'Edie, I want you to spend the rest of the day reading up on everything to do with Ingrid Blackwood, and I want you teed up, ready to go, if we get the nod.'

She turned back to me, her own phone already wedged between her shoulder and her ear.

'Look, Tessa. You ballsed up. There's no other way of

saying it. This interview has taken months to set up and I can't afford to take any more risks. I thought you'd be a safe pair of hands.'

Then she broke off, as whoever she'd called picked up.

'Isabella? It's Natalie Dawson. Look, this is slightly awks, but we've got a bit of a *situation*.'

She turned pointedly away and I slunk out of her office, humiliation blazing on my face.

I sat down at my desk without meeting anyone's eyes. I was still finding it hard to believe what had just happened, how things could have gone so horribly, sickeningly wrong.

28

After the Ingrid Blackwood debacle I debated not going in to finish my stint on *Silk* magazine, but I couldn't risk being labelled unreliable and alienating the few magazine contacts I still had. I felt useless. Worse, I felt I'd let everyone down.

In the end, Edie, the deputy features editor, had done the interview that Ingrid Blackwood's publicist had tacked on to the end of the day as a personal favour to Natalie. She'd turned up at the office the next morning, phone in hand like a conquering hero.

'Didn't you think she was just such a lovely person, though?' she asked me. 'So down to earth. She ended up giving me loads of extra time. We just clicked. Isn't it fab when that happens?'

When I'd left the office on the Friday afternoon, Natalie had called me in.

'Thanks for all your hard work, Tessa,' she'd said, with a smile that stopped somewhere around her cheekbones. 'Now you can go back to semi-retired bliss.'

I'd known then that my days of working in a magazine office were done.

Back home, I'd gone over and over the mystery of the

strange phone call. Someone had known I was going to be at that hotel at that time, but all the people I'd asked – Kath, Mari, Em, Rosie, even Phil – had denied any knowledge of it.

The mad thing was I couldn't shake off the idea that it was Stephens, that he'd somehow found out where I was and staged an emergency call to sabotage my interview.

And yes, I knew I was paranoid. Which wasn't surprising. After his angry *I won't forget* message when he'd been kicked off his football team, I was hardly sleeping at all at night now. Every noise outside, every pipe gurgling, or branch scratching against next door's roof, brought me shooting upright, convinced he was out there, watching me.

Watching Em.

One night I kept hearing footsteps on the roof over my head and leapt to my feet, sure Stephens had somehow managed to scale the drainpipe and was preparing to come down through one of the upstairs windows. I ended up fetching a broom from the kitchen, gaffer-taping my phone to the handle and pressing the video button to record, leaning out of my bedroom window to hold it up to the roof. But when I watched the footage back I could see that a television aerial had fallen over and was hanging down by its cable, rolling to and fro across the slate tiles whenever the wind picked up.

On the Wednesday after my disastrous week at *Silk*, Frances rang. She'd been thinking about me, she said. Wondering how the date with Nick had gone in the end, and how I'd got on at the magazine office.

I was touched by her concern. Despite the busy life she projected on Facebook and Instagram, I had the feeling Frances was lonely. When you got to my age, there was a temptation to attribute to attractive younger people an inbuilt shield of invulnerability. In reality, I was all too aware of the wretchedness of being a carer to someone you loved, watching them grow weaker in front of your eyes. And her best friend moving away must have left a void in her life.

Frances was at work but suggested meeting that evening in the pub where we'd met before. I'd noticed before that she seemed much happier talking in person than over the phone. I knew some people were just like that, preferring to see expressions, and body language, connecting in a visual way that was impossible down a phone line.

'I feel bad keeping you away from your mother,' I told her. 'You know I'm happy to come to you, if that's easier.'

But Frances assured me she was happy for an excuse to be out.

'Mum is going through a really good patch at the moment,' she told me that evening, when we were both settled into a table at the back of the pub. 'Her MS is very up and down. Some days she can't get out of bed unaided, and other days you wouldn't know there was anything wrong with her at all. But she never complains. She has a huge heart.'

'She's like you, then.'

'Hardly.'

'Don't do yourself down. Not many people would have put themselves in danger by helping Em. Look at the ones who drove past without stopping. And you didn't have to keep in touch with her afterwards. Don't shake your head, I know Emma offloads on to you things she believes she can't say to me, and I just want you to know I'm really grateful.'

Frances's eyes got quite shiny then, as if she was fighting back tears.

'Thank you for saying that, Tessa. But you know I just did what anyone would have done. And Emma is such a lovely girl. You're obviously a great mother.'

I frowned.

'I don't think you'd say that if you knew the full story. I've made some huge mistakes with my girls.'

'Yes, but you always loved them. That's the key.' She paused. Then: 'Have you heard about the cloth-monkey experiment?'

I shook my head.

'We learned about it at school in psychology. Basically, this American scientist bred baby monkeys in a lab, taking them away from their mothers when they were tiny. Then he made two surrogate mothers, one out of bare wire and one out of a frame covered with cloth. And the telling thing was that, even though the wire-framed mother was the one holding a bottle with food, it was the soft mother that the monkeys clung to. The need for a mother's comfort is so instinctive, isn't it? So deeply ingrained.' Her amber-flecked eyes gazed into mine so intently I had to look away.

Finally, we got on to the subject that was preoccupying me. I explained what had happened at work. The humiliating interview with Ingrid Blackwood, the mystery phone call that had eaten into my allocated time.

'I know it's crazy, but I keep thinking about the timing of it and wondering if Stephens is mixed up in it all.'

Frances gazed at me levelly and I took a long sip of my sparkling water and tried to loosen the knot of unease that was growing tighter the longer she took to respond.

'Maybe you're not so crazy,' she said eventually. 'Do you know what spyware is, Tessa?'

This, I was not expecting.

'Isn't it some kind of software jealous husbands and wives put on their spouse's computer to keep tabs on them?'

'Exactly. Except you don't have to physically access the computer. You can send some programs remotely via a link in an email. If the other person opens it, *pfff*, you're in.'

'What do you mean, you're in?'

'I mean you can see everything the other person is doing on their computer – what websites they're visiting, what documents they're printing. And, obviously, their emails too.'

I stared at her. What she was talking about was so beyond the realms of my reality. Frances worked in that field – data, computers, tech – so she'd know all about it. But for someone like me, it seemed like a different world.

'But surely that's James Bond stuff.'

'Not at all. It happens all the time. Some unethical businesses even do it to try to track consumer behaviour and then sell the information on to other companies so they can tailor their advertising towards the things people are specifically interested in. Stephens has already managed to send you one email via your website – the photograph of your house. How do you know he hasn't done it again?'

'But I would have seen. I don't get many messages at all via my website, maybe two or three a week. And I haven't had . . . *oh.*'

I stopped short, remembering the message I'd had a couple of weeks before from a journalism undergraduate who'd said how much she enjoyed reading my work and then used the 'I know it's a cheek but would you mind reading this feature I just wrote' line. Normally, I'd have just dashed off a one- or two-line reply explaining I was on a deadline and wishing her the best. But I was curious, and the message had been so complimentary I'd clicked on the attachment and was confused to find some garbled, nonsensical text like you get when your computer can't read that particular format. There was a link there too, which I'd also clicked, thinking it might open up the feature in a different format, but again I hadn't been able to make head nor tail of it. I'd sent a curt email back, telling her to resend in a different format but hadn't heard anything more and had forgotten all about it.

After I related this to Frances, her expression grew serious.

'Sounds like you've been had, Tessa. Look, do you want me to come round and take a look? I'll be able to tell straight away if there's any malware or spyware on there and, if there is, I can clean it up for you.'

I nodded, numbly. It was only slowly dawning on me what this could mean. Stephens had read the emails I'd sent to Natalie at work, and to Ingrid Blackwood's publicist. As well as the ones to Kath and Mari. He knew what a big deal that interview was for me. And he knew where it was and when.

It's no exaggeration to say I felt violated. The thought of his meaty fingers pawing through my innermost thoughts, of him knowing what I was going to do ahead of time, being one step in front of me in my own life. Reading my Twitter posts, my Facebook messages, the silly jokes I sometimes sent to Em in the middle of the day. It was unthinkable.

Frances saw my distress and leaned forward to put a hand on my arm.

'I'm working from home tomorrow. I'll come over in the morning and we'll sort all this out. In the meantime, make a new email account and access it only from your phone or your desktop. Just to be on the safe side. And start keeping a record of everything – times, dates. You'll need it all written down to get the police to take notice.'

I stared at her, open-mouthed.

'I can't go to the police and say, *Oh, by the way, someone rang me at a London hotel and didn't leave a name, but I believe it's actually James Stephens spying on my every move through my computer.* They'll think I'm crazy – well, even crazier than they think I am already.'

'No. But if you start building up a convincing dossier showing every single thing that's happened, it'll get to the point where there's too much evidence to ignore.'

I hadn't seen Frances so animated before. Though she kept her voice steady, a dull pink flush was spreading up her neck from her chest. It struck me then how much it really mattered to her that justice was done, that the right outcome was achieved. Her passion left me feeling shallow by comparison.

'How did you know,' I asked her, as I drained the last of my drink, 'that I'd been working at the magazine?'

'Oh, Em told me.' Frances was already on her feet and gathering her things to leave. 'She's very proud of you.'

On my way home I tried to call Rosie again. We'd taken such a huge step forward by meeting up that time in the café, and then she seemed to have backed away again. I knew I couldn't pressurize her but I was terrified of losing momentum and her slipping away again.

This time she picked up but sounded distracted.

'Sorry, Mum. I'm in a rush.'

'Hot date?'

Even as I said it, my faux-pally tone grated. I wasn't Rosie's pal. I hardly qualified as her mother these days. But Rosie was clearly at that stage of a new relationship where any opportunity to talk about it was not to be missed.

'Maybe. Yes.'

Encouraged, I dared press further.

'So it's going well?'

'Ye–es.'

'Hope you're going to be nicer to this one than you are to most of your admirers.'

It had been a family joke since school days, when the boys who had crushes on my elder daughter were invariably given short shrift, that Rosie was impossibly hard to please when it came to potential suitors. Even the few that made it out on a date were usually 'let go of' within a few weeks, as if they'd run foul of their probationary period. She had high standards for everyone, that was the problem – boyfriends, me, but most of all herself.

'This is completely different.'

'How so?'

'He's nothing like all the others. He's a proper grown-up.'

'Oh. Well, that's great.'

In truth, I was taken aback by the excitement she was unable to disguise in her voice. If things hadn't been so delicate between us, I might have sounded a note of caution. She was still so young, so vulnerable to hurt.

I sent up a silent prayer to this unknown boy. *Please be kind to her.*

Back home, Dotty hurled herself at my legs. She was still subdued after her ordeal, but the cut on her belly was healing. The vet said it probably looked worse than it actually was but he hadn't been able to tell us what might have made it. 'Perhaps she tried to jump over a rusty fence, or lay down on broken glass,' he'd suggested.

'Or someone did it deliberately?' I'd asked.

'That's also possible.'

Giving her a final scratch behind the ears, I went into the kitchen and opened my laptop, acutely conscious of the possibility that Stephens might be shadowing my every move, seeing through my eyes.

The thought took hold of my throat and squeezed.

I switched on to the webcam so that I could watch my parents. If Stephens really was tracking everything I was doing, he'd already have seen them, so I wasn't exposing them to any new danger. And if he was logged on at this moment, I reasoned that watching two elderly people doing nothing would surely bore him into logging off again. Even so, I couldn't help viewing them through a stranger's eyes, which left me feeling both protective and embarrassed.

My mother was in her usual chair, watching *East-Enders* with such rapt attention that the plate of food she had on her knee had slipped, baked beans sliding off on to the floor, forming a lumpy orange puddle on the carpet by her feet.

She'd clearly dressed herself today and was wearing an old grey T-shirt of mine with a faded photograph of Bob Marley on the front that I left at their house to sleep in which she'd teamed with one of her fancier skirts, a knee-length blue velvet number she used to wear to parties.

There weren't any parties these days.

Dad was nowhere to be seen, and I waited with growing anxiety until I heard his voice in the kitchen. 'Have you finished, love?' he asked her, coming to the doorway. I saw he had his insulin pen in his hand, as if in the middle of giving himself his injection.

His face fell as he saw the beans pooling on the carpet next to Mum's feet and pity tugged at the hem of my heart as his features slumped into an expression of sheer exhaustion.

A beeping noise alerted me to a new text message. My laptop was synced with my phone, so I opened up a new window to read the text on screen, keeping one eye on my parents. It was from Rosie, but the brief flare of pleasure from seeing her name was extinguished when I read her message.

OK, *in the interests of full transparency, I might as well tell you b4 Dad does that new man is kind of a rough diamond & was in trouble with law in past. But he's completely different now. Runs own business. Reads Guardian!! So plse DON'T WORRY.*

I sat frowning at the screen as something niggled like incipient toothache at the back of my mind. Something more than worry about what my daughter was getting into.

Almost instantly came a second text. *I really like this one, Mum. FINALLY! So try 2 b happy for me!*

I began typing a reply. *Thanks for letting me know. I really appreciate it.* But now something occurred to me and I broke off as a cold web of dread spun itself around me.

No, I was being ridiculous. Paranoid. I continued typing. *I AM happy if you're happy, darling.*

I clicked send and shut down the window, selecting 'sleep' on the pull-down menu. Then it was just me, looking at my own reflection staring back from the depths of the blank computer screen.

29

I tried to push my suspicions from my mind. But it was no use. The more I thought about it, the more it seemed to make a sickening kind of sense. The timing, the little details.

On impulse, I picked up my phone and shot Rosie another text. *Out of curiosity, what does new man do?* I half expected her not to reply. The truce between us was still tissue-paper fragile. If I pushed too hard, it might tear to shreds. But again I'd underestimated the headiness of those early stages of romance, when it's all you can think or talk about.

Why, you already worrying about his prospects? Haha. Not really sure what Steve does. Nothing creative (sorry 2 disappoint). Some kind of building trade. Anything else? Nearly at pub now 2 meet him. Want me 2 ask him how much he earns & inside leg measurement??

A lump of ice formed in the pit of my stomach. I could no longer ignore the horrible conviction that Rosie's new man was Stephens.

Everything added up. If it really was him, chances were he wouldn't use his real name. But Steve would be an obvious pseudonym to choose. And 'building trade' was vague enough not to identify him but also close enough to the truth that he'd be able to bluff convincingly. She'd said he worked for himself. And God knows he'd definitely been on the wrong side of the law.

Still, I couldn't quite believe it. What Frances had suggested was bad enough, Stephens combing through my private messages. But targeting my daughter, just to get revenge on me? Surely he wouldn't?

Then I thought about the football coach and how his mouth had set into that tight, thin line when he'd heard what Stephens had done, as if he wasn't entirely surprised. I thought about the old lady dwarfed by her doorway and the young girl in the police-station waiting room with the biro'd heart. I remembered those lumps on Emma's scalp. He'd already targeted one daughter. Would he really baulk at targeting another? Did I really think he wouldn't retaliate for everything I'd done?

I called Rosie. The phone rang six times then went to voicemail. I hung up and immediately tried calling her again.

'Pick up,' I said out loud. 'Pick up, pick up, pick up.'

'First sign of madness.'

'What?'

I'd completely forgotten Em was in the house and had half shot out of my chair.

'Talking to yourself. First sign of madness. Who are you so desperate to get hold of, anyway?'

'No one.'

I clicked off my phone quickly.

Em raised her eyebrows and I realized she probably thought there was a new man on the scene.

If only it were that simple.

For a moment, I was tempted to tell Em everything. Worry for Rosie was pressing down on my chest so I could hardly breathe. But how would it help Em to know that her older sister might be out somewhere with the very man who attacked her? I knew my younger daughter's propensity for taking responsibility for things that were way beyond her control. When the World Cup was on, she had to leave the room if a match went to penalties, holding herself somehow accountable for the misery of whichever player failed to score. She would see this as her fault, for bringing Stephens into our lives.

As soon as Em had gone back upstairs I started calling Rosie's number again, but each time the voicemail message snapped on.

Call me, Rosie. As soon as you get this.

Rosie, it's urgent. Please call.

I sent Rosie text after text but didn't get an answer.

In desperation, I called Phil.

'I've got a horrible feeling Rosie's new boyfriend is the same guy who attacked Em.'

'I beg your pardon?'

In my agitation, I couldn't remember how much I'd told Phil of what had been going on. Very little, it turned out. As I hurriedly filled him in, my words coming out in a hot, impatient rush, there was a resolute silence from the other end of the phone. Then:

'Have you any idea how crazy you sound?'

'I know it sounds like the plot of a really bad film, but there are just too many coincidences.'

The ice in my stomach was spreading along my veins, up through my body. Where was Rosie right now? What might he be doing to her?

Another silence. But the next time Phil spoke his voice carried a new note of uncertainty.

'I just don't get any of this, Tessa. How would this man have found Rosie in the first place?'

'She was listed on my Facebook profile. He could have tracked her down through that.'

I didn't add that, if he really did have access to my laptop, as Frances had suggested, Stephens would be able to find out any detail about all my friends and family. I was still trying to prove to Phil that, contrary to what the vindictive anonymous note had alleged, I was a steady, responsible mother. Steady, responsible mothers did not have spyware installed on their computers.

'Bloody hell, Tessa. How can you be so careless about what you give away? Oh, hold on a minute . . .'

'What? What's happening?'

'I think that's her now.'

I heard Phil's voice, muffled, shouting Rosie's name. Then – *oh, the relief!* – the sound of Rosie saying, 'What do you mean, where've I been?'

There were more raised voices, but I couldn't make out the words. Then Phil came back on the phone.

'She's not happy.'

'Put her on the phone. I'll explain.'

A pause. More voices arguing in the background. Then:

'Mum? Just what the *fuck*?'

I was too happy to hear her voice to mind how angry she sounded.

'I'm really sorry, darling, only I have a horrible feeling this guy you're seeing might not be who he says he is.'

'Is this because I'm leaving uni? Because I can tell you

now that has nothing to do with Steve – I made up my mind ages ago.'

'No, it's nothing to do with that.'

'Oh, so it's because he made a couple of mistakes when he was a teenager and he doesn't work in a nice office wearing a nice suit.'

'No, Rosie. I'm not like that.'

'What, then?'

'I think he might be the same man who attacked Emma.'

Stunned silence. Then a snort of laughter.

'I don't believe this, Mum. I really don't believe this.'

'How did you meet him?' I asked her.

'If you must know, I went to see Hamish's band playing at a place in King's Cross and he was there. We got chatting at the bar. It was completely random. He didn't *groom* me, if that's what you're thinking.'

'How many Facebook friends do you have?'

'What?'

'Go on. Five hundred? A thousand?'

'I don't know, somewhere in between.'

'So if someone sends you a friend request, you usually accept.'

'If we've got mutuals, sure. But I don't post private stuff on there. I'm not an idiot.'

'What about events? Did this gig in King's Cross get flagged up as an invitation in your events section? Did you click the box that says "going"?'

'I don't know. Maybe. It's not a crime. Loads of us did.'

'So any one of your friends would have got a notification saying Rosie Hopwood is going to an event in London on this particular date at this particular time?'

Now Rosie had had enough.

'Oh, for God's sake, Mum. Will you listen to yourself? You know, I really missed you over the last six months. But this kind of bullshit is why I had to have a break from you in the first place. Why can't you just accept that none of this is about you – not the guy I'm seeing, nor the attack on Em. I'm really sorry you lost your job, and then Dad pissed off and left you, but you have got to stop trying to create dramas in my and Em's lives just to fill up the empty spaces in your own.'

'Rosie, I—'

But she was gone.

I sat at the table, momentarily skewered by doubt. Might she be right? Was this whole thing an attempt to position myself back at the centre of Rosie's world after all these months of feeling excluded?

For one brief moment I allowed myself to taste the sweet relief of accepting that none of it was real, that everything that had happened since Emma's attack was somehow my doing.

But I knew the truth.

My daughters were in danger.

I watch you.

It's ironic, isn't it, given everything I've done to get as far from you as possible, that I should spend so much of my life checking your movements?

Because I couldn't stand you following me, I've ended up following you.

I watch you on Facebook and Instagram. I track you through LinkedIn. Did you know you accepted my request to join your network? Probably not, as I used neither my real name nor my real picture.

I see who you're connecting with. I see where you go. And because I know you, because I know your little habits and your way of looking at the world, I can read between the lines of the story you tell in public.

I watch you to keep us safe, my boy and me.

Tonight I have my laptop open in front of me and I have half an eye on the television screen on which is playing an episode of a Netflix series about a man who is on trial for murdering his wife. It is a real case and I watch it despite myself, despite knowing that true crime is the last thing I need in my life. Bodies at the bottom of stairs. Questions of motive, of opportunity. Of guilt.

How well do we ever really know anyone else? When they visit the pathologist on screen, it's Matt's body I see there under the sheet.

Yet I can't switch it off. The need to see justice done burns a hole in my brain.

At the same time, I am scrolling down your Instagram feed. Looking at the photos you have chosen to show to the world, the face you are presenting.

There is a photograph of you in a pub. Or it could be someone's house.

You are smiling, looking up at the camera.

I double-click on the picture and enlarge it until your face takes over the entire screen, and then I keep enlarging until you disappear altogether into a blur of pixels.

30

By the next morning, I was calmer. I'd seen from Face-book that Stephens was DJ'ing at a club in Coventry that night, so I figured Rosie was safe from him at least for today.

Frances arrived after breakfast, bringing with her a smell of Acqua di Parma and a bag of fresh croissants from the artisan bakery in Muswell Hill. In all the furore over Rosie and Stephens I'd forgotten the arrangement we'd made for her to come over to check out my laptop and was momentarily taken aback to see her on the doorstep.

I told her about Rosie's new man, hoping she'd dismiss my suspicions like Rosie had done, but instead her expression turned serious.

'If you're right, this isn't just abstract words on the internet any more, Tess. He's invaded your actual life, involving your kids. You should go to the police, get Rosie to—'

'I can't involve Rosie.'

'But she could—'

'Can we please drop the subject?'

It came out harsher than I'd intended and Frances's cheeks flushed pink.

'Of course. Sorry.'

While Frances got to work on the computer, I went to sit outside in the garden. It wasn't really warm enough, but the sun was out, and I felt I needed to be on my own for a minute or two. It had been another night when sleep taunted me from the end of the bed, always out of reach, and now I felt wrung out and bone weary. I heard my neighbours two gardens along chatting quietly to each other in Greek and a woman singing through the open upstairs window of the house backing on to ours, and I envied them their nice, normal lives.

Frances appeared in the doorway. 'Sorry to tell you, I did find evidence of spyware installed on your laptop. I can't be sure how much he had access to but I'm afraid you should probably assume he's seen everything that's on there.'

'Everything?'

I felt light-headed with disbelief. I thought of the emails to Nick, of my parents shuffling around their living room in Oxford, of all the things that related to the girls. I had photocopies of both their passports stored on my desktop. Might he be able to do something with those? The thought brought on a rush of nausea.

'I've gone through and cleaned up what I can and installed a spyware protection program to detect any suspicious activity and get rid of it. But I'll need to take your phone, too, I'm afraid.'

'My phone?'

'To see if that's been breached as well.'

'You mean he could have been listening to my conversations?'

Frances scrunched up her face in sympathy and nodded.

I handed over my phone and my passcode, feeling once again sick and violated.

Frances seemed to understand how I felt and didn't try to give me false reassurances, for which I was grateful.

'I'll be as quick as I can,' she said, disappearing back into the house.

When she emerged some forty minutes later, she was smiling.

'Good news, your phone is fine,' she said.

I was suffused with relief. It was horrific enough knowing Stephens had been in my computer, but for some reason my phone felt so much more personal.

Frances seemed nervous. Tentative. I was filled with remorse for having been so tetchy.

'Thanks, Frances. You've been really kind. Listen, I'm sorry I was so short earlier. The pressure of this whole situation—'

'You don't need to explain. I understand. I really do.'

Acting on impulse, I asked Frances if she'd like to come for a walk with me and Dotty. The dog had been curled up in her basket since Frances arrived and seemed generally out of sorts, but she recovered once she saw her lead in my hand. As Frances had the car, we could drive up to Highgate Woods, which boasted a café in the middle, where I offered to buy us both brunch as a thank-you for all her technical help.

Frances drove the ten minutes to the woods, which

were, anyway, practically on her way home. You can tell a lot by the way someone drives, I always think, and Frances was calm and confident, considerate but also assertive, pushing out into a gap in the traffic when we were turning right on to the main road, ignoring the furiously tutting woman in the SUV who'd had to brake to let us through.

The woods were glorious in the spring sunshine, full of dappled shadows and lush green leaves and odd clear pockets where golden light pooled on the grass and the ridged mud.

'You're so lucky, Tessa,' said Frances, bending to pick up a stick to throw for Dotty, who retrieved it then brought it straight back to me. 'You have so much love around you.'

I stopped still then, too surprised to carry on. Since Phil had moved out, it had seemed to me that the idea I'd long held in my heart of our tight, loving family had been exposed as being as hollow and as easily shattered as a Christmas bauble. So to hear Frances talk about love in the context of me and my life took my breath away.

And yet, might she have a point?

True, I didn't have the life I had expected. I'd had to say goodbye to the career I'd spent thirty years building, the home I'd thought I'd grow old in, but I had my daughters – well, I would have, once I'd made peace with Rosie. I had my friends. Even Phil was still around, though admittedly not quite in the capacity I'd thought he'd be.

'But you have love, too, Frances, don't you?' I asked her. 'Your mum sounds wonderful.'

'Oh yes, she is. I know I'm lucky too. It's just that it's only the two of us, really. Friends and boyfriends have had to take a back seat over the years. It was different when Claudia was still here. She lived in the flat downstairs. But she moved away and now life can be quite lonely.'

It was what I'd suspected, and I was touched that she'd entrusted me with the truth. We walked on in silence for a while, the only noise the birds tweeting in the trees overhead and the distant shouts of the children that carried on the breeze from the playground on the other side of the woods.

'Tessa, you can tell me to mind my own business if you like, but what happened between you and Rosie? I can see you adore each other, but I also sense there's been some sort of a rift.'

My first instinct was to deny it or tell her to mind her own business, but then I stopped myself. I'd spent the last few months in denial, and look where it had got me. My daughter in danger, and me unable to reach her.

I took a deep breath.

'I don't normally talk about it.'

'Oh goodness.' The sweet, old-fashioned exclamation left me unexpectedly moved. 'If it's painful, please don't say any more. I'd never have asked if I thought it would upset you.'

'I'm not upset, I'm ashamed.'

Frances glanced over and I was glad we were walking side by side so I didn't have to meet her eyes. I felt hot and sticky suddenly, way more than the April weather warranted.

'After Phil left, the girls missed him more than I can

say. I could see how upset they were, and how hard they were trying not to show it, out of concern for me. And that just made me feel worse, the idea that my children were worrying about me when they ought to be grieving for themselves and what they'd lost. And I suppose I over-compensated. I took them out all the time, though God knows I shouldn't have been spending money at that point. I was constantly waking them up in the mornings with stupid, bright suggestions. "Let's go to Brighton for the weekend." "Who fancies a day in town, shopping, then lunch?" "Shall we move all the furniture round and repaint your rooms?"'

I glanced at Frances, who had a strange, faraway look on her face.

'You're a good mum, Tessa,' she said.

I shook my head.

'Not really. I was all over the place emotionally. Bursting into tears for no reason, drinking more than I should. Playing Coldplay at full volume.'

It was meant as a joke, but Frances didn't crack a smile.

'What I'm trying to say is I wasn't consistent. At a time when they probably needed consistency more than anything. I was too desperate to please. We'd just moved to the Bounds Green house and I knew the girls were upset at moving away from all their friends. Oh, I know it's not far, but they'd been so used to being able to walk round to call on their mates and now they had to negoti-ate night buses and make advance arrangements. They both had important exams and I was so worried about how all the upheaval would affect them.

'Then, on top of that, I was still reeling from Phil

moving in with Joy, just a couple of roads away from our old home. I got it into my head that the girls would decide to go to live with him because he had the big house back in the same place where all their friends were. And it just poleaxed me, you know. The thought that I could lose everything.'

We had arrived by this time at the clearing in the middle of the woods where the café was. Dogs weren't allowed into the garden area, so I tied Dotty to the fence just by the gate, where there was water and shade, well away from a Great Dane dozing on its side, and nabbed a table nearby where we'd be able to see her. I wasn't taking any more chances.

I left Frances sitting outside with strict instructions not to take her eyes off the dog while I went in to order our food.

When I returned to the table I was half hoping she might have forgotten what we were talking about so I wouldn't have to continue, but she fixed her warm brown eyes on me expectantly.

'You were saying, Tessa?'

I sat down heavily, weighted by my own sinking heart.

'It was a Friday night in the September after we moved, not long before Rosie was due to go to Manchester to start uni. Both girls were out. Em was with Phil. Rosie had chosen to go out with her friends instead of seeing him.'

I didn't tell Frances how I'd been quietly smug about Rosie's decision or about how I'd turned down the chance to go out with Kath and Mari so I could stay home and play the martyr, hoping to win points with my girls by being the perfect mother in contrast to their home-breaker dad.

Sometimes, now, when I look back at the way I behaved, I can't blame Phil for leaving.

I explained to Frances how I'd stayed home to watch something on Netflix and treated myself to a bottle of wine and a pizza. Rosie rang about eleven thirty. She and her friends had gone to a party in Stoke Newington which turned out to be really boring and needed a lift home. Two of them had Uber accounts but one was overdrawn and another didn't want to be the last in the cab on her own. It was raining and horrible out, and they just wanted to get back. "Please, can you pick us up, Mum?"

'I know I should have just said no, but I hadn't drunk *that* much,' I said now. 'Just three or four glasses. And it wasn't far. I knew the route like the back of my hand.'

Frances paused, fork in hand.

'Plus, you wanted to make her happy.'

'Exactly. Which is ironic, given what happened.'

Frances waited expectantly. I took a deep breath.

'I picked them up. Rosie and two of her friends, Kaz and India. I'd known them since they were all small. I knew India's parents, Anna and Joe Cunningham, a little bit, socially. The girls were on good form, glad to be escaping from the boring party, full of excitement about starting their new university lives. I was just so pleased to feel useful, and to listen to them chatting about the evening and who had had too much to drink and who had copped off with whom. Glad that they felt comfortable enough with me to be able to do that.

'We drove back up Green Lanes. Rosie was in the front seat, the other two behind. It was raining really heavily, so I had my wipers on full, which made it hard to see properly. We got to the junction by Wood Green station just as the lights ahead turned orange. I didn't feel drunk. You have to know that. Or I'd never—'

Frances nodded, but stayed quiet.

Shame beaded on my skin like sweat, and I felt unbearably hot, despite the cold breeze.

'I wasn't speeding, but the rain made the road slippery so I made a split-second decision.'

'Not to stop.'

I nodded, unable to meet her eyes.

'But I misjudged the timing and by the time I went through the lights were red. And, just our luck, the driver at the head of the queue of traffic coming from the right was in a tearing hurry and anticipated the lights.'

I remembered the terrible noise of metal crunching and the loud thud of something hitting the back of the driver's seat.

'It took me a few seconds to realize that noise was India, who hadn't had her seat belt on. She'd been flung forwards by the impact and had landed half on, half off the back seat with her arm bent behind her. There was blood coming from her head and she wasn't moving.' My voice tailed off to a whisper. 'I thought she was dead.'

'And the others?'

Frances was leaning forwards over the table, her food quite forgotten.

'The man in the other car hit his head and was taken to the hospital, but he was okay, thank God. And the other girls just had cuts and bruises, like me. But they were in shock. Kaz was screaming, "Oh my God, oh my

278

God, oh my God," over and over. It was the worst thing, you know, the very worst. Sometimes, even now, if I close my eyes, I can still hear her. Rosie was deathly pale. She had her hand over her mouth. I reached for her, but she shrank back as if I was going to attack her. I asked her if she was okay, but she was just staring at India and then she looked at me, and said, "What have you done, Mum?"

'And then the police were there – the policewoman who'd recognized me at Em's ID parade – and the ambulance, and I was being breathalysed and I knew before they even said anything that it was going to be bad. And I was taken away, and still Rosie wouldn't even look at me.'

'And was she dead? India?'

The question was so shocking, I blinked, momentarily disoriented.

'No. I mean, thank God. She had concussion and a broken arm.'

'But she was okay.'

Frances had relaxed again, gone back to her food, and I felt strangely deflated. True, nobody died, thank God, but this was still the worst thing that had happened to me in my life.

'It was a bad break on her right arm. So it was a big setback. She ended up deferring her university place until the following September. I was prosecuted and fined and banned from driving for a year.'

I didn't tell Frances about the savage jolt of pleasure I'd felt after the conviction, how I'd welcomed the punishment, wished only that it had been harsher.

'And Rosie wouldn't speak to you afterwards.'

'Only through Phil. She said she felt ashamed and

embarrassed in front of her friends and their parents. She felt that I couldn't love her if I was willing to risk her life and her friends' lives.'

'Teenagers can be quite sanctimonious.'

'Yes, but she was right. I deserved it. And more. She started uni not long after the accident and spent most of the Christmas holidays in Italy at the home of one of her new uni friends, so this is the first chance I've had to make amends. And now I wonder if I've just made everything worse.'

I glanced over to check on Dotty, as I had done periodically throughout this difficult conversation, reassured to see her familiar black-and-white shape through the fence of the café, although she was sitting in an odd position, pressed up against the wood. There was a woman standing next to her, tall and upright with strong features and a mouth set into a line, who seemed to be staring at us quite intently over the top of the fence. She was wearing an orange silk scarf looped around her neck.

'Do you know that woman?' I asked Frances.

'Which woman?'

Frances looked around blankly.

'The one over . . . oh, never mind.'

The woman had disappeared.

'Now I can see why you're so protective of Em,' said Frances. 'But you know, Tessa, what's done is done. You can't go on punishing yourself for ever. And going after Stephens won't make your daughters forget about the car accident. The two things won't cancel each other out.'

She was right. I knew she was. On some level, I'd allowed myself to see this thing with Stephens as a chance to make amends and prove myself worthy as a mother. Wipe the slate clean. Ridiculous, when I looked at it like that.

Still, now it had gone this far, and Rosie might be involved, I couldn't back out.

Back home, I sat at the kitchen table and called up Facebook Messenger.

Please, I wrote to Stephens. *Please don't hurt my daughter.*

I hated begging, but if it made him think twice about involving Rosie in all this, then I didn't care. Hell, I'd prostrate myself at his feet to protect my daughters. A part of me almost welcomed the idea of that kind of abasement. At least then I'd be doing something. It was this passive limbo that was so impossible to deal with.

From nowhere, I heard Phil's voice in my ear: *This isn't about you galloping in to save the day. In actual fact, it isn't about you at all.*

After that I sat motionless for half an hour or more, waiting for a reply that never came.

31

The night after my conversation in the woods with Frances, I lay awake for hours. I'd bottled my shame up inside me for so long that, now it had finally been released, it felt like it had burned a channel through me on its way out, leaving behind a trail of singed and painful tissue.

Whenever I closed my eyes, I saw India in the back of my car, blood matting in her blonde hair from a gash in her head, arm bent at a ghastly angle behind her, unmoving. I heard Kaz screaming, 'Oh my God, oh my God!' And worst of all, Rosie's ashen, terrified face: 'What have you done, Mum?'

So when I got up the following morning I was like a ghost person, my body functioning with negligible input from my brain. I felt hollowed out, as if someone had scooped out the contents of my head with an ice-cream spoon.

The only thing I could think about was Rosie. She still wasn't answering my calls, so in desperation I called Phil.

'She's fine,' he said coolly. 'She's upstairs in her room.'

Stupid how much it still hurt that my daughter had a room in a house that wasn't mine.

'Well, can you ask her to call me?'

'Tessa, this is between you and Rosie. I'm not getting involved.'

In the end I sent a text.

Please look at this photograph and tell me if it's your new man. This 'Steve'. Then I cut and pasted a link to Stephens's Facebook page.

It wasn't ideal. I'd wanted to be there with her when she saw the picture, so I could give her support if she needed it. I knew she'd fallen hard for this new man, and I also knew what it took for my eldest daughter to make herself so vulnerable, how deep the hurt would go.

There was no reply. I waited five minutes. Ten.

I tried to do some work. After the disastrous interview for *Silk* I knew I was unlikely to get more work from them, and the last of my redundancy money had now gone.

A newspaper had commissioned an idea I'd suggested, inspired by Dotty's disappearance, on the emotional toll of pet-owning, but I was finding it hard to concentrate for long enough to come up with a decent opening. Finally, I got started, and was just getting into a rhythm when the doorbell shattered my focus.

From the silhouette through the frosted diamond-shaped glass panel of the hideous front door, I could see it was a woman, dressed in dark clothes. Irritation bubbled up inside me. We got a lot of God Squad callers, standing on my doorstep thinking it was perfectly acceptable to interrupt whatever I was doing in order to ask the kind of personal questions you wouldn't dream of asking even members of your own family. Are you afraid of death? What do you believe in?

So *invasive*.

I flung open the door in an accusatory way.

'Oh. It's you.'

Joy stood on the doorstep, wearing a fitted jacket in the softest black leather and a pair of black trousers with high-heeled boots in a buttery suede. Her ash-blonde hair was twisted up so that the ends tumbled adorably over the clip, the front section falling just so over her face.

The woman my husband left me for.

'I'm sorry to intrude like this, Tessa. I know I probably should have called you first, but I knew you wouldn't want to see me.'

The nerve of her.

'Absolutely right, I wouldn't. And if you don't mind, I'm busy trying to earn a living. I don't know if you've heard, but my husband left me, so money is quite tight.'

'Look, I don't blame you for being antagonistic, Tessa, though I had hoped it might be easier after so long.'

Her voice was lower than I'd imagined. But then I'd only ever heard it one time. Screaming at me, 'Once and for all, can you just leave us alone!'

It's ironic, because I hadn't even been doing anything that time, just walking past. It was just the final straw that broke the camel's back, after all the phone calls, and the letters that used to pour out of me in the middle of another sleepless night which I'd stuff through their letterbox, a coat pulled on over my pyjamas.

I have no excuses, really. Except that it just seemed like the end of everything. I felt as if my life was imploding, like one of those black holes that swallow themselves up, folding in on themselves until they don't exist.

It wasn't Phil I was so scared of losing. It was me.

Now, when I think back to the woman I was then, I don't recognize her.

'I'm here about Rosie,' said Joy, and I felt a quickening of my heart, remembering the link I'd sent and thinking how badly Rosie must have taken it to have sent Joy here on her behalf.

I stood back to let Joy inside, wishing that Dotty wouldn't give her quite such an ecstatic welcome and feeling childishly pleased when I saw strands of white fur clinging to her expensive-looking trousers.

I took her into the living room, reluctant for her to see the kitchen which I considered the heart of the house, where Em's exam schedule and various family photos were stuck to the fridge.

She didn't have the right to see who I was when I was most myself.

Joy glanced at the dark grey sofa with its dusting of dog hairs before opting for the leather armchair instead. She was so perfectly put together. Her figure neat and firm – well, she did meet my husband in the gym, after all.

Up close, she wasn't exactly pretty – her features were too heavy for that. But she was what would once have been called handsome. Her make-up was that understated, 'natural' look that I knew took hundreds of pounds' worth of cosmetics to achieve. Her nails were neatly manicured. I was momentarily thrown by the long scratch on the back of her right hand before remembering that she ran an upmarket florist's.

I sat down opposite her on the sofa, trying not to mind my toothpaste-spattered sweatpants and ancient jumper. At least I wasn't wearing one of Phil's old T-shirts he'd left behind. He'd told me to bin them but I hadn't got around to it and occasionally threw one on. Just for old times' sake.

Worry for Rosie wound itself around my heart but I forced myself to remain silent. Let Joy be the one to speak first. I imagined Rosie had sent her to fetch me, as I no longer had a car. And I'm not proud to admit that there was a part of me that relished the idea of the woman who'd replaced me having to ask for my help, forced to acknowledge that when Rosie was at her neediest it was her mother she turned to.

'Look, Tessa, I know we got off to a rocky start, which is probably only to be expected, given the circumstances. But I want you to know I love Rosie and Emma very much. They're very special girls. And I want the best for them, just as you do. Isn't it time we put aside our differences and worked together, for their sakes?'

Joy was sitting in the chair, her long legs together and sort of folded to the side, like Princess Diana, I swear to God.

I focused on her legs and the way she was sitting and how I'd read somewhere that the royals sat like that so that there was no chance of an intrusive camera lens capturing more than it should, because I didn't want to hear what Joy had to say and be forced to agree with her. Not on anything.

Her expectant smile dimmed as my silence stretched on.

'It's not the same man,' she said suddenly.

Now, I looked up.

'The link you sent. The DJ. That's not Rosie's new boyfriend. In fact, she couldn't believe you'd imagine he'd be her type. She's actually pretty upset about it.'

'But—'

Whatever I was about to say was washed away by a wave of conflicting emotions. Relief that Rosie wasn't, after all, mixed up with Stephens combined with anguish at how far this would set back our tentative rapprochement and, underneath it all, the thin whine of panic about what it meant that I'd made such a colossal misjudgement.

I stood up.

'I'll go to her now.'

'No, Tessa, I'm afraid you can't.'

The fury I'd been keeping at bay swept over me like a rash.

'You don't intimidate me, Joy. Rosie needs me.'

Still, Joy remained seated.

'I'm really sorry, Tessa, but Rosie doesn't want to see you right at the moment. She says she wants a break from the drama.'

I took a step back.

'Drama? But that's ridiculous. Everything I've done for the last two decades has been about creating a calm, happy life for my children. Everything.'

'Well, don't forget you had a career as well. It wasn't only about the children.'

'Don't you dare judge me for that. You, of all people.'

Joy held up her hands in surrender.

'I'm not judging. Not at all. I admire you for the way you managed to carve out a name for yourself at work and bring up a family at the same time. It's not easy. I didn't go back to work until the twins were in secondary school – I couldn't have managed, so I take my hat off to you. Genuinely. All I'm saying is that your job must have been very exciting, a real adrenaline rush, and since you haven't been working—'

'I'm what? Creating drama purposely by pissing off my own kids?'

Was I so angry because I could hear the echo of that school mums' WhatsApp conversation? *Sometimes I think Tessa thrives on the drama.* Who'd said that? Mel? Ayesha?

'No, not at all. Look, I'm not expressing myself very well. I'm just saying there was bound to be a period of *readjustment* after you left work, where things might not have gone completely to plan.'

'And do you think maybe my husband having an affair and walking out on me might have made that *readjustment* just a tiny bit harder?'

Joy sighed. Close up, her face looked a lot older than it had appeared all those times I'd watched her from across the street, with a latticework of fine lines fanning out from her eyes and upper lip.

Phil must really love her. The thought arrived with a painful jolt. Up until now, I'd convinced myself, in some deep part of me, that it was her physical attractions that had drawn him in and that once he got used to those, or they lost their appeal, he'd grow bored and regret the choices he'd made.

But now I could see that she was just ordinary. Like me. Sure, she made the very best of herself, but underneath the perfect make-up and the gym-toned skin she was just another middle-aged woman with black shadows on the inside corners of her eyes muddling through, as we all were.

I felt something shift inside my head, a realigning of the tectonic plates of my hostility and sense of betrayal. There was a gap created after they'd moved that I probed carefully, as with a missing tooth, finding there, in place of the hatred, a curious indifference that felt almost like peace.

'Rosie will come around in time,' Joy said wearily but not unkindly. 'She's a strong character. Just like her mother, I suspect. But this is her first experience of being in love and she just wants everything to be perfect. Give her some space. She loves you an awful lot.'

I don't know if it was the generosity of that last sentence, or that gentle, unexpectedly James Stewart-esque adjective 'awful', or just the fact that someone, anyone, was offering me some comfort, telling me it would be all right, or just the bloody hormones again, but I found myself suddenly weeping.

'I just want to turn back time, you know?' I said between sobs. 'Just wrench back the fucking clock. Why can't I do that? Why?'

I knew on some level, even then, that I would regret this the next day. Falling apart in front of Joy, of all people. But now I'd abandoned myself to it there was no way to stop, like sliding down a sandbank, the only option to close my eyes and just give myself over to falling. If Joy had come closer, or made some attempt to comfort me, humiliation would have cracked me clean in two like a coconut, but to her credit she stayed calmly on her side of the coffee table while I grieved for a life I hadn't realized I wanted until after I'd let it go.

I am in a soft-play centre called World of Fun. It is hell on earth.

I sit at a table that is bolted to the floor and sip vending-machine coffee that tastes like hot and nothing else. But Henry is loving it, and every time I look at his face, shiny with excitement, with those two perfect circles of pink in his cheeks like a storybook child, I know that I would do this a hundred days in a row, two hundred, just to see him so happy.

I have my phone out and I am scrolling through social media. I have developed a habit now. First, I go through my own pages. And then yours.

I do Twitter first. You have retweeted a couple of things. A clip of a comedian I've never heard of, a joke about Brexit.

Then I go on to Instagram. And my heart stops.

There is a photograph of Matt. My Matt. He is wearing a T-shirt we bought together on our honeymoon in New York. It was the happiest I'd ever been in my life. I'd waited so long to be with the love of my life. But he was so worth it. In the picture he is smiling in that half-dreamy Matt way, his lips full under a two- or three-week

*black beard. I hated that beard. But God, I loved that
mouth.*

Underneath the picture you have written: Thinking of
my mate Matt – kind, funny, great listener, terrible cook.
Nearly a year since we lost him and I still think of him
every day. Please, guys, talk about how you're feeling.
Don't bottle it up. #Samaritans #SuicidePreventionLine
#BetterOutThanIn #MissYouMatt

*For a moment I think I will vomit. Right here on this
plastic, wood-effect table. With the air ringing with the
screams of excited children.*

*Your photo has twenty-seven likes, and three com-
ments.* Dude, I know this particular pain well. You're
not alone, *reads the last one.*

*Matt continues to smile out at me from my phone
screen. I see the scar on the bridge of his nose from a
long-ago motorbike crash, and the chickenpox dent
above his left eyebrow. I remember how it felt those
weeks before he died when he stopped smiling at me.
When there were only pleas and anger and accusations
and more pleas. He'd aged ten years in just a couple of
months, looking nothing like this relaxed, smiling Matt
in the photo.*

*'Mummy, watch me!' commands Henry, standing
feet apart on a yellow padded plastic platform, looking,
in his Superman outfit, like he has just conquered a
mountain rather than climbed a three-foot-high red
nylon net.*

*So I do. I watch my boy. But I am thinking about
you. I am thinking about the message you are sending
me. That it is not over. It will never be over.*

32

Three days after Joy's visit I was still cringing whenever I remembered how I'd broken down in front of my husband's girlfriend. Over the previous two days I'd cycled from anger with her for putting me in a position where I'd wound up indebted to her, to anger with myself for being so weak and then gratitude to her for being so tactful.

Now, I felt strangely empty and realized it was due to the space at my core where my animosity towards Joy had once lived. Its loss left me feeling lighter, but unmoored, as if the slightest gust of wind could blow me away.

The day after seeing Joy, I'd been racked with self-doubt, going over and over what had happened, wondering how I'd been so terribly wrong about Stephens and Rosie. Paranoia had made me jump to conclusions that seemed preposterous now I was able to think them through rationally. Stephens was about to have a baby. Would he really go to the lengths of seducing a young girl, just to get back at her mother? Plus, the timings were all out. I could see now that Stephens would have had to have planned to target Rosie from the second he found out about her. None of it made sense. And yet I'd been so quick to believe it.

What else might I have talked myself into?

But as the weekend had gone on I'd started to feel better. Even though Rosie still wasn't returning my calls, I knew she was safe. And that was the main thing.

By the Monday, I'd resolved to make a new start. I'd invited Nita over for a drink and a chat that evening. Since I'd told Frances the story of my crash with Rosie and her friends, it felt as if someone had pulled out the plug of shame that had been blocking up my throat and kept me from communicating with the school-mum network. I hadn't forgotten what I'd read on that WhatsApp chat, but some of Rosie's friends' mothers had been my bedrock through the long, fraught years of the girls' early childhoods. I'd frozen them out since the accident, out of shame. Now, belatedly, I wanted to seek them out to apologize and explain, and I needed Nita's help to do it.

I cleaned the house, realizing as I started just how long it had been since I last did it properly – when Frances came round on the day of the ID parade, maybe. There were balls of Dotty's fur collected in corners and I found a couple of rogue kernels of popcorn under the coffee table. I scanned the CD rack and found a CD of Oasis that I hadn't played in years and blasted it out while I ran Henry the Hoover around and Dotty hid behind furniture, the better to launch attacks on this age-old enemy.

When this album was first in the charts, Phil and I had just moved in together – weekends where we wouldn't get dressed from Friday night to Monday morning.

Enough. Enough. Enough.

I sang over the sound of the vacuum cleaner, the lyrics

magically coming back to me through the lost years. Everything felt lighter, better, now I was free of the iron ball of resentment that had chained itself around my ankle ever since I first found out about Joy.

I called Nick on impulse.

'Want to meet for lunch?'

Less than an hour later we were perched side by side on stools, looking out of the window of a tiny coffee shop in Lamb's Conduit Street, ten minutes' walk from the university where Nick had lectured for the last twenty-two years.

'At least tenure lasts longer than marriage,' I joked.

His face froze.

'You wouldn't laugh if you knew how hard I tried to make my marriage work,' he said coolly. 'I loved my stepson so much. I'd have done anything to spare him from being hurt. After my divorce, I felt like such a failure.'

I'd upset him. I was such an idiot.

'I know what you mean. I'm so sorry. I didn't mean to make light of it.'

To my relief, he smiled and reached out to take my hand.

'No, I'm sorry. For being a cantankerous old git.'

The nerve endings in my fingers tingled where they touched his.

'What happened with your ex?' I asked, emboldened by the gesture of intimacy.

Nick shrugged. 'Out of the blue, she announced she wasn't happy. Said she was going to take her boy to stay with her mum for a while as she needed space. Omitted to mention that she'd been screwing her ex-husband – one of my old friends, to add insult to injury – for the last six months. He was the love of her life, apparently. Sorry.' He squeezed my hand. 'Nothing less attractive than a bitter middle-aged man wanging on about his divorce.'

Nick was supposed to leave after forty-five minutes but in the end it was well over an hour before he reluctantly rose to meet with a first-year undergraduate who had plagiarized his mid-term paper in its entirety from an online essay-mill site.

'I honestly think they consider us to be such old crocks we don't know how to check the internet,' he said.

I put on a puzzled face.

'What is this internet of which you speak?'

When I made my way home again I felt as if my very bones were glowing.

It was going to be all right. From now on, things would be okay again.

Em came home from school and surveyed the newly mopped kitchen floor, the sofa with the plumped cushions.

'Are you feeling well?'

'Yes, why?'

'All this housework. I thought you must be having a funny turn.'

'Very droll.'

I looked at Em fondly and she smiled, and for a minute or two it was just normal, a mother and daughter sharing a joke at the end of a school day. Then:

'Oh, by the way, Frances is coming over in a bit. You don't mind, do you?'

I was taken aback by the twinge of annoyance that shot through me at the news. Not that I had anything against Frances. How could I, when she'd been so helpful? And of course, we owed her so much. It was just that I'd temporarily allowed myself to forget everything that had been going on, to feel as if I'd turned a corner. But Frances would bring it all with her. Treading Stephens into my freshly mopped floors and my newly vacuumed carpets.

'No, of course not. She's not staying long, though, is she? Only Nita's coming over later . . .'

'A quick catch-up, she said.'

It was sweet, really, I told myself as I took Dotty out for her evening walk. Nice for Emma to have someone else to confide in who wasn't family.

But still, I wished she'd picked some other night.

Frances had already arrived by the time we got back and was sitting with Emma at the kitchen table, the two of them talking in low voices, their heads close together. She had her hair up in a round, shiny brown knot like a large conker. She looked up and smiled, the gap between her front teeth coming as a surprise, as it always did.

'Tessa. So good to see you.'

I became aware of a pressure on my leg. Dotty pressing herself against my calf. Since she came home from wherever she'd been, her moods were unpredictable. Could dogs get PTSD? I wondered.

We sat and chatted for a while, but I was conscious that Nita was coming over soon and I wanted to finish getting the house in shape. I was very fond of Nita, but it wasn't the same as with Kath or Mari, where I knew they accepted me exactly the way I was. With Nita there was a conditionality. Not that I felt she'd judge me or I wanted to impress her, but it felt important that she should know I was capable. Respectable, if you like. It was like that with people you met through your kids, that sense of responsibility to present yourself in the best light, not to let the side down.

But that was okay. Some friendships just asked more of you than others.

'Have you got any work you should be doing?' I asked Em, smiling to show I wasn't nagging.

'Not really. Well, I guess I have got an English assignment due tomorrow, but . . .'

Em tailed off, embarrassed. I knew she'd hate to make Frances feel uncomfortable.

'Please get on with whatever you need to do,' said Frances. 'Don't feel you have to stay down here because of me. I've got to leave soon anyway.'

'If you're sure,' said Em, standing uncertainly by the door.

'Go on,' said Frances. 'And remember, any time you need anything, someone to talk to, I'm just on the end of the phone.'

She can talk to me.

At least I didn't voice the petty thought out loud.

When Emma left I expected Frances to go too, but instead she settled back in her seat.

'And how are you feeling now, Tessa?'

I stifled the urge to glance at the kitchen clock.

'Oh, fine. Well, good, actually. Rosie's still mad at me, but she'll come around. Stephens has been really quiet. You know, I don't want to tempt fate, but I feel like this whole thing might finally be over.'

Frances bit her lip, and when she looked up there was an expression of concern in her eyes that her weak smile couldn't disguise.

'I hope you're right, Tessa. But I'm still worried he's planning some kind of retribution for you getting him thrown off the football team. Men like him don't tend to let things like that go. And even if he isn't, it doesn't alter the fact that he's right here. Just a few streets away from you, from Emma. Can you ever really feel secure?'

A drawstring was pulled tight across my chest when she said that, but I tried to smile.

'I just have to put it out of my head. I mean, when you think about it, there's no tangible difference now from when this whole thing started. We always knew it was a good bet that the man who assaulted Em would turn out to be local. We had a chance to stop him with the ID parade but after that failed we just had to accept there was nothing more we could do. Which is exactly the position we're back in now.'

I didn't bring up the failed ID parade to score a point. Honestly. But I could see it had stung.

'Obviously, you have to do what's best for you.'

'That's just it. This is what's best for me. I feel normal again, Frances, for the first time in weeks. I feel . . .'

I was interrupted by the arrival of Nita, who swept in holding a big bunch of tulips and a bottle of wine.

'Oh,' she said, stopping short in surprise at seeing Frances. 'I didn't know we would have company. How lovely. We met before, didn't we? Up at the Palace?'

Again, I hoped Frances would take this as her prompt to leave. I wanted some one-on-one time with Nita.

Frances, however, showed no signs of moving and

happily accepted a glass of wine, despite what she'd said before about not drinking during the week. I didn't, although I was sorely tempted. Not drinking was part of my private penance to Rosie and her friends. It wouldn't be for ever, just until I forgave myself a little more. The conversation around the table was pleasant but stilted, never really dipping beneath the surface. I didn't want to talk to Nita about what had been going on with Stephens. I needed her to feed back to the others that I was doing well. Stable. So I was on tenterhooks in case Frances gave something away.

Forty-five minutes passed. An hour.

Nita asked me about Nick, and I felt weirdly self-conscious, remembering how Frances had thought he might not actually be real.

'Things are going well, believe it or not,' I said now, shy as a teenager. But still there was a twinge of pleasure at having proved Frances wrong.

'It's so exciting,' Nita declared. 'I adore a good love story, don't you, Frances?'

Frances smiled tightly. 'A bit early to call it love, don't you think?' she said.

I felt oddly embarrassed then, as if I'd allowed my emotions to run away with me.

'You're right,' I said. 'It's early days and I'm certainly not taking anything for granted. It's not even two years since I split up with Phil and I'm still not sure I'm completely over it. To be honest, I wonder if you ever do really get over something like that.'

Finally, Frances looked up at the clock.

'Oh, crikey,' she said, rising to her feet. 'I should be getting back. Can I give you a lift home, Nita?'

Nita looked taken aback.

'No, you're fine, thanks. I think I'll just hang on here a little longer.'

'Right. If you're sure.'

Still, Frances hovered in the doorway.

'Okay,' she said eventually. 'I'll just nip up to say goodbye to Em and then I'll head off.'

After she left the room Nita waited a few seconds to give her time to go up the stairs and then turned to me with raised eyebrows.

'I thought she'd never leave.'

There was a creaking noise then, from out in the hallway, and we looked at each other in panic, Nita's mouth falling open in an 'o'.

A few moments later came the sound of the front door closing.

'Oh my God, do you think she heard?' Nita had her hand half over her mouth. While Kath would have found the whole thing funny, Nita looked horrified. She wasn't used to being thought badly of.

Remorse ran through me, warm and sickly as treacle. Frances was only trying to help. And even though she'd never say it, I'd formed the impression she needed these short periods of respite from her home and her mum and her carer responsibilities.

'Don't worry,' I told Nita, 'I'll call her tomorrow to smooth things over.'

Still, unease crept like damp into my bones and I could not shake it off.

33

I took Dotty out to Alexandra Palace and sat on one of the benches that line the top path. This is the path that runs along the top of the hill, directly across the road in front of the Palace. From there I composed an unnecessarily long text to Frances, saying I hoped she hadn't felt excluded the previous night and explaining that Nita was an old friend I hadn't seen for a while and we had a lot of things we needed to talk through.

After I pressed send I stayed on the bench, gazing down the steep grassy slope in front of me to the path that ran along the middle of the park, and then over the trees towards the lower path and the bottom park, and then on to where London lay spread out across the horizon like a street trader's wares. The sun glinted off the glass-pyramid-topped roof of Canary Wharf Tower while the silver needle point of the Shard pierced a cobalt-blue sky.

God, but my city was beautiful sometimes.

Frances's reply came through a couple of minutes later. *Please don't worry. I understand completely.*

Thank God for that.

Feeling instantly lighter, I called to Dotty and we

started descending the steep tarmacked path that led through the grass. Halfway down, I stopped.

On the middle path just below us, bisecting the path I was on, an imposing figure stood, staring up. Her straight hair, neither brown nor blonde but an indeterminate shade in between, was tucked behind her ears and there was a slash of orange around her neck. A shiver rippled through me as I recognized her. It was the woman who'd been watching Frances and me at the café in Highgate Woods.

I called to Dotty, who'd scampered on ahead, and she came bounding back, tail wagging in expectation.

'Silly girl,' I said softly, bending to clip her lead on to her collar.

When I looked up again the woman had gone.

I hurried down to where the woman had been standing, at the crossroads where the middle path that was slung around Alexandra Park like a belt crossed over the steep path I was on. There was no sign of the woman in either direction but I noticed, off to the right around fifty yards ahead, a rough trail through the trees that separated the middle path from the lower one.

We set off down the winding trail, but Dotty didn't want to go that way so our progress was slow and by the time we reached the lower path there was no sign of the woman.

All the way home I tried to convince myself it hadn't been the same woman we'd seen before, or if it was, it was purely coincidence. Highgate Woods and Alexandra Park were popular local dog-walking spots; it wasn't unusual to see the same faces in each location. But still I couldn't completely shake off that chill of recognition.

As I fished in my bag for my keys, my phone rang. A number I didn't recognize.

'Tessa? It's Joy. Can you come over? Something's happened.'

Something's happened. The repeat of the phrase Frances had used on my doorstep that first awful night she'd brought Emma home made the flesh freeze around my bones.

Twenty-five minutes later I was walking up that black-and-white tiled pathway to the wide front door with the stained-glass panels on either side, ducking my head under the low-hanging wisteria. Shame coated me in a damp sheen and I had to stop to run a hand over my clammy face, remembering how I'd been here before in those early febrile days after Phil's departure. Banging on doors that refused to open to me, convinced that if the people behind them could just see my face I could somehow force back time like a faulty shop shutter, and Phil and the girls would step through and come home with me and none of it would have happened.

Em's face at the window upstairs, mouthing, 'Please go home, Mum.'

I closed my eyes.

Up ahead, the front door swung open. There was Joy, barefoot, in a way that spoke of underfloor heating. Wide-legged navy trousers and a matching navy camisole with a long, soft cream cashmere cardigan draped over the top.

'How is she?' I asked.

'A bit heartbroken,' said Joy. 'He didn't give her any warning, that's the worst thing. She thought things were going so well, and then he just ended it out of the blue.

By text. She'll be all right. She's made of strong stuff. But right now she needs her mum.'

My skinny jeans stuck to the backs of my thighs as I stepped forward. I'd never made it this far before. In the past, I'd been stopped at the door or, after Joy's patience ran out, Phil would cut me off at the gate.

The hallway was wide and square with a staircase of polished wood that swept up around it. Through an open doorway at the back I glimpsed a vast white-floorboarded kitchen with a central island and concertina glass doors along the length of the back wall.

Joy led me into a living room at the front dominated by the biggest, deepest corner sofa I'd ever seen in a vivid pink velvet, piled high with cushions. The rest of the room was pared back in shades of white and cream. I took in the white plantation shutters I'd stared at from the other side all those times, trying to imagine what lay behind them.

As I sat down in a corner of that enormous sofa, a willowy blonde teenager with braces across her teeth poked her head round the door, trying not to stare too obviously. I'd never really given much thought to Joy's twins, but now I felt embarrassed at the things they might have seen in that fraught period after Phil moved in.

That wasn't me, I wanted to say to this girl. *That was someone else.*

'Fetch Rosie, would you, Izzy?' asked Joy.

The girl nodded and disappeared.

'Your girls must think I'm crazy,' I said, trying to laugh.

Joy didn't reply.

Rosie appeared, also barefoot, wearing pyjama bottoms

and a sweatshirt, even though it was late afternoon. I tried not to mind how comfortable she looked here, how at home.

A small, ungracious voice in my head whispered, *No wonder she doesn't want to live at your house.* But I drowned it out. It was time I started taking responsibility for the things that had happened.

I knew that.

Rosie's hair was greasy at the roots and pulled back into a messy ponytail, and her eyes were puffy. I got up to hug her and, after a moment or two, her arms closed around me and she leaned her head on my shoulder.

'I'm so sorry you got hurt, RoRo,' I said, using an old family nickname that stemmed from Em's early attempts at pronouncing her sister's name. 'And I'm sorry about before, thinking Stephens had got to you. I should have given you more credit.'

She nodded and sank down on to the sofa, her expression so much that of the little girl I used to drop off at school or friends' houses, determined not to cry, that my heart felt bruised with love.

'I'll go and make tea,' said Joy, slipping out of the room. I was grateful for her tact as I sat down next to my daughter, who seemed so terribly fragile.

'Mum, why doesn't he want me?'

Rosie's voice was thick, as if she had something in her mouth, and something inside me ripped apart like an old sheet.

'Oh, darling. He's a fool. You're worth ten of him. Twenty. Thousands. I know this hurts now, but eventually you'll find someone worthy of you and then you won't even think about him any more.'

I squeezed her shoulder hard, as if I could force her to share my optimism, but when I looked down her lovely face was pale with misery.

In the end, Rosie came back home with me for the night, wearing a coat over her pyjamas.

I helped her into bed as if she were a child. It had been so long since anyone went into her bedroom I'd almost forgotten what it looked like. After the crash, when she didn't want to talk to me, it was just too painful a reminder of everything I'd lost.

Luckily, it was all there, just as she'd left it that last time before she went to the party in Stoke Newington. The bed still made up with her favourite vintage-style floral duvet cover, the sheepskin rug on the floor, even a novel waiting on the bedside table, bookmark in place. A pair of battered Doc Martens, so old the leather had cracked across the widest part, sat untouched under the desk.

I pulled the duvet over Rosie and sat on the edge of the bed, smoothing her hair.

'Sorry for being such a wuss,' she said in a small voice.

'Don't be silly. It's good to have you home,' I said.

When she was asleep, I went downstairs and opened up my laptop and watched my parents for a while on the webcam, to take my mind off everything. Once again, my father looked tired. My mother was telling him off about something. 'You never listen,' she said. 'That's your problem. You'll never amount to anything if you don't listen.'

I wondered who she thought he was. Perhaps some long-distant version of himself.

My dad rubbed a hand over his eyes and suddenly I

was consumed with anger at the unfairness of it all. Contemporaries of theirs were still going on cruises and taking up yoga and joining the University of the Third Age. Why my parents? Why were they the ones reduced to this horrendous half-existence? They'd worked hard all their lives, tried to be decent people, and now here was my mum in a constant state of confusion and fear and fury at people who weren't even there, and my poor dad, not in the best of health, and worn to a thin shaving of his former self, his whole day spent parrying demands and abuse.

A hot rush of despair surged over me. Why was life so bloody vindictive? The last years should be a reward for all the good things you'd done, and instead there was indignity stacked on indignity, like a teetering pile of rotting trash.

Why should people like Stephens, who thought of nothing but themselves and their own selfish wants and pleasures, be strutting the streets in all their swaggering power and virility and vigour while my parents were semi-prisoners in their home?

I clicked off from my parents and rang Nick, leaving a long, rambling message when it went to voicemail.

He texted back almost immediately, saying he was out with one of his colleagues.

Are you OK? You sounded weird, he asked.

Fine, I lied. Then I put my head in my hands and wept.

34

That night I lay awake for hours. I was still worrying about my parents, the way my father's face sagged, as if his very muscles had given up. I picked up my phone to check the Granny-Cam and found a new email from Nick. He must have sent it when he got in, still worried by my voicemail message. I tried to compose a reply but couldn't find the words I wanted to say. I started telling him how I'd convinced myself that Rosie's new man was Stephens, but it looked so ridiculous written down. Paranoid. So I told him instead about Rosie's break-up and my quiet joy at having her home again, but then it felt wrong to be talking about my daughter's private affairs to someone she didn't even know and I ended up deleting the whole thing, feeling vaguely ashamed of myself. I was so overwrought with emotion and exhaustion I even found myself questioning whether I should be embarking on a new relationship when my children still needed me so much.

Early in the morning I crept to Rosie's open door and watched the duvet rising and falling with her breath. In the clear light of the new day my perspective shifted, the soul-searching of the previous night giving way to a cautious optimism. My daughter was back home where she belonged. Anything felt possible.

While I made her breakfast, Rosie admitted she was already regretting dropping out of uni. She'd been feeling unhappy in Manchester for a while because she didn't feel it was the right course for her, and then meeting Steve had just reinforced her decision to leave. 'I'm just waiting for a call from the head of the criminology department at uni,' she said. 'He's going to tell me what extra assignments I'd need to do to go straight into year two in the autumn.'

I smiled at her but knew better than to make a fuss. If Rosie felt everyone wanted her to follow a certain course of action, that was often enough to convince her to do something else entirely. It was just the way she was.

Rosie left just before lunchtime, giving me a tight hug at the door that made me well up.

'God, you're burning up, Mum,' she said, pulling away.

'Good old menopause,' I replied, blinking away the tears and arranging my mouth into a determined smile.

The good humour engendered by my unexpected reconciliation with my elder daughter and her admission that she was thinking of going back to uni carried me through to the afternoon.

I was working on a new feature on the unexpected bonuses of finding yourself single in middle age. When I'd first been commissioned, I'd inwardly laughed a hollow laugh at the whole concept, but the more I thought about it, the more I decided that, actually, there were some positives to Phil not being here. I did what I wanted, when I wanted. And yes, it wasn't always wise, but at least I had agency now. I could make my own choices and my own mistakes. Marriage was such an endless dance of compromise and negotiation.

And now that we were nearly two years out, and the pain of rejection was fading, I could concede that Phil might have had a point when he'd said our marriage had run its course. A memory came to me suddenly of him coming straight to a dinner party after being away working for a week and me seeing him arrive across the room and thinking, *Well, how strange. He could be anyone.*

While I missed a lot of things about being with someone, I realized to my surprise that I didn't actually miss *him.*

So it wasn't being single that I had an issue with so much as the timing of it. If it had come when I was still at the height of my career, I might have taken it more in my stride. Instead, I was still reeling from redundancy and the fiftieth birthday which followed so close after as to make the two things inseparable in my mind. Then after the separation came the house move and the car crash, and the estrangement from Rosie and from the local mums who might otherwise have been a support system.

I sat down at the kitchen table with my laptop and dashed off an introduction. I was pleased with the tone of what I'd written. It was always hard to write first-person features that struck the right note of being warm and honest without lapsing into self-pity.

An alert sounded on my computer to show a Skype call coming through. Kath. She quite often called around now, when she was sitting in her office having a cup of tea in that mid-afternoon slump time.

The screen showed her behind her extremely untidy

desk, piled high with box files and papers and mugs and a packet of cotton-wool pads next to a plastic bottle of nail-varnish remover. She was wearing a leopard-print top and her red hair was piled carelessly on her head and held in place with a tortoiseshell clamp.

I told her about Rosie staying the night and she gave a little cheer. Kath knew how much losing Rosie had destroyed me. Then I took a deep breath and filled her in on the latest with Stephens. How he'd attacked another girl and I'd reported him to his football coach. She listened with an expression of building disbelief. When I got to the part about the spyware, she exploded. 'Fuck's sake, Tessa!'

I grimaced. 'I know. I know. You don't need to say anything.'

'Yes, I bloody well do. You know this is crazy, don't you? The whole thing. You have got to stop with this. You don't know who this guy is. You don't even know if he *is* the right guy.'

'Of course he's the right guy. Why else would he be sending anonymous notes and threatening photographs?'

Kath ignored me. 'And whether he is or he isn't, he's a nasty fucker either way. Why are you involving him in your life and your daughters' lives? It's almost like you're looking for trouble.'

That hurt. Something that clearly showed in my face, because when Kath resumed talking she was less antagonistic.

'It just beggars belief, that's all, Tess. I mean, for decades, you sail serenely along – great career, great job, great family. Then, suddenly, *boom!* You hit fifty and you're living in a bloody *Die Hard* movie, crouching behind a car while bullets whizz past your head.'

TAMMY COHEN

'Yeah, thanks for the sympathy. But thankfully, apart from the spyware thing, he's been really quiet recently. I don't want to tempt fate but I do think he might have got bored now and moved on.'

Kath's expression was sceptical. 'From what you say, I wouldn't bank on it.'

Kath made me promise that this would be an end to it. That from now on I'd give Stephens a wide berth.

'Draw a line under the whole thing,' she told me. 'And that includes getting shot of your new groupie.'

It took a few seconds for the penny to drop.

'You mean Frances?'

Kath knew about Frances intercepting me before my date with Nick, and I'd texted her about how awkward it had been when Frances overstayed her welcome the night Nita was over.

'That's her. Look, I know she's been nice to Emma and everything, and yes, it was bloody handy that she knew how to de-bug your computer, or whatever you call it, but what you need now more than anything is to get everything back to normal for you and the girls, and the last thing you want is a needy hanger-on. Time to detach now and get on with your own life. There's a limit to how grateful a person can be expected to be.'

I hesitated. On the one hand, I felt I should defend Frances and, of course, I was grateful to her, as Kath said, but if truth be told, I was starting to feel a little *crowded* by her. I felt hypocritical even thinking it, knowing I'd done my bit to encourage the relationship – all those times I'd turned to her in place of my oldest friends. But in my mind she was inextricably associated with Stephens, and Kath was right, if I wanted to put a

312

distance between me and him, it might mean withdrawing from her as well.

Then Kath wanted to talk about Nick and I found myself relaxing, describing how comfortable I felt in his company, how often we'd been speaking since we went on the date and how much we made each other laugh.

'Stop, or I'm going to gag. Seriously, Nick sounds like a Very Good Thing. I'm happy for you. You deserve this. Don't fuck it up.'

After Kath had gone I realized that talking about Nick had made me miss him. I knew he'd be at work so I sent him an email.

Are your ears burning? Just been talking about you. And before you ask, yes, it was all good. I'm going soft in my old age.

After I signed off I went back to work. I was feeling uplifted by the conversation with Kath and the memory of that hug with Rosie, but despite what I'd said to Kath, I couldn't completely shake off my concerns about Stephens. Was he quiet because he'd had enough – or because he was planning something new?

I kept glancing at my inbox, waiting for Nick to reply. Usually, he responded within an hour, even if it was a quick message sent from his phone between lectures. But today there was nothing.

At 4.30 p.m. I sent him another message. *Is everything ok?*

Finally, at quarter to six, his name appeared in my inbox and I breathed a sigh of relief. But pleasure turned rapidly to bewilderment and then utter dismay as I read his message.

I don't really know what to make of this, Tessa. After

your email last night I've been racking my brains to work out how to respond. Or even whether to bother responding at all.

What email?

I tried to remember what I'd written last night. I knew I'd tried a few times to formulate my thoughts into some sort of sense but, as far as I was aware, I'd given up and deleted the lot. Or had I?

Sick with nerves, I went to my sent message folder. Sure enough, an email had gone out to Nick Lambert the previous night at 2.37 a.m.

I clicked on it with an ominous feeling of dread. Why couldn't I remember having sent it?

Loads of stuff going on here, I'd written. *To be honest, it's probably not the best timing for me to get into another relationship. My girls need me. I'm not even sure I'm fully over my husband yet. Sorry, but better to nip it in the bud now before anyone gets hurt.*

I read the message with growing confusion. I knew I'd been in a weird state the night before, half dead with tiredness but also hyped up by what had happened with Rosie. I'd spent a while trying to compose a message, struggling to find the right words, not even sure by the end what it was I wanted to say, but I'd deleted everything, surely?

Yet even as I protested to myself the doubts started creeping in. I had been in a volatile mood last night, full of fear. I'd lain in bed for hours while anxiety ate a path through my veins, beating myself up about all the things I should have done differently. I know there had been a point at my lowest when I'd questioned what kind of a mother I was, not to be able to protect my daughters from a man like Stephens, and been angry for allowing myself to even think I might be happy with Nick while the people I loved most in the world were suffering.

Was it so unlikely that I'd put some of those fears into words in a message to Nick? Wasn't it within the bounds of possibility that I might, in my sleep-deprived state, have hit send without even intending to?

Or perhaps I *had* intended it. Perhaps it was me self-sabotaging because, at heart, I didn't feel worthy of someone like Nick.

I'm so sorry, I wrote back now. *I was very emotional last night and I think I got myself into a bit of a state. I have no recollection of even sending that message. It certainly isn't how I feel. Can you just forget you ever read it?*

There followed an agonizing wait while I refreshed my inbox every few seconds. Then, finally, a new message from Nick. Just one word.

Sure.

I could feel his hurt and confusion through the type and had to refrain from sending another message apologizing all over again. I'd call him in the evening, when he got home from work, and try to explain.

Only how could I explain what I hardly understood myself?

35

It broke my heart a little to see how thrilled Em was that Rosie had spent the night in our house. Though, obviously, she'd seen a lot of her older sister at Phil's house, and the two were constantly in touch on WhatsApp, I knew she'd missed Rosie being part of our lives here.

'I was thinking, I could clear out half of my wardrobe so Rosie could hang her clothes up in there,' she said now. 'I feel bad that she only has room for a chest of drawers and that tiny cupboard.'

'I wouldn't worry, Em. She always said it made sense for you to have the bigger room as she was away at uni so much.'

'Yeah, but . . .'

Whatever argument Em had been planning to make was lost to the ringing of the doorbell.

Instinctively, I was on guard, Kath's warning about Stephens still fresh in my mind.

'I'll go,' I said, determined to beat Em to the door.

I could tell from the shape through the glass that it wasn't him, but when I opened it my relief was tempered when I found Frances standing there, brandishing a bottle of wine in one hand. Sancerre, which I used to love, but rarely drank as it was so expensive.

'I thought you might need this,' she said as I stepped back into the hallway to let her in. 'Em told me there'd been some drama with Rosie.'

'I don't drink any more,' I said. 'Not since the crash.'

'Just a small glass won't hurt. It's practically medicinal.'

'No, really.' It came out more sharply than I'd intended. 'But thank you. It was a really kind thought. Why don't you have a glass yourself, for both of us?'

I got a glass down from the cupboard and passed Frances the corkscrew. Em was quieter now we had company, finishing her dinner in virtual silence, speaking only to tell Frances that, yes, she was working hard, and yes, it was infuriating how older people always said how much harder exams were in their day. After their initial closeness following the attack I wondered whether Emma might also be starting to find Frances an unwelcome reminder of an incident she would far rather put behind her. Then I remembered that it was Em who'd told Frances about what had been going on with Rosie. So there was still a bond there, of sorts. Still, Kath's description of Frances as 'needy' had lodged in my head and I could not shake it free.

I'd worried Frances might feel awkward after her visit a couple of nights before when Nita had been here and the three of us had made stilted conversation, but if she did, she certainly didn't show it. She couldn't have overheard Nita's 'I thought she'd never leave', I decided, which was a huge relief.

After Em finished eating and washing up the pots, she

hovered by the sink until I put her out of her misery by telling her she ought to go upstairs to work if she had things to finish.

'Yes, don't feel you have to hang around,' said Frances. 'I'll pop up to see you before I go.'

As soon as we were alone Frances moved her chair closer so that she could reach out and lay a hand on my arm.

'How are you, really?' Her head on one side. Eyes locked on mine.

'I'm fine, Frances. Honestly.'

I hoped she couldn't hear the note of irritation in my voice. The truth was, I felt conflicted. Frances had been so supportive since the attack, and of course I could never forget that it was thanks to her courage that a far greater trauma had been averted. But sometimes she seemed so *invested* in us. I remembered what she'd said in that bar in Peckham about how the Chinese say, if you save someone's life, you're now responsible for them. Did that mean she intended to stay in our lives for ever?

The sound of the house phone startled both of us. Only one person ever rang on the house phone.

'It'll be my dad,' I said, glad of the interruption. 'Do you mind if I get it?'

Without waiting for a response, I snatched up the handset from its cradle on the kitchen worktop next to a neat row of cookery books with faded Post-it notes poking up between their pages.

'Hello, love,' said my father. 'Your mother and I were just wondering how you are.'

It ripped me apart a little bit, that 'your mother and I'.

Even though I knew, if I turned on the webcam, she'd be sitting in her chair watching the television, oblivious.

'I'm fine, Dad,' I said. 'And you?'

I turned to look at Frances, who flashed me a small, pinched smile. *Sorry*, I mouthed, putting my hand over the receiver.

I let my father talk for a few minutes. He was telling me about a diatribe my mother had launched at the new care assistant that morning. He was laughing, but in that way people did when they knew they could just as easily cry instead. He'd always been so unfailingly polite, my dad. Always believed that a person could be measured by how much respect they gave to those around them. I knew my mother's rudeness would have bruised the very core of him.

His voice had that slight tremor I'd noticed recently, that sense of being strung so tight the words reverberated off the surface of it. If Frances hadn't been there, I would have quizzed him more closely about how he was doing, how much closer to the edge he had stepped since the last time we spoke, but I was conscious of her scrolling restlessly through her phone.

'Dad, I'm sorry, can I call you back? There's someone here.'

'Oh, yes. Righto. My apologies, love. I should have asked.'

He sounded so small and forlorn I wished I could climb through the telephone line and put my arms around him.

'Sorry about that,' I said to Frances when I'd put the phone down. 'My parents are a bit of a worry.'

'It's quite all right, Tessa. I understand completely.'

I remembered too late about her ill mother.

'God, I'm an idiot. Of course, you know all about it with your own mum.'

She nodded wordlessly.

'Look, Frances,' I said, sitting back down at the table. 'While you're here, there is something I've been meaning to discuss with you.'

I felt a tug of treachery as I saw her eyes light up, and she leaned towards me as if in expectation of a confidence. Why did things like this have to be so difficult?

'It's just that, well, please don't take this the wrong way, but this is a really important year for Em at school and she needs to focus on work and put what happened to her out of her head as much as possible. And I'm afraid you're a reminder of it. So I think it's better, that is, I think it would make sense if . . .'

'If I faded out of the picture a bit,' said Frances.

'Yes, that's what I was trying to say, very clumsily,' I said, sagging with relief.

'Please don't worry, Tessa. I get it. Really. I mean, I'll always feel bonded to Emma, and I suspect she will to me, too, after what happened. But I'm happy to give her space for the time being. And besides, it gives the two of us a chance to spend more time together. I hope you don't mind me saying this, but I think you could do with a friend.'

She wasn't making this easy for me.

'That's really sweet of you, and you know I've been so grateful for your support over the last weeks. But the thing is, I really need to give some proper attention to my girls and to my parents. My mum and dad are struggling.

Well, you heard me on the phone, didn't you? They really need me to be around more. I'm worried about my poor dad.' I swallowed back a twinge of guilt, thinking about how hard my dad struggled not to be a burden. And here I was using him as an excuse to wriggle out of an association that was becoming inconvenient. Still, I continued: 'To be honest with you, Frances, I don't even have time for my . . .'

I bit back the words 'real friends' just in time.

'. . . for all the other people in my life.'

For a moment I worried I might have offended her. She blinked her eyes a few times in quick succession, bit down on her lip.

Then she smiled.

'Oh God, I'm with you there. Life is so stressful, isn't it? So hard to fit everything in.'

I could have kissed her for being so understanding.

After Frances had finally gone, popping up to see Em quickly on the way out, as she'd said, I dashed off a text to Kath.

Just chucked Frances. Feel like a cow!

Then I also made my way upstairs to see Emma. She was on her bed, her laptop on her thighs, a pair of outsize headphones covering her ears.

I perched on the mattress next to her and stroked her head, my fingers seeking out that soft fuzz of new growth in the circular patches where the hair had fallen out.

'You know, darling, it's lovely you and Frances have got so close, but I'd have preferred to keep Rosie's love life between us.'

Em's eyes grew wide and I rushed to reassure her.

'It's okay, really. I understand that you have a connection with Frances. And I know we owe her so much. I'm just saying we could maybe do with creating a little bit of distance, just while we focus on repairing our little family.'

'I think she's lonely,' Em said then, looking miserable. 'That's why she likes coming here.'

I leaned forward and gave her a squeeze, becoming tangled up in the cord of the headphones.

'You're such a softie,' I said, into her hair. 'Don't ever lose that.'

The conversation with Em discomfited me. Frances *was* probably a bit lonely. She had to spend long periods of time looking after her mum, and her best friend had moved away. I remembered the glib text I'd sent to Kath and wished I hadn't written it.

My guilt was compounded when, an hour or so later, I saw Frances had posted a new photograph to her Instagram page, a selfie with Em she must have taken when she nipped up to see her on her way out.

Funny how the world works in such a random way, she'd written. *This is E, and I can't say how we were thrown together, as it's not my story to tell. But I know we'll always be an important part of each other's lives.* #SoulSistas #UnbreakableBond

36

When people talk about the menopause, it's about the hot flushes and the mood swings. What no one tells you about are the pains that shoot up your legs suddenly in the night, like electric shocks. What no one tells you about is how long a night can seem when every second that passes is a different regret dredged from the mud of the past. They don't mention the mornings when you feel at once both heavy but also hollowed out, as if you've spent the night pushing a boulder up a hill, only for it to slip right back down to where you started.

I was still worried about Em and worried about me and what it said about my state of mind that I'd been so ready to believe Stephens had targeted Rosie. That message I'd sent him, *Please don't hurt my daughter*, was like a bad taste in my mouth I couldn't get rid of. I agonized that I might have upset Frances, but also, conversely, that I hadn't made myself clear enough.

'I'm a horrible human being,' I told Nick as I put the hummus back in the fridge. We had fallen into a habit of talking on the phone in the early afternoons when he was on lunch break at the university and Emma was still at school. Since my weird late-night email earlier that week I'd questioned whether a note of wariness had crept into his voice that wasn't there before, but I told myself I was just being paranoid.

'You're not horrible. It's only natural you should want to ringfence your family, after everything that's happened.'

'Yes, but we owe everything to Frances. If she hadn't come along . . .'

'Then maybe someone else would have.'

He was right, but then Nick hadn't been here that night Frances appeared on the doorstep, with her arm around my sobbing daughter. He hadn't felt that gut-tearing wave of gratitude that swept over me as I realized what had happened, and what worse things might have happened if she hadn't come along. In that moment, I would have given that woman anything. No reward could possibly be enough for what she'd done.

And now here I was, trying to pull away from her, just because I had failed to set any boundaries.

After Nick had rung off, I made myself a cup of tea and sat down in front of my computer, scrolling idly through my social media timelines. Emma was going out after school and for some reason having an un-broken stretch of time to work always made me less productive rather than more. Twitter was full of out-rage. Another male celebrity had just fallen foul of the #metoo movement, and Piers Morgan was embroiled in a new controversy. I clicked on my Facebook page with trepidation, still half expecting some vitriolic message from Stephens, but all was calm – just the usual posts about cute pets and endless pictures of other people's holidays. The faces we paint on to our real ones to show to the world.

I finally got down to work but struggled to write. Frances was still very much on my mind. Had I upset her? Had I got my message across? Worry for my parents was also a constant distraction, throbbing like toothache under the surface of my thoughts. Finally, late afternoon, when the sun was low and, through the window, our concrete yard was entirely in shadow, I gave up and logged on to the webcam in my parents' house, my heart sinking as I found my mother in mid-rant at my father. Hard to believe now that they'd rarely said a cross word to each other all the time I was growing up.

'You're lazy. You've always been lazy. Lazy lump of lard. Sack of potatoes. *Nincompoop!*'

I smiled at that one. When was the last time anyone even used that word?

My dad was in his usual chair, legs stretched out, fast asleep.

Amazing how he could sleep through that racket.

Now Mum picked up her stick from next to her chair and started prodding him with it.

'Wake up, mister. I'm hungry. Mister, wake up.'

Her voice was completely different now, wheedling, like a young child's. And I realized she'd completely forgotten who he was. Who she was too. How did he bear it?

Prod, went the stick into his thigh. *Prod*, into his arm.

Unease stirred inside me like a waking cat.

'WAKE UP!' my mother screamed, leaning over to jam the stick into his stomach.

Nothing.

Oh no.

Oh no oh no oh no oh no.

I ran for my phone, which I'd left in the living room, praying that when I got back I'd see my dad stretching and coming blearily back to consciousness. But when I glanced next at the screen he hadn't moved.

Scrolling frenziedly through my contacts, I found the entry for Sandra, my parents' key-holding neighbour.

'I think something's happened to my dad!'

Sandra stayed on the phone while she dug out the key to my parents' house. Meanwhile, I watched the screen with my stomach knotted. My eyes were fixed on my dad's chest. Was it moving?

My mother had given up her onslaught on my father and was engrossed in whatever was on the television.

'I'm just going in now,' Sandra told me, and a second or two later I saw her ash-blonde bob onscreen entering my parents' living room from the hallway.

She hurried over to the armchair where my dad was and knelt down beside him, holding his hand. As soon as I saw her face, I knew. I just knew.

'Oh, Tessa.' Sandra's face as she looked up at the camera was already shiny with tears. 'I'm so sorry.'

My mother, who up until now had been oblivious to what was going on, now turned to Sandra.

'Have you come to make my tea, dear? I'm starving. They don't feed me here.'

I didn't look at her. My eyes were still glued to the unmoving figure in the chair.

'Tessa, I'm going to ring off now,' said Sandra in a low, unsteady voice. 'I need to call the doctor. Get things sorted. I assume you'll be coming straight over?'

I nodded numbly. Then remembered she couldn't see me.

'Yes. But Sandra . . .'

'Yes?'

'I can't see his face. Is he peaceful? Did he suffer?'

'No, Tess. He looks grand.'

She rang off then. But I carried on watching without sound as Sandra, still on her knees, jabbed numbers on her phone keypad and my mother, agitated now, continued to berate her from her chair.

I put out a fingertip and traced the length of my father's leg that stretched out from the chair.

A hole opened up in my chest and I felt myself falling through it.

37

'Thank goodness you're here, Tessa. They won't let me see your father. They're keeping him from me.'

It was one of the great ironies that, at the very time when the detachment from reality that dementia brings would have been of most benefit to my mother, it decided to temporarily loosen its grip.

'I'm so sorry, Mum. He's dead. He's gone.'

'But gone where? He wouldn't leave me without saying anything.'

It was the day after Dad's death and we had spent the whole morning going around in the same heartbreaking circle.

At least Mum was spared the worst of it, unaware that my parents' GP, Dr Ali, believed Dad had deliberately overdosed. The dial on his insulin pen had been turned up to ten times its normal level.

'I'm afraid rates of depression in patients with diabetes are twice as high as in the normal population,' Dr Ali had told me the previous evening. He'd been at the house when I arrived, overseeing what needed to be done. 'And add to that the circumstances of your father's life – a full-time carer to a woman who, let's be honest, wasn't always as kind as she could be.'

He'd seen my face.

'Not through any fault of hers, of course. What I'm saying is that your poor father had a lot on his plate and perhaps it all just got too much for him. Even the strongest of us have moments where everything seems overwhelming.'

Guilt had flooded through my veins, until I thought it might drown me. I knew I hadn't seen as much of my parents as I should have done over the last two tumultuous years. I had thought I was doing them a favour, wanting to shield them as much as possible from the mess of my life. Because I kept watch on them from afar through my computer I'd fooled myself into thinking I was in constant touch and yet, for them, it was as if I wasn't there at all. Completely absent during those long stretches between visits.

And all the time, my father had been battling demons of his own, unsupported. How selfish I'd been. Too caught up in my own misery to notice anyone else's.

Something occurred to me then.

'Did you know my father had depression?'

Dr Ali had looked uncomfortable. 'It was something we had talked about. He was taking a low-dose anti-depressant to manage his moods.'

I'd stared at him then, too shocked to speak. My father, the man who'd refused paracetamol even when his appendix was about to burst, had felt unhappy enough to willingly take pills every single day, above and beyond the insulin he was obliged to take for his diabetes. And I'd known nothing about it.

There would be a post-mortem to determine the exact cause of death, but Dr Ali wanted to prepare me in advance.

'He would have slipped into a coma without knowing what was happening,' Dr Ali told me, trying to give what reassurance he could.

My one crumb of comfort as I'd lain in bed last night in what had once been my bedroom was that at least Mum's dementia cushioned her from the grief I was going through.

And yet, when I'd woken blearily after just a couple of hours' sleep and heard her in the kitchen and rushed downstairs, I'd found her, for once, heartbreakingly alert.

'Tessa, love,' she'd said, trying to mask her consternation with a smile, as she'd done at times of crisis throughout my childhood. 'I was just looking for your dad. He seems to have disappeared.'

Throughout the day she'd become increasingly querulous, barely hiding her fear, but still frustratingly compos mentis. True, she thought I was the younger version of me, still living at home and subject to parental rule. And she refused to hear that my father was dead.

'What do you think has happened to him?' she asked me now, seemingly for the hundredth time. I looked over at her pale blue eyes, which were watery with worry, and something inside me caved in like a mountain of flour.

'Perhaps he's been held up at work,' I said.

The change was instantaneous, the tight lines around her eyes relaxing and her entire face lifting so that she looked ten years younger.

'Oh yes. That will be it. Silly me.'

On impulse, I got up and threw my arms around her. She was sitting in her usual chair in the living room, so I had to crouch down. Her narrow, wasted frame felt like a bunch of old twigs in my arms.

'Well. My goodness. What have I done to deserve this?'

We weren't normally a physically demonstrative household, but I could tell she was pleased.

'I love you, Mum.'

She blinked at me, a pink flush of pleasure spreading over her soft cheeks.

'And, naturally, I love you too. But if you're just being nice to me so I'll excuse you from homework, you can think again, young lady. Now, off upstairs with you.'

I went upstairs and called Phil.

'How are the girls taking it?'

I'd spoken to both Em and Rosie the previous evening, assuring them their grandad didn't suffer, listening to their gulps and sniffles while trying to hold it together for their sakes.

'Oh, you know. They're pretty cut up. You know how much they loved your dad. And don't forget, this is their first experience of death. It'll take a while to sink in. More to the point, how are you, Tess?'

I told him then about what Dr Ali had said. Speaking the words aloud made them suddenly, horribly real.

'I don't know what to say,' said Phil finally. 'Poor Ian.'

'I feel so guilty. I had no idea he was so low.'

'Oh, come on, Tess. You've had battles of your own to fight. Don't give yourself a hard time. It's weird, though . . .'

He tailed off.

'What's weird?'

'I just would never have thought your dad capable of it. I mean, he was always so responsible. He had such clearly defined notions of duty, didn't he? Remember how he took two months off work to look after his own father when he was dying all those years ago, not long after we first met? And I know from the girls that you tried to persuade him to get some kind of respite care so he could come and visit you in London, and he always refused. I find it so hard to believe he'd have abandoned your mum like that. Sorry. That sounds like I'm blaming him.'

'No. I know what you mean. I can't believe it either. I wouldn't have imagined in a million years my dad would ever have left Mum on her own, or left me to shoulder the burden of looking after her. But I guess he just wasn't himself. Depression does that, doesn't it? Alters your personality?'

'What will you do now?'

I tried to sigh, but grief was a weight crushing the air out of my chest.

'I don't know. Prepare for the funeral. Start looking at care homes for Mum.'

'You've decided, then.'

'I can't look after her at home, Phil. You know that.'

His voice was soft when he replied.

'Yeah. I know.'

I went downstairs, where Mum was engrossed in watching *Mrs Brown's Boys*. As I sat down in the seat that used to be my father's, she let out a volley of laughter, echoing the laughter of the studio audience. I wondered if she even knew what she was laughing at.

I sent a message to Nick. For once, not trying to be witty or smart. I'd already spoken to him that morning to tell him what had happened, my voice straining to get past the lump in my throat. Now I sent him just five words.

I wish you were here.

Kath had called and left a voicemail. She was crying, I could tell. She and Mari had both loved my dad. 'Let me know if there's anything I can do,' she said. 'Oh, and Tess—' Then she'd paused and I could hear her ragged breathing down the phone line. 'It doesn't matter. I'll tell you when I see you. I'm so sorry.'

I typed her a quick reply saying I couldn't face talking at the moment but giving her the details of the funeral. I'd need all my friends around me.

The following day was Sunday, and I felt disconnected from myself, as if I was an actor in my own life and everything that happened was some sort of play or performance, one step removed from reality. Phil drove Emma and Rosie over for a few hours and I was glad of the company. Their warm, fierce hugs were a physical reminder of the life I felt so distanced from.

The girls were red-eyed and sombre. It was the first time they'd come up against the awful irrevocability of death. In a world where everything was re-doable – marriages, GCSEs, career paths – the finality of their grandfather simply ceasing to exist had come as a devastating shock.

Mum showed little interest in their arrival, submitting to their hugs with bad grace, impatient to get back to *Countryfile*.

'Where's Grandad?' Em whispered to me, wanting to know where the body was being held.

'Oh, we won't be hearing from that one. He's dead,' said my mum conversationally, without turning her attention from the television screen.

How much did she know, really? I wondered. And how much did she simply choose not to know?

After they all drove back to London, I went to bed early, not long after Mum. Exhaustion encased every bone in my body in lead. But still, sleep eluded me. Every time I closed my eyes I saw my dad as he had been when I was a child. Fit and vigorous with fair, curly hair that, to his frustration, sprung straight up from one side of his parting while lying perfectly flat on the other. I saw him squeezed into the tiny pink chair in my bedroom after I'd woken up from a nightmare and had refused to sleep unless he was there, I saw the back of his head over the top of the car seat in front as he drove, his big, soft hand snaking back to hold mine when we stopped at traffic lights.

When, finally, I fell asleep, long after it had got light, I dreamed I saw him sitting on a rooftop, but a far younger version of him than I had ever known, a version that came from an old photograph. He was wearing shorts and a loose, white short-sleeved shirt, his long limbs nut brown from a long-forgotten holiday, just perched on a rooftop across a whole span of rooftops.

Out of reach.

I woke up just an hour later, my face sticky with tears.

After a long conversation with the social worker who oversaw my parents' care, I drew up a list of potential care homes that catered for people with dementia. Sandra came round to look after Mum while I faced the soul-destroying task of touring around them all.

In one, a smartly dressed old man sat by the front door with his coat neatly folded over his lap and a bag by his feet.

'Have you seen my daughter?' he asked me anxiously. 'She's coming to take me home. I've had a lovely time at this hotel, but I want to go home now.'

'His daughter lives in New York,' confided the uniformed care assistant who was showing me around. 'She hasn't visited in over a year.'

In another, an elderly woman came out of a toilet and shuffled slowly down the corridor pushing a walker, her underpants around her ankles.

Every place I visited had that institutional boiled-cabbage smell, over-laced with urine and bleach and a thick fug of inertia, but the staff – middle-aged women, back in the workplace with no qualifications apart from years of keeping a home and kids, or young Eastern Europeans or Africans – were kind, on the whole, if weary and overworked. And the residents at least appeared safe.

One of the homes was only a few streets away from my parents' house. Just twenty-two rooms, bright and modern and relatively fresh-smelling with a lovely garden out the back. In the lounge three women watched a daytime chat show in companionable silence. The manager was young and full of ideas for innovations she was going to introduce. The cost was eye-watering, but I tried not to think about that. Just as I tried not to think about leaving Mum here on her own – whether or not she'd even be aware of where she was.

'Don't worry, we'll look after her,' said the young manager, reading my emotions in my face.

Back at the house, my mother was again agitated.

'She's been looking for your father,' Sandra explained. 'She thinks he's gone out to the pub and left her behind.'

To my knowledge, my father hadn't been to the pub in years, apart from the odd occasion when we all went as a family group.

'He went to the door and then that was it. Off he went,' said Mum crossly. 'Not so much as a goodbye. Selfish man.'

Sandra gave an 'I've been here before' sigh and said, 'I told you, Judy, it's not his fault, he's—'

'Why did he go to the door, Mum?'

My mother arched her sparse eyebrows over her pale eyes, as if astounded by the stupidity of the question.

'Because someone rang the bell, of course.'

A finger of unease ran up my spine.

'Who was it?'

'Well, Douglas, I should say. Always leading him into trouble.'

I sighed, shoulders slumping. Douglas was my dad's younger brother, who'd dropped dead of a heart attack more than a decade before.

It was like this with my mother. Me always wanting to believe she understood more than she was letting on, until I came right up against the dead end of her condition.

I noticed a huge bouquet of flowers propped up in a bucket against the back wall of the living room. Plump white and green tea roses and blousy blue hydrangeas were crammed in with delicate lilac wax flowers and sprays of white baby's breath, all wrapped in acres of cellophane.

'They came while you were out,' said Sandra. 'Gorgeous, aren't they? Must have cost a fortune.'

Nick, was my first thought, and I felt a surge of warmth

as I unwrapped the cellophane and extracted the card from its creamy-white envelope.

So sorry to hear your news, Tessa. Please let me know if there's anything I can do. Sending love and strength, Frances.

Instantly, warmth was washed away by guilt.

Frances had called while I was on the train to Oxford the day of my father's death, staring rigidly out of the window as tears rolled down my face. I'd sent her a terse text a few hours later, explaining what had happened and how I'd be tied up making arrangements for the next couple of weeks. At least that was one positive thing about this whole hideous business, I remembered thinking, that it provided a natural breathing space where the girls and I could regroup and Frances would step back.

But now here were these over-the-top flowers.

She must have got the address from Em. I knew it was kind of her but, in my fraught state, it felt like yet another thing I needed to be grateful to her for.

The flowers were too tall for any of my parents' vases, and I clattered around the kitchen flinging open cupboards and drawers before dumping them finally back in the plastic bucket, much to Sandra's consternation.

'A beautiful bouquet like that, it seems criminal.'

I left the flowers on the floor of the kitchen, out of sight.

On the train, Henry presses his nose to the window and keeps up a commentary of what he is seeing. 'There's a field. There's another field. Look, Mummy, a sheep!' I love him and am exhausted by him in equal measure. More so because we are on our way to the cemetery, and that always makes me tense, as though there isn't sufficient air inside me for all the breaths I need to take.

There is a young woman opposite and she smiles at me conspiratorially as Henry prattles on, but I look away and pretend I haven't seen.

Ironically, the first time I visited the cemetery was with Matt. We stumbled across it, literally, while wandering around Coldfall Woods, a gap in the perimeter fence opening up on to a seemingly secret graveyard, the headstones mellow with age and lichen.

'Wow,' Matt had said, as we wandered around, amid graves that seemed to grow out of the woodland itself, a mossy stone angel, weeping under trailing ivy, and glimpsing in the distance a church spire, grey against the winter blue sky. 'When I go, this is where I want to end up.'

What would that younger me, swaddled in love and a

striped woollen scarf, have said if she'd known that, just a few years later, we would bury him right there? Not in the wild, overgrown section where all the ancient graves and tombs crumble into the earth, but in the part nearer the church, the newly dug graves laid out in neat rows, marble tombstones gleaming like jewels.

When we step into the graveyard, from the more conventional road approach, Henry runs ahead to see Daddy. He has brought a picture he painted at school that he can't wait to show him. He is so proud of that picture, and the idea of leaving it pegged out by stones on each corner, to be torn to pieces by the wind and the rain, breaks my heart.

I turn the corner into Matt's row.

'Look, Mummy,' says Henry, who is already lying on the ground spreading out his painting. 'Someone very kind has left a present.'

The teddy bear is glossy and new, with shallow yellow glass eyes that glint where they catch the light. It is box fresh, as if recently placed.

I remember your face as you shyly handed me the parcel. 'I know it's a bit naff,' you said as I unwrapped the velvet elephant, skin soft and smooth as grey moss. 'But I thought you might like it.'

Holding the teddy bear as far from me as possible, as if it contained a bomb that might explode at any moment, I place it on the grave at the furthest end of the row.

'Why are you putting Daddy's present on someone else's special place, Mummy?'

Henry is sitting up, frowning.

'Because this poor man doesn't have any presents. Daddy would have wanted to share, wouldn't he?'

Henry thinks for a moment, and then nods.

After that, Henry talks to Matt about his teacher and next-door's new puppy, but I don't listen. My eyes are scanning around the graveyard, up one row, then the next. There's a figure in black some distance away and my heart stops for a moment, but when I look closer and see the stooped back and white hair, I realize it can't be you.

But you have been here. To this place, of all places. And I will never be free of you.

38

The day of the funeral, it poured with rain.

Mum was in a subdued mood, submitting to everything I asked of her like a docile child.

The previous night, she'd woken in the early hours, upset. Crying and hitting herself repeatedly on the head until I'd knelt down on the carpet next to her and pressed her hands in mine.

We travelled to the crematorium in the back of a funeral car, along with Rosie and Em, who'd arrived the previous night. 'Why do people think it's okay to stare?' asked Rosie crossly, as a woman standing on the pavement craned her neck to see inside the car. 'I feel like we're some sort of art installation.' But I didn't blame them. Death was kept so separate from us these days, as if it might be in itself contagious, so when we did butt up against it we gawped in fascination.

My mother was wearing a midnight-blue woollen dress and the threads of my heart snagged, remembering how we'd bought that dress together for her cousin's funeral. Could it really be just six years ago? We'd met up in John Lewis on Oxford Street. Spent a couple of hours shopping. Had lunch in a little Italian café in the back streets. Were there clues, even then? If there were, I didn't see them. She'd always been a bit ditsy in that 'where are my glasses?' type way. There was nothing new. Nothing to set alarm bells ringing.

Phil was waiting for us outside the crematorium. I was grateful for the long hug he gave me and the steadying fact of his presence. I was so sleep-deprived my thoughts were like balloons drifting off into space before I could quite grasp them. Phil felt like an anchor weighting me to the here and now.

There was no sign yet of Kath and Mari. Though I hadn't been able to face talking to them on the phone, I realized now how much I was relying on them being here to get me through the ordeal of the funeral. They'd loved my dad, both of them having complicated relationships with their own fathers, and had often told me over the years how lucky I was. But more than that, they'd been at all the other big life events since we met – my wedding, at the hospital straight after the girls were both born, the night Phil moved out – it was inconceivable to think of going through this without them.

Other mourners arrived, though not many. I'd known it would be a heartbreakingly small gathering. So many of my parents' friends were now dead, and the pair of them had become semi-reclusive over the last tortuous year or so of my mum's illness.

I looked at my phone. Only five minutes to go. My oldest friends were cutting it very fine.

The guests from the preceding funeral spilled out of the crematorium in a wave of dark clothing, some holding tissues to their noses.

A man in a black suit and with the kind of bluish

complexion that spoke of long, sunless days cloistered indoors, appeared discreetly by my shoulder to tell me the room was now empty if I wanted to take my pew.

After one last glance around, searching in vain for a flash of distinctive red hair, I led the way inside.

The service was low key. I read a Seamus Heaney poem my dad had loved. Phil gave a speech, recalling a few favourite family anecdotes. There was a hymn.

I was sitting in the front row, with my mother. Phil sat behind with the girls.

I kept turning around to smile encouragement. They looked so pale, both of them – and so young. It was too easy, caught up in the day-to-day stress of living, to lose sight of the children they'd so recently been.

Earlier, I'd managed to have a little chat with Rosie on our own in my parents' dated 1980s kitchen. 'How are you feeling now – about Steve?'

'I'm okay.' She smiled weakly, as if to prove her point. 'To be honest, Grandad dying has put it all into perspective, really. I hadn't known him long enough to get properly emotionally involved. I was stupid to get so upset. I think it was just the rejection that hurt, you know?'

Of course I knew. When did she get so wise, my daughter?

Now she was sitting stiffly next to her father, pressing her lips together to keep from breaking down.

Next to her, Em's head was bowed. At first I thought she was crying and I was just about to lean back to touch her knee when I realized she was hunched over her phone, texting. Just a few furtive taps and then she put it away again, but I turned back to face the front feeling a tug of disappointment.

I knew she was upset, and I was sure her friends were being lovely and supportive, but couldn't she have managed without her phone just for forty-five minutes?

A door opened at the back of the room and I gazed expectantly, waiting for Kath and Mari to pile through, breathless and apologetic, having taken a wrong turning or having had to go back for something they'd forgotten. But the figure who darted inside, wearing a plain black dress and a solemn expression, resembled neither of my oldest friends.

Grief and shock meant there was a delay before I placed her, and, when I did, my chest felt suddenly tight.

Frances.

Seeing me looking, she gave a small wave and slid into one of the rows at the back. I caught Em's eye, and she shrugged, glancing pointedly at her phone, which is when I realized it must be Frances she had been texting with just moments before.

I turned to face the front, my emotions all over the place.

I'd been so longing to see my friends, and it certainly wasn't Frances's fault that Kath and Mari had let me down. And yet, what was she *doing* here? She had never met my parents. She barely knew me.

After the service the mourners stood outside in small knots. I had my arm linked through my mum's and various people I half recognized came up to tell us how sorry they were, and what a lovely man my dad had been.

My mother, for once, stayed silent, accepting the condolences with a fixed smile. Frances appeared over the shoulder of a woman who'd once worked as my dad's PA

344

and was in the process of recounting a long and touching anecdote about how supportive he'd been when her husband was ill.

'I'm Frances Gates, a friend of Tessa and Em's,' said Frances, after the woman had moved away, taking my mother's limp hand in hers. Then she turned to me.

'Tessa, I was so sorry to hear about your dad. I know how much he meant to you. I hope you don't mind me coming. I just wanted to show support to you both. I asked Em for the details. I knew you'd be busy.'

'No, of course I don't mind. That's very kind of you. And thanks for the lovely flowers too.'

My voice was as cracked as parched earth.

Everyone was invited back to the house for sandwiches and tea. Sandra and her daughter had made the food – 'We did some egg ones, because we know your Rosie is vegetarian' – and I was so grateful to her I cried, which set her off too, and soon we were both in floods of tears.

Mum, who was more animated now that we were back on familiar territory, had decided this must be my wedding reception and wandered around the room graciously greeting guests and asking if they'd come far and saying what a lovely couple Phil and I made. When she got to me, she whispered:

'Do you think people are enjoying themselves? I worry it seems a bit flat.'

Phil came over, asking who Frances was, then insisted on being introduced so he could thank her for what she did for Em and give her a hug.

'What a nice woman. It's very good of her to come,' he said afterwards. I didn't reply.

I jumped as someone tapped my shoulder and felt a surge of hope that it might be Kath and Mari, finally arriving, with a story about how the satnav had taken them to completely the wrong place, but when I turned around it was Dr Ali, who had come to pay his respects.

'I'm afraid I only have twenty minutes or so. I'm on my lunch hour,' he apologized, his eyes liquid in his craggy face. 'But I wanted to come. Your father was my patient for twenty years, you know. I liked him immensely.'

'Thank you.' I was embarrassed but not surprised to find my voice clogged up with tears.

Dr Ali waited, giving me time to compose myself.

'I have the post-mortem results, if you need to discuss them.'

I nodded. I'd known, of course, that the post-mortem was being carried out – we'd had to wait a few days before Dad's body was released for cremation. But I hadn't wanted to think about the results until the funeral was over with. It was all just too much.

'It's as I told you, I'm afraid. An intentional overdose of insulin. The dial on his pen was turned up from ten to a hundred and the autopsy bore that out.'

'But he could have made a mistake, couldn't he? His eyesight was awful. He could easily have mistaken a hundred for ten if he had the wrong glasses on.'

'Indeed, although it doesn't explain why he was tampering with the dial in the first place.'

Dr Ali's tone was kind and calm, but firm, closing the door on any question of doubt.

I nodded again, unable to speak.

'Ian was a fine, courageous man who devoted his life

346

to looking after your mother, but you know, everyone has their breaking point. You must not think it is any reflection on how much he loved his wife or his family. He was just tired, I think.'

I was grateful for the doctor's delicacy. His precise way of speaking seemed to lay the facts gently to rest.

But after he'd gone I walked into the kitchen and opened the kitchen drawer where, for the past God knows how many years, my father had kept his diabetes equipment, and stared into it as if I might find answers there to the questions I couldn't even face asking.

39

'Don't you worry about it, Mum will be happy as Larry here with us, won't you, dear?'

The care assistant had a large, lumpy frame but a wide, generous smile and, once I'd got over the strangeness of her referring to my mother as Mum, I warmed to her.

My mother, meanwhile, had found the remote for the television that stood on a chest of drawers on the far side of the room and was busy hopping through the channels, seemingly unperturbed to find herself in these new, unfamiliar surroundings. I'd brought photos and a rug and a bright, striped duvet cover to make the room feel more like home, but she had shown no interest in anything apart from the TV.

Well, good. Far easier to cope with the guilt of leaving her here if she was oblivious to what was going on around her.

'I'm going to have to go now, Mum,' I said, reaching over to give her a hug.

Already I could feel my guilt at leaving and my relief at getting away pulling in opposite directions, forming a tourniquet around my heart.

At first I thought she wasn't even going to reply, leaving me free to slip quietly away, but as I reached the door she called out, stopping me in my tracks.

'You're leaving me, then, are you, just like he did?'

Remorse skewered me to the spot while the care assistant shot me a sympathetic look, which I ignored. But before I could explain again to Mum about Dad being dead rather than just having gone AWOL, she continued.

'Went to answer the door, didn't he? And then, *pfffff.* Silly old fool.'

Something niggled at the edges of my mind.

'Who was it, Mum? At the door?'

But now her attention had wandered. She looked at me, blinking. Then stared at the door to her room, which was open to the corridor.

'Well, there's no one at the door. Who were you expecting?'

Her pale eyes were wide, making her appear as guileless as a baby, and I was seized again by the depth of my treachery in leaving her in this place.

'She'll be fine,' said the care assistant, seeing something stricken in my face. 'We'll take good care of her.'

By the time I let myself into my parents' house an hour later, having spent the intervening period ensconced with the home's manager, filling in interminable forms and trying not to look at the monstrous amounts of money I was committing to every week, I'd talked myself into a more objective frame of mind. My mother was in the very best place for her, I told myself. I'd visit regularly. I'd done the right thing.

I walked into the living room, pleased with the way I was managing to put a distance between myself and my emotions. Here I was, aged fifty-two, quietly competent, getting on with the things that had to be got on with.

I set about tidying the place up. Though my parents had a cleaner who came in once a week, my mother would often get agitated at the thought that a stranger – she always claimed not to recognize the cleaner from one visit to the next – was handling her things. 'Don't touch that, it's worth thousands!' she'd shriek when the poor woman tried to pick up an Ikea fruit bowl to dust underneath, or the novelty ashtray they brought home from a tacky Corfu souvenir shop. As a result, the house had a tired, surface-clean feel, as if ornaments had been wiped around and things swept hastily into drawers.

My smugness at the way I was coping with everything lasted right up until I made myself a coffee and opened the kitchen cupboard and saw the mug I'd given my dad on his birthday a few years before, with a photo of him and Mum on their fortieth wedding anniversary, flanked by a heartbreakingly young Em and Rosie, all smiles and laughter lines and gratitude for everything they had. He'd been so pleased with that mug, insisting on drinking his morning coffee from it. And Mum had teased him, calling it his kingly tankard.

A dagger of loss sliced through me, cleaving apart my skull and chest, leaving my heart exposed, and I dropped to the floor, curling up there and howling with pain.

I would never see my father again. The blunt fact of it sucked the air from my lungs.

Nor would Mum ever again be the laughing, teasing woman in the photograph – the one who'd brought me up. Life had lurched forward into a different gear and there was no reverse, no going back.

I'd never felt so alone. Not only was I missing my parents, but also my friends. I'd been so hurt when Kath and Mari had failed to show up to the funeral four days before. I'd waited for them to get in touch to apologize, but there had been nothing. Just a text from Mari the next day, saying, *Hope yesterday wasn't too traumatic x*, and one from Kath with just a kiss. No 'sorry', no explanation. Nothing. It was as if they didn't consider my father's death to be that much of a big deal.

Well, I wasn't about to make the first move, if that's how little they cared. But that didn't mean I wasn't devastated by their behaviour. Even Frances, who I hardly knew at all, had made the effort to come, invited or not.

After I'd cried myself out, I dragged myself to my feet, my eyes coming to rest once again on the drawer that held Dad's diabetes equipment.

I opened it and stood gazing in. Dr Ali had taken the insulin pen my dad had been using. But here were test strips and lancets, plus a meter to test his blood sugar levels, a packet of glucose tablets and a box to dispose of the old needles.

Something snagged in my mind as I slid the drawer shut, and I went back into the living room to dig out my laptop, which was charging on the floor next to the television.

Guilt stopped me from sitting in my mother's usual chair, as if I might find it still warm.

Instead, I sat on the floor with my back against the sofa they'd hardly used and double-clicked on the icon that launched the webcam. For a crazy second when the picture came on I wondered who on earth that was making themselves at home in my parents' sitting room, until I remembered that, of course, it was me.

351

When I'd first got the Granny-Cam app, I'd subscribed to an extra video-recording function which meant footage could be stored for up to thirty days. It was only a year since I'd been made redundant and I still expected to go back into full-time work, so I wanted the option of coming home from work and being able to replay the footage of whatever had happened during the day so I could check that the carers had been doing what they were supposed to.

I started rewinding the footage, speeding backwards to the day of my father's death (could it really be just two weeks ago?). Once I'd reached the right day, I pressed play at a random point in the afternoon. There was my father, kneeling on the floor in front of my mother's chair, helping her on with her shoes while she gazed vacantly ahead. The sight of him, living, breathing, still so alive, splintered me into tiny, sharp pieces.

He was wearing the jumper I'd bought him for Christmas two years before, pale blue and kitten soft. I knew exactly how it would smell. That mix of the sugar-free mints he liked to suck and the peanut butter he would eat directly from the jar when no one was watching, the Head & Shoulders shampoo he used every morning on the full head of hair he was so vain about. And that other, sweet, musky smell that was completely his own.

My head was full to the brim with missing him.

For a few seconds, I almost gave in to the temptation to sink back to the floor, rocking, as I had done in the kitchen, but then I steeled myself, knowing how easily a spontaneous outpouring of grief could turn into abject self-pity.

I started fast-forwarding the tape, looking for the

point when someone came to the door, holding down the forward-arrow button so long my finger started to go numb. Nothing. I sighed. Another one of my mother's flights of fantasy. I was about to give it up when something caught my attention.

I rewound the tape. The clock in the top-right-hand corner said 16.47 when my father looked up from the book he was reading and exchanged a few words with my mother, whose expression had suddenly become one of sly coquettishness, and who was patting the back of her thinning hair as if in anticipation of a gentleman caller.

I saw my father get stiffly to his feet, turning down the corner of the page in his book before placing it face down on the chair. I smiled to myself when I saw that he was reading *Bleak House* yet again, despite all the new books I'd sent his way over the years, accompanied by effusive descriptions of why he'd enjoy them.

Dad made his way out of the living room. Though the door he exited through was ajar, frustratingly, it wasn't open wide enough for me to have a view into the hallway.

A minute went by. Two. Then Dad reappeared in the living room, walking with purpose to the sideboard, where he opened a drawer and withdrew an old Oxo tin where he and Mum had always collected change they didn't want to carry around with them. My heart broke as I watched him rummage around inside and realized someone must have come collecting for charity.

He always was a soft touch.

Dad was facing the camera as he picked out coins. I could tell by the stiffness of his fingers that his arthritis must have been playing up that day. He'd pulled the door half closed behind him, obviously so the visitor couldn't see what he was doing, though his innate politeness wouldn't have allowed him to shut it completely.

Mum was saying something. Twisting around in her chair to speak.

And that's when I saw it.

A dark blur moving in the background.

I pressed stop, and then rewound, and something hard and sharp lodged in my throat.

There! There it was.

Quick, but unmistakable. A shadow moving across the open doorway to the hallway, too dark to see clearly, but tall and obviously human. Then, a few seconds later, the same thing in reverse, a shadow passing the other way, back towards the front door.

I didn't know what it meant, but something felt badly wrong. Had my parents been victims of a callous conman, pretending to be collecting for some good cause or other, taking advantage of my dad's brief absence to mount a lightning-fast robbery?

Getting up, I checked that the webcam in the corner of the living-room ceiling was recording, then crossed the room and went out to the hall, making sure the door was open at the same angle as it had been in the footage from the day my dad had died. Then I crossed from the front door to the bottom of the stairs, which were to the right of the hallway, assuming an opportunistic thief would have nipped up to the bedrooms to pocket some jewellery or bedside cash.

But when I played back the footage of the last few minutes, I realized the angle of the open doorway made it impossible to see any movement at all.

That only left the kitchen, which was to the left of the front door as you came in, the side closest to the living room. But what on earth would a thief be hoping to steal from a kitchen?

Even then, dread was crawling over me like a rash, but I refused to acknowledge it. I made my way once again into the hallway and crossed from the front door to the kitchen.

Watching the footage back was like a replay of the original film.

Someone had come to the front door, created an excuse to distract my dad, then slipped into the kitchen while his back was turned.

Less than an hour later, my father had taken his insulin pen out of the drawer and injected himself with a fatal overdose.

It couldn't be true. I must be imagining things. Grief was making me paranoid, so I saw connections that weren't there, just as I had when I thought Stephens was Rosie's new boyfriend.

But it didn't matter how hard I tried to rationalize it, or how ridiculous I told myself I was being. My mind kept coming back to the same conclusion, as if drawn there by a magnet.

Stephens had been in my computer. He'd seen the letter I'd written for the new carer, which set out every detail of my parents' lives.

He knew where they lived.

He knew where my dad kept his medication and what the correct dose was.

What if it was him?

40

'Do you think maybe you should see someone?'

'What do you mean?'

'Like a counsellor.'

Nick saw my face and immediately added: 'It wouldn't be surprising if you're not thinking straight after everything you've had to cope with recently.'

'You think grief has made me bonkers?'

'Not bonkers. Just very sad and perhaps a little bit paranoid.'

We were sitting in Soho Square, on one of the few patches of grass that hadn't been commandeered by achingly trendy media types – men with bushy beards and long shorts and colourful T-shirts with tasteful logos, women whose skin and hair gleamed, and whose eyes were hidden behind dark glasses, their lips fuchsia or flame red – or by the kind of scabby pigeons urban England specializes in.

Nick had nipped out of work for lunch so we'd bought sandwiches from Pret A Manger to eat in the grubby mid-May sunshine. The air was thick with fumes and ambition, the heady promise of a London summer.

'I know it sounds far-fetched.'

Nick shook his head.

'Listen, you just lost your dad. That's hard enough on its own. Then you learn he might have done it deliberately. Of course you're going to want that not to be true. Of course you're going to look for other explanations. Anyone would. But don't you think it might be the grief taking over? And probably a bit of misplaced anger as well. You're mad at your dad for dying and for leaving you with the guilt about putting your mum into a home. But you can't let yourself admit that because he's dead and you miss him so much.'

Instantly, my eyes were blurred with tears, my Pavlovian response to any scrap of sympathy. I was already realizing that losing my dad was never not going to hurt. Bereavement wasn't something you could be cured of with a course of antibiotics.

Nick shifted towards me and put his arm around me and I leaned my head gratefully on his shoulder. It was embarrassing how much I craved human contact. Not in a sexual way, just in the way of having someone care, someone put their arms around me and give me the comfort I could no longer get from my parents.

I missed Kath and Mari more than I could say, but their behaviour made me question just how close we really were. After the texts they'd sent the day after the funeral, I'd waited for them to contact me, expecting to pick up the phone and hear Kath's voice: 'Sorry I've been such a dick.' But there was nothing. And their silence hurt me in a fundamental way I couldn't express, like I was a giant game of Jenga and someone had taken the bottom bricks out so now the structure of me appeared to be built over an empty space.

'But what about the blurry figure in the hallway?' I asked Nick.

My voice sounded small and whiny to my own ears.

'It could have been anything, Tess.' His thumb stroked my shoulder while he spoke. 'The shadow of the front door swinging in the wind or a person passing on the road outside. Look, go to the police. Tell them what you saw. Show them the video. Then at least you'll have done what you can.'

'But you think they'll think I'm crazy. Like you do.'

Nick gave my shoulder a squeeze.

'I don't think you're crazy, Tess. I think Stephens is a nasty piece of work and you've zoned in on him because it's too painful to focus on all the other things – your dad, your divorce, everything.'

He put his hand on my chin and gently turned my face towards his so he could kiss me on the lips, and all my fears and sorrows temporarily melted in the hot rush of my body's response.

'You're not crazy at all,' he repeated softly when we finally pulled apart. 'You're gorgeous.'

His eyes were so blue I had to look away.

The thing about grief is it doesn't follow a neat, linear pattern, starting off at a peak and then tapering off to nothing over time. Grief is like one of those lines on a monitor you see on TV medical dramas, with jagged spikes that come out of nowhere. You can't plan for it. You can't anticipate it. It's not like packing an umbrella for a predicted shower.

You can have a couple of days where the world seems almost back to normal. You're actually interested in what's going on around you. Things exist in their own right, not just in reference to the person who is no longer around to experience them. *I'm getting over it*, you think, relieved. *The worst has passed.*

Then, the very next morning, you awake feeling as if an elephant is sitting on your chest, crushing your ribs so your breath comes out in painful, thin gasps, and nothing has any point. Not the eggs you were going to make for breakfast, or the make-up you were going to put on to face the day.

After I said goodbye to Nick on the southern corner of Soho Square, I felt better than I had done in days. Of course the shadow I'd seen at my parents' house the previous week would turn out to be nothing. And I was sure he was right that blaming Stephens was just a diversionary tactic to spare myself from facing the things that were still so raw.

I could still feel the warmth of Nick's arm around my back, and my lips tingled from our goodbye kiss.

So I was fine, relatively speaking.

Until I started wondering about Nick and whether this might actually turn out to be the start of something. And that got me thinking about Phil and how badly that had ended, and how sad my father had been to see me floundering in the aftermath. 'I'd love to see you find someone to make you happy,' he'd said. And now, no matter what happened, he never would. Whoever I found next, whether it was Nick or someone else, they'd be someone my dad would never know.

The realization came out of the blue, poleaxing me as I came out of Dean Street ready to cut down Old Compton Street. I turned towards the plate-glass window of the old-fashioned whisky and cigar store that had been there for as long as I could remember, as if fascinated by the bottles on display. But really, I felt lacerated by grief.

Things would change, and I would become a different person from the person my father knew. Yet he would stay always the same.

After I'd collected myself I walked briskly on to Leicester Square Tube, but grief was a stalker, dogging my footsteps. No matter how fast I walked, it stayed right behind me.

Leaning against the glass partition on a crowded Piccadilly Line train on the way home, I spotted a man further down the carriage who looked just like my dad when I was young – broad-shouldered and thrumming with purpose, bouncing softly on the balls of his feet. I closed my eyes to block him out, but now I found myself thinking again about that shadow moving across the doorway behind my father's back as he scrabbled in his old coin tin.

It couldn't be Stephens, I told myself. Nick was right – that was just me inventing wild theories to take my mind off the fathomless chasm of loss that had opened up like a trapdoor in the centre of my life.

Nevertheless, I got off the Tube at Wood Green station, the longer route home that took me past the police station. Even right up until I arrived there I wasn't sure I was actually going to go in. I started walking past, determined to go straight home, but that image of the moving blur in my parents' hallway stopped me in my tracks when I'd gone a few yards up the road, and I turned back, borne on a sudden tide of rage.

'Mrs Hopwood. How are you?'

Detective Byrne's greeting was polite, but there was a new guardedness in his manner.

'You're going to think I'm crazy,' I began, knowing instantly that it was the worst possible way I could have opened the conversation. Still, now I'd started I had to press on, bringing Detective Byrne up to date on what had been happening: the death of my father, the blurred shadow on the webcam footage.

The detective's face grew still as he listened to me, his expression setting hard as concrete.

When I'd finished he rubbed his middle finger slowly across his right eye. Then he looked at me.

'Mrs Hopwood. I'm sincerely sorry for your loss. I lost my own father last year to cancer and I still think about him every single day. *However . . .*' He emphasized the last word and then left a pause which said everything I needed to know about what was going to come next.

'This obsession with James Stephens – and make no mistake about it, obsession is what it has become – has got to stop now. If it continues, you could find yourself facing a harassment charge and a possible custodial sentence.

'Read my lips. I'm only going to say this once. The man from the CCTV footage on the night your daughter was attacked was *not* James Stephens. I'm not really supposed to tell you that, but I don't want to see you getting into any more trouble, and if I lodge a formal complaint from you, that's the way it will go.

'Go home, Mrs Hopwood. Grieve for your father. Look after Emma. And please get some help. There are people trained to deal with this kind of trauma. Find one of them.'

I felt numb as I left the station. The fact that Byrne's last comment echoed Nick's words almost exactly disturbed me. Was I really losing hold on reality? Was it a psychiatrist I needed, rather than a policeman?

On the walk back I kept going over what the detective had said about Stephens not being the suspect they'd identified from the CCTV footage. Hadn't there been something strange about the way he'd phrased it? As if the man from the CCTV might turn out to be separate from the man who attacked Em?

And, thinking about it, what was to stop him lying to me about it? As far as the police were concerned, the case was closed. They'd spent the resources and hadn't got a result. The last thing they wanted now was me raking it all up again, causing a public nuisance, making more paperwork.

I liked Detective Byrne, but I knew my accusations were making him nervous.

Nervous enough to lie to my face?

At home, I sat down at the kitchen table and, out of habit, went to the computer to watch my parents on webcam before remembering there was no one there to watch.

Then I put my head in my hands while rage and guilt erupted from me in an almighty howl of pain.

When the doorbell sounded I ignored it. To be honest, I was in such a state I couldn't even be sure the noise wasn't in my head. Then it sounded again, a longer ring this time.

I thought of all the people I didn't want to see on my doorstep. James Stephens had once stood on the pavement opposite and taken a photograph of my house and

362

my dog. It might be him. Or else Frances, and I really wasn't in the mood for her. Then I remembered the night of the attack, when I'd found Emma sobbing on the doorstep, and how she claimed to have been standing there for ages.

I hurried to the door and flung it open.

For a split second I stared at Kath and Mari as if they were strangers, while all the hurt and upset of the last week surged to the surface. And then suddenly I crumpled and they were both scooping me up, their arms around me, and we were all crying.

'Why didn't you come?' I asked when we were finally back inside the house and sitting huddled up together on the sofa, as we had so many times over the three decades of our friendship.

'Come where?'

Kath was looking at me in surprise, her eyes startlingly blue against her cheeks, which had gone the deep puce colour they always did in the sun – the perils of being a redhead in a country where heat is not introduced incrementally, giving your skin time to adjust, but rather flung about like a squash ball, one day there, next day gone, new tans peeling off like flaking paint.

'To the funeral, of course. I waited and waited for you to show up.'

Now they were both gazing at me in astonishment. 'But you specifically told us not to come,' said Mari, leaning back so she could survey me properly. 'In your email you said you were keeping the funeral deliberately small. Family only. And you didn't feel up to talking to either of us yet. You just wanted a little space and time to yourself to grieve "with your nearest and dearest".

363

I remember the exact words you used, because, well, we both found them pretty hurtful, to be honest.'

'Yeah, I was all for getting in the car and going straight over and having it out with you there and then, but Mari convinced me to give you some time.'

I was looking from one to the other, waiting for the fog to clear and everything to fall into place, the explanation that would make sense of what they were saying. I knew the issue would turn out to be with me, because grief had made mincemeat of my thoughts. And yet nothing shifted.

'I didn't send you anything like that,' I said. 'The last message I sent was a text with all the details of the funeral.'

Now Kath and Mari exchanged a look.

'But the email came the day after that text. You said you'd been thinking a lot about it and you'd decided to limit the funeral to just family.'

'That's ridiculous.' I was getting upset all over again. 'I'll prove it to you.'

I marched into the kitchen and grabbed my laptop, bringing it back to the sofa. Logging into my emails, I went straight to my 'sent' folder and scrolled back a couple of weeks. I didn't have to go far – I'd hardly sent any emails since Dad's death.

'Stop,' said Mari, leaning over my shoulder to point at a message in my 'sent' folder.

It was there. Exactly as they'd described. A brief, abrupt email telling them I'd changed my mind about the funeral, that it was to be a small, private affair. Exclusively for family.

'But I never wrote this,' I said. 'I wanted the two of

you there more than anything. I was so devastated when you didn't show up.'

Mari was looking at me strangely.

'Tess, you've been under a lot of stress recently. Are you sure . . .'

'*I didn't write this*,' I repeated, almost shouting in my frustration. 'It doesn't even sound like me. I don't know what happened, but . . .'

I stopped short.

I *did* know what had happened.

Whatever software Frances had put on my computer to counter the spyware Stephens had installed, it hadn't worked. He'd been able to get my new email password to send messages as if he were me.

I suddenly remembered that strange email I'd supposedly sent to Nick. The one I had no recollection of writing.

The world tipped sideways and I felt myself falling.

41

Everything felt like it was happening to someone else. Someone who looked a bit like me but couldn't be me because the actual me was packed away in a padded box where nothing could get through to her.

The mystery email left me shocked and so shaken up that Mari and Kath insisted on staying with me until Em came home. Even then, they were reluctant to leave, especially once they'd heard about the blurry shadow I'd seen on the webcam, crossing the hallway.

Did I imagine the look that passed between them when I told them what I suspected – that Stephens had deliberately tampered with my dad's medication to get back at me?

'I think you should talk to someone,' Mari said, in an echo of Nick and Byrne. 'You're not yourself.'

'Good,' I said grimly. 'Myself is the very last person I want to be.'

After they'd finally gone, Em brought her laptop and books down to the living room. She didn't know about the weird email or how my dad had died, but she sensed I was fragile.

'You don't have to keep watch over me, darling. I'm fine,' I said.

'I know. I just fancied a change of scene.'

It bothered me that she so obviously thought I was about to break.

'You know how much I love you, don't you?' I told her, feeling suddenly awkward. 'You know I've only ever wanted to keep you safe.'

Em nodded, looking as if she was about to cry.

'I miss Grandad,' she said.

'Me too.'

That night I felt emotionally exhausted and, for once, slipped gratefully into sleep almost as soon as I got into bed, only to dream again of my father. I was chasing him through a cityscape, knowing I had to catch him to stop him injecting himself, but even though he was old in my dream, as he had been before he died, he was always just out of reach.

I woke with my heart thumping, the sheets drenched in sweat, then lay awake for hours, too scared to close my eyes.

'I think I'll go and visit Grandma today,' I told Em over breakfast, trying to sound like it was something I was looking forward to, rather than dreading.

It was a mixture of guilt and frustration that was driving me to Oxford. I knew I was unlikely to get any answers from my mother, but in the absence of anyone else who might be able to provide proof that I wasn't going completely mad, that someone *had* come to the door just before my dad died, she would have to do. Besides, I was still beating myself up about having left her in the home, even though there hadn't been another choice.

By the time I was on the Tube to Paddington, I was regretting my decision. I still felt strangely detached from my life, as if I were doing everything from a distance, operating my body remotely. What help could I be to my mum in this state?

The train had just pulled away from the platform when I heard my ringtone from my bag.

'Kath, I'm on the train,' I said before she could speak. 'So it might cut out at any time. Listen, I know you're worried about me after yesterday, but I'm fine now. Honestly.'

'I am worried. But that's not why I'm . . .'

A shadow as we passed into the tunnel and dead air on the other end of the line.

When we emerged, I tried calling back, but her phone was busy, obviously calling me. After a few minutes of this, my phone rang again.

'Sorry, Kath. We got cut off. What were you saying?'

'I meant to tell you yesterday, but then it went out of my head. The thing is, don't be cross, but I did some checking up on Frances Gates.'

For a moment I thought the crackling line had caused me to mishear.

'Frances? Why would you do that?'

'I just think there's something strange about the way she's latched on to you and Em. I thought it was worth finding out a bit more about her.'

I was nonplussed. Yes, it was a bit odd that Frances had turned up at my dad's funeral. But a part of me still felt protective of her. As if saving Em from Stephens had made her family, with the allowances that confers.

'And?'

'I remembered you said she worked at some investment bank called Hepworths. So I called them.'

'What do you mean, you called them? God, Kath, I hope you haven't been making trouble for her at work.'

'No. I just wanted to confirm that she really does work there. And guess what?'

An icy finger traced its way along my spine.

'She hasn't worked there in four months. So, then I rang them back again and pretended she'd applied to me for a job and given them as a reference.'

'Kath! For fuck's sake, that's completely unethical.'

'No, it isn't. They're not to know any different. Anyway, the first woman I spoke to in HR gave me the official line – how long she'd worked there for, the date she left. Nothing contentious. But then, listen to this, about half an hour after I'd hung up, the phone goes and it's this guy from Hepworths. Reluctant to give his name at first, but said he wanted to give me an unofficial "heads up" about Frances. That's the phrase he used. He said she'd—'

I cursed under my breath as the train hurtled into a tunnel and the line once again cut out. The woman opposite me glanced up from her laptop and gave me an empathetic 'what can you do?' shrug.

By the time I finally got back to Kath, she told me she was about to go into a meeting.

'But what did he say? The guy from Hepworths?'

'Just that Frances had been "borderline inappropriate". That was how he described it. Nothing that put her in breach of company law, I don't think, but she'd . . . oh, hang on a minute, Tess.'

I could hear the sounds of voices in the background. Then Kath came back on the line:

'Sorry, Tess, but I really have to go. I'll call you tonight, okay?'

After Kath had rung off I couldn't settle. I stared out of the window, determinedly not catching the eye of the woman opposite, who seemed to be waiting for an excuse to say something.

I was so fixated on Stephens and what he might be capable of, I just didn't have the emotional energy to start stressing about Frances as well. If I was honest, my pride was a little hurt that she hadn't felt comfortable enough with me to admit she'd lost her job, but maybe she was just embarrassed. Obviously, she'd left under some sort of cloud, so I couldn't blame her for not wanting to talk about it.

Still, I felt uneasy, and whenever I thought about what Kath might have been about to tell me, I felt a pressure on the underside of my ribs.

My discomfort intensified when my phone beeped with an incoming text message and Frances's name appeared on the screen, almost as if she knew Kath had been checking up on her.

She wanted to know how I was. She was concerned about me, she wrote. Grief could be so destructive. If I ever needed to talk, I knew where she was.

Suddenly, I felt short of breath, as if I was being suffocated.

On impulse, I dashed off a reply.

Frances, please don't be offended, but I think I need some time to focus on me at the moment. And on Em and Rosie too. I'll get back in touch when things are on more of an even keel.

After I'd sent it I felt guilty, but also lighter, as if I'd offloaded an unwanted task I'd agreed to do for someone else. I knew we owed Frances a massive debt, but her presence in our lives was feeling increasingly intrusive.

When I arrived at the care home I had a chat with the manager, a tall, skinny woman with very straight blonde hair cut into a blunt fringe and eyes that had the give-away bulge of a thyroid problem. She reassured me Mum was settling in perfectly well.

'She's even made a friend,' the manager said proudly. 'There's a lady in here your mother knew some years ago, apparently. It's the gift that keeps on giving, really. Every time they meet each other they've forgotten about the last time, so they get to be delighted about their reunion all over again.'

Mum was in the lounge when I arrived, on the end of a row of armchairs in which sat an assortment of old women in various stages of diminishment. She was wearing a jumper I'd never seen before with a jazzy black-and-gold diamond pattern on it. They were in front of one of the biggest televisions I had ever seen, which was blaring out a cookery programme.

I crouched down in front of Mum and tried to get her attention.

'Mum, it's Tessa,' I said, taking her hand. It felt shockingly fragile, something made from tissue paper.

My mother hardly glanced at me. Her eyes stayed trained on the television.

'Are you the physiotherapist?' her neighbour, a tiny, hunched figure, asked hopefully.

371

'No,' I said, smiling. 'I'm her daughter.'

'Only my knee has gone again,' the woman went on, as if I hadn't spoken. 'I've been doing those exercises, but it just went. *Pop!* Just like that. *Pop!*'

'No,' I said again. 'I'm her daughter.'

A woman two chairs along leaned painfully across.

'Your mother is wearing my jumper,' she whispered conspiratorially. 'The laundry woman is clueless, I'm afraid. I've tried to tell her, but she won't listen.'

I wondered if either of the women was the friend of my mum's from her old life. If so, I wondered if the two of them ever questioned what had happened to the women they used to be.

I waited until the programme was finished and then asked Mum if she wanted to come for a walk. To my surprise, she got straight to her feet and followed me docilely out of the lounge and through the lobby, with its photo montage of residents in party hats posing with visiting schoolchildren or local celebrities.

Outside was a large, square lawn bordered by flower beds and a path that went around the entire perimeter with wrought-iron benches at each corner. I led Mum to the only one which was in full sun. Despite her fair skin, she'd always loved the warmth, never caring if she burned.

I still wasn't completely sure what kind of mood she was in, but when an elderly man passed by on the opposite side, pushed along in a wheelchair by a young male carer, my mother suddenly called across to them, 'This is my daughter, you know. She edits a magazine.'

I looked at her in astonishment. I hadn't imagined the pride in her voice. It didn't matter that she was two years behind the curve with my employment history. She knew who I was.

'Mum. Are you okay?' I asked, as we sat side by side on the bench. I still had her papery hand in mine.

'I don't like my room. The bed is too small.'

'That's because you're missing Dad.'

It was the wrong thing to say. Mum snatched her hand away and I could tell she was growing upset.

'I don't want to talk about that,' she said, her face pink and mottled.

'No. Okay.'

Yet it wasn't okay. She'd seemed so lucid moments ago, but I could see the window of opportunity closing.

For a while we sat in silence, feeling the sun on our faces. Then I tried again.

'Mum, you know that day. The day Dad died.'

'I told you, I don't want to talk about that. You mustn't talk about that.'

'Someone came to the door, didn't they? Dad got up to answer it.'

'Yes. Can we talk about something else now?'

'In a minute, Mum. I'm so sorry, but this is important. Did you see who it was?'

My mother had started rocking gently, forwards and backwards, forwards and backwards.

'Mum. The man at the door. Did you see who it was?'

Now she stopped suddenly and looked straight, urgently, into my eyes and I was convinced she was about to tell me what I wanted to know. But then:

'No.'

Hope drained out of me. Stupid, really, to have thought she might be able to help.

'No. Okay, Mum. You didn't see him. We'll talk about something else now. Tell me about this friend of yours you've met in here.'

But my mother was still sitting rigidly, a frown on her face. She was clenching and unclenching her hands in agitation, and I realized, with a rush of love that threatened to dissolve me completely, that she was straining to help, to overcome the obstacles of her own crumbling mind.

'I meant no, there was no man,' she said, her whole body tense with the effort of remembering. 'The person at the door was a woman.'

I am on the sofa with Henry. He is snuggled into my side and I have my arm wrapped around him and I can feel how much he has grown over the last few months. The round belly I used to blow raspberries on has completely flattened out, and I can feel his bones through the skin of his narrow shoulders. I remember a time when he could sit against the back cushions with his legs straight out in front of him, but now they dangle off the edge.

We are watching the DVD of Paddington 2. *Again. Or rather, Henry is watching it and I am on my laptop, checking up on you.*

It is a while since I have allowed myself to do this. The grotesque teddy bear at the graveyard left me shaken for days and I was determined to put you out of my mind. But I need to know where you are, what you're doing. Who you're with.

Your Twitter account is mostly retweets of other people. Occasionally, you comment on a book you've read or a film you've seen. You never say anything contentious. You could be anyone. Going about your life. Ordinary.

Only I know the truth.

And ordinary doesn't come into it.

Your only update on Instagram is an arty photograph of a lawn sloping down to a lake whose surface glitters in the sunlight and a cluster of thick green trees beyond. I recognize the view from Kenwood House, on the northern edge of Hampstead Heath.

It's tough living in the Big Smoke, *you have written, with an icon of a winking face.* #SummerintheCity #GreenSpace #NoFilter

Next I turn to Facebook, putting your name into the search box. I only need to type the first letter and it goes straight to you. That's how often I look. The page loads up.

The photograph is still there and, even though I've looked at it so many times over the last few weeks since I first noticed it, there is still a roaring noise in my head and my mouth feels dry.

It is clearly a selfie, judging by the angle it is taken from. The camera is being held up above you at arm's length and you are smiling, showing that gap in your teeth that makes me want to smash a hole through that smile. You are wearing a coral-coloured jumper that I recognize.

How many lies did you tell me, wearing that jumper? I wonder.

But, as ever, my attention does not linger on you. Instead, it is drawn to the young woman next to you. A tangle of thick brown hair, split at the ends in that way girls' hair gets when they can't bear to get it cut. Pale face, no make-up. The tell-tale bumps of spots on her chin.

She is smiling, a weak sort of smile, and leaning into your arm, which is around her shoulders.

Is it my imagination or do her brown eyes seem troubled? Anxious? I peer more closely and now she seems to be looking straight at me. Asking for something.

Asking for help.

'Mum, you're hurting me.'

I realize I am squeezing Henry's shoulders, and I release my grip, planting a kiss on the top of his head.

'Sorry,' I say. 'Silly Mummy.'

But when I look back at the screen the unknown girl is still looking at me.

Funny how the world works in such a random way, *your post reads.* This is E, and I can't say how we were thrown together, as it's not my story to tell. But I know we'll always be an important part of each other's lives. #SoulSistas #UnbreakableBond

I close my eyes and remember how you'd bought me a necklace on our friendsiversary, as you called it.

'Creepy,' *was Matt's verdict.*

'Don't be idiotic,' *I'd told him.* 'Just because you don't have the gene for sentimentality.'

I'd worn the necklace a few times, just to make you happy. But the chain was too short and felt constricting.

The girl in the picture isn't wearing a necklace, but she has that look of someone who does not feel comfortable. Someone lumbered with an intimacy they have not asked for.

Whoever this E is, I know you will not let her go.

Just as you will not let me go.

42

Walking to get the train, anxiety was a sharp stone lodged in my shoe. Even installed in my seat, my thoughts still churned.

I tried to calm myself by looking at the whole thing rationally. There was no proof that whoever had come to the door of my parents' house had anything to do with my dad's death. And certainly, it was ludicrous to suggest it might be someone I knew.

Still, I couldn't stop my brain whirring.

Stephens worked as a painter and decorator and part-time DJ. Why on earth hadn't I questioned before whether he was likely to possess the technical know-how he'd need to remotely install spyware on my computer and so infiltrate every aspect of my life? I'd seen the way he expressed himself online, the language he used, the spelling. Could he really have composed those emails, masquerading convincingly as a middle-aged mother and journalist?

Wouldn't it be more likely to be a woman, someone who'd got close enough to me to observe my life and my relationships, someone who was well versed in technology, perhaps even someone who worked in IT?

Someone like Frances.

I got out my phone and googled 'spyware'. I read about how it was indeed possible to install a spying program on someone else's computer through a link contained in an email, as Frances explained had happened to me when I clicked on that file I was sent through my website. That would give someone access to my computer.

Spyware could also be installed on a phone, I read. But this would have to be done manually.

Instantly, I had a flashback to the morning Frances had come round to check my computer.

'I'll need your phone,' she'd said, standing in the doorway.

And I'd handed it over.

Arriving at Paddington, I exited on to the main road and walked until I spotted a little shop selling reconditioned computers and phones.

I went in and bought the cheapest pay-as-you-go phone they had in stock plus twenty pounds of credit.

'Lots of people get these, as a second phone,' observed the man behind the counter, putting it in a bag with a knowing look. I realized as I got out on to the street that he must have thought I wanted to use it to conduct an affair.

'Kath, what was the name of the guy you spoke to at Frances's work?'

Even over the sound of the traffic, I could hear my voice sounded urgent and high-pitched.

'Dean something or other. I'll look it up. What's up, Tess? Why are you ringing on a different number? And why do you sound so weird?'

'I'm on my way back from seeing Mum. Kath, the

person who came to the door just before Dad died was a woman.'

I don't know what I expected then – that Kath would immediately jump ahead as I had done to the worst possible conclusion? Instead, there was a pause and then:

'And?'

'And what if it was Frances?'

'Oh, come on, Tess. Get a fucking grip. I mean, I know Frances has done some odd things, but it's a huge leap from social misfit to murderer.'

'But think about it. Frances works with computers. She knows all about that kind of stuff. She was the only one with the opportunity to put a spying program on my phone.'

Kath paused again, considering.

'Even if you're right and she has some weird obsession with you that makes her want to know everything about you, there's still no reason for her to target your parents, is there?'

I had to admit she was right. Now I was thinking more clearly, I could see how wild the connections were that my mind was making. It was the lack of sleep, I supposed, blurring the edges of my brain and allowing my thoughts to spiral unchecked.

'No, I guess not,' I said grudgingly. 'I'd still like to talk to this Dean bloke, though. Frances has become so involved in our lives, and I realize I know so little about her.'

Dean Baverstock didn't sound happy about being contacted to discuss Frances Gates.

'I'm at work. Look, what I told your colleague was completely confidential. I could get into real trouble for this.'

I took a deep breath. 'Kath isn't my colleague. She's my friend. And she's worried about me.'

I quickly outlined my acquaintance with Frances. How close she'd become to Em.

'My daughter's only sixteen years old. I just want to know who she is letting into her life.'

'I don't take kindly to being lied to, Mrs Hopwood.' Dean had lowered his voice, and now there was a drop in background noise, as if he'd been in an open-plan office but had now taken his phone somewhere quieter. 'However, if I were you, I'd be giving some serious thought to ending that relationship.'

Standing outside an estate agent's window, I leaned on the glass, staring at the ridiculously priced houses in the display without seeing them.

'What exactly did she do to get sacked from Hepworths?'

Dean made a noise as if he were sucking air in between his teeth.

'Not sacked. Not officially, anyway. We had a *restructuring* and her position was surplus to requirements.'

'But really . . .'

'Really, the bosses wanted her out. Well, they knew the rest of us would walk if she didn't go.'

I rubbed my forehead with my hand, as if trying to manually shift the blockage that was stopping me from thinking properly. I just couldn't reconcile the Frances I knew, the one with the gap in her teeth and the shiny hair, with the social pariah he was describing.

'You still haven't told me what she actually did.'

Dean sighed.

'Look, it's not easy to put a finger on, all right. And it

was something that happened over time so that none of us really noticed at first. We all liked her to start with. She seemed so eager to help.'

'So what changed?'

I was growing impatient to get off the phone. Worry was twisting itself around my bones and I wanted to get back to my house and to my daughters.

'We got a new CEO, a woman who, let's just say, is pretty exacting. Things started to go wrong. We're a relatively small company, and though we'd had the odd disaster over the two years I'd been there, there was nothing like this. Every other week it seemed there was a new crisis – the systems crashing and wiping out all our data, or a breach of security, or all the prices being a digit out so we traded for half a day at well below what the shares were worth. And each time, Frances would quietly and efficiently step in and save the day.'

My other phone started vibrating in the pocket of my bag, signalling a call coming through, and I willed it to stop so I could concentrate on what Dean Baverstock was saying.

'One time, two of the client managers were called out to separate meetings with prospective new clients in different cities hours away – meetings that turned out not to exist. And while they were gone the CEO came in with various specially invited guests expecting a presentation from one of the absent managers on a new multimillion-pound merger of two key accounts. Apparently, the whole thing had been set up by email and, though the manager swore blind he had never made any such arrangement, it later turned out to be right there on his digital calendar. Anyhow, guess who stepped up to the plate to give the presentation in his place?'

'And you think Frances engineered all this – to impress the new boss?' In my bag, my phone beeped an alert, but I hardly registered it.

'Nothing was ever proven but . . .'

I heard the sound of a man saying something in the background and then Dean's voice, muffled as if he had his hand over the phone. When he spoke again, it was in a completely new tone. Brisk and detached.

'Right. Well. I hope that's been useful. Please get in touch if you have any further queries.'

I still had loads of questions, but I knew I was being dismissed. I also knew Dean Baverstock had stuck his neck out by telling me this much, so I thanked him and said goodbye.

The Tube home was busy. A man sat in the seat next to me with his legs spread wide apart, oblivious to how I was having to squeeze my own legs to the side to avoid clashing with his.

My mind was tying itself in knots trying to make sense of everything.

What I knew for sure was that Frances had been lying about her job. But that wasn't a crime. Plenty of people would be embarrassed about being made redundant, especially if there'd been bad feeling before they left.

Other than that, everything else was pure specula-tion. Yes, it was true Frances had the credentials and the opportunity to put spyware on my computer and phone and to intercept my messages, but there was no proof that's what she'd done. And true, Mum had said a woman came to the door just before the shadow appeared in the hallway and before Dad injected himself with a lethal dose of insulin. But as I knew only too well, my mother's recollections were far from reliable. And even if the visitor had been a woman and had, like a scene from a bad horror movie, sneaked into the kitchen while my dad's back was turned to tamper with his medication, what evidence was there to link her to Frances? I'd been happy to make that leap when I thought it was Stephens, an ex-con, tracking my every move, out for revenge. But this was Frances we were talking about, with her cashmere jumpers and her ill mother.

And yet there was a persistent pinching on the raw ends of my nerves, as if something bad was coming.

Hurrying home from the Tube, I took out my usual phone to call Em, but when I clicked the home button I saw she'd been trying to get hold of me.

I remembered then that there had been an incoming call while I was on the phone to Dean Baverstock, but when I tried to get back to Em it went straight to voicemail.

Trying to quell my growing uneasiness, I rang Rosie, but she sounded distracted.

'I'm just waiting for a call from the head of the criminology department at uni,' she said. 'Fingers crossed I'll be able to go straight into year two in the autumn.'

'I'm so pleased.'

'Are you okay, Mum? You sound tense.'

For a moment I considered telling her about my new fears. It would be such a relief to talk to someone about it all, but I knew she was in a hurry and I didn't want to burden her.

'I'm fine, darling. I've just been to see Grandma, that's all, which is always a bit unsettling.'

After I'd said goodbye to Rosie I tried Em again, sighing when she didn't pick up. This time I left a message, even though I knew she rarely listened to her voicemails.

'Hello, sweetie. Can you call me when you get a chance?'

I found myself walking more quickly, needing to be home, hoping that I'd find Emma there, curled up on the end of the sofa, watching the telly while absently twirling a hank of hair around her finger in that way she did, her phone on silent. But when I turned the corner into our road I noticed there was someone standing in our front garden.

The blood in my veins turned to ice as I drew closer and recognized the distinctive orange silk scarf around her neck.

43

Claudia Epstein had the look of someone who slept with the lights on. Her grey eyes were set deep into dark shadows and darted around on constant alert and, even when seated at one of my kitchen chairs, she held herself very upright, every muscle seemingly tensed, as if poised for flight.

She had refused a cup of tea, though she grudgingly accepted a glass of water. Even that was toyed with rather than drunk.

'I asked my mum to pick my son up after school for me,' she said. 'It's the first time I haven't gone in myself and I'm worried how he'll cope.'

'I'm sure he'll be fine,' I said. 'Kids are so resilient.'

It's the kind of thing parents say to each other. But even as I was saying it I realized it wasn't true. Children might bounce back up faster than the rest of us, but their scars are just as deep. And being young, those scars last longer.

I glanced at my phone, willing Em to come home.

I'd known as soon as she introduced herself outside on the doorstep that Claudia was the one Frances had mentioned from time to time, although her age took me by surprise. I'd expected her to be younger, like Frances. 'You're the friend who moved away. She talks about you often,' I'd said.

'Friend?' Claudia had repeated, looking at me as if I'd slapped her.

'You've been following me,' I told her now in my kitchen. Accusatory.

She didn't deny it.

'I saw a picture of Frances with your daughter. On Facebook. I followed her to your house and came to warn you. I know what she's capable of.'

Something pulled itself tight inside me then. What exactly *was* Frances capable of?

'So why didn't you?' I asked her. 'Warn me, I mean. You had the opportunity. Maybe not in Highgate Woods when I was with Frances, but that time in Alexandra Palace.'

She looked fleetingly guilty.

'I was afraid,' she said simply. 'I'd spent so long running from her, I was afraid of letting her back into our lives.'

Now she started telling me the whole, terrible history of her relationship with Frances Gates.

'We moved into a garden flat in Muswell Hill about four years ago. My son, Henry, was just a baby. Frances lived upstairs.'

'With her mum?'

Claudia gave me a funny look.

'Just Frances. We met the day we were moving in. It was hectic. My husband, Matt, had rented a van and it was packed to the gunnels with all our stuff. I'd driven over with Henry and was helping Matt unload the van while Henry was asleep in the communal hallway, tucked out of the way in his car seat under the table where we piled up the post.

'All of a sudden, this woman, Frances, appears from the house with Henry on her hip. "Poor little fellow was screaming his head off, so I took him out," she said. "Hope that's okay." I felt awful then. I hadn't heard a thing.'

I imagined Frances smiling her wholesome, gap-toothed smile, bouncing a stranger's baby on her hip, and I shivered.

'After that, Frances was in and out all the time. Matt wasn't sure about her right from the off, thought she was too intense, but I was grateful to have her around. I was an older mother. None of my friends lived nearby. I was lonely when Matt was at work. Frances was really helpful at first, minding Henry while I did the shopping or even on the odd occasion Matt and I went out in the evening. We thought we'd really landed on our feet.'

'Until?' I asked, checking my phone again.

'Until things started happening.'

'Things? What things?'

Claudia ran a hand across her forehead and I noticed how smooth it was and realized she was younger than I'd first thought. I'd put her at around my own age, but I thought now she was at least five or even ten years younger.

'It happened like a dripping tap,' she said finally, fixing me with her cool eyes so that I couldn't look away. 'So gradual I didn't notice it. Frances appeared subdued around Matt. She moved away when he stood near her. One time she asked me if I trusted him, but when I wanted to know why she backtracked completely and told me to forget she'd said anything. I found things as well. A receipt tucked in between the pages of a novel Matt was reading, for dinner in a fancy restaurant I knew he and I had never been to. Another time a business card for a boutique hotel inside one of his jacket pockets.

'What you have to understand is I was so tired all the time. Henry was a terrible sleeper. I wasn't myself. My thoughts were all over the place.'

I nodded in silent recognition. In this, at least, I could empathize.

'So you confronted him?'

'Not immediately. But I did change towards him. We started arguing a lot. I was constantly testing him. Like I said, I wasn't thinking straight. All these little things were clocking up in my subconscious.' Here she broke off to make a ticking noise while tapping the side of her head. 'But I wasn't really aware of them. Except I must have been to an extent, because why else would I have gone snooping on his computer?'

'Snooping?' I repeated dully.

'I think I justified it by telling myself I needed to find something on his laptop – a household bill, maybe. I'm not sure. I remember opening up any files that had unfamiliar names. Frances and I had had a conversation some time before where she'd told me that when people try to hide stuff on their hard disk, they use really generic, deliberately dull-sounding terms like "admin" or else a series of random letters or numbers. You know how she works in computers, so she knows that kind of thing. Most of Matt's files were completely innocuous, but then there was one which had numbers rather than a name and, when I clicked on it, I saw it contained around five or six jpeg images.

'I wasn't really focusing. I was already feeling guilty for having gone into Matt's laptop. I opened up one of the images, and for a few moments I couldn't make sense of what I was seeing, like my eyes were sending the message to my brain but my brain wasn't processing it. I opened up another. And another. Waiting for the explanation to come into my head.'

'So?' Anxiety – about Frances, my dad, Em going AWOL – made me impatient. 'What were the images of?'

'A woman's naked body. No head, just the anatomical parts. The usual tawdry tale, I'm afraid. Different pornographic poses on the same bed.'

'So what did you do?'

'Closed the file. Shut down the computer. I suppose I was in shock. I knew then that Matt was cheating. And that if there had been one, there had probably been others too. The next time I saw Frances, I asked her point blank if Matt had ever tried anything on with her. I'd remembered the way she behaved when he was around. How she never seemed to want to be in the same vicinity as him.'

'And what did she say?'

'She refused to answer me. And that was all the answer I needed. I told Matt he had to leave. By this time, we hadn't been getting on for a while. I showed him the photographs on his computer and he swore blind he had never seen them before. He said someone else must have put them there.'

I was thoughtful then, remembering the email to Nick saying we ought to nip our relationship in the bud and then the message that had gone out to Kath and Mari telling them not to come to my dad's funeral. An image came into my head of Frances bent over my laptop that morning she came round to check for spyware on my computer. Those competent fingers flying over the keyboard.

'So Matt moved out and instantly went into a spiral of depression. He'd suffered that way before when he was younger, before I met him. Had a breakdown as a student and ended up on a psych ward for a few weeks. I missed him like an amputated limb, and so did Henry. Frances was around all the time, fussing over me. But I wanted my husband. And I was worried about him, despite everything. I told Frances I was having second thoughts, said everyone made mistakes in their lives. That's when she took a deep breath in, as if she had something unpleasant to say, and then she told me she'd seen Matt out with another woman, having dinner in a Muswell Hill restaurant he and I used to go to in the early days. She hadn't wanted to upset me, she said. That's why she hadn't mentioned it before.

'So that was that. I couldn't take any more. I told Matt I wanted a divorce. He looked so awful I almost caved in, but then I thought about those disgusting photographs, and Frances saying she'd seen him with someone else while I'd been pining after him, and I hardened my heart and walked out.

'Two days after that conversation, a woman out walking her dog near Tring came across Matt's car parked in a lay-by with all the doors and windows locked and the remains of a burnt-out portable barbecue in the back seat. Suicide by carbon-monoxide poisoning, the coroner said.'

Had I suspected where the conversation was heading? Looking back, I think I had. There was something hollowed out about Claudia, as if a fundamental part of her had been scooped out and discarded.

Her story made me forget my own for a minute, my worries about Em fading in the face of Claudia's crushing sadness.

'How did you find out about Frances?' I asked her now. It was just a given that this was why she was here – to tell me what she knew about this woman who'd wormed her way into my life – and my daughter's.

'It was a few days after Matt died. I wasn't coping well. I felt so guilty and sad, and every time I looked at Henry it was like tearing a fresh strip off my heart. I came up to see Frances and she was in the middle of a work call. She'd taken time off work to be with me, even though I hadn't asked her to.

'So as not to disturb her, I waited in the hallway for her to finish. The door to her bedroom was open. I'd never been in there before. She usually came down to me, because of Henry, I suppose. Anyway, that's when I saw it.'

'Saw what?'

'The bedspread from the photographs in that hidden file on Matt's computer. The naked ones.

'The woman was Frances.'

44

My thoughts reeled. Frances, with her freshly scrubbed complexion and her childlike desire to please. I couldn't believe it was true.

And yet, already, the spreading nausea in the pit of my stomach told me it was. I remembered how Frances had more than likely overheard Nita saying, 'I thought she'd never leave,' and yet still she'd come back for more. Determined to stake her claim on our lives.

'When I could finally think joined-up thoughts again, I started doing some digging on Frances,' Claudia continued. She seemed to be finding some sort of release in this unburdening and I had the impression talking about this was new for her. 'I tracked down a cousin of hers through social media, a man called Michael, who talked to me reluctantly, only after I told him about Matt.

'He said Frances had always been "odd". That was his word. He said her dad had left when she was young and she'd been brought up by a narcissistic mother who never gave Frances the attention she craved.'

'But that's not true!' I exclaimed. 'She's always talking about her mum's kindness.'

Claudia gazed at me levelly.

'Have you never told yourself that if you repeat a lie often enough you can make it true?'

I thought of the lie I'd told myself about my marriage. That we were happy. That Phil had destroyed something whole and good, rather than something already irredeemably cracked.

'Only one time did her mother make a fuss of her, her cousin Michael told me,' Claudia went on. 'It was after Frances got into the local paper when she was a child for doing some small act of heroism, which of course her mother then managed to turn around so it became about her. *So proud of my heroic daughter.* That sort of thing. After that, Frances would apparently create dramas deliberately to recapture her mother's attention and approval. Once, an aged aunt's handbag went missing at a family party and everyone searched for hours before Frances produced it with a flourish, getting all the thanks and gratitude, even though Michael had seen her hide it herself. Another time she was at one of her mother's friends' houses and their dog somehow got out of the front door and it was Frances who triumphantly brought it home.'

I remembered Dotty then, coming home with a gash in her stomach, and a sour taste came into my mouth.

'Frances told me she lived with her mother,' I told Claudia now. 'She said she had MS and she was her carer. She said they were close.'

Claudia frowned at me. 'Frances's mother died a few months before Matt and I moved in.'

I felt out of my depth then. Floundering. All those times Frances had talked about her mother, how nurturing she was. It had all been a lie.

'So why didn't you cut her off?' I asked Claudia now. 'Once you knew what she was like?'

'I tried, but don't forget she lived upstairs. She knew when I was at home and would come round, knocking on the door, asking why I wouldn't see her any more. I challenged her about the photographs, but of course she denied knowing anything about them. And when I tried to find them again on Matt's computer, they'd vanished.'

I thought about all those evenings Frances had babysat alone in Claudia's flat. The access she'd had to their computers, their lives. It all made a sickening kind of sense.

'Then one day I was in the kitchen making tea and Henry was in the garden splashing about in the paddling pool. I had my eye on him the whole time. But all of a sudden there was this hammering at the door and Frances was screaming that Henry was in danger, and I ran out to the garden and saw he was holding a big, jagged piece of glass. Frances said she'd seen him pick it up from the end of the garden, by the bottom fence. But I knew.'

'You knew what?'

Of course, I already understood what Claudia was saying, only I didn't want to hear it. Didn't want to think it even.

'I knew she'd dropped it from her kitchen window. Probably aimed it directly at the paddling pool.'

'That can't be right. No one would . . .'

I didn't finish.

I remembered that shadow passing my parents' living-room doorway. How Frances had turned up at the funeral, desperate to be involved. And now I remembered something else. How I'd tried to gently push Frances away a couple of days before my dad died, using the excuse that my parents took up so much of my time. Oh God, had I signed my father's death warrant?

'Did you tell the police?' I asked Claudia.

'Yes, but when they questioned Frances she reminded them how I'd complained a few months before about the student house that backs on to ours. They used to throw butts of joints and those metal capsules of laughing gas over the fence and I'd made an official complaint to the police. "They must have chucked a broken bottle over this time," Frances told the policeman who came to her door. "Thank God I happened to be looking out." '

Claudia told me how she'd put the flat up for rent then, and moved out a few days later, to a place near enough that Henry could still go to the same nursery but far enough to put some distance between them and Frances.

'But then she found us. I went to pick Henry up one afternoon and there she was, with her hand on his shoulder, chatting to the head of the nursery. I can't explain to you how it felt. This clammy fear that came over me that we'd never be free of her.'

I didn't tell her that she needn't explain to me how it felt.

'That's when I knew I had to move away completely. Cut all ties. I moved to Surrey to be near my mum. Ever since then I've been constantly watching over my shoulder. Questioning Henry about who he's seen and talked to.'

'What about the police?'

'What could I say? That there were photos that don't exist any more of a woman's naked body on a similar bedspread to hers? That my boy picked up a piece of glass from the garden? That my husband killed himself because I wouldn't believe him?

'You know, some days, I even question myself. Can I really be sure it happened this way? Is she really as dangerous as I think?'

I had a strange feeling then, a clawed hand grasping at the skin of my back as she said that word: 'dangerous'.

I grabbed hold of my phone again in case Em had called and I hadn't heard it, but there was nothing. In desperation, I went to our WhatsApp group chat to send her a message telling her to contact me. Which is when I saw she'd sent a message earlier that day.

Belatedly, I remembered that bleeping sound from my bag while I was talking to Dean Baverstock on the pay-as-you-go phone.

Frances asked to come round but I know she's starting to get on your nerves, Em had written, *so in the end I said I'd go to hers instead. Taking one for the team. You can thank me later.*

I remembered the text I'd sent that morning telling Frances that I needed to focus on me and my girls. That rush of guilt and relief that came afterwards.

'Do you know where Frances lives?' I asked Claudia Epstein urgently.

'Of course I do. I lived there, remember.'

'Can you take me?'

Claudia was already shaking her head.

'Sorry. I can't go back there. Not to that place. Not to where Matt and I were so happy.'

'Please,' I grabbed her hand. Her fingers felt thin and dry. 'I haven't got a car. I think my daughter is in danger.'

Claudia held my gaze for a few moments, while the world seemed to stand still, then gave the briefest of nods.

We climbed into her ancient Volvo. There was a child seat in the back and a selection of picture books that Claudia gathered up hastily and shoved into the glove compartment, as if trying to protect her son's privacy.

The drive to Muswell Hill took only ten minutes, but it felt like hours. Every red traffic light we stopped at had me pressing my nails into my palms, wondering where Em was. Why she wasn't answering her phone.

'Just up here,' said Claudia. Then, almost immediately, 'Oh!'

I followed her gaze to where a knot of people was standing outside a house with a large clematis in the front garden. They were gazing up at the top floor, where black smoke was billowing from an open window.

45

'The fire brigade is on the way.'

The woman who told us this was in her forties and wearing sweat pants and sheepskin slippers, as if she hadn't been intending to leave home today. Her voice was fast and flustered and a purple rash of excitement extended over her chest and neck. She was shouting to be heard over the screeching of the smoke alarm.

'It's just awful because my neighbour Frances, who lives in that flat, had just nipped out for milk and came home to find it on fire and, before we could stop her, she ran back inside. She said someone was in there. A visitor.'

I looked at the ground, where a half-empty plastic carton of milk lay in a white puddle of its contents. A numbing chill had overtaken me, so it took several seconds for my mind to catch on that visitor meant Emma.

'Oh my God!' My hand was over my mouth, my blood rushing in my ears.

The woman, misunderstanding, turned to me. 'We all tried to stop her,' she said, as if I was holding her to blame. 'She insisted on going in.'

TAMMY COHEN

I lunged towards the open front door, which was half wreathed in smoke, but Claudia held me back.

'It's not safe,' she said. 'And if Frances is on her way back with Emma, you'll only get in their way. The stairs are quite narrow and it's pitch black in there.'

Still, I strained to get free.

'Look!' Claudia shouted.

A figure was materializing from the smoke-filled doorway. At first it was just a dark shape but, as I watched, with every single one of my muscles knotted, it slowly revealed itself to be Frances, her face blackened, her normally smooth hair standing up in a halo of singed frizz around her head.

My eyes moved past her to the doorway, waiting for the second figure to follow, but nothing else moved.

'Where is she?'

Frances was bent double and coughing, her shoulders heaving, but her head shot up at the sound of my voice just inches away.

'Tessa? I'm so sorry. I tried. I really tried.'

The words were deep rasps that tore from somewhere raw in her throat. Her face was a mask of horror, her eyes wide with shock as she caught sight of Claudia behind me.

But even before Frances had finished speaking I was moving towards the doorway.

I heard Claudia's voice shouting for me to stop and someone put their hand on my sleeve trying to pull me back, but I shrugged them off. All I could see was that awful black, gaping mouth of a doorway through which, somewhere inside, my daughter waited for me.

Just before I plunged inside I heard Frances's distinctive

rasp cut through the air behind me. 'Keep going straight, Tessa. All the way ahead.' At the same time, someone thrust something at me – a wet towel – which I snatched without thinking.

The hallway was thick with smoke and I instinctively ducked low to the ground, holding the towel over my head. I could just make out the bottom of the staircase, and I crawled up on my hands and knees with the towel draped over me. The noise of the smoke alarm as I ascended was deafening.

Adrenaline was an electric force running through me, powering me into action. My brain, as if aware that the instinct for self-preservation would override everything else if left unchecked, seemed to have switched itself off, so I was merely a collection of limbs and muscles acting without volition.

At the top of the stairs, by another open doorway, which I assumed to be the front door to Frances's flat, I hesitated and fumbled in my pocket for my phone. The screensaver came up and I was able to click on the flash-light icon. The beam didn't extend far into the black smoke, but it was enough to see a few feet ahead along what looked to be a long corridor.

By this time I could feel the intense heat of the fire and, even with the towel pressed to my face, the acrid smell of smoke was getting into my nose and throat. I was fighting the urge to cough all the time. Further up ahead, through the black smoke I could make out a flickering sliver of orange at floor level.

Ahead.

Wasn't that exactly where Frances had told me I'd find Em?

My phone was growing hot and I turned it off. I knew on some deep, primordial level that if I stayed where I was I would never get moving again, so I forced myself forward, crawling along the corridor, my breathing fast and shallow.

The smoke alarm stopped abruptly, leaving a thick, ominous silence. I unwrapped the towel from my face to shout Em's name and a wall of heat hit me. As I took in air to shout again, smoke burned the back of my mouth. A spasm of coughing stripped my throat raw and I turned my head to the side to be sick.

Again I forced myself forward through the black smoke in the direction of the orange strip, until I was stopped in my tracks by a sharp, shooting flare of pain in my temple. When I felt around I realized it had been caused by the corner of a low table or bench.

As I edged around it, I could feel blood trickling down my forehead, but I pressed on. By now I was struggling to breathe and had lost all sense of direction. All I knew was that I needed to keep going straight ahead towards that orange glow, which, it occurred to me now, must be the fire blazing behind a closed door.

If Em was in there, she had no chance.

Yet still I went on. I knew now that I'd probably die in here. I could feel the smoke scalding my lungs, making breathing increasingly painful. My eyes were streaming and my eyeballs felt as if they were burning. But I couldn't, wouldn't, leave there without my daughter.

I crawled on, but more slowly now. Realizing it was all but impossible. I remembered the heart-wrenching accounts of survivors of the Grenfell tragedy, how people had talked about door handles scalding their palms.

And even if I managed to open the door, surely the flames would burst out and engulf me in seconds.

My breathing had changed now, becoming noisy and laboured, and it felt as if everything was closing down, like my body was a dark building in which all the lights were being extinguished one by one.

All of a sudden my fingers encountered something. I felt around uncertainly, and then my heart was suddenly pounding inside me, reminding me I was still alive.

It was a foot. I was holding Em's foot.

You are staring at me, your eyes wide in your smoke-blackened face.

This wasn't part of your fantasy plan. I see it instantly. You have not considered that your victims might find each other. Share stories. Swap notes. Find the cracks in your lies through which the truth trickles out.

Everything is about external validation for you. You are scared that we will make you confront what lies inside yourself.

Your neighbour has draped a blanket around your shoulders and is fussing over you, but you keep sneaking looks at me.

'Claudia,' you say at one point, in a voice like scraped rust, struggling to be heard over the screaming of the smoke alarm. 'I really tried to reach her.'

You are in shock, I can see it. You know you have gone too far.

For a moment I almost feel sorry for you.

Almost.

Then I remember Matt and how he'd said to me once, 'All my life I've felt I was waiting for something, and now I know I was waiting for you.' And I remember

Henry's face at the funeral. Tear-stained and tired and asking for Daddy.

I look up at the house, where the black smoke billows, and I think of Tessa voluntarily plunging in there to save her daughter.

Love is strong, I think to myself. Love is the strongest. And you will never know that. Although you will always suspect it, which is what will keep you searching for it.

I know now that, whatever happens today, I am done with running. Done with hiding.

Love is strong and you will not win.

46

Heart hammering in the pitch darkness, I followed the shape of Em's body that I knew so well, my hands travelling up her leg to her chest, leaning my head close to her ribs, hope exploding inside me when I heard a faint heartbeat. I shook her shoulders.

No response.

Em appeared to be lying in a doorway with her legs extending into the corridor, which is where I'd stumbled on her.

I tried dragging her by the feet, but her torso got caught on the corner of the door.

I raised myself up, only to be hit by a wall of heat. The temptation to drop back down again was overwhelming, but I forced myself to stay semi-upright and squeeze through the doorway so that I could lift Em by the arms into a sitting position and manhandle her around the doorframe and into the corridor.

The heat from the door at the end was now unbearable, and I understood on some instinctive level that the flames would burn through at any moment.

I manoeuvred Em so that I was crouching behind her

with my hands under her arms and started dragging her backwards. The blackness was absolute and I couldn't get my bearings, and breathing was now like scraping knives across my throat and chest.

Light-headed from lack of oxygen and coughing more or less constantly, I found a doorway that I thought must be the door to the flat and was just about to go in when I remembered the table I'd bashed into in the corridor on my way in. Had I passed that yet?

Blindly, I carried on moving backwards, dragging Em along with me until I hit the edge of the table. Squeezing clumsily past it, I felt myself growing weaker, the hope and adrenaline that had borne me this far slipping away.

I slowed to a standstill, fighting for breath.

I wasn't going to make it. It was too hard. I was simply too weak.

That's when I heard it. A low moan.

Em. My daughter. My baby. She was still alive.

The sound gave me a burst of new energy, as if a battery that had been run down almost to nothing was put back on to charge.

I started up again, shuffling backwards along the corridor, dragging Em with me, no longer conscious of direction or time or anything except the need to keep going. I no longer registered the coughing or the searing pain in my throat. All I knew was that I was trapped in a dark tunnel of pressure from which I could never escape.

And then I was aware of a change in the density of the air, a cooler pocket that my damaged lungs tried to reach towards. I took a big step back and then I was falling. The walls came to meet me in the blackness. *Em*, was the thought that filled my head, though I don't think I managed to say her name out loud. I hit my arm on a hard surface, then my head.

And after that there was nothing.

47

'I'm very sorry. I know you were hoping for different news.'

Detective Byrne looked genuinely regretful at what he had just told me, and I knew I should put on a brave face for his sake, but I couldn't hide the visceral impact of his words.

'I was expecting it,' I said, when I was able to speak. 'But still I hoped . . .'

I didn't need to finish. We both knew what I had hoped.

'The fire investigation service has ruled that the blaze started accidentally, so there are no charges for Miss Gates to answer.'

It was what Frances had claimed from the beginning. She had lit a scented candle on top of a low bookcase in the living room where she and Em were sitting. She hadn't given a second thought, she'd said, to the canvas print on the wall above the bookcase. Nor had she had any idea that leaving the spent match lying across the top of the candle would act as an accelerant to the flame. She'd only wanted to make the room nice for her visitor, she'd said.

And there'd definitely been no sign of fire when she'd nipped out to get milk.

TAMMY COHEN

Em had confirmed it. My girl who couldn't lie, speaking in a painful croak from her hospital bed.

Em had been sitting on the sofa leafing through a magazine, with the bookshelf behind her on the back wall near the door to the corridor. Frances had been playing music loudly through her iPhone speakers, so Em didn't hear the initial crackles of flame. At first the scent from the candle was so strong it had masked the smell of the canvas burning and setting fire to the wooden clothes horse leaning up against the wall. By the time the smoke alarm sounded and Em looked up, the air behind her was thick with smoke and the sofa arm was on fire.

'Why did you close the door to the living room when you went out for milk?' the police had asked Frances, after ascertaining that the only smoke alarm in the flat was in the corridor from which all the other rooms led off. If the door had been open, the alarm would have sensed smoke much sooner.

'I've always done it,' she'd said. That eager look she had. So keen to help. 'To keep the heat from escaping in winter when the radiators are on. It was second nature.'

When Em had jumped to her feet, she'd felt lightheaded and sick from the smoke she hadn't been aware she was inhaling. By this time, the entire back of the room was ablaze and the air was dense and black and acrid.

Her first thought had been to escape through the window on the other side of the room, but by the time she reached it the fire had taken hold of the wooden shutters and the whole frame was burning.

So instead she'd grabbed a heavy woollen throw off the sofa and wrapped it around herself, covering up her thin cotton T-shirt and dived through the flames, grabbing for the door handle, the red-hot metal melting the top layers of skin on the palms of her hands – an injury for which she was still receiving treatment even now.

As the black smoke poured out into the corridor, she'd panicked and pulled the door shut behind her in an attempt to stop the fire spreading, plunging her instantly into total darkness. By now she was struggling to breathe and totally disoriented. She tried to feel her way along the wall, but her hands were burnt and painful. Stumbling upon the doorway to the kitchen, she became convinced it was the door to the outside, and by the time she realized her mistake she was too weak to double back, which is when she must have passed out.

'And Claudia?' I said now to the policeman who'd gone out of his way to come around in person to update me on the case. I no longer cared how desperate I sounded. 'The nude photos. Surely that's enough proof that Frances mounted a deliberate campaign of harassment against Claudia's husband?'

Detective Byrne glanced down as if embarrassed. I noticed the patch of psoriasis on his wrist was inflamed and weeping, as if he'd recently given in to the urge to scratch.

'The photos no longer exist. And even if they did, I'm not sure what law Miss Gates would have broken by sending them.'

It was the same story with the things Dean Baverstock had told me about how Frances always seemed to be conveniently around in a crisis, and with the tissue of lies she'd spun me about caring for her ill mother. Strange behaviour, to be sure; reprehensible, even. But not criminal. And as for what I suspected had happened to my father, well, that was speculation and nothing more. My mother wasn't capable of providing evidence and the inquest had ruled his death a deliberate overdose. There was no evidence that a crime had taken place, let alone that friendly, eager-to-help Frances Gates who'd never met either of my parents might have had anything to do with it.

Even the anonymous letter that had been sent to Phil had revealed no further clues, a cursory dusting of the envelope producing just one full fingerprint, which was found to belong to Phil himself.

'I know you don't want to hear this, Mrs Hopwood,' Detective Byrne continued now, 'but we can't ignore the fact that Frances Gates went back into the building to rescue your daughter and sustained nasty burns to her own arms in the attempt.'

'But don't you see, that's exactly what she does?' I said, exasperation making my voice higher than normal. 'She fixates on people and creates dramas so that she can sweep in and save the day. She probably placed the candle under the canvas deliberately and waited until it was just about to catch fire before making an excuse to leave. Em wouldn't have noticed. She had her back to it and the music was on.'

'Why would Ms Gates want to set fire to her own flat?'

'Maybe she didn't expect it to spread so quickly. Maybe she thought just the canvas would burn and she'd go charging back in to put it out and win Em's eternal gratitude – and mine – except it got out of hand.'

Detective Byrne fixed me with his sad brown eyes.

'I hope you're not going to accuse her of somehow engineering the attack on your daughter too?'

I sighed then. Defeated. 'No, of course not. That was purely opportunistic.'

'Right place, right time?'

'Wrong person,' I added ruefully.

The man who'd attacked Em had been caught. He'd tried to do the same thing to another girl just a couple of miles away in Tottenham and two men who happened to be driving past had stopped and wrestled him to the ground until the police arrived.

He wasn't Stephens.

He didn't even look that much like Stephens. The cleft in his chin was far less pronounced, and his eyes were brown, not green. All he had was a jacket that looked similar and the kind of flashy ring lots of men wear. He hadn't killed anyone, it turned out, though he had been in prison for common assault. An earlier charge of possession of a firearm with intent to cause violence had been dropped on a technicality. There are a lot of men like him walking the streets. People with histories that would keep you awake at night if only you knew.

And Number Eight wasn't Stephens either. Just a random bloke who'd volunteered to be part of the police database.

Stephens had made another complaint in the end. The message I'd sent when I thought he was Rosie's new boyfriend, begging him not to hurt my daughter, had freaked him out. The police had interviewed me and half-heartedly attempted to make a case that I had a vendetta against him. They wanted me to admit that I'd planted the seed in Em's head after the ID parade that Number Eight was definitely her attacker and had made her so paranoid that he lived nearby that she'd seized on the first local guy she saw who looked anything like the man in the police video. But they hadn't pursued it.

Stephens's police record spoke for itself. Besides, I think the blisters on my arms put them off.

But I'd thought about it a lot since then. How quick I'd been to go along with it all, transmuting the flimsiest of supporting evidence – the w-shaped chin, the jacket with the white logo, Frances's own unequivocal identification – into incontrovertible proof.

Sometimes I wondered if I'd been so desperate to make amends for the car crash with Rosie, and the marriage break-up and not being there for Em when she'd needed me, that I'd invented a scenario in which I would be the one to protect and save my children.

Perhaps Frances and I weren't so different after all.

Even all those weeks later, I found it hard to separate what had been Frances and what was Stephens. Logically, I knew that the sinister photograph of the front of my house with Dotty framed in the window was Frances's doing, and the malicious note Phil received calling me an unfit mother (oh, how well she knew what buttons to press), but still my mind persisted in clinging to that other, more familiar narrative, where Stephens was the bogeyman I needed to keep my children safe from. It made things so much simpler and less frightening.

I'd thought about contacting him. Stephens. To apologize.

Then I'd remembered the man who'd died because he couldn't control his temper and the threatening messages he'd sent: *I won't forget.*

I'd have liked to see his grandmother again, though. Just to explain.

I looked at my phone to check the time. Later that evening I was introducing Nick to Kath and Mari and I needed time to get ready. Our relationship was still at that magical early stage where I wanted him only to see me at my best.

At least the shadows under my eyes had faded a little since I'd started sleeping again. Only a few hours a night, to be sure, but it was a start.

Detective Byrne got to his feet from the chair where he was sitting in our kitchen – the same kitchen in which he'd stood all those months ago on the night Em was attacked.

'You look after yourself, Mrs Hopwood,' he said.

It was one of those things people say, but with him I felt he meant it.

Em arrived home as we were saying goodbye on the doorstep. I saw the anxiety in her expression as she recognized the policeman and knew she would be panicking about what fresh trouble his presence signified. I stepped forward to put my arms around her.

'Everything's fine, Em. Detective Byrne was just updating me on things.'

Two months on from the fire, Em's hands had lost the bandages she'd worn during those first awful weeks, but the skin was tight and shiny, though we'd been told that would eventually heal. Similarly, the effects of the smoke inhalation had all but cleared. She'd needed an inhaler in the immediate aftermath and we'd joked about her secret hope of being stuck for ever with her new deep, raspy, sexy voice. And both of us were still comparing notes daily on the colour of our phlegm, which had gradually lightened from black to toffee-coloured and now almost clear again. But apart from that, you'd hardly notice anything different.

The emotional scars, though. It'd be a while before we knew the extent of those.

As Detective Byrne drove away, we turned back into the house, my daughter and I. Rosie would be arriving shortly to keep Em company while I was out with Nick. Em insisted she didn't need babysitting, of course. But I wasn't taking any chances.

'Honestly, Mum,' she'd said earlier, 'what do you think is going to happen?'

I'd thought then of the fire, how I'd been convinced we were both going to die, and of the shadow passing my parents' open doorway. I thought, with the usual poker-hot flare of rage, of my dad, who'd only ever done his best, and my mum in her single bed at the nursing home, snatching at words and memories, trying to anchor herself to a world that no longer made sense. I thought of Em's face after the attack and the bumps that came up like eggs on her scalp under her hair, and Rosie crying herself to sleep, heartbroken. I thought of the blood on Dotty's collar, and the gash in her stomach that had faded now to a thin pink scar. I'd been back to Frances's house to ask her neighbour if she'd ever seen her with a small black-and-white dog, but she'd looked at me as if I were crazy. 'She risked her life to rescue your daughter,' the woman told me. 'You should be thanking her, not blaming her.'

The truth was, none of us knew what was going to happen from one day to the next. Life was random. People were unpredictable. We were all of us so fragile.

'You're right,' I said to Em. 'Nothing's going to happen.'

I didn't tell her I'd installed the webcam from my parents' house in the light-fitting in our hallway.

Just in case.

I am watching you.

I follow you on Instagram, on Facebook, on Twitter. I chose my online persona carefully – an older woman. A friend of a friend of a friend. A teacher with a close family and an interest in galleries and exhibitions. I trawled the internet for the right photograph. Middle-aged, smiley, but not too smiley, if you know what I mean. Someone you'd have to work at getting to know. Someone who doesn't offer friendship on a plate. Someone you'd want to impress.

I didn't approach you until I'd already been befriended by several of your online friends, so there were enough mutuals.

I knew you'd be on your guard.

And now I'm in, I watch what you do. Where you go. Who you go with.

I know you might find that hard to believe, after the lengths to which we went to get you out of our lives. Claudia and I joining forces together. Bringing your cousin Michael to confront you with all the lies you told.

It was the mention of your mother that drove you

away in the end. Nothing else shamed you, not what you did to Matt, or to Emma, or my poor dad. When I think of it, that shadow in the hallway, I still feel I could tear you apart with my bare hands, limb from limb, force the blade of a knife through that gap in your teeth and twist.

But you denied it all. Not you in the nude photos, the fire an accident, my dad's death suicide, just as the coroner said.

But your mother was more than you could bear. Having to admit she was dead and that you would never have the chance to force her to love you? You were prepared to give us up, rather than do that.

But still I want to keep tabs on where you are in relation to me, and to Em and Rosie and the other people I love, to know that they're safe.

I saw when you got that new job at the health trust. They clearly didn't speak to Dean Baverstock. Or maybe he's just decided to keep quiet about it all now. It's not really his business, after all.

I saw when you moved to Clapham. I guess your insurers must have paid out for your Muswell Hill flat in the end. I went past it the other day, you know. It has been rebuilt. The scorch marks all covered over in fresh white paint. It looks like nothing untoward ever happened there. They did a good job.

I click on your Instagram now, as I do several times a day. And this is when I see it. A photograph of you in a pub, sitting next to a woman. She is about my age, attractive, relaxed and smiling, holding up a glass of rosé wine as if making a toast, and looking straight at the camera.

But you, you are looking at her.

My new boss, *you have written*. Better look busy! #LOL #NotReally #BestBossintheWorld

You look so normal in your blue-and-white striped Breton top and your conker-shiny hair and your butter-wouldn't-melt smile.

They must have thought they'd lucked out when you turned up for the interview. So keen to help. To be useful.

But I know.

I know what you did.

Acknowledgements

There are certain events, both good and bad, that shape the landscape of family life. In January 2014, my daughter, Billie, was followed off a bus on her way home from a party by a man who then tried to drag her off the main road, hitting her repeatedly around the head when she resisted. Thankfully, a passer-by shouted from the other side of the road and the man ran off.

That story is hers to tell. What is mine is the feeling of utter powerlessness that followed. The intense but useless rage as I sat in the police station while they played the ID parade video, knowing that somewhere on that tape was the man who had done this to my daughter. The visceral reaction to one of the participants, followed by incredulity when Billie was unable to make an identification. Then the worry when she came home from school weeks later and said she thought she'd seen the man who did it emerging from a doorway locally. Or was it the man from the video? She couldn't be sure.

Luckily, that's where my and Tessa's experiences diverge. There were no more sightings. There was no more contact from the police. Our lives went back to normal and the attack became just another chapter – a dark one, to be sure – in our family's ever-expanding history. My daughter is in her last year of university and has travelled widely since then, sometimes on her own, always looking forwards, never behind, just as it should be.

There's a refrain in my house and among my long-suffering friends: *I expect you're going to put that in a book*. So the first and biggest of thanks goes to Billie for giving me permission to use this horrible moment in her life as the spark for this story. And for relinquishing ownership of it, allowing me to fashion someone else's narrative out of the seed that had been hers. She is strong and brave and resilient and, if karma has any decency, only good things will happen to her from now on.

I'd also like to thank the detectives from the Met police who dealt with my then-teenaged daughter with kindness and empathy. In the intervening years, the station where the ID parade took place has been closed, along with many others, and I feel a little pang of sadness every time I go past its whited-out windows. And a shout-out also to Victim Support. My daughter decided she was fine (and she was), but it was reassuring to know there was help if she needed it.

Huge thanks to Lucy Morris and Felicity Blunt at Curtis Brown, who read and re-read draft after draft of this story, making bacon-saving suggestions and gently steering me away from the deadest of ends. Some of the key scenes and turning points stem from an intense but productive brainstorming session with the two of them, which gave me the inspiration I needed to push on and finish the book. Agents are the best, and these two are the best of the best. Thanks also to Melissa Pimentel at Curtis Brown, whose job it is to convince foreign publishers to buy my books. Whenever I see her name in my inbox, my heart does a little dance.

Transworld has been publishing me since my debut in 2011, and I am so lucky to work with the brilliant team there. *Stop at Nothing* represents my first experience working with editor Frankie Gray, and I'm grateful for her thoroughness, perceptiveness and deftness of touch and for understanding how paranoid authors can get waiting for feedback and our pitiful need for reassurance. Natasha Barsby also read multiple drafts of the book and suggested ways to make it stronger, and for that I'm truly thankful.

There's little point in writing a book if no one ever gets to hear about it, and that's one of the reasons I love my publicist, Alison Barrow, so very much. No one spreads the book love quite like Alison. She's also innovative and kind and one of the best-read people I know. Swapping book recommendations with her is one of my very favourite ways of distracting myself from work.

Thanks also to copy-editor Sarah Day, who unwittingly sparked a Twitter storm after correcting the phrase 'you've got another thing coming' to 'you've got another think coming'. It blew my mind – and the minds of thousands of Twitter users too, apparently – when I googled it and found she was absolutely right, so thanks for sparing me the shame of that and my myriad other mistakes. Thanks as always to Kate Samano for overseeing the copy-edit, and to Jo Thomson who designed this book's magnificent cover which I fell in love with at first sight.

I know nothing about fire safety, so a big thank-you goes to Steve Westley of Shrewsbury Fire Station, who advised me on the fire scenes at the end of the book (and to Jenny Blackhurst, who introduced us). And also to Dr Roma Cartwright, who suggested the diabetes storyline. Rebecca Bradley is a former police officer turned crime writer who now offers a service advising on police procedure and I'm grateful to her for patiently answering all my many queries on policing. It goes without saying that any mistakes in any of these areas are absolutely my own.

The writing community is incredible. So many writers have helped with this book, in terms of providing either practical writing advice or emotional support or gin or all of the above. So I'd like to thank Amanda Jennings, Colette McBeth, Marnie Riches, Lisa Jewell, Anna Mazzola, Fiona Cummins and Clare Mackintosh, as well as all the Killer Women and the Prime Writers and the Cockblankets and the NLW. I went on three wonderful writing retreats during the writing of this book, having never been on one before in my life, and now I am a retreat convert. So gratitude goes to Julie and Steve at Ponden Hall and to Janie and Mike at Chez Castillon, as well as to the staff at the brilliantly eccentric and magical Gladstone's Library. Also to Angela Clarke, Rowan Coleman, Julie Cohen, Polly Chase, Kate Harrison, Cally Taylor, Callie Longbridge, Tamsyn Murray, Cari Rosen, Karin Salvalaggio, Rachael Lucas and everyone else who kept me company on those retreats and bombarded me with drunken title suggestions in the early hours.

Thanks, too, to the bloggers and the reviewers who do such brilliant work in championing the books they love and getting the word out. With retail space for books decreasing all the time, word of mouth has never been more crucial.

My family and friends put up with a lot. Not only with me plundering their lives for inspiration for books and working at weekends and on holidays, but also dealing with the inevitable mood slumps that come at thirty thousand words into a book when the plot has ground to a halt and self-doubt is raging. So thanks to Rikki, Mike, Roma, Juliet, Mark, Mel, Helen, Jo, Maria, Steve, Sally, Ed and Dill. And to Sara, Colin, Ed, Alfie, Simon, Emma, Margaret, Paul and Ben. And, as always, to my children, Otis, Jake and Billie, of whom I'm ridiculously proud. And special thanks to Michael for reminding me, whenever I insist this is the very worst book anyone's ever written, that 'you always say that'.

Finally, thank you to the readers. I'm so grateful to everyone who buys my books or borrows them from the library (authors get a small amount for each loan). There is so much instant entertainment on tap in all our lives – Netflix, TV, YouTube, social media. I find it hugely cheering that people are still choosing to read.

Book people make the world a better place. Fact.